★ GHOSTS OF WAR ★

Also by Brad Taylor

One Rough Man
All Necessary Force
Enemy of Mine
The Widow's Strike
The Polaris Protocol
Days of Rage
No Fortunate Son
The Insider Threat
The Forgotten Soldier

Short Works

The Callsign
Gut Instinct
Black Flag
The Dig
The Recruit

GHOSTS OF WAR

BRAD TAYLOR

A Pike Logan Thriller

DUTTON
— est. 1852 —

DUTTON
—— est. 1852 ——
An imprint of Penguin Random House LLC
375 Hudson Street
New York, New York 10014

LIBRARY OF CONGRESS CATALOGING-IN-PUBLICATION DATA
Names: Taylor, Brad, 1965– author.
Title: Ghosts of war / Brad Taylor.
Description: First edition. | New York, New York : Dutton, [2016] | Series: A Pike Logan thriller
Identifiers: LCCN 2016014171 (print) | LCCN 2016021059 (ebook) | ISBN 9780525954927 (hardcover) | ISBN 9780698409774 (epub)
Subjects: LCSH: Special operations (Military science)—Fiction. | Terrorism—Prevention—Fiction. | BISAC: FICTION / Espionage. | FICTION / Action & Adventure. | GSAFD: Adventure fiction. | Suspense fiction.
Classification: LCC PS3620.A9353 G49 2016 (print) | LCC PS3620.A9353 (ebook) | DDC 813/.6—dc23
LC record available at https://lccn.loc.gov/2016014171

ISBN 978-0-525-95492-7

Printed in the United States of America
1   3   5   7   9   10   8   6   4   2

Set in Sabon LT Std
Designed by Cassandra Garruzzo

For the LuLus—and especially Christie—who are bound together by friendship and are forever more #LuLuStrong

Never strike a king unless you are sure you shall kill him.

Ralph Waldo Emerson

No one starts a war—or rather, no one in his senses ought to do so—without first being clear in his mind what he intends to achieve by that war and how he intends to conduct it.

Carl von Clausewitz

I know not with what weapons World War III will be fought, but World War IV will be fought with sticks and stones.

Albert Einstein

★ GHOSTS OF WAR ★

1

The Old Town, Fredrikstad, Norway
Four months ago

The Range Rover made the turn onto the final road, a long stretch of gravel ending at what looked like a moat surrounding a fortressed town. In front of the water, two men in uniform stood next to a fire barrel, compact assault rifles slung over their shoulders, hands hovering above the barrel to ward off the chill. The driver slowed instinctively. The passenger said, "Keep going. Don't give them any reason to suspect anything."

The driver huffed slightly, strangely giddy at the turn his life had taken.

Suspect? Right. I'm sure they won't wonder why an American in a business suit is traveling with an Arab wearing ratty jeans. Or why I'm sweating like a whore in church in the middle of winter.

The American continued at reduced speed, using the melted snow on the roadway as an excuse, doing whatever he could to slow the inevitable showdown. The Arab said, "Easy. Very, very easy. You get us through this, and you're free. Remember that."

"Okay, okay. What do you want me to say? Should I tell them who I am?"

The American prayed the man with the gun would say yes, because he was sure there was a massive manhunt for him involving security agencies from at least two countries.

The Arab said, "No. Of course not. We are tourists like everyone else coming down this road."

The Arab caught the disappointment on the driver's face and smiled. "Remember, only one of us inside this vehicle is afraid to die."

The American nodded, wiping the sweat off his upper lip. He pulled into the checkpoint and lowered the window. One officer approached while the other began a sweep of the undercarriage with a mirror on a shaft. The American gave a nervous smile and waited.

The policeman said something in Norwegian. The American said, "I'm sorry. English?"

With a heavy accent, the policeman said, "Business here?"

"We're just visiting. We wanted to see the fortifications of the old town. Maybe go to the museum."

"Okay. But the museum is closed."

The American knew that. What was going on in the museum was the primary reason the man to his right held a gun. He felt nauseated and overwhelmed. Beads of perspiration rolled down his face despite the freezing air, a direct result of being squeezed between two armed men, one using subterfuge and the other standing out in the cold precisely to penetrate the charade. He had nothing to do with either, but that would matter little when the bullets began to fly.

He stammered, "C-can we just see the old town, then? Surely the square isn't closed."

The officer studied him for a moment, then said, "Car registration, please."

The American felt the panic blossom. He had no idea if the vehicle even had valid registration, or where it would be stored. But the Arab did. Right hand held low, hiding the pistol, he used his left to dig through the glove box, pulling out a leatherette envelope and passing it through the window.

The policeman took it, saying to the American, "Are you all right?"

He wiped his upper lip again and said, "Yes, fine. A bit of a cold, I think."

The policeman said nothing, studying the forms inside the envelope. Still looking down, he said, "What is your name?"

The American knew whatever he said, it wouldn't match the forms the policeman held. The Arab knew it as well. The American stammered for an answer and caught movement in his peripheral vision. His brain recognized the nightmare a millisecond before the pistol went off right next to his face, the explosion consuming the inside of the vehicle, splitting his eardrums apart.

The policeman's head snapped back, blood spouting out, and his body crumpled. The American screamed, crouching down and covering his head. The Arab turned to find the other policeman. He was outside the passenger window, frantically attempting to bring his rifle to bear, the mirror dropped to his feet. The Arab fired through the window, shattering the glass and hitting the policeman in the chest, the bullet sending up a small puff of goose down from his jacket, belying the destruction wrought beneath.

The policeman whirled in a half circle, then fell to the ground, crawling toward a ditch and clawing at the rifle on his back. The Arab exited the vehicle and stalked over to him, putting a boot into his back, pinning him in place. He yanked the man's head up by the hair, placed the barrel of his gun against the back of the policeman's skull, and pulled the trigger. A plug of gore exited the man's open mouth and stained the snow underneath.

The American sagged against his seat, the absolute violence destroying any vestige of hope he might have had for self-defense. The Arab calmly returned to the car, walking around to the driver's side. He said, "Get in the passenger seat."

The American did so, numb. The Arab slid behind the wheel and rolled up the window. He locked the doors, then began digging beneath the driver's seat. He pulled out a small box the size of a cigarette pack with a thin wire snaking back under the seat.

He flipped a switch on the box and a tiny light turned green. The American said, "What is that thing?"

The Arab bared his teeth and said, "Your ticket to paradise."

He put the Range Rover into gear and drove across the small moat, entering the ancient fortress.

For all of his fear and naïveté, the American was not a stupid man. He knew what the little container represented. The Arab's intentions had become painfully clear. *This isn't a hostage situation. They never wanted me.*

He was riding in a homemade cruise missile. A mobile bomb directed by a thinking, breathing human being. And he was going to die. None of the power of his position would alter that.

The vehicle made a left turn as soon as it crossed the moat, the Arab with one hand on the wheel and one holding the weapon aimed at the American. As if he could do anything now. He was close to catatonic, rocking forward and back in the passenger seat. Begging for a miracle.

The vehicle picked up speed, racing down the asphalt lane, the brick and stone buildings constructed centuries ago a blur outside the window. The American heard the Arab curse and opened his eyes. He saw the Arab staring into the rearview mirror. The American rotated around and caught sight of a man on a motorcycle right behind them. A rider on a BMW, closing in on the bumper, no helmet, long hair blowing in the wind.

A man the American thought he recognized, but that would be impossible. Even so, he began to hope.

The driver began chanting in Arabic, stoically reciting something over and over. A brick wall, protection for a courtyard built long ago, appeared outside the passenger window. *The museum.*

They reached the end of the lane and the Arab whipped the Range

Rover around the turn, tracking the brick wall. The American saw the entrance to the museum about two hundred meters ahead, a gaggle of men in suits walking to cars parked outside.

And another BMW motorcycle headed right toward them.

The bike raced by the entrance, security men shouting as it passed, brandishing weapons way too late.

The motorcycle grew larger, playing an insane game of chicken. To their left was an ancient berm; to the right, the brick wall of the museum. There was no way to avoid each other. The Arab dropped the weapon and put both hands on the wheel, then floored the accelerator. The American shrieked, jamming his foot against a nonexistent brake pedal in the passenger footwell.

The motorcycle kept coming, the rider helmetless, his jaw clenched and teeth bared.

And the American recognized him as well, but couldn't believe it. There was no way that man was here.

They closed within fifty feet and the biker yanked his handlebars, diving off as the motorcycle went into a slide, spraying gravel as it sliced into the ground.

The Arab screamed, jerking the wheel and slamming the vehicle into the berm. The world tumbled into a kaleidoscope of images. Sky, tearing metal, ground, shattered glass. The American slammed into the door, then the roof, coming to rest upside down on the seat of the Range Rover, the vehicle sliding to a stop on the passenger side. He heard nothing but the ticking of the engine.

The Arab to his right began to stir, slowly rising up and searching for the box, and the American realized he had seconds to alter his destiny. He slapped his hands on the man's wrist, and the Arab punched him straight in the mouth, knocking him back. He rose up, the siren call of self-preservation pushing him forward, and he heard multiple cracks, the Arab's face popping open as if someone had driven in fishhooks and then ripped them out.

The Arab toppled over in the seat, the box held in his hands.

The American sat still for a moment, stunned, the steam rising from the engine, one wheel still grinding as it rotated freely. He looked out the windshield and saw his savior. The man from the rear motorcycle, a huge grin on his face, holding a smoking gun.

The American sagged against the seat, unbelieving. After two hours of hell, he was alive. He floundered in the seat for a second, getting his feet underneath him, then began the climb toward the driver's door above him, a smile plastered on his face. He jerked the door handle, found it unable to open, but the window above him was shattered and clear. He clawed his way over the body of the Arab, struggling to escape through the sliver of daylight, hearing shouting from the front.

He looked through the stars in the windshield and saw his savior screaming at him to stop. Confused, he simply grinned, and continued on. The man shouted again, now frantically waving his arms. The American paused, wondering what was causing the concern. He looked down, and saw his foot on the small box. An innocuous thing, held in the hand of the dead Arab. He lifted his foot, and the box fell out, a long, long drop to the other side of the vehicle.

The last thing he experienced in his mortal life was a flash of light. No heat, although his body was consumed by fire a millisecond later.

2

Washington, DC
Present day

Colonel Kurt Hale held his badge against the access panel and was granted entry with a chirp and a green light. The drop bar in front of him silently rose. He put the car in gear, rolling downward into the garage, the darkness forcing him to remove his sunglasses. He swung around the deck, pulling into a spot labeled CEO, sitting right next to a small atrium housing an elevator. Adjacent to the glass doors was another smart-card reader and a simple brass placard proclaiming BLAISDELL CONSULTING, looking like a hundred other such power signs littering the lobbying/consulting landscape of Washington, DC.

What was beyond the elevators was anything but a lobbying firm, unless the chosen form of persuasion was a flashbang or an assault rifle.

Kurt killed the engine and said, "Probably should enjoy this. My next parking spot won't come with a label."

Removing his tie in the passenger seat, George Wolffe said, "Aww, come on. It wasn't that bad. You want this to be realistic, maybe we should invest taxpayer dollars for some fake stockholders to scream for your head."

A quiet man with a whimsical sense of humor, George had lived a lie his entire professional life. His business cards read CHIEF OPERATIONS OFFICER, which fit into the Blaisdell Consulting charade and was a title that rolled off his tongue more comfortably than his real one: Deputy Commander, Project Prometheus.

Because nobody spoke the true name out loud.

Kurt shook his head and said, "No. This was different. It's been four months, and the Taskforce hasn't conducted a single operation. Even if they don't come right out and say it, mentally they're shutting down. Guy George scared the piss out of them, and they'll use the upcoming election to pull the trigger on us."

"What if Hannister wins?"

Kurt scoffed and said, "Well, that would be something, but only in an alternate universe. He's getting obliterated in the polls on just about everything, even his personality. Did you see that hit piece from Politico asking if people could tell the difference between him and a wax figure of himself at Madame Tussauds? He's cooked, and with him, so are we."

George opened the door and said, "Well, they have a point. He *is* about as exciting as a ball of yarn."

A little melancholy leaking out, Kurt said, "This place was just hitting its stride. What a waste. Fucking Guy George."

Halfway out the door, George Wolffe sat back down, seeing the strain the last few years had brought his friend. Having walked the tightrope of clandestine operations, eschewing the very oversight rules he had once championed, George saw that Kurt felt responsible for the debacle they were now in. Before it had always been for the greater good. Now Kurt Hale could no longer make that claim.

George said, "Hey, cut that out right now. Guy wasn't your fault. You did what you could. At the end of the day, he was right. The real heat came because of that asshat Billings. You tried to save him, tried to do the right thing, and it's going to cost us. But it isn't a done deal yet."

Kurt tapped his hands on the steering wheel and said, "I hope you're right, because I don't think I can go shine a seat in the Pentagon for real. Pretending to do it is bad enough." He turned and looked at his longtime friend and ally. "What will you do? I mean, if worse comes to worst?"

"Go back to the CIA, I guess. Although I've burned most of my bridges there. Probably end up as a reports officer in one of the new Mission Centers looking at climate change."

Kurt laughed and said, "Well, at least they know where we stand."

George pushed open the door a second time and said, "That's true. Nobody on the Oversight Council can say you play politics. Even if that briefing may have been one of your last."

Project Prometheus was decidedly unique, operating outside the normal intelligence community and defense establishments, which is to say, it operated outside the view of just about anyone in the United States government who usually oversaw such activity. A polite way of saying it was an illegal organization, albeit one sanctioned by the president of the United States. But it wasn't completely autonomous.

A panel of thirteen individuals, each handpicked by the president from both the government and the private sector, approved all phases of operations. They required quarterly briefings on all activity, and Kurt and George had just come from one such update. One that had been less about counterterrorism operations and more about damage control.

It had been brief and brutal, but Kurt Hale, for all his tactical acumen at special operations, understood the reasons why. Four months ago a Taskforce Operator named Guy George had gone rogue, applying his lethal skills on a personal vendetta and killing three members of the government of Qatar. The officials had provided financial support to the nascent growth of the Islamic State in Afghanistan, and part of that support had caused the death of his brother.

And Guy's unilateral response had precipitated the death of the United States secretary of state, Jonathan Billings.

It was a killing that had been splashed throughout the world stage, with the subsequent investigation one would expect. All that would have been fine and good, except Kurt Hale had launched a Taskforce team to prevent the killing, without sanction, and the fallout was threatening to expose the extralegal force, along with a possible jail cell for every member of the Oversight Council.

Kurt had tried to start the meeting off by asking for authority to continue surveillance of a suspected financier in Mali, and had learned how naïvely optimistic he had been.

The president himself, Peyton Warren, had cut him off, saying, "Kurt, come on. We're nowhere near ready to continue with operations. Get to the heart of this meeting. What's the state of play with the motorcycle rentals in Norway?"

Kurt had absorbed the rebuke, and saw that everyone in the room was hanging on the answer. Afraid for the skin they had in the game.

"Sir, there's been no change from the last update, and honestly, there won't be a change. The bikes were rented under aliases with credit cards that end in a PO box in Sacramento, California. We had four cutouts before that. There is no way to find a link between who rented the bikes and who was riding them."

Alexander Palmer, the president's national security advisor, said, "Yeah, but that in itself looks strange. It *looks* like an intelligence operation, which is something the Taskforce said would never happen."

Kurt said, "Whoa. Wait. We can ensure we get out clean before an operation, but that statement is predicated on our operational footprint. A slow burn to build the infrastructure and accomplish the mission. This was a hostage rescue—something we don't do. Secretary Billings put his *own* life in danger, and I had the assets to attempt saving his life."

He paused a beat and saw his words were having no effect. Exasperated, he said, "It didn't work out, and now you want to accuse me of not preparing? Maybe I should have just sat on the sidelines. Let the suicide bomber destroy the peace talks. At least then I wouldn't be having this conversation while letting other terrorists go free."

3

President Warren held his hand up and said, "Okay, okay, calm down. Nobody's faulting the effort, but the fallout is something different. We've officially entered the silly season of a presidential election, and the questions arising from Billings's death are almost overpowering. I can only shrug so long before it looks like I'm hiding something."

Left unsaid was that the shrug was tainting his vice president, Philip Hannister, the man who'd recently picked up the proverbial election staff and was running for the president's seat. Forget about the opposition—he was now getting hammered by his own party as ineffectual and/or a liar.

Kurt said, "Sir, it's the best we can do. There's no way to crack what happened. No way the Taskforce will be exposed, but those questions are going to remain. All we can do is shrug. Deny. Hell, ask them to look. They won't find anything."

Palmer shook his head at the pat answer and said, "What about the diplomatic security guys? The ones protecting Billings? They saw Taskforce activity."

Kurt was incredulous. "You're asking *me* to explain that? I don't own them. You do. Who's the next SECSTATE? Who's the acting now? Read them on and start getting control of your own house."

And in the facial expressions of the Council he saw how far the fear had seeped. How little power he actually held.

President Warren said, "I've got a man I'm thinking of. Woman, actually, but I'm not reading her on to Project Prometheus. The last two nominees got hammered hard enough at the confirmation hearings until they quit, and honestly, I'm not that confident on this one. I don't see the need to expand the circle at this stage. Anyway, by the time she gets through the confirmation process—if she gets through—it won't matter."

Won't matter? Why? The answer was clear, even as he asked it. The president was saying, *We're shutting this experiment down.*

Kurt tried one more time. "Sir, what happened in Norway shouldn't stop us from continuing. We have a couple of targets that pose a clear and present danger to US interests. I'm just asking for Alpha authority. Asking to explore."

President Warren said, "No. I'm not even putting it to a vote. Jonathan Billings's death has caused a firestorm, and like it or not, your attempt to prevent it is wrapped up in that. If we're exposed, it'll be catastrophic. You're still on stand-down."

"Sir . . . did you see the reports of Russian ex-KGB trying to sell uranium to terrorists in Moldova? This is not the time to stop Taskforce activities. If anything, we've become more necessary."

Palmer scoffed and said, "Come on. The FBI caught them. We found them through traditional channels. The world is returning to level, where traditional means matter more than Taskforce efforts. We didn't have the Taskforce during the Cold War, and we did okay."

Kurt chose his words carefully, not wanting to antagonize a Council member. "Maybe. Maybe not. The FBI broke up a one-time plot, but the shitheads were then put into the host country's justice system. Ex-KGB. How hard do you think that was? They're going to be released in months, if they're not out already, and we got no intelligence from it. Let me hunt those guys and we'll do some real good."

Kurt waited on someone from the Oversight Council to back him up, but no one did, preferring to stare at their hands or the tabletop. The silence stretched out for a beat, then was broken by President Warren. "You may have a point, but at this stage we just can't risk it.

Too many people are curious and looking into our activities. They haven't found anything yet, but they might, and I can't give them another thread to start chasing. What happens if something goes wrong on the next operation?"

"Sir, it won't."

"And you can promise that? You did, in fact, recruit and train Guy George, did you not?"

Kurt had no answer to that, because there was none. The unit, which had begun as an idea in a presidential candidate's head, had come full circle. President Warren no longer believed.

After an uncomfortable silence, Kurt said, "Sir, whatever Guy did, at the end of the day, he was right. Secretary Billings is dead because he was stupid, not because Guy George was wrong. Let's not forget that had he not done what he did, the peace meetings would have been destroyed, and Billings would still be dead. The only reason the Task-force *could* react was because of Guy."

The words held no sway, and Kurt quit trying, spending the rest of the meeting answering multiple questions about the death of Secretary Billings and the status of various cover organizations that might be exposed. After the meeting, he'd walked down the granite steps of the Old Executive Office Building, in the shadow of the White House, feeling like he'd failed his men.

Driving back to their office, he'd all but mentally given up, but now, entering Blaisdell Consulting, he felt a newborn drive for the unit he'd helped create. A gnawing desire to save it from destruction.

He exited the car, seeing that George had already keyed entry and was holding open the door. George said, "Hurry up. I don't want to explain an alarm because I was acting like a gentleman."

Kurt slid through the door, walked across the atrium, and pushed the elevator button. When George reached him, he said, "The hardest thing is going to be telling the men. I have a team waiting on an EXORD for a simple bugging operation, and I have to tell them no.

They aren't stupid. They're going to understand something's not right."

George barked a laugh and said, "If you mean Johnny's team, I'm sure his stint in Jamaica isn't going to cause any angst. All that means is he gets another day of poolside fun."

"I was thinking about Pike. The active-duty guys can take care of themselves, but Pike and Jennifer deserve an answer with enough time to prepare. If the Oversight Council turns off the tap, everyone else can go back to where they came from. Pike and Jennifer are going to be hung out to dry."

The elevator doors opened and George said, "You going to tell him today?"

"I hope to. He's up here doing some sort of business development for his company. I asked if we could meet, but I don't know if I'm going to make it now. Too much crap going on."

George keyed the access panel, then pressed the button for the third floor. He said, "I wouldn't worry about Pike landing on his feet. He'll figure something out—if it's even necessary."

They rode in silence for a moment, then Kurt said, "You remember all that studying we both did on the Office of Strategic Services? Not wanting to repeat any mistakes they made when we stood up the Taskforce?"

"Yeah?"

"Don't you think it's ironic that in the end, we're going to end up just like them? Disbanded and thrown to the wolves because the threat is deemed not worthy?"

The car came to a halt and the elevator doors opened. George exited and said, "We aren't there yet. There's a lot of time before the election, and something may happen to alter any calculations of our worth."

Kurt simply nodded, exiting the elevator. George caught his arm, made sure nobody else was in the hallway, then said, "You believe that, right?"

"Of course I do. I just don't know if it will matter in the end. Politics trumps security every time."

George let the doors close behind him and said, "Until security drives the politics. Remember, there are a lot of assholes out there who need killing, and only one organization designed to do that."

4

★★★

The sun was still above the horizon, fighting to remain, but had started its inexorable dip, the Black Sea below the helicopter reflecting its light, lending a spectacular flare of orange and red hues to the imposing grandeur of the palace perched on the cliff above it.

The helicopter went feet dry and swept inland, directly over the top of what could only be described as a work of architectural excess. A massive, ostentatious structure of granite and stone that sprawled over 160 acres, from the air it looked like something created from the botched memories of Marie Antoinette and the Mad Hatter. Or from a man who was fervently attempting to reconstruct the power of tsars of old. Springing out of the thick woods on the Russian coast, the building had an opulence that reflected an earlier time, when money and influence were meant to be displayed.

The AugustaWestland AW139 crested the eastern facade, flew over the top of a courtyard large enough to host the World Cup, then zeroed in on four helipads five hundred meters away.

Sitting in his leather seat, the chill fading from the untouched glass of vodka in his hand, Simon Migunov took one look at the mansion and realized whom they were going to meet.

He had never been to the Black Sea Estate, but of course he'd heard about it. Everyone in Russia had, but only a select few were allowed to actually visit, and for good reason: It was where any decisions were made that fell outside of the official records of Russian history. Which was a misleading distinction, as the true history of modern Russia was precisely decided here, outside of any official organ, at a place that not even the Russian press would admit existed, even though it could be seen from satellites as clearly as the Great Wall of China.

Any sordid event that threatened to sully the rarefied air of the State Duma was discussed and decided here, under the canopy of a mansion that itself had been built using pilfered and hidden funds from the state. The stone construct, in fact, was the perfect embodiment of modern Russia.

The thought was unsettling to Simon, as were the two security men at the back of the helicopter, looking bored even as their jackets bulged with potential death.

Simon glanced at his . . . boss? peer? friend? and nodded at the courtyard below. Viktor Markelov smiled and said, "I told you it was important."

"You said nothing of the sort. You said we were negotiating natural gas extensions with the Baltic states."

Viktor flashed yellow teeth, then downed yet another shot of vodka. He said, "The Baltic states are on the menu, but their representatives won't be here. They aren't necessary for this conversation."

Victor Markelov was the vice president of external business development for a Russian conglomerate called Gazprom, the largest oil company on Earth. Which, while impressive, didn't really do the organization justice. It was actually the largest company, oil or otherwise, on the planet. A quasi-state-run entity, it controlled the massive amount of natural gas flowing out of Russia and, in so doing, was a hammer used in Russian foreign policy.

To put it bluntly, Gazprom was a weapon. An enormous beast that couldn't really be compared to any other corporation on Earth, unless one turned to fiction, where it looked more like something James Bond would fight, with Blofeld at the helm.

Part profit-driven corporation, part state-run politics, part mafia-controlled interests, its whole was something that couldn't be adequately described. But, Simon knew, it could certainly be leveraged.

Simon represented the seedier mafia side. Viktor was on the corporate side—the money side. Noticeably absent in the posh helicopter was anything resembling the state.

That, Simon concluded, resided in the mansion by the sea.

The helicopter settled onto the second pad to the left, the others empty, the only thing visible a small caravan of black Mercedes. The chosen vehicle of the elite.

As the engines wound down, Simon said, "Have you been here before?"

"No. This is my first time."

Simon flicked his head to the rear, toward the armed men, and said, "We must be careful. This meeting may be about more than gas."

Simon's tendency toward such vigilance was born from direct experience. A Russian Jew, when the Soviet Union disintegrated he had been barely cresting twenty years old, scraping a living out of petty crime on the streets, but with a wily intelligence and a knack for survival.

The wall fell, and Simon had plied his trade in the chaotic free fall of the Soviet state, becoming a powerhouse working for an oligarch, using whatever levers he could to crush anyone who opposed him. Eventually, he had become the powerful head of an ever-expanding organized crime syndicate, working hand in glove with the new "democracy" of the Russian Federation. Then, as if on a whim, he'd been arrested by those same men. He'd spent a hellish year in a Moscow prison when his agenda no longer fit the desires of the state. Twelve months later, with no reason given, he'd been released.

He'd learned much during that time, the most important thing being that the state was fickle and could turn from provider to punisher at any moment. He was now back on top with Gazprom, doing enough underhanded business to end up on the FBI's Ten Most Wanted list, but he understood his entire life was lived on a brittle shelf of ice. The man they were to meet inside the mansion had almost had Simon executed once, and Simon felt an irrational terror that he had voluntarily given himself over for a second attempt.

Viktor smiled at the concern on Simon's face and said, "We have nothing to fear. I told you this would be a surprise. We are about to step into history. We were invited here because of what we have done with Gazprom. You for your inroads into the true power of the states, and me for my official expansion. We'll seize the day. Seize what is offered tonight."

Simon glanced again to the rear, where the security men were, and said, "Careful what you seek, Viktor. I have seen what catching the tiger brings."

Viktor slapped his leg and said, "Nobody cares about your prison time. That was the old days. When the oligarchs ruled Russia. This is a new age, where we rule. Gazprom is the single biggest weapon Russia has. We execute using our power. *Our* power. Not Russia's."

Simon was amazed that Viktor actually thought his position brought him leverage. But, then again, he'd been burned once by the same hubris.

Viktor unbuckled his seat belt, and the three nameless aides to his left did the same. Simon sat for a moment, reflecting, letting them exit first.

In his youth, he'd worked as a dealer in an unauthorized poker den, carving a living out of the concrete and steel of a new Moscow and hiding his Jewish past. The men in the games would just as soon cut your throat as look at you, and he'd learned something significant from the manager who'd allowed him to deal the cards: If you couldn't recognize the sucker at the table, more than likely it was you.

He exited the aircraft behind Viktor's entourage and in front of the security men, taking a seat in a Mercedes limo next to a guy with a bulging neck wearing a suit that didn't quite fit.

After a short drive, they pulled into the courtyard they'd flown over and entered the fantasyland that was modern Russia—if one were in a position to appreciate it. They walked through two gigantic wooden doors into an atrium that looked like a caricature of opulence, something from a Hollywood movie set, as if someone were trying too hard to show off their wealth. The only thing missing was a naked woman and a midget giraffe from a vodka commercial.

They climbed a granite stairwell wide enough for two cars to drive up abreast, the *clack* of their heels the only noise bouncing in the hall. Simon's trepidation increased with each step.

They reached the top and entered a hall with a dining table the size of the landing deck of an aircraft carrier, the far end set for six.

The security men motioned for them to sit, then retreated to the walls behind them. They did so, staring uncomfortably, no words spoken.

After a brief interlude, another entourage entered, four men striding as if they were late for a meeting, breaking the plane of the room with a purpose. Behind them was the man. The president of Russia, Vladimir Putin.

It was only the second time Simon had met him, and the first hadn't ended very well.

5
★★★

At Putin's entrance, the only thought that stabbed through Simon's brain was, *This is it. I'm dead.* He had no reason to think that, other than the memories of a year in a Moscow prison at the whims of a man who did whatever he wanted with the lives under his control. But it was enough.

While Simon and the others from the helicopter tried to compete for who could jump to attention the fastest, the men of the president's party stopped at an unoccupied chair like a rehearsed parade, the president at the head of the table. He took a slow look around the room, then said, "Thank you for coming here with such little notice."

Viktor said, "By all means, Mr. President. We serve at your pleasure."

Viktor glanced at Simon with a smile on his face. Simon wanted to smash it off. He now understood who the sucker was at this meeting, but he had no idea why he'd been chosen. He'd learned his lesson. Learned not to cross the path of the Russian government. Or he thought he had.

What had he done? He had several operations in play that could have drawn unwanted attention, but each would have taken no more than a whispered word and he would have quit. Stopped completely. What had he done to draw the ire of the president of Russia?

The president said, "I'm glad you feel that way. Tonight, we will do a lesson in trust. Something I have found valuable. A way to learn that no matter what we do individually, we do so as part of a greater system. Yes?"

Simon nodded weakly. Viktor said, "Yes, yes. By all means."

Putin said, "But first, a toast."

As if by magic, a man appeared with a bottle of vodka, poured a shot for each man, then set the bottle on the table.

Putin raised his glass and said, "We live in a complicated world, do we not? And yet sometimes we make it more complicated than it needs to be. A bear in the woods does not hesitate, searching for a decision. He either attacks or runs. Simple. So let us become like the bear. To simplicity in all things."

Simon raised his glass and said, "To simplicity," then downed the vodka in one gulp, wondering what hidden meaning was within the toast. No sooner had he set his glass on the table than the waiter began filling it again. A Russian tradition.

When the waiter had completed his rounds, Putin raised his glass again and said, "But the bear fights alone, and we do not. The wolf is a better analogy. When they attack, they do so because they can trust the member to their left and right. Trust that they will do what is right for the pack. We do the same, do we not?" He glanced around the room and said, "To trust."

They downed their second glass and the security men came forward, each carrying plastic zip ties.

Putin said, "Trust is the cornerstone of our existence. Without it, Russia would have been lost long ago. I need you to trust in this test."

The security men began cinching Simon's wrists to the wooden arms of the ornate dinner chair. Simon offered no resistance, noticing they took care to place the ties over the cuffs of his jacket. When they were done, the security men stepped back again. Simon saw that everyone from the helicopter was cinched like him.

President Putin spoke again. "I trust you men to work for the interests of the Russian Federation. I give you that trust."

Simon felt sweat gather underneath his arms. He glanced at Viktor and saw the man grinning stupidly.

Putin continued. "I see that Ukraine has stated that they will no longer buy natural gas from Gazprom. That unless we lower our prices, they will turn to the European Union for their energy needs. And now Lithuania and Estonia are rumbling the same way."

Viktor flexed his hands and said, "Sir, they always say that. They have no choice but to use us. Nobody in the EU can compete with us."

"They had no choice before, but they have been diligently working on a gas line. Something you failed to stop. Something I trusted you to stop. Even Belarus is talking to the West now."

For the first time, Simon saw Viktor react, realizing he had skin in the game. He said, "Sir, yes, they are trying to wean themselves, but they cannot. We own all their energy needs. If we were to turn off the gas, they would freeze. Belarus would go bankrupt without our help, and they know it." He glanced around the room for support, finding none. His voice cracking, he said, "Sir, we rule them with Gazprom. We rule them. . . ."

The president walked around the table, tapping the wood and saying, "Yes. Today, that is true. But tomorrow is a different story. Because of you. Isn't that correct, Simon?"

Simon jerked upright at his name, unsure of what to say. His role in Gazprom ended at feeding the organized crime beast. He had no control over who or what did anything on the world energy markets. But he also knew his life hung in the balance.

He said, "Sir . . . perhaps you are correct."

Viktor's eyes flew open, looking at Simon in shock. And Simon saw the cards in his hand for the first time, realizing he was not the sucker in the room.

Putin said, "I know I am."

The security men sprang forward, slapping a swath of clear plastic cling-wrap over the face of each Gazprom executive and pulling their heads backward, the plastic covering the mouths and noses of the men. Everyone except Simon. They wrapped the heads until each man was shrouded like a modern-day mummy.

Simon sat still, watching the men writhe and fight, their hands locked to the chairs. Putin said, "It's a shame, really. So many Gazprom men having a heart attack at the same time. Or perhaps it will be a leak of carbon monoxide in a hotel. Either way, there will be repercussions. Investigations of Gazprom chemical uses."

And Simon realized why they'd used the flex cuffs over the suit sleeves. No bruising.

Simon sat in a surreal silence, surrounded by the opulence of gold and granite, watching the men to his left and right die horribly, while the president of Russia clinically studied the suffocation. Eventually, the men ceased moving. At a simple flick of Putin's wrist, the security men began dragging them away. His hands still locked to his chair, Simon waited.

Putin said, "Simplicity, as I said before. Firing them or arresting them on charges would have left them licking their wounds, looking to return the favor in the future. Do you agree?"

Simon caught the trap before he spoke. If he said yes, he was agreeing to his own death because he had been spared once before. If he said no, he was doing the same thing.

Putin didn't wait for an answer. He asked, "Do you believe in Russia?"

"Of course I do. I have proven that over and over again."

"I know. You have been placed in prison for crossing me. Incorrectly, as it turned out. I regret that. Do you harbor any ill will because of it?"

Simon had no illusions of what had happened to him. He had been doing the bidding of the state, and when his actions had been deemed a risk—because of the man in front of him—he had been hammered. The Russian system wasn't built on guilt or innocence, but on who was more powerful. But he was not stupid enough to say that now, with his hands locked to a chair and four of the most powerful people in Russia now dead.

He said, "Of course not, sir. On the contrary, I appreciate the state realizing I was innocent."

Putin picked up a butter knife from the table and played with it, saying, "You know it was I who released you."

"Yes. Of course I do."

Putin pointed the knife at the retreating corpses and said, "You understand why I did that? Understand the threat they represented?"

Unsure of what to say, Simon retreated. "If you thought it was necessary, I'm sure it was."

Putin said, "I mentioned the wolf because I respect its dedication. Respect its loyalty to the pack. Do you?"

Sweat building, Simon, unsure of what turn the conversation had taken, said, "Yes. Of course."

"Do you know the Night Wolves?"

The biker gang? What do they have to do with anything? He didn't voice that, instead simply saying, "Yes, I do. I have business with them on a frequent basis. They are what is pure with our own society."

Putin said, "We live in dangerous times. NATO is encroaching on our terrain every day. They cause one after the other of our former allies to join them. They fight us in Syria and prepare secretly for the demise of the Russian Federation here in Europe. You heard me mention Belarus. Have you any contacts there?"

Simon fought to keep up with the turns of the conversation. "Yes. Naturally, I have some elements there, but not in the government."

Putin smiled and said, "The government is precisely my concern. The people of Belarus are a part of Russia, and yet the government continually makes overtures to the West. The Baltic states are letting NATO put military capability on our doorstep, and Belarus prevents us from building our own bases, despite the wishes of the people. The people are Russian. A part of mother Russia just like Crimea, yet the government of Belarus denounced our intervention into that area. They are vacillating cowards."

Simon was growing more and more confused by the discussion. He had nothing at all to do with the geopolitics of the Russian Federation. He knew, of course, of the discussions of a union between Belarus and Russia—an ongoing struggle to join the two entities into one that had been executed in fits and starts since the demise of the old Soviet Union—but he certainly didn't understand the intricacies.

Putin leaned across the table, and Simon felt the full force of his commitment. "I cannot let Belarus fall into the hands of the West. They agree to treaties with us, then break them. Agree to cooperative engagement with an outstretched hand, then clench the hand into a fist, spurning us. We can no longer wait for their government to do what is right. Now is the time to strike. NATO and the United States are stretched thin by Syria and the rest of the Middle East. China is testing them in the Pacific, and ISIS threatens them at home. They have no tolerance for further foreign entanglements, especially with a country such as Belarus. In Ukraine, I saw what they would do given the chance, and the answer is, very little. Like in Crimea, the people of Belarus will welcome us. All I need is a reason to go in."

Simon nodded, finally realizing where the conversation was headed.

Putin said, "You, dear Simon, will give me that reason. Just as you did once before."

6

★★★

Jennifer came back to the table carrying a couple of rum and Cokes and a bottle of Corona. She handed the beer to Knuckles and gave me a plastic Solo cup, saying, "Great choice. Nothing like getting fired in a dive bar."

Jennifer and I had come up to DC from Charleston because of a strange request from a couple of Israelis we knew. Although saying it was a "strange" request was redundant. Like saying, "Come to a *complete* stop," because every damn request from those two was strange.

Of course, I couldn't come to the nation's capital without grabbing a beer with Knuckles. That would have been sacrilegious.

Kurt Hale had heard Jennifer and I were in town and had asked for a meeting, and I knew it was because of the current hand-wringing about the Taskforce. Usually, we ended up in a coffeehouse somewhere in DC, but this was a special situation. And with it came a special destination. A place called the Rhino Bar on the main drag of M Street in Georgetown. A wing bar with chipped tables, rickety metal stools, and rowdy patrons.

My kind of place, but this time I could blame Knuckles. He'd picked it.

He said, "What's wrong with this establishment? It's in the heart of Georgetown. There are rich folk all over the place. It's not like I took you to the slums."

Jennifer held up her plastic cup and said, "A, they can't afford real glassware. B, the floor sticks to my shoes when I walk. C, they don't even have Bacardi. It's some rotgut rum."

I said, "Beauty is in the eye of the beholder, and anyway, we didn't have a choice. Aaron doesn't want to cross Rock Creek. According to him, it's some sort of no-man's-land border and he's forbidden from entering DC proper. Here, apparently, is okay."

"This is still DC. Didn't you tell him that?"

I took a sip and said, "Of course I did. Well, I told Shoshana, but there's no reasoning with her. To them, this is not Washington, DC. Maybe someone should email the Mossad a link to Google Maps."

Aaron and Shoshana were operatives formerly employed by a Mossad project called Samson, something they referred to as a "special operations team," but it bore little resemblance to what we Americans called SOF, because its entire range of operations encompassed killing someone. Put bluntly, they were a hit team. Born out of the heritage of the Israeli Wrath of God operations in the '70s, they'd run around the world smoking anyone who was trying to harm Israeli interests.

They'd left the services of the Mossad a couple of years ago and set up their own private intelligence business. A cutout, really, because in truth most of their money came straight from a black budget in the Knesset for operations that were deemed too sensitive even for the Mossad. Not unlike the company Jennifer and I ran, only our money was from a different black budget.

We'd first crossed paths on an operation in Istanbul a few years ago, when I'd tried to kill Shoshana. Later, in Amman, Jordan, on a different mission, she'd tried to return the favor. Since then, we'd become fast friends and had quasi-sort-of started working together, on occasion. In this case, Aaron had contacted me out of the blue saying he might have a "business proposition," and requested a meeting "in Washington, DC, but out of the capital."

Since we were doing nothing with the stand-down of the Taskforce, and it gave me a chance to drink a beer with Knuckles, I'd agreed. There was no telling what the meeting would be about, but we could always just say no. Kurt's request, on the other hand, was a complete blank, but it would be good to see him as well.

Jennifer said, "So, Knuckles, why does Kurt want to see us? We haven't been operational since we got back from Norway. Is there finally movement with the Oversight Council?"

Currently checking out the co-eds walking down M Street, Knuckles didn't hear the question. Jennifer followed his gaze and rolled her eyes. "So the choice of bars becomes painfully clear."

Knuckles was a fashion-plate, long-haired, male-model-looking guy with a hippie vibe that women found irresistible. For some reason, they always looked at me as a Neanderthal, failing to see that, as a Navy SEAL, he was exactly the same.

Jennifer said, "Knuckles? Hello?"

He whipped his head back, a little embarrassed, and said, "What?"

"I said I can see why you picked this place. Would you like a napkin for the drool? Why don't you just go out on the sidewalk and say hello instead of playing peeping tom? We'll wait."

Jennifer, on the other hand, had always seen right through him. Just like she had with me, when she recognized that, past my craggy exterior, I was all warm and fuzzy inside, which is why we were together.

Okay, that's not exactly true. I don't have a craggy exterior.

Knuckles said, "Ha. Believe it or not, I'm off the market. I'm seeing someone."

Jennifer perked up, sensing a potential conversation about something other than guns or four-wheel-drive vehicles. She arched an eyebrow and said, "Really? Who would that be?"

He slid a finger in the condensation from his beer bottle and made a trail on the table, clearly not wanting to talk. That got my attention. I said, "Well? Who is it? You haven't mentioned anyone the last four months."

He said, "It's Carly."

Carly? I said, "Carly Ramirez? How? She's in Greece."

He sighed and said, "She's not. She got reassigned right after our operation there. Her career took a hit when the thing with Guy George blew up. She got in a little trouble because of it. She's back at headquarters. She called, and . . . one thing led to another."

Jennifer and I said nothing, processing the information, and Knuckles took it as an indictment. He said, "It's not what you think. We didn't plan it or anything."

Carly Ramirez was a CIA case officer who had dated Knuckles's best friend, a man with the callsign Decoy. He'd been killed in Istanbul on the same operation on which I'd met the Israelis, and through a confluence of events, Carly had ended up helping us try to stop Guy George in Greece four months ago. Intimately involved in the debacle that had caused the stand-down of the Taskforce, she'd apparently been jerked back home to protect our cover, and now Knuckles believed we thought he was sleeping around on his best friend.

Which was sort of nutty, but I could see that he felt some guilt.

Jennifer said, "Hey, we're not judging. I was just surprised. Decoy would approve, you know that."

Jennifer had been standing next to Decoy when he'd taken a round to the head and had killed the man who'd done it, so her words held some weight.

Knuckles smiled, and I decided to dig into him a little bit. He'd been a stickler against fraternization in the ranks, and it had taken him quite a few missions before he'd grudgingly agreed that my relationship with Jennifer hadn't harmed our operations. The last I'd heard, Kurt Hale was looking to recruit Carly into the Taskforce fold, and turnabout is fair play for all the grief he'd given me.

I said, "Screw what Decoy thinks. How on earth can you date someone you work with? You damn hypocrite."

Knuckles laughed and said, "She's still CIA. The Taskforce is on complete manpower hold, no new members. We even canceled the next Assessment and Selection. Kurt Hale never offered her an invitation, so you can stow all the fraternization crap. We're just taking it slow and easy. Nothing permanent, but honestly, I was afraid to tell you."

I immediately forgot about his love life, zeroing in on his other statements. "What do you mean, they canceled A and S? Why?"

"I don't know, but honestly, I'm worried. I think the Taskforce is coming to an end. I wouldn't be surprised if that's what Kurt's going to tell us. Guy George scared the hell out of them, and with the election coming up, I think they're afraid to do anything. When the new administration comes in, I think we're gone."

In my heart, I'd known the same thing, but just didn't want to face it. We operated outside the US Constitution, and sooner or later, such a unit either mutates into something dangerous or is expunged. Or both. Since we hadn't mutated quite yet, I'd just assumed we'd continue on as soon as everyone quit worrying about Guy George, but apparently others thought we'd already become too great a risk. Our actions in Norway hadn't been exactly clean, and so the powers that be were worried about their collective asses. The easiest way to salvage that was to cut the Taskforce away.

As if to punctuate the thought, my phone vibrated with a text.

Pike, how long are you in town? I can't make it out today.

I said, "Speak of the devil. Kurt just canceled the meeting."

I texted back, **Not sure. Depends on what happens at my other meeting. With Knuckles now. What's up?**

I didn't like the response: **Let's just say you might want to look hard at that business proposition. I'll have no work for you for a while.**

I replied, **A while, or forever? Knuckles told me about A&S.**

I got the little bubble on my phone and waited for the reply. At least it had some vote of confidence, as it came in all caps: **A WHILE. NOT FOREVER. Talk soon.**

I showed the phone to Jennifer, then passed it to Knuckles, saying, "What's that mean for you guys?"

Knuckles was still on active duty with the Navy, sheep-dipped at some do-nothing job on the Navy rolls while he actually acted as my second-in-command for our team. The other operators were also either active-duty military or CIA. Jennifer and I were unique in that we were civilians, with a civilian company.

He said, "For now, nothing. We're just sitting around twiddling our thumbs. We aren't even allowed to conduct exercises to keep our skills up. Long-term, I guess we'll all just go back to where we came from. Although the thought of going back to big Navy makes my skin crawl. I'd end up on staff at WARCOM wearing a uniform."

Jennifer held up her phone and said, "Just got a text from Shoshana. They're on M. Should be here in a couple of minutes."

I nodded and said to Knuckles, "How much more time do you have until twenty?"

"A couple more years. At least I'm getting a paycheck. What are you guys going to do?"

I said, "Hey, Grolier Recovery Services still exists. The Oversight Council can't shut that down. We'll just take our show on the road until they pull their heads out of their asses and let us start operating again."

He laughed and said, "Real archaeological work? Without the Taskforce paycheck, you'll starve within a year."

Grolier Recovery Services was the company Jennifer and I had founded after I'd left active duty. Ostensibly, we facilitated archaeological expeditions around the globe, not by doing the actual digging— that was up to whoever hired us—but by providing liaison with the US embassy, site security, and coordination with the host nation.

Honestly, Knuckles had a point: We'd done only a few contracts where the customer was an actual, real research entity—and one of those had simply been a billionaire who wanted to play Indiana Jones.

Most of our money came through the Taskforce, using our business as a cover to penetrate denied areas and put some terrorist's head on a stake.

Jennifer stood and I saw Aaron Bergman enter the bar, looking around for us. She waved and I said, "That was the past. I think GRS might be on the verge of a banner year."

7

The dim lighting providing barely enough illumination to see his boss, Mikhail Jolson said, "You don't seem yourself. Did everything go okay with the meeting?"

The music was overpowering, forcing Mikhail to speak above a whisper, but that cacophony was precisely why this meeting place had been chosen. There was no way any listening devices would be able to parse what was said on the small balcony. Well, that was one reason the place had been chosen. The young girls dancing below, all struggling to catch the attention of one of the men in the rarefied air above them, were the other reason.

Even so, Mikhail took care to use a language rarely heard around Moscow. Speaking Yiddish like Mikhail, Simon said, "No. It most decidedly did not go as well as expected."

President Putin had stuck to the Russian tradition that once a bottle was opened, it had to be emptied, and in between shots of vodka, Simon had learned his tasking and the help he would have from the Russian state to ensure success. What was left on the table, besides the empty bottle, was what his fate would be once the mission was complete.

Simon had flown back to Moscow in the executive helicopter alone, save the pilots; the empty cabin seeming much larger with the absence of the Gazprom staff. It was a brutal reminder of how thin the line was between life and death in modern-day Russia. How little of it he controlled, even with his vast empire.

The boss of a criminal enterprise that stretched from Moscow to New York to the Levant, he could order the death of just about anyone, and yet his own life was forfeit to a megalomaniac in charge of Russia. And that was the crux.

If he were ever to be free, truly free, he would have to deal with Vladimir Putin. And if his last tasking by Putin was any indication, he would have to do so now, before the president began sweeping away the evidence like he had before. Simon was sure he wouldn't be lucky enough for even a jail cell when the event was completed.

A waiter stuck his head into the small balcony, a look of surprise on his face when he saw both men, mistaking Mikhail for a body-guard. He couldn't be blamed for the confusion, as Mikhail was fit, with jet black hair and black eyes that were constantly scanning, his hands resting near his open jacket. He could have been a bodyguard, and would most certainly act like one if any trouble appeared, but that was not his duty.

In contrast, Simon was pasty and bordering on corpulent, his jowls flowing out over the collar of his suit, looking vaguely like Alfred Hitchcock, which is to say he fit the template of the men occupying the adjacent balconies, and yet he knew why the waiter stared.

The nightclub was reserved strictly as a playground for the billion-aire oligarchs who dotted the landscape of Russia. To prevent drunken shootouts that had occurred in the past, the hired help waited outside, while the barons—the women called them "Forbes"—sat inside and drank the night away, picking and choosing whom they would take home, the security provided by the nightclub by mutual agreement.

Simon pulled a wad of money out of his pocket and waved the waiter over, saying, "This is Mikhail, my associate. I will have some more men visiting who do not fit the profile of the others here. Sergio has their names at the door, and there will be no trouble."

He handed a note to the waiter, who saw the denomination and smiled, nodding his head and retreating.

Reverting back to Yiddish, Simon said, "If only our business was to find a mistress, life would be much easier."

Mikhail smiled and said, "No, it wouldn't." He waved a hand to the floor of women all vying to be called up to one of the balconies. "Once they get their claws in you, it's demand, demand, demand. Apartments, cars, vacations. Better to just find a whore for the night."

Simon said nothing, drawing on a cigarette. Mikhail waited a beat, then said, "Will your meeting upset what we have planned in Poland?"

"No. Not at all, but it might upset my ability to spend the proceeds."

Mikhail didn't respond, and Simon crushed the embers of his cigarette, then laid everything bare. "Putin wishes to take over Belarus. He has engaged me to do so. He wants to attack his Su-27 squadron in Baranovichi."

Mikhail looked astounded, his mouth hanging open. When he found his voice, he said, "Take over? You mean the country? I thought Russia was building a base at Babruysk."

"They're trying to. Belarus is still dragging their feet, and one of the sticking points is that Russia wants to use a large contingent of infantry to protect the base. Belarus, of course, sees that contingent in a different light. They see nothing but a Russian threat, and so they maintain that they can protect their own terrain."

"So Putin is going to attack his own people?"

"Yes. There is a squadron of aircraft in Baranovichi. He wants me to destroy some planes, kill people, generally cause havoc, then leave evidence of provocateurs behind. Chechens allied with the Islamic State. He'll proclaim it his right to defend what's his, and then he'll roll in with everything he's got over the protests of the Belarusian government, using his forces to 'protect' the other airbase in Babruysk and the two Navy radar relays. When he's done, he'll have effectively boxed in Minsk. From there, he'll own the country. Truthfully, he has the support of enough of the population to make it happen. It'll be a bloodless coup. Well, bloodless except for the men he wants me to kill to make it happen."

Mikhail said, "Putin's a shit, but I can't believe he'd want you to actually kill his own soldiers. Are you sure you aren't reading into what he wanted?"

Simon let a smile slip out, tainted with sadness. "Do you remember the apartment bombings in 1999? When Vladimir Putin was a newly appointed prime minister?"

Simon waited while Mikhail searched his memory, saying, "You were still working intelligence in Israel, but it made a splash on the world stage."

Mikhail nodded, the story coming back to him. He said, "Yes, Chechen terrorists killed hundreds of people in three apartment complexes, which led to the second Chechen war and the destruction of Grozny."

"Mostly true. It *did* lead to the second Chechen war, and also to the election of one Vladimir Putin to the presidency, the first time, but it wasn't Chechens. It was the Russian FSB, all for the express purpose of starting a war."

Mikhail scoffed and said, "Yeah, yeah, we heard those stories in Israel, but there was no proof of that. Just conspiracy theories."

Simon took a sip of his drink and said, "I am the proof. One of the bombs didn't go off because FSB men were arrested trying to plant it. They claimed it was an unrelated exercise. I know differently. I was involved in the planning and execution of the operation."

Mikhail said nothing, absorbing the information. Simon said, "Can you get me back into Israel, with your connections?"

"No. Not now. It was all I could do to get you out the last time. The Shin Bet has you at the top of their list. Christ, you're on the top ten of the American FBI. Even if the Shin Bet wanted to leave you alone, you'd be arrested by pressure from the United States. We're going to have a hard enough time keeping your name off what we get in Poland when it's sold. They smell you on it, and nobody will touch it."

Simon sagged back against his chair, then said, "That's what I expected. Which leaves only one option. Putin has to go."

"What are you talking about? Just do the job. Who cares about Belarus?"

Simon leaned forward, his eyes burning. "The last time I 'did the job,' I went to jail for a year of hell. The others, the ones closest, like I am now, were killed. And Putin's only become bolder. Christ, I just saw him kill four executives of Gazprom because they weren't selling enough gas. I do this and I'm dead. There is nowhere I can hide. He'll start cleaning up immediately, even as his tanks are rolling into Belarus."

"Wait, wait, I'm still a little confused. We're businessmen. How are you supposed to execute a coup in Belarus? Who are the foot soldiers? FSB agents?"

Simon barked a mirthless laugh. "No. Putin's smarter this time around. There won't be any FSB men arrested at an inopportune time. He's using the same men we deal with for our protection network. The Night Wolves."

"You've got to be kidding. Those nutcases? That's insane. He gives them a match and they'll turn it into a bonfire. At least he can control the FSB."

The Night Wolves were ostensibly nothing more than a motorcycle gang, but while its roots began with a Harley Davidson, its DNA had become much more. Springing forth during the *perestroika* days of the old Soviet Union, it had started as a small group of men clinging to the identity of Russia beyond the constructs of the USSR. Since then, it had grown to over five thousand members with an ultra-nationalist bent that saw enemies of Russia in every corner, a paranoid group with the strength to enforce their will.

In one respect, the club was different from the so-called one-percenters of American biker gangs such as the Hells Angels or the Mongols, in that it had embraced a nationalist identity fully in lock-step with President Putin. Far from being chased and hunted by the law enforcement of Russia, it was encouraged to the point that it had become a quasi–state arm, and was used to crush any potential protests in Red Square, with the culmination of President Putin himself riding in a Night Wolves rally.

Wrapping themselves in the Orthodox Church and having a rabid belief in Russian superiority, the group had achieved a mythical status as the final protectors of Russian sovereignty. Under whispers of state control, they had actively participated in the annexation of Crimea, providing its members as "volunteers" driven to return the peninsula to the Russian homeland. Three had officially been killed in the fighting, and had been hailed as heroes.

The titular head of the Night Wolves was a man known as the Surgeon, either because he had once been a doctor, or because—as the myths held—he was good with a knife. Neither could be proven to any degree, but both were just as likely to be true.

Simon said, "Yes, you're right. The Night Wolves *are* uncontrollable, and that's exactly what I'm counting on. I'm going to give them Putin's mission, and Putin's support, but I'm going to spur them on for something greater."

"What do you mean?"

Simon said, "There's only one way Putin will be removed. Only one way he'll cease to be a threat to me, and that's if he oversteps his bounds as president."

The waiter entered the room, leaned over, and said, "Your other guests are here."

"Please show them up." When the waiter had left, Simon said, "I'm going to need your help as well."

"Doing what?"

"Starting World War Three."

8

★★★

Aaron entered the bar by himself, letting the door close behind him. He stood for a moment, then caught Jennifer's wave. He started to come our way and I wondered what had happened to his satanic partner. Okay, that was a little mean. Truth be told, although I'd never admit it to anyone but Jennifer, I was sort of sweet on her.

Knuckles said, "Should I go?"

I said, "Not unless you want to. I've got no reason for you not to hear what he has to say. Aaron might have a different opinion, but you might as well finish your beer."

Jennifer hugged Aaron and said, "Where's Shoshana?"

He flicked his head to the street and said, "Window shopping. Looking at some bag worth much less than they are charging."

I said, "She actually shops? For useless shit like Jennifer?"

I didn't mean it to come out that way, but it did. Jennifer gave me her disapproving teacher glare, and I was starting to backpedal when the door opened again. The little angel of death herself entered, carrying a new purse the size of a small duffle bag, and I saw Jennifer break into a smile, which was something I still had to wrap my head around. They were so far apart it was like night and day, but for some reason, they connected.

A tall, waifish woman of about five foot nine, with black hair cut in a pageboy, Shoshana was all sinew and muscle, like a snake, with no womanly curves. In contrast, Jennifer looked like something from a California surfing calendar, with a shape to match. Gray eyes, dirty blond hair held in a ponytail, she routinely turned heads wherever she went. Next to her, Shoshana looked like she had stepped out of a Charles Dickens novel, and the contrasts didn't stop with outward appearances.

Jennifer had a moral compass that was black and white, unerringly telling her the limits of what she was willing to do to accomplish our mission. Shoshana's compass was broken beyond repair. She would do *whatever* was necessary, no matter who was harmed in the process.

At least, that's what I thought. Jennifer seemed to feel differently, and believed I was selling Shoshana short. And maybe I was, but it was only because I saw myself when I looked into her eyes. But given Jennifer's unbending sense of right and wrong, if she believed it, it might be true. That compass had proven true with me once upon a time. I just didn't want to test the theory, because on the last mission where I'd done so, Shoshana had threatened to kill me. Even if we were friends.

I had to admit, though, I missed her.

She glided over to the table in her predatory way, taking in the entire room without appearing to, looking for threats. She hugged Jennifer even as she was eyeing the bartender, still assessing her environment. It made me wish I'd have planned for Knuckles to leap out of the rafters. Of course, that might have ended up with him dead, so I guess that wouldn't have been too funny.

She let go of Jennifer and said, "Nephilim. You look good. A little fatter than last time. Jennifer must be feeding you well."

What the hell? Her face revealed nothing but innocence.

Over her shoulder, Jennifer glared at me, telling me not to go off, so I didn't. While the statement wasn't accurate, I wasn't even sure it was an insult in her eyes. Lord knows, I couldn't get her to quit using my given name, even when she knew I hated it. She seemed to think it was some talisman of good luck.

Aaron was grinning at the jab, but remained silent, knowing that he had no control over his little assassin. He never did, until push came to shove, and then she followed him into hell simply because he asked.

I smiled and held out my arms, saying, "You want to test the fat man, Carrie?"

Which is what I called her to return the favor. On our last mission together, my team had taken to using *Carrie* as a callsign for her because she was something straight out of a Stephen King novel, down to some scary ESP-type ability she seemed to possess. It was supposed to be an insult, but she took it as a compliment.

She hesitated for a moment, and I could feel her reading me. Penetrating me. It was always disconcerting, but I was getting used to it. Then she hugged me harder than necessary, surprising me, squeezing and resting her head on my shoulder. She said, "I missed you. You and Jennifer."

I said, "Yeah, I bet you missed Jennifer. Always wanting what you can't have."

Jennifer believed Shoshana was a lesbian, but I wasn't convinced. Either way, Shoshana routinely tried to aggravate me by hitting on her. Jennifer took the flirting in suffering silence, like a family pet caught between two small children fighting over who gets to throw the ball.

Shoshana laughed and said, "You didn't hear? I'm married." She held out her left hand, and I'll be damned if it didn't have a ring on it.

I said, "Seriously? Who's the lucky . . . person?"

"Aaron, of course. Who else?"

Aaron looked embarrassed and said, "It's for the business proposition I wanted to talk to you about. We're working as a husband-and-wife team."

Shoshana beamed and winked, saying, "Yeah, it's *only* for the mission."

I swear, those two were the most complicated couple on the entire planet. And that was *including* Jennifer and me. Aaron loved her with his entire being, and she loved him back, but it would never be physical. At least according to Jennifer. With the wink, I was wondering if Jennifer wasn't off base, but with Aaron's embarrassment, whatever was happening was still a mystery, even to him. Only Shoshana knew, and she wasn't telling.

Because she was a psycho.

Knuckles downed the rest of his beer, shook Aaron's hand, then said to me, "Well, I'm outta here. I'll tell Kurt we talked."

Shoshana looked him in the eyes, then said to Aaron, "He can listen. Maybe he can help us too."

Knuckles said, "Oh, no. You guys do whatever you want, but I've got enough work to keep me busy."

Shoshana flicked her eyes from him to me to Jennifer, then settled back on Aaron. She said, "That's not true."

Knuckles's mouth fell open, and Shoshana said, "I don't mind him coming. We might need him."

Knuckles looked at me in amazement and I said, "Wait, wait, what the hell are we talking about?"

Shoshana started to say something else, and Aaron held up his hand. She closed her mouth and took a step back from Knuckles. That had never, ever happened. I said, "Well, well, looks like you've learned some discipline."

Shoshana settled her eyes on me and said, "I've always had discipline, but it never involved you. We've never needed you before. You and Jennifer. We need you now, and Aaron is afraid you'll refuse if I aggravate you. So I promised not to do so until you agree. Then I get to do what I want."

I looked at Aaron and said, "What is she talking about?"

"Like I said, we have a business proposition. It doesn't require your skill. It only requires your company."

"What's that mean?"

"Have you heard about the fabled Nazi gold train in Poland? The one that's supposedly buried in a secret tunnel?"

9

★★★

Out of all the things I had thought Aaron might say, this had not been even remotely in the ballpark. I said, "Did you say ghost train? No, actually, I haven't. Have you heard about Area 51? Jennifer and I have been there. They don't really have any aliens."

Jennifer said, "I've heard about it. I thought it was a hoax. Some guys said they used ground-penetrating radar to locate the train, but the government says they're frauds and there is no train."

Leave it up to Jennifer to have a clue what the Israelis were talking about. She was constantly reading *National Geographic* and other, more obscure anthropological and archaeological magazines, and seemed to be tracking all attempts by modern man to penetrate the past. If it had anything to do with history, she almost always knew exactly what that history was. But this was a bit much.

She saw my expression and said, "He's talking about something real. Not just pulling your chain for a smart-ass response."

Shoshana nodded and said, "It's real, all right. And they've found it. No hoax. The government just wants the treasure hunters to go away, because they've already emptied the contents."

Jennifer said, "What? They can't do that in secret. The train probably held millions of dollars of property belonging to someone else."

Shoshana's eyes glowed and she said, "Exactly. It also held something more valuable to us."

I held up my hands and said, "Wait, wait, damn it. Someone explain all this to me."

Jennifer looked at Aaron, and he gave her permission to lecture me. "Okay, it's really pretty simple. You know about the horrific roundup of the Jews in Eastern Europe, right? How the Nazis hunted them and then sent them to the concentration camps?"

I said, "Yeah, yeah. I know the history of World War Two. You can speed it up."

"Well, when they boarded the cattle cars, they lost everything they had, from famous artwork owned by the richest Jewish citizens to the meager wedding rings of the poorest. Everything valuable was taken, and as the Jews were taken from each city, their valuables were loaded onto trains and shipped west to Germany. Some of the trains were captured—for instance, one famous train in Hungary in 1945, with forty-four cars loaded floor to ceiling with gold products—while others were known to exist but have never been found."

I said, "And someone thinks they've located one of these missing trains, buried underground? Why would the Nazis do that?"

Jennifer looked at Aaron and said, "You guys clearly know more than me on this train. Want me to continue?"

Shoshana said, "Oh, yes. Please do. It's not often we get to feel superior to Pike."

Knuckles snickered, and I said, "Like you know about this."

"I'm not the one they're trying to hire, but given your lack of knowledge, I'd be suspicious of paying you anything."

Aaron said, "Jennifer?"

Jennifer patted my hand and said, "Okay, knuckle dragger, you do know about the fighting in Eastern Europe, right?"

Now on more comfortable ground, I said, "Yeah, I'm pretty sure I can hold my own there. Warsaw uprising, Stalingrad, what do you want to know?"

"Project Riese?"

Now I was getting aggravated. I had no idea what that was. Shoshana grinned, which didn't help my mood.

Jennifer smiled at me, knowing it would defuse my anger. Which it did. I noticed Shoshana staring intently at the small exchange, as if she were studying a couple of lizards in a jar.

Jennifer said, "That wasn't a fair question. Riese wasn't a fight. It was a system of tunnels built into the mountains in what's now western Poland. In World War Two, it was German territory. Anyway, to make a long story short, Hitler was building a gigantic complex—*riese* in German means 'giant'—for reasons unknown and debated to this day. Some say it was a final command complex for the führer, others that it was for building next-generation weapons. A sort of Hydra-like complex straight out of the Avengers, except it was real. And a lot of it is still unknown."

I took that in and said, "So this complex might be hiding the missing trains?"

"Well, that's what the treasure hunters say. They claim they found one of the trains in a previously unknown tunnel that had collapsed. They even had radar images to prove it." She turned to Aaron and said, "But the last I heard, the government explored and found nothing."

Aaron said, "That's because they don't want a riot over claims, like happened with that Hungarian train you mentioned. They found it, but it wasn't forty-four cars loaded with gold. It was one car, and it held a couple of cases of gold products, mostly candlesticks and that sort of thing, some artwork, and something special to us."

I said, "What?"

"There might be a very, very old Torah from a synagogue in Plonsk, Poland. David Ben-Gurion's birthplace."

Even I understood the significance of that. Ben-Gurion was the father of Israel. It would be like finding a bible owned by George Washington.

He continued, "If it's the right Torah, it will be over four hundred years old."

Scratch that. Make it a bible that had been passed down for generations until it reached Washington's hands.

Aaron said, "It is something the State of Israel would very much like to confirm, but they can't do so openly. Officially, they don't know it exists, which is where you come in."

"Us? We're not Jewish."

"No, you're not. But you *are* the owners of Grolier Recovery Services. A facilitation company for archaeological work."

"And?"

"And Poland would never let in a group of Israelis to look at the Torah. They'd be petrified we'd raise an alarm and cause trouble over the entire find. But they don't have an issue with a husband-and-wife team from the United States who happen to be experts on ancient Jewish texts, especially when they're being escorted by such an esteemed company. You did, after all, find a pyramid in the Guatemalan jungle."

I brushed off the blatant flattery, saying, "And this husband-and-wife team would be you and Carrie here?"

Shoshana nodded and said, "Yes. We just want to use your cover to make us legitimate. Get us over there to take a look."

"How do you guys even know all this?"

"Let's just say that certain elements of our government have determined all this, and that the Polish government is trying to ascertain what they found. They've made discrete inquiries to various universities asking for help in determining the provenance of some of the artwork, and we managed to interject ourselves into the flow for the Torah."

Meaning some idiot in Poland had actually contacted an expert in Israel, and they, in turn, had reported back to the Mossad.

"So all we do is fly over there with you, look important, then fly home?"

"Basically, yes. That's it. Look, Poland's intentions aren't evil. They're just trying to do the right thing without a firestorm. Taking it slow and easy. We'll take a look at the Torah and report what we find. Israel doesn't want to cause a fight without reason, but if it's real, they *will* get it back."

Sounded simple, but one part of the whole scheme was blank. Jennifer caught the same problem, asking, "But who's going to do that? Determine if it's real? None of us have that ability."

Aaron said, "We have tracked down survivors from that synagogue. The Torah has identifying markings. And we have Shoshana."

I said, "Shoshana?"

She nodded, and said, "All I need to do is touch it. I'll know."

A part of me wanted to roll my eyes at the magic mumbo jumbo, but a deeper, primordial part believed. I don't know how, but Shoshana had a weird, freakish ability to read intent from a person simply by studying them. I'd seen her do it, and it was real. I couldn't see how it extended to inanimate objects, but hey, it was their dime. Who was I to question?

I looked at Jennifer, and she shrugged, saying, "We're not doing anything in Charleston."

I said, "Knuckles, you want to take some leave? Earn a little money?"

Aaron seemed unfazed by the suggestion, which should have sent my radar up, but I figured he was just willing to do anything to get our commitment. After all, he wasn't footing the bill.

Knuckles said, "Nope. You guys go ahead. I'm staying right here. Flying for eighteen hours just to look at an old scroll isn't my idea of fun."

He stood up, flipped some bills onto the table, and said, "Call me if it turns into high adventure."

I grinned and said, "Will do."

He walked out saying, "I'll let Kurt know you've found at least a week's worth of employment."

To Aaron I said, "When would we need to fly?"

"Well . . . I've taken the liberty of using your company name and address already. The Polish antiquities department is expecting us in two days."

It took a second to find my voice, unsure if I should be flattered or aggravated. I finally said, "You're kidding me. You were that sure we'd sign on?"

Aaron grinned and said, "I wasn't, but Shoshana was. And I've learned to trust her instincts."

Bouncing up and down on the balls of her feet, looking more like a kid waiting on ice cream than the lethal killer she was, Shoshana said, "So you'll do it?"

I looked at Jennifer and said, "You mean spend a week with you and Aaron acting like a married couple? How on earth could I miss that shitshow?"

Shoshana beamed, for some reason taking it as a compliment. She said, "I've been studying you and Jennifer. I'm getting really good at it. I just can't decide if I want to be the pure one that suffers through, like Jennifer. Or like you."

I said, "The pillar against the wind? The protector of all that's sacred?"

She scrunched up her face and said, "No, no. Is that how you see yourself? Get real. I mean the cranky asshole of the relationship."

Jennifer and Aaron both started laughing. Aaron said, "I only told her not to aggravate you until you agreed."

Shoshana leaned in and kissed me on the cheek. I ignored her, waving for the check, saying, "You don't need any practice at being the cranky asshole."

10

★★★

The Russian girls continued dancing below. Inside the alcove, the dim light failed to hide Mikhail's shocked expression at Simon's statement. Simon said, "Yes, you heard me correctly. We need to alter the balance of power. Running and hiding won't do me any good. Putin will find me wherever I go, just as he did with Alexander Litvinenko. But, unlike Alexander, I have no intention of dying of radiation poisoning in a London hospital. I will die of old age in Moscow."

Mikhail said, "I can't help with this. I understand your plight, but that is not mine, at least not yet. We have had good business together, but you're asking me to commit suicide."

"No, I'm not. The world is sick of Vladimir Putin. He barges around like a bear in the woods, from Syria to the Ukraine, and he's made the West afraid with his actions. They're on a trip wire after Crimea."

Mikhail grimaced and said, "There is an old adage: 'If you shoot at the king, make sure you hit him. If you bury him, make sure he's dead.' That is not us. We *cannot* take on the president of the Russian Federation."

"*We* can't, but there is an undercurrent of unease in Moscow. Men who are worried about Putin's global escapades. Men of power. These men will do anything to retain what they have, even if that means removing Vladimir Putin and his entrenched circle. But they need to be convinced that such action is in their best interests."

"And how are we to do that?"

"We will provoke the West. Destabilize the already fragile lines of war. If it appears that Putin took it upon himself to initiate hostilities for political gain, he will not be allowed to remain in control, especially if NATO is on the verge of crushing the entire Russian Federation. He is a powerful man, but not a god, and he will be sacrificed when it's deemed expedient. Just like he is planning to do with me. NATO and the oligarchs in Moscow will accomplish our goals for us. All we need to do is light the fuse."

Still not convinced, Mikhail had started to reply when there was a knock on the door to their little alcove. Simon held up a finger and said, "I believe that's our book of matches."

The door cracked open and Simon saw the same waiter stick his head in, saying, "Sir, the men you have on the list arc here, but they refuse to put on—"

That was as far as he got before he was shoved rudely out of the way. Two men pushed past him, both looking decidedly different than the rest of the patrons in their thousand-dollar suits. One had a full beard, the other an unkempt goatee. Wearing jeans and jackboots, both sported leather vests adorned with a multitude of patches, the back of each vest taken up by a large depiction of a howling wolf's head, flame coming from the neck as if it had been launched from a cannon.

The lead man said, "Simon, the weasel here has an issue with our colors."

Simon rolled his eyes and stood up, waving another bill. He pointed to a couch and said, "Sit." To the waiter: "It's okay. They won't cause any trouble."

The waiter took the money, hesitated for a fraction of a second, as if contemplating forcing the issue, then decided discretion was the better part of valor and silently left the room.

Simon waited until the door had closed again, then turned and said, "What did I tell you about the dress code? Why do you insist on making a scene? Being remembered?"

The leader held up his hands and said, "Honestly, I just thought you were recommending. I didn't know wearing a coat and tie was a rule."

Simon sat down, pointed at the other man and said, "Who is this?"

"Oleg. He's the one with the skill you asked for."

Simon nodded, then said, "Mikhail, meet Kirill Zharkov. The leader of our little cell of Night Wolves."

Mikhail stuck out his hand and said, "Yes, yes, of course. We've spoken over chat and text, but never met."

Kirill shook the hand, thinking, then said, "Mikhail? You're the man who turned us on to that little opportunity in Volgograd, is that right?"

Mikhail nodded, and Simon said, "Which brings us to why you're here. Opportunity, but not for profit. For the motherland. The president has a special mission, and has asked for you to carry it out."

The words had an effect on the two men. Kirill said, "Like he did in Crimea?"

"Exactly. Are you prepared to fight for Russia?"

Kirill became agitated, slapping his hand on the table hard enough to make Simon wonder how much vodka he'd had in the last hour. "Of course! President Putin has had his hands tied too long. He's trying to make us what we should be, and he's stopped by weaklings in our own government. It turns my stomach. We've suffered one indignity after another at the hands of the West. What is it you wish us to do?"

Simon saw Mikhail roll his eyes, and he snaked his hand under the table, tapping Mikhail's knee as a reminder. He slid one glare Mikhail's way, then told the men the broad strokes of what was expected of them. After he was done, he said, "Do you have any qualms about that?"

"No. I think it's perfect. We'll do our part."

"You might end up killing Russian soldiers. It's not necessary, if you can blow up aircraft instead, but it might happen."

Kirill said, "I'm not sure why that matters. We're prepared to give our lives for Mother Russia. So are they. Who cares who pulls the trigger, if the end result is for the greater good?"

Simon saw Mikhail squeeze his eyes shut as if he were warding off a headache, and leaned forward to block Kirill's view, sliding a cell phone across the table. He said, "Okay, then. The president himself will provide Russian uniforms to penetrate the base. You did as I asked, and your men have all served, correct?"

"Yes. Of course. It's hard to find someone in Russia who hasn't served."

"That's not what I meant. I mean you've served beyond the minimum conscription. You have people who can act like they know what's happening in the military. Not some asshole who spent two years stealing from his command and never even learned to put on his uniform correctly. You'll have to bluff those same people at the gate."

Kirill said, "We can. My cell has many veterans. We know how to act like we're still in the military. You provide the uniforms, and it will be no problem. But that's not the final issue. We escape as Russians, and we still have blame to give. What about the Chechen artifacts? How will we do that?"

Simon was surprised at the forethought, believing that the Night Wolves would not understand the totality of the attack, and that he would have to spoon-feed the solution. He was pleased.

"The president will post the attack on some of their social media sites. They will claim credit even if they don't want to. You will also get certain weapons to leave at the scene. These weapons will have biometric traces on them from known Chechen terrorists on the loose. It will be enough to drown out any protests of innocence."

Kirill took that in, then said, "Okay. All that makes sense, but it doesn't explain why you wanted Oleg. The Buk radar operator."

Simon knew he was now brushing up against treason. Stepping out into the void.

He took a breath, glanced at Mikhail, then said, "This mission isn't the only one, which is why you must get in and out without casualties or compromise. There will be another one. When you are through with Belarus, you will travel back to Ukraine. Remember the shoot-down of MH17? The civilian aircraft?"

For the first time, Kirill looked uneasy. He said, "Yes . . . but that wasn't us. That was Ukraine."

Simon waved his hand and said, "Whatever happened before, this time it will be you. Your team will take over a Buk M1 currently in Eastern Ukraine. After Russia has secured our airfields in Belarus, you will destroy a NATO warplane. The ones that are always buzzing about to show us how strong NATO is."

Oleg's eyes widened and he said, "There is a ceasefire in eastern Ukraine. The president himself agreed to it. If we shoot, we will cause a war."

Simon turned on the heat as if he were a missionary burning with the gospel, the truth fighting to escape. An ability he'd learned to mimic fairly well in prison, when every proclamation had to evince true fever.

"Exactly. That is *exactly* right. They will come to fight, but it won't be because of *Russian* provocation. They will simply make it so in their own minds. The president needs to be able to plausibly deny he did this, but he *wants* a fight. NATO is too weak to secure the Baltic states, and if they provoke a response because of one misguided missile fire, he is more than willing to take them up on it. It will be self-defense."

Oleg remained silent. Kirill slowly nodded and said, "That is genius. Pure genius. We will regain all our lost lands."

Simon sagged back in his chair, relieved. "Precisely. And with troops already in Belarus, it will be a short hop to success. But you must travel in secret. Nobody can know Russia was involved. From this moment on, outside your team, you cannot even talk to your Night Wolves brothers. *Nobody.* Is that understood?"

Simon could tell both Oleg and Kirill were caught up in the secrecy and scope of the plan, reveling in being chosen. He repeated, "Understood?"

In unison, they said, "Yes. Of course."

He said, "Russia cannot have any connection to either attack. Because of this, Mikhail here will provide you with Israeli passports."

Mikhail snapped his head up, and Kirill said, "Israeli? That's crazy. Why? We can get into Belarus as Russians, and Ukraine is no problem."

"One, because I just told you: no Russian connection whatsoever. Two, because it might not end with those operations. We need to guarantee a strike from NATO, and this might not be enough. Yes, you can get into Belarus, but you can't get in anywhere else as Russians. Poland, Slovakia, you name it—they all suspect the Federation. Other countries don't have our love of the motherland and require a visa for Russians, but none do so for Israel."

Feeling Mikhail's glare, Simon glanced at him and said, "You can do this, correct?"

Mikhail gritted out, "Yes. Give me a few days."

Simon smiled and said, "Then it's settled."

He poured a shot of vodka for all in the balcony and raised his high.

"To Mother Russia. May she keep us in her embrace forever."

Oleg and Kirill repeated the toast and slammed the vodka home.

Mikhail left his on the table.

11

★★★

The hotel was small, no more than ten rooms, but clean. Built to look like an extension of Ksiaz Castle next door, it hadn't held up nearly as well, with the modern attempts at stonework starting to crumble. I didn't really care one way or the other—it had a bed, and I was smoked.

We'd spent one night in DC, then flown out the following afternoon. With a layover in Paris, we'd made it to Warsaw by eleven A.M., local time, having spent all night in the air. I'd arrived tired and cranky, because apparently, while our business was sorely needed, it wasn't needed enough to get us first-class tickets and I'd been saddled with a middle seat next to a hyperactive child. And our trip wasn't over when we landed, as we still had four hours to the Polish border area where the castle was located. Aaron had reserved two rental cars, and off we went, driving through the Polish countryside.

I made Jennifer do the driving because she needed the experience working in a foreign environment—future operations might depend on that knowledge. And I was tired and cranky. . . .

I pushed my carry-on to the corner of the room and flopped onto the queen-size bed, saying, "Man, I might take a nap while they co-ordinate."

Jennifer put her carry-on next to mine and said, "Don't think you'll have the time. Aaron seemed anxious to get this started."

"Yeah, but he doesn't know where to go to find his point of contact, and nobody speaks English. He'll be a while, trust me. It'll take Shoshana thirty minutes just to get those trunks to their room."

"I was going to ask you about that. Why do you suppose Aaron and Shoshana brought such large suitcases?"

When Jennifer and I had flown from DC, we'd packed for five days at Aaron's request, and all that fit into a couple of roll-aboards. Aaron and Shoshana, on the other hand, had brought suitcases large enough to allow a permanent change of station.

Eyes closed, I said, "I don't know. They did have to come from Israel, so maybe they've been on the road for a while."

"Shoshana's was heavy. I picked it up off the belt at baggage claim, and it's got to be close to overweight. What do you think is in there?"

I opened my eyes and said, "What are you asking? Maybe it's shoes, shampoo, makeup, and a hair dryer. She is a female after all."

Jennifer slapped my thigh and said, "Shoshana? You think she's packing like a Real Housewife from Beverly Hills? Come on." She slid in next to me and said, "Scoot over."

I slid over to the right, allowing her room on the bed, and propped a pillow behind my head. I said, "Who can figure out what those two are up to. Maybe they came from a hit straight into this mission."

Poking through a brochure, Jennifer said, "I hope we get to tour the castle after we do whatever it is we're supposed to do."

I chuckled and said, "Maybe we'll get a discount on admission."

Ksiaz Castle had been built in the thirteenth century, and as such, Jennifer had immediately become interested in reading its history. It had changed hands many, many times and was finally confiscated by the Nazis in 1941. From there, it became the heart of Project Riese, with some speculating that it was to be a final headquarters for Adolf Hitler. The ghost train had been found in a tunnel in the nearby Sowa Mountains, but the plunder had been brought here, to Ksiaz, because it already had a formidable security presence to protect the castle and museum, and its distance away from any town or city facilitated the secrecy the Poles wanted to preserve.

Jennifer said, "Let's go look at it now, while Aaron is tied up with the museum staff. I don't want this to end up like every other Task-force operation, where I'm always left hanging."

We used our company as a cover to facilitate counterterrorist operations—much like we were doing today—which usually involved some plausible, concrete archaeological find around the globe, and Jennifer always studied up, becoming excited about seeing the site. Un-fortunately, about nine times out of ten, Jennifer ended up doing far more meat-eating commando operations than plant-eating archaeo-logical work.

I said, "This isn't a Taskforce operation. We'll get to see the castle. I promise. In the meantime, I'm taking a nap."

I closed my eyes again and, as if on cue, heard a knock on the door. I muttered, "*Shit.*" Jennifer sat up and said, "It's open."

Shoshana came in, took one look at me, and said, "Wake up, sleep-ing beauty. Time to earn your pay."

I swung my legs over the side of the bed and said, "No way did Aaron wade through the Polish red tape that fast."

Shoshana smiled and said, "Correct. You are the wader. Bring your business credentials, and don't forget your passports."

Jennifer dug into her bag. I rubbed the sand out of my eyes. She stood up holding our documents and I said, "Okay, Carrie. Let's go earn some money."

She looked at Jennifer and said, "He doesn't travel well, does he?"

Jennifer opened the door and said, "He would be much more amenable if we were allowed to survey the castle afterward. For our business."

Shoshana gave a weird little grin and said, "Oh, I think that's going to happen," then walked through the door. Jennifer looked at me with a *what the hell does that mean?* expression. I just shrugged.

We walked up the cobblestone path that intersected the castle courtyard, the landscaping looking remarkably like that of the Over-look Hotel in *The Shining*. In front of us, the castle loomed over the courtyard, built onto the side of a mountain, with sheer walls drop-ping two hundred feet down. I have to admit, it was a little impressive.

Shoshana led us through the front doors, past the tourist ticket booths, and into the castle gift shop. She ignored the lady behind the counter and walked to the rear, entering a room packed full of furni-ture for sale. I'm not kidding. It was like an antique flea market, with wooden desks, chairs, and bookshelves all for sale, as if the average tourist would stop in the gift shop and say, "Wow, I like that two-thousand-pound oak table. I'll take it!"

At the far end, next to a desk with an inkwell and quill on it to show it was worthy of the antique title, Aaron stood next to a man in a security uniform. Aaron saw us enter and smiled, waving us for-ward.

12

★★★

After introductions, I turned the business explanation over to Jennifer. She gave a little canned speech on our company—complete with a history lesson of the castle to showcase our knowledge. The man looked at her documents and our passports, then nodded his head, apparently suitably impressed.

He asked a couple of questions about security and Grolier Recovery's history on maintaining nondisclosure, and Jennifer named a few digs we'd been on that had never made the news, assuring him of our discretion.

Satisfied, he turned to Shoshana and Aaron introduced her as his wife, the supposed expert. He shook her hand, but asked no questions, making me wonder if Aaron hadn't already laid that groundwork with a fake diploma from a fake Hebrew school.

Bona fides complete, the man spoke in heavily accented English, "You may call me Nacek. I am in charge of security for the find, and as you can understand, I may let you look at the Torah within, but nothing else. Agreed?"

Aaron said, "Of course. We were invited here by the Polish government for that express purpose. Where is Dr. Kowalski?"

"He is waiting for us right now. Please, follow me."

He led us out of the flea market and into a large marble hallway. We wound back around the ticket booths, Jennifer looking longingly at the carpeted stairs leading upward to the castle proper. We entered another hallway, this one looking more modern, with offices on the left and an incongruous bank of steel elevators on the right. It was clearly off the beaten tourism tracks. Nacek stopped next to an ancient oaken door that was only about six feet high, made back when men weren't nearly as tall as they are now.

He knocked on the door, and we breathlessly waited. Well, everyone but me waited breathlessly. I wanted a beer.

It opened, and a skinny man of about twenty-five poked his head out. I saw Shoshana draw up, staring intently at him, then glance at Aaron. The man was only in the doorway for a split second before another man appeared, this one grizzled and old.

He said, "I'm Doctor Kowalski. You must be Aaron?"

Aaron said yes, and shook his hand. We did the circus of introductions, and then were led into a small office with low ceilings. In the middle were two oaken chests, closed. In front of them was a table with a scroll sitting on it. The Torah.

I watched the guy Shoshana had pinged on, but he seemed to be nothing but paid security, and had sauntered to the back of the room, reclining in a chair. Bored with the proceedings.

I looked at Shoshana, and she was still feeling something from him. She didn't show it outwardly, but she was on fire. I could tell.

They went through a dance of putting on cotton gloves, talking about the Torah, and then Shohana inspected it, looking for the markings they had learned. I watched closely. As soon as she touched it, it was over.

She glanced at Aaron and simply nodded, then proceeded to recite a bunch of memorized things about old shit, Torah markings, and the synagogue in Plonsk, ending with, "There's no way to tell completely, of course, without a comprehensive examination, but we can help with that as well."

Dr. Kowalski said, "This *is* the examination. Can you not conclusively prove it's from the synagogue in Plonsk? Is it not the one we thought?"

Shoshana surprised me, as I would have expected her to just rip his head off at the sharp tone, then walk out. Instead, she sounded exactly like an expert. "Sir, it fits everything we know about the Torah in question. It is definitely centuries old, and it matches the description in its sheepskin and markings, but there's really no way to know without bringing it to the people who actually used it. And those people are only in Israel. As I said, I can facilitate that, and maintain discretion. Nobody will know it came from the gold train, and nobody will question when it returns here. They'll think it's from a museum."

Dr. Kowalski sighed and said, "I thought as much. Unfortunately, I'm not authorized for such a move now. I'll take your information and get back to you."

Aaron tried one last time. "Surely a simple trip with the Torah would do no harm? I'm positive I could arrange the travel free of charge."

Kowalski nodded and said, "Yes, yes, that would be the easy thing, but then we'd be traveling out every other day with paintings, candlesticks, and rings. We wanted to do the opposite and have each confirmed here, where we have control. I cannot risk a firestorm because of rabid idiots on the Internet. I'm sorry, but I promise I'll take your recommendation higher."

The doctor shook his head and grinned, saying, "Truthfully, the government doesn't know what to do. They want no blood splashed on them because of the find. They wish it had remained hidden forever."

Aaron nodded sagely and said, "I completely understand. I'm grateful you allowed us to see it, and wish you the best in its disposition. Rest assured, you have our discretion."

Kowalski smiled and said, "Exactly why I asked for you. There is nothing better than working with academics who are outside the political spectrum. When can I expect your report?"

"Two days, at most. You'll have it before we leave."

He held his arm out and said, "Come. Let me pay for your meal. Talk about other things."

We left without another word, Shoshana taking one last glance into the room, staring at the milquetoast in the corner.

We ate at the restaurant adjacent to the castle, getting some typical Polish fare, which suited me fine. What I didn't like was what had just happened. Something had occurred, and I wasn't sure what it was. We spent the entire lunch talking about the bloody history of the castle, with Jennifer leading the way, and by the end of it, all I wanted was to ask some questions of the Israelis in private.

We paid the bill and walked back to the hotel, Jennifer talking about the Torah with Aaron, and Shoshana weirdly walking right next to me. Rubbing up against my body and glancing into my eyes every thirty seconds. I knew it wasn't because she was itching to tell me a good joke. I stopped and said, "Okay, you two, what's up?"

Shoshana said, "Nothing. Aaron and I are going to Wroclaw. This took much less time than we thought, and we have a nicer hotel there, about an hour away."

I said, "This hotel's fine, and I'm sick of traveling."

"We can't plan in this hotel. Too close to the castle. And it might be monitored."

I glanced at Jennifer and said, "What on earth are you talking about?"

Aaron said, "Our flight out isn't for two days. I'll pay for you to leave tomorrow, if that's what you'd like, or you could stay in Wroclaw, with us."

I stopped, knowing this was the endgame. I said, "I'm not looking forward to jumping right back on a plane, but it depends on what you have planned."

Jennifer looked from me to Aaron, not saying a word. Shoshana said, "You aren't that stupid."

I said, "Apparently I am. What is it you want?"

I knew the answer even before I asked for it. Knew that mission success was much more than utilizing our cover organization. They wanted our skill.

Aaron glanced at Shoshana and she nodded. He said, "We're going to steal that Torah. And we could use your help."

13

★ ★ ★

Mikhail popped an olive into his mouth and said, "Some team of Jewish experts came to the castle today and looked at the Torah."

"From Israel?" asked Simon. "I thought your contact said that would never happen."

"No, some husband-and-wife team from America, facilitated by a company called Grolier Recovery Services. I checked them out, and they're legit. They've done stuff like this before, but the team recommended sending the Torah to Israel for confirmation. You know if that happens, they'll keep it."

Simon said, "The Poles know that as well. They won't let it happen."

"They'd better not. That Torah is my payment. I already have a buyer in Vienna."

"I'll reimburse you from my stake if that happens. From the rest of the gold we obtain."

"Even so, we should move the operation up. Do it tomorrow."

"Are we ready? Can we do that?"

"Yes. The team is here, in Warsaw, and the plan is set. It'll be easy. We roll up to the northern face of the castle right at the base. There is a road that leads to an underground loading zone. We meet our man, get the uniforms, get in an elevator, ride up, and secure the trunks. We load them, move back down, and leave. Outside of removing the other two hired men, we'll avoid the entire security apparatus. It's not going to get any better if we wait."

Simon took a sip of wine, then said, "And you trust this inside man?"

"No. Of course not. But I trust the men I brought from Israel. You'll get your gold. That I know. If we wait until after your crazy plan in Belarus, I can't predict the outcome."

Mikhail fished another olive from the bowl, and Simon remained quiet for a moment. When he spoke again, it was from a different perspective.

"Do you have any qualms about stealing from the deceased of the Holocaust? Does that bring you any pause?"

Mikhail waited a beat, then said, "I have no connection to the Holocaust. My family moved to Israel in 1919. I'm fourth generation. The people who own the goods in that train are long gone. Whoever ends up with it will be stealing it, I'm sure. It'll happen in a courtroom, or with me. No. I have no qualms."

He took a sip of his whiskey and said, "But you ask as if you do. Your family felt the death. Felt the pain. Are you having second thoughts?"

Simon raised his glass and said, "I would, but if the camps taught anyone anything, it's that survival is based on the ability to manipulate your surroundings. To make your own destiny. My grandfather survived the camps by sheer will and cunning. No. I don't have any qualms. But I never served in Israeli intelligence. I've been fighting my entire life for survival. I'm a de facto Israeli citizen, but I feel no connection to the country. It only allows me to pursue my business."

"Then we are agreed."

Simon set the glass down and said, "Why did you leave the Mossad? I've dealt with them before, and they are all true believers. What caused your fall from grace?"

Mikhail chuckled and said, "Why does anyone leave any intelligence organization? What causes most falls from grace?"

"A woman? You couldn't keep your dick in your pants?"

Mikhail's glare became harsh, and he said, "Yes. It was a woman, but not because of sex. Because she was a traitor. Nobody would listen to me, and it ended badly. She was moved within the building, and I was moved out."

He relaxed and said, "Make no mistake; before being true believers, the Mossad is a bureaucracy. I was a true believer. The bureaucracy won."

He ate another olive and said, "And now, I ply those skills for you."

Simon said, "Good enough, but I worry about your commitment. If you're willing to turn on your country, why should I think you won't turn on me?"

Mikhail scoffed and said, "I have never turned on Israel. Nothing I have done has affected them. It's only enriched me." He jabbed his small fork toward Simon's face and said, "You are the last man who should be accusing me of turning on my country."

Simon laughed and said, "Yes, I suppose you're right. Survival for self will always supersede anything else, but truthfully, I don't think of Putin as being a part of my country. I love Russia, but not from the bottom of a pit with a bucket to shit in. I don't expect you to understand. Only obey."

Mikhail nodded and said, "Fair enough. So we trust one another about as far as we can throw one another. You provide me what I want, and I do the same."

Simon glanced at him and said, "Mikhail, I would never turn on you. You and I are of the same build, with the same goals. But you didn't appreciate me leveraging you for passports for the Night Wolves, and that causes concern."

"I don't like being played. I didn't like you throwing me into your little plan for World War Three without asking, but I got the passports, did I not?"

"Yes. You did. And Kirill is on the way. Maybe you're right. Maybe it's smart to do our mission in Poland earlier."

Mikhail downed the last of his whiskey and said, "No doubt. That gold train plunder will be inaccessible after Kirill lights the fuse."

14
★★★

We were sitting in a pub called Whiskey in a Jar, forced to drink nothing but Coca-Cola because of the potential mission parameters. I said, "You made a decision? I mean, if Aaron comes back with what we asked for?"

Jennifer fiddled with her straw and said, "No. On the surface it seems like the right thing to do, I suppose, but I don't know about working for the Israeli government. I mean, is that even legal? I feel like a mercenary."

"It's not about the money. You know that. I could care less about the cash."

She looked into my eyes and said, "There are more forms of payment than just money. Do you crave the excitement of the mission, using the purpose as a cloak to allow you to operate?"

I chuckled, because she knew me too well. I said, "I honestly don't know. But you're in the same boat, except you're more worried about breaking trust with Shoshana than the purpose of the mission."

Earlier, standing inside the courtyard to Ksiaz Castle, I immediately told Aaron there was no way we were helping him—meaning the State of Israel—steal an artifact from another sovereign country. Especially not as Americans. I said I was sorry, but that was just the way of it.

Shoshana looked at me with a touch of sadness, then turned to Jennifer, asking her the same question. Imploring her as a way to get to me. Jennifer was torn by the look, and glanced at me for support. I shook my head, telling her no.

Aaron said, "Don't decide here. Let's go to Wroclaw, and let me lay out what we know. At least let me show you the plan, so you can make an informed decision."

We drove the hour to Wroclaw in our separate cars, mostly in silence. Pulling into the parking garage for the Sofitel hotel on the outskirts of the Wroclaw old city square, Jennifer said, "Separate cars. Large suitcases. Reservations for hotels in two different cities. The cryptic talk from Shoshana. They were planning this all along."

I pulled into the first available spot and said, "That thought has crossed my mind. And it pisses me off."

We met in Aaron and Shoshana's room, to find Shoshana's suitcase open and displaying a selection of thin nylon ladders and assorted climbing gear. On the bed was a historical blueprint of Ksiaz Castle. Standing behind the bed was Shoshana, looking contrite.

I shook my head and opened my mouth to speak but Shoshana cut me off, saying, "Yes. We tricked you, but not completely. Don't tell us no out of revenge."

I said, "Revenge? Jesus, you are a piece of work. How about I say no because it's stupid? Like you knew I would have in Washington, DC?"

Aaron said, "Wait. We didn't completely trick you. We *did* need your company for the mission, and I really had hoped to convince him to send the Torah on his own volition, but he declined. That truly would have been the better way."

Jennifer said, "He didn't decline. He said he had to send it up to his boss. Why don't you just wait for the no instead of jumping into a theft?"

Shoshana said, "The Torah isn't going to be there much longer. None of the things recovered are. Someone is going to steal it, and the Torah will be lost forever."

"How do you know that," asked Jennifer, "and why didn't you say something like this to begin with? Why all the lying?"

Aaron said, "We didn't know. I swear, we didn't know."

And I realized what had happened. "The man in the room. The one Shoshana zeroed in on." I turned to her and said, "You saw something in him."

She nodded, the earlier fire coming out of her eyes. "Yes, I did. He's working with someone. He had an aura coming off him like a pile of rotten meat. He's planning to steal the trunks."

I heard the words and held up my hands, sick of the mental-magic crap. "Come on, there's no possible way you can read that intent in someone. I'm sure he's probably a bad guy, but maybe he's stealing from the petty cash drawer at the ticket booth."

Shoshana slitted her eyes at me, saying nothing. Aaron said, "Look, I don't expect you to believe, but I do, and I'm breaking into that castle tonight. I could really use your help. Both yours *and* Jennifer's."

I pointed at the climbing gear and said, "You need Jennifer to establish an anchor outside?"

"Yes."

In a past life, Jennifer had been a gymnast, and had actually trained with Cirque du Soleil. She could climb up anything short of plate glass—and even that would be doable if she were given a little help.

"And you need me . . . ?"

I let the question trail off.

Shoshana said, "Why does anyone need you, Nephilim? Why would we ask for your particular skills?"

I was disgusted at the question, because I knew. And it didn't make me happy. "To break some heads."

She smiled and said, "Yes. Your abilities are formidable in that sense, but that's not why. You bring with you the ability to succeed no matter how bad things have become. You bring something we cannot. I can't describe it. But it's real."

I looked to see if she was just blowing smoke up my ass, but she appeared completely sincere.

I said, "That's not me. You're remembering Tirana. When Aaron and I saved your life. It wasn't me. It was luck. Period. Luck doesn't follow a person. I've been in fights when luck went the other way. When people died. When *you* would have died."

She looked me in the eyes, boring in, reading me. I could actually feel it. She said, "Nephilim, we need you tonight. I can't explain it other than to say *I* need you. Aaron doesn't agree. He thinks we can do this on our own, but I won't do it without you."

She looked at Jennifer and said, "You and Koko. I don't know why, but it's critical."

I paused, not sure how to respond. It was pretty compelling, even if it was a little crazy. I finally got out, "Okay, okay, I hear you, but what if we get caught? Get arrested? You'll have Israeli help. Jennifer and I will be hung out to dry. I can't risk that. Imagine the headlines— 'Grolier Recovery Services Arrested for Breaking into Ancient Castle to Steal Holocaust Gold.' Apart from spending some time in a Polish jail, we'd never work again."

Aaron said, "I can fix that. If I can assure you that you will not— as you say—be hung out to dry, will you do it?"

I said, "Like I would trust that word. Your government will hang me out as soon as I'm not viable."

With steel I had never heard from her, Shoshana said, "You're wrong."

Jennifer raised her head at the statement, sensing a shift in the conversation. I remained silent.

Shoshana looked at Aaron, then at me. She shifted toward me, sliding in a way that made me wary. She came close and looked me in the eye. I tensed, and she said, "If I say you will be protected, you *will.*

Even if it means my life. Listen to Aaron. He does not lie. I know it. I follow him because of it. Do not sell us short."

Shoshana snaked her hand into Jennifer's and squeezed without looking at her. Jennifer felt the touch and I saw the conflict on her face. Her wanting to do what was asked.

Aaron simply looked at me, knowing how much weight the words held. Understanding there was nothing he could say that would mean as much. I shook my head and sliced through the emotion. "We aren't doing shit until I see what brilliant plan you've come up with."

Aaron smiled, the tension cut, and said, "It really is brilliant in its simplicity." And he stood over the blueprints and laid it out. In the end, there wasn't much to it. If everything went right, we'd be in and out without issue. The only problem was if something went wrong. But I'd dealt with that before. I asked some questions about cameras and other surveillance, and Jennifer asked some about the facade of the building, but all in all there really weren't a lot of moving parts.

I told him Jennifer and I needed to discuss the proposal, and that he needed to bring some assurances we'd be taken care of if the worst happened, then we left the room. Jennifer and I wandered the old square looking for a restaurant or café to stop and talk in. That's when I saw the sign for Whiskey in a Jar. The perfect place.

Well, Jennifer would rather have found some old Wroclaw bakery, but I texted the location to Aaron, short-circuiting her ability to say no.

We were on our second plate of fries, and the Cokes were growing warm—because apparently ice is a rarity in Europe—and we still hadn't made up our minds.

Jennifer rubbed my arm across the table and said, "Maybe we do the job. For them. It's not that hard, really, and it would mean a lot to Shoshana."

I said, "She's fucking crazy. You want to risk our lives for that?"

Jennifer said, "No. Of course not. But she's *not* crazy. We've done several operations with her, and she's *always* right. Scary right. I think we should."

I said, "You sure?"

"Well, you'd get some high adventure out of the trip. Make that flight worthwhile. But only if we get the support from Aaron."

Before I could answer, Shoshana came into the bar, squinting her eyes in the gloom. Aaron followed close behind. I said, "Looks like we're about to find out."

I waved and they came over, Shoshana beaming like she was a cat with a cornered mouse. Aaron said, "Well?"

I said, "Well, what? I'm the one waiting on an answer."

"You are in. We have a lawyer in Warsaw. One with highly placed connections. You'll be covered and shuffled out without drama, provided we don't do any permanent harm to anyone."

I simply nodded.

He repeated the question. "Well?"

I looked at Jennifer one final time. Shoshana went from me to her, then started bouncing on her toes, a smile on her face. "They say yes."

I rolled my eyes and said, "Can you turn that crap off for one minute and at least let us be the ones to say it? Just for formality's sake?"

She ceased moving and made a concerted effort to stop the grin, looking for all the world like a child. Nobody said a word. Shoshana leaned over and kissed me on the cheek, saying, "Thank you."

Jennifer smiled at that. She said, "Yes, we'll do it."

15

★★★

The car drove by the front gate at a steady pace, like a tractor dragging a plow. It neither slowed when the harsh lights of the gate came in view nor sped up once it was back in the darkness. It did nothing to give anyone concern that reconnaissance was in the works. Not that the guards would have believed it, no matter what the car did. The driver could have parked out front and pulled out a video camera, and the men manning the gate would have remained listlessly behind their drop bar and chain link. They couldn't be faulted for that. They were, after all, on a military base in the heart of the last dictatorship in Europe. The 61st Fighter Airbase, Baranovichi, Belarus.

In a country nearly impossible to enter as a tourist, with a secret police still enamored of the legacy of the Stasi and the KGB, Belarus was a dinosaur. An aging relic of the Cold War where "Let me see your papers" wasn't a satirical comment, but a daily occurrence. It would be preposterous for anyone to believe one could attack a military base in the heart of the state without substantial help from those same forces.

Unless one had help from forces that were just as good, and just as vicious.

Kirill Zharkov said, "Misha, keep going another mile. The turnout will be on the left."

Misha said, "Same old Belarus. I'll bet those weapons aren't even loaded."

From the back, Oleg said, "Yes, getting in will be easy, but we still need to get out."

Kirill said, "We'll drive right through that gate in the chaos."

"What if they lock it down?"

"They'll be looking for Chechen insurgents. Not Russian officers."

Oleg remained silent. The headlights hit the gravel turnout, and Misha pulled into it, finding a rutted dirt road. He bounced down the track for about seventy meters, until he was hidden in the wood line, then stopped. He flashed his lights and received two small blinks from a flashlight thirty meters away. He pulled forward, getting off the track far enough to allow another vehicle to pass.

Kirill exited and met the man with the flashlight, standing next to a Belarusian army lorry. They shook hands and Kirill said, "Dmitri, really good to see you. I was worried you'd have issues. Any trouble?"

"No. Minsk is no different than Moscow. Weapons and uniforms were right where they were supposed to be."

"You sure you weren't identified? Followed?"

"Would I be sitting out here in the woods if I had been? The Israeli passport was a genius idea. Two days of shopping and they quit looking at us."

Kirill nodded. "Good enough. The special weapons are here as well?"

"Yeah. Two AK-74s in cloth bags. A note on them says not to touch them. What's that all about?"

"They were collected off a battlefield in Dagestan. They have the fingerprints of a Chechen warlord." He smiled in the dark and said, "The FSB has been keeping them for a special occasion."

The other two men from the car came forward. Oleg shook Dmitri's hand and said, "Where's Alik?"

Dmitri hooked a thumb at the lorry and said, "Changing. Getting promoted by about ten ranks from what he was when he was booted from the army."

Kirill laughed and said, "Everyone, do the same. Guard shift is in one hour. We need to be through the gate before then. I want to attack during the change, when there's confusion on who's in charge of what."

Thirty minutes later, they were all dressed as Russian air force officers, Kirill the ranking man as a major, the rest captains and lieutenants. It might have been more imposing—and thus easier to penetrate—pretending to be a higher rank, but there was only a single Russian Su-27 squadron here, and that meant very few high-ranking members of the Russian military. Someone of that rank would be remembered—and questions would flow afterward. Captains and lieutenants were a dime a dozen.

Kirill gave the command to load, and they bounced down the lane, passing the car they'd used for reconnaissance, Dmitri driving with Kirill in the passenger seat. The other men were in the back, weapons under a blanket. They hit the blacktop and began retracing their steps.

They saw the glow of vapor lights in the distance, like a small stadium in the woods, and Kirill tensed up. He said, "Remember, you defer to me. I don't want to see your temper tonight. I outrank you, I'll do the talking."

Dmitri nodded and said, "I understand. But if they give us any shit, I'm killing them."

Kirill laughed and said, "It won't come to that. Remember your time in the military? Would you have given a shit about a couple of drunk officers showing up?"

The full glare of the vapor lights hit the windshield as they came around the bend. Dmitri said, "I'd have killed them, too."

He pulled the truck straight up to the drop bar as if he belonged, which Kirill knew was half the battle. Act like you're confused, and you'll get a strong response. Act like you're in charge, and people will let you be in charge. He knew no soldier wanted trouble from his commander for being a jerk at the gate. Especially to Russian officers on a Belarusian base.

A guard popped out of the small shack next to the drop bar and came forward, his AK-47 slung over his shoulder, a flashlight in his hands. Kirill leaned over and presented his Russian credentials outside the window. As if he'd done it a hundred times in the past. The guard took one look at the uniforms and that was it. He didn't even bother to turn on his light to see the identification. He waved behind him, and the drop bar rose.

Dmitri muttered, "Well, that was easy."

16

★★★

His statement was belied a mere five minutes later, as they took a wrong turn and ended up on the main post, with Belarusian airmen working the midnight shift looking at the lorry curiously. They drove around a traffic circle and back out, headed the way they had come. Kirill cursed and said, "Where the hell is the airfield? We need to find the Russians."

Dmitri said, "We'll have to stop and ask."

"Are you fucking crazy? *Ask* where our squadron is? At two in the morning?"

Dmitri saw a vehicle coming toward them and said, "Yes. We're drunk Russians. Nothing new."

He leaned out, and acting like he was inebriated, asked directions to the cantonment area for the Su-27 squadron. The man in the car laughed at the predicament and gave them instructions. In short order, they were driving parallel to the flight line, the runway to the right and a distant glow in front. As it got closer, they saw open-bay hangars with the dual-fin Su-27s inside, sleek killers posted to Belarus as a hedge against the West.

Kirill said, "There you go. That's the target."

Dmitri said, "We got another checkpoint."

Kirill refocused to the front of the vehicle and saw a barricade of orange cones manned by a single Russian.

Kirill said, "Shit. Get ready. We might not bluff our way through this one."

They pulled up, and a Russian airman came forward, clearly confused at the Belarusian truck. He saw Dmitri's uniform, and, in a semi-joking manner, said, "Why is a lieutenant driving a truck?"

Kirill wasted no time, leaning over and shooting the man in the face with a Makarov PM pistol, the gunshot shattering the night. He watched the body drop, then shouted, "Let's go!"

The lorry jumped forward, flattening the cones and racing down the sliver of blacktop to the hangars. The men in the back began shouting questions, wondering what had happened. Kirill separated the canvas behind the cab and said, "Get the RPGs ready. We're attacking now."

Dmitri pulled onto a pad adjacent to the hangars and killed the engine. Nobody from the Russian side of the base reacted. Time slowed back down. Kirill opened the door and jumped out, saying, "Misha, Alik, Oleg, let's go."

He heard them scrambling over the gate at the back, then saw them run around, two holding RPGs and AKMs and one with the bags of AK-74s. Alik tossed Kirill an AKM, then readied his RPG, looking at him for instructions. Dmitri came around the cab, taking another AKM and waiting on Kirill for a command.

Kirill was astounded that nobody had reacted. He'd expected to have to fight his way in and then blast his way out. The silence was deafening. He said, "Dmitri, take the far side security. I'll hold the near. Misha and Alik, shoot the first aircraft, then the second. Destroy them both. Oleg, scatter the weapons next to the maintenance bay."

Dmitri scampered to the other side of the hangar, disappearing into the darkness. Misha and Alik looked at Kirill, and he said, "Well? Do it."

They took a knee, aimed their RPGs, and let them fly. It was surreal, like a practice range, the men kneeling just outside the lights of the hangar, the bird sitting stoically waiting for the punishment. The rockets sputtered out, streaking toward the twin tail fins of the jet, then impacted in an explosion of metal, followed by the ignition of the fuel, turning the hangar into an inferno.

The men whooped and yelled like kids at a fireworks display, then reloaded. Kirill said, "The next. Hit the next."

He noticed Oleg and said, "What are you waiting for? Get rid of those weapons. Be sure not to touch any metal."

Oleg turned to go and they heard Dmitri's weapon fire on full automatic. He shouted something and Kirill said, "Go, go!"

To the two grenadiers he said, "Shoot! Blow up the next one!"

They slid the rod of the grenade home, then took a knee. Kirill saw Dmitri bouncing back, still firing on full automatic. The grenadiers released their deadly missiles, and the second aircraft was engulfed in flames. Kirill said, "Shoot it again," then raced over to Dmitri, crouched behind an aircraft tractor, seeing three shadows in the distance firing at them, none appearing too intent on pressing the assault.

Kirill slid in next to Dmitri and grabbed his shoulder, saying, "Come on. Let's go!"

"They saw me. I was in the light."

Kirill paused, then said, "You sure?"

"Yes, I know it. They were shouting at me in Russian, calling me by my rank."

Kirill turned and shouted, "Alik! Over here."

Alik scuttled over to them, the RPG launcher awkwardly banging against his knees. Kirill said, "I need a grenade on them. Before others come and they can tell them what they've seen."

Alik glanced across the tarmac, seeing the three Russians crouched behind a row of barrels, occasionally cracking rounds their way, none coming close to them. He said, "They aren't hitting anything. We got the aircraft."

"They've seen Dmitri and his uniform."

Alik started to say something, then closed his mouth. Kirill said, "Kill them."

"They're Russian."

"Yeah? So?"

Alik said nothing more, simply loaded another rocket. He sighted, then let it fly. The rocket-propelled grenade struck the center of the stack of barrels, the explosion shredding the three soldiers.

Dmitri shouted, "Yeah!"

Kirill said, "Let's get the fuck out of here."

They sprinted back to the lorry, Oleg and Misha on the outside, nervously holding AKMs. Kirill said, "Did you drop the weapons?"

"Yes. Near the maintenance bay."

Kirill nodded and said, "Everyone load up. Dmitri, you drive."

They started to move when a truck with an open bed came flying around the corner, bouncing into the light of the flames, revealing it was loaded with Russian and Belarusian security. Oleg shouted, "Shit!" and turned to fire. Kirill knocked the gun down and shouted in Russian, "There! They're getting away! Across the tarmac!"

The vehicle skidded to a stop next to them, and a captain jumped out, waving a pistol. He saw the flaming inferno, then took in the uniforms. He said, "What the hell happened?"

"Chechens. Chechens blew the shit out of everything. They killed the man at the gate and then started shooting rockets. They escaped that way. They're on foot. You can catch them."

The captain shouted at his men, then said, "Sir, can you secure this area? Make sure none of them are still here?"

Kirill nodded, and the vehicle raced off, men hanging on with gun barrels bristling. Looking for an enemy that didn't exist.

Ten minutes later, the lorry was at the front gate. There was double the manpower from before, but no cohesive control. The men ran back and forth as if the movement alone were progress. Kirill grabbed one and talked to him, spreading more rumors, and then they were through, gaining their freedom simply by speaking Russian.

17

★★★

I felt someone lightly tap my thigh, then heard Shoshana whisper, "It's time."

I shook the sleep out of my head and saw Jennifer slipping a backpack over her shoulders, now wearing skintight black Lycra leggings and an Under Armour top, courtesy of the Israelis. Surprisingly, it fit her perfectly. As if they knew who would be wearing it.

I stood up and saw rain running down the window. I said, "That's not a good omen."

Aaron, wearing jeans and running shoes, handed me a tiny headlamp and a leather sap filled with small lead shot. He said, "It was threatening to come down since we drove up, but it's just a drizzle."

The sky had been overcast on the nighttime return, making the narrow blacktop leading to the castle bitterly dark. This time we'd traveled in a single vehicle, Shoshana behind the wheel, Aaron in the passenger seat. Jennifer and I were in the back, now part of their team. Which made me wonder when I'd crossed the border into lunacy.

Through the trees, I'd seen the glow of lights and said, "You sure it's not going to look strange for a car to pull up this late at night?"

Aaron showed me the parking pass we both received earlier in the day. "Not when we have a room. We park, go upstairs, and act like we're simply going to bed."

"You didn't check out?"

Shoshana said, "Why would we do that when we fully intended to come back?"

I shook my head at the subterfuge, and Jennifer grinned.

The parking area for the hotel was a little cramped shelf overlooking the valley the castle protected, requiring us to wind down a steep, potholed road running parallel to a stone wall. After bouncing around hard enough to cause the headlights to jostle like a drunken man waving a flashlight, we'd pulled off the road to the left, entering a small courtyard packed with about seven cars, all parked without any semblance of order.

Aaron said, "Another reason to come in later. We won't get blocked in by someone."

I said, "Yeah, that would suck for the getaway."

We'd exited the car and Aaron had led us to the stone wall. As I crossed the road, I saw it ran low around the side of the mountain, ending at what looked like an arched tunnel under the castle, a single lightbulb over the top illuminating the entrance.

Aaron leaned over the wall and said, "That's our access path."

He'd told us earlier that we'd be walking to the castle, and I could see a footpath paralleling the road, but lower on the slope, with benches every hundred feet or so for a walker to take a rest and gaze out into the valley.

I followed it as far as I could in the darkness, but couldn't see where it came out next to the bottom of the castle.

Aaron pointed and said, "That's why we need you, Jennifer. The office is on the first floor—ground level where we came in, but we'll start the climb two floors below that, and you'll have to go one floor higher, because there aren't any external windows to access on that floor."

The castle was vaguely illuminated with a scattering of outdoor lights, and I could make out the ancient stone of the walls. Jennifer studied her potential path in the dim light and said, "I can do that."

Shoshana smiled and said, "That was never a question."

I said, "Let's get some sleep. We might need it."

We'd returned to the room and I'd tried to nap, but it seemed we'd only been in the room for about fifteen minutes before Shoshana had tapped my thigh.

I looked at the window again and said, "Koko, you sure you can make that climb freehand with the rain?"

She cinched the pack down and pointed to a window on the other side of the room. She said, "It looks like it's coming south to north, and it's only a drizzle. I'll bet the walls on the north are dry."

Aaron said, "She's only going about four floors."

"And what if the window's locked? She'll have to go higher."

"It's not. I told you. The window was built centuries ago. Nobody thought it needed a lock. At any rate, if it is, she comes down, because that window height is the length of the ladder we had made."

I said, "You had the ladder made for that window?"

He looked embarrassed and said, "Well, yes, when we first started studying how to access the castle. We didn't know where the Torah was located, but that didn't mean we couldn't plan entry."

Shoshana handed me some thin gloves and a black balaclava and said, "Now we know where it's located."

I took the items and she said, "No fingerprints, no pictures."

I said, "I thought there weren't any cameras. You said they used roving guards."

Aaron said, "That's true, but remember, we can't terminate anyone. You meet someone, they'd better be able to remember it tomorrow."

I muttered, "Just great," and Shoshana said, "Don't worry. I've got a good feeling about this. You're my lucky charm."

I said, "That instills *so* much confidence in me."

Aaron turned out the lights, then opened the door. Jennifer grinned and said, "Showtime."

I have to admit, her confidence was infectious, making me smile as well. Aaron said, "I do appreciate this. We'll most definitely owe you one."

I exited onto the wooden balcony and said, "Believe me, I plan on collecting."

We slipped down the walkway to a narrow stairwell, keeping to the shadows and circling away from the bar in front. It was close to two in the morning, but no way did we want to run into some inebriated patron coming back to his room.

We went through the parking lot, and I saw that none of the cars had moved, all still jammed together like a drunk valet had parked them. We reached the road and sprinted over it one by one. As I crossed, I glanced toward the castle and saw a black van, nose out, illuminated at the edge of the tunnel.

Aaron was already lowering Shoshana over the side, letting her drop the seven feet to the path. I crouched against the wall and said, "There's a new vehicle. Someone's shown up since we arrived."

Jennifer came across, crouching next to me. Aaron glanced toward the castle and said, "Did you see movement?"

"No. Headlights are off, but it's definitely there."

Shoshana hissed from the far side, wanting to know what the holdup was. I looked at Aaron, then tapped Jennifer, getting her up on the wall. I leaned over, holding her hands, and she walked down three feet, looked up at me and nodded. I let her go.

I turned back to Aaron to find him staring intently down the road. He came back to me and said, "What is your gut saying?"

"It's trouble."

"You want to abort?"

I flashed my teeth and said, "And spend another night with your sociopath? No. We can handle trouble. I think it means we'll have more active patrolling than we thought, even if it's a cleaning crew. We just need to be on our toes."

Aaron took that in, then slowly nodded. He said, "I appreciate the honest answer. This was your chance to quit."

I hoisted myself on the wall, looked down to determine the drop, then said, "I've never quit anything in my entire life. And lord knows I would rather face some Stormtroopers who can't shoot than your damn wife."

Before he could answer, I let go.

Aaron landed softly five seconds later. He said, "Okay, everyone knows their positions. Jennifer first, get the anchor in, me next, then Shoshana, Pike last."

We'd all talked about this endlessly, but I understood he was reaffirming the fact that it was his Op. He was in charge. I nodded, and we took up a slow jog down the path, the drizzle settling on us until we broke past the castle itself. True to Jennifer's prediction, it was dry, the stone blocking the weather.

We ran by the tunnel, the van right above us, then reached the back of the castle, with Aaron stopping at a modern drainage pipe running from the face of stone and down into the valley. We took a knee and Jennifer tested the pipe. Shoshana said, "Told you. This will be a cakewalk. You have your own ladder for the first two floors."

Jennifer glanced up at the pipe and the ensuing climb, then looked at me. I said, "Too late now. Unless you can't do it."

She grinned and said, "You know I can do it. Last chance to back out."

I fist-bumped her and said, "Then let's go."

Before I could stop her, she leaned in and kissed me on the cheek, saying, "See you at the top."

She leapt up on the pipe, scrambling like a monkey in a zoo. In seconds, she was two floors up, and began climbing using the rock of the castle. Satisfied, I returned my eyes to the team, seeing Shoshana staring intently at me. I said, "What?"

"You never would have let her show affection like that before."

"So? What's your point?"

"I'm just studying. Trying to decide what part of the relationship I want to be."

I looked at Aaron and he rolled his eyes, the patient uncle with the kid who wouldn't quit annoying him. I said, "The husband-and-wife mission is over. Nobody cares what your marital status is anymore."

The nylon ladder rolled down, slapping on the stone right between us. Shoshana said, "I'm not talking about the mission. I'm talking about life."

I looked at Aaron again, and he pretended to be engrossed in testing the strength of the ladder, studiously ignoring the conversation. He found it strong and began climbing. I took the bottom rung and pulled it taut, giving him a solid platform instead of a swinging mess. And getting me away from the conversation with Shoshana, just like he'd done.

The ladder quit shaking and I glanced up, seeing it empty. I said, "Your turn, Carrie."

She grinned and said, "You have no idea what to do with Koko. You're just like Aaron."

She said it like she'd discovered something profound about the human condition. I said, "Get on the fucking ladder. Why do you always do this right before a firefight?"

She pulled herself up on the rungs and said, "I appreciate you helping. It means a lot to me and Aaron. I just wanted to say that in case this goes bad."

Incredulous, I looked up at her and said, "I thought you said this was going to be easy?"

She started climbing after I drew the ladder taut and said, "No. I said you brought luck. I'm not sure this is going to be easy, but I'm positive it will be worth it."

In seconds, she was out of earshot, climbing past the floors. I felt the ladder go slack and looked up. She was gone. I began the climb myself, wondering what the hell she was talking about.

18
★★★

I reached the sill of the ancient window, the glass open wide, strong seams of iron between the opaque panes. A foot-long hunk of granite extended out, giving me purchase. I pulled myself up and swung inside, dropping lightly to the ground. We were in a room with velvet ropes on the doors, the interior full of archaic renaissance furniture and massive murals on the walls. I saw Jennifer crouched to the left of the window, her job pretty much done. All she had to do was wait; then, after all of us had escaped, she'd drop the ladder and free-climb back down.

The two Israelis were near the door, listening and looking like bank robbers with the balaclavas over their heads.

Jennifer smiled at me, pumped with adrenaline after the climb. I grinned back and patted her Lycra-covered thigh, whispering, "Hero of the day again."

She said, "It was easy."

I turned serious. "This goes south, you get the hell out of here. Don't wait on me or anyone else. Get out and down."

Her smile faded and I said, "Shoshana's not nearly as confident as you thought. I don't know what they know, but they've lied to us from the start. Just get out."

She nodded, then said, "What about you?"

"I'll pull my security position, but trust me, if this thing goes sideways, I'm right behind you."

She nodded again, saying, "See you in a few. Don't do anything stupid."

This time I was the one who leaned in. I pecked her on the cheek and said, "Too fucking late for that."

I duckwalked toward the door, sliding my balaclava over my head and seeing Shoshana staring at me again. I reached her and whispered, "What now?"

"You kissed her."

"No, I didn't. I was whispering in her ear about what a pain in the ass you are. I didn't want you to hear."

Aaron chuckled and said, "Okay, we're going down one floor. Everyone remembers the floor plan, right?"

Shoshana and I nodded. He said, "We get down there, and Pike provides security to our rear. Shoshana and I will acccss the door. There are four security guards on this floor, but only one on the trunks in the admin area. We reduce him as a threat, then pop the locks to the door and get the Torah. We come right back to you, and we're out of here."

I said, "Sounds good. Let's get it done."

He nodded and slipped out the door, Shoshana right behind him, moving down a wide hallway lined with portraits of old dead guys. I brought up the rear, feeling naked without a firearm, but understanding the fact that if I had it, I'd probably use it. And I could handle anyone who showed up.

We kept to the wall, sliding against it to a large staircase. Aaron slipped down it, the carpet muffling his steps, reaching the next floor. We paused at the base, and Aaron whispered, "Left." He pointed at the wall across from the staircase, a point where I could dominate anyone coming and going, and said, "You, there. Shoshana, on me."

I slipped across the hall, taking up a position in the shadows, the winding staircase in front, the opening to the castle lobby on my left. I watched them slink down the same hallway we'd entered earlier in the day, then pulled out my lead-filled sap.

Anyone entered, and I had to take them out, but not permanently harm them, which wasn't exactly a perfect science. And because we had luggage that had been X-rayed every step of the way, Aaron hadn't even brought a Taser. I only had my hands and a lead-filled weapon from a bad mafia movie.

I sat still, breathing through my nose and constantly scanning left and right, waiting on their return. I expected to hear shuffling footsteps. What I got was a gunshot, loud and echoing down the hallway. Then two more.

Shit. What happened to no guards being armed?

I slid toward the hallway, my head swiveling behind me, keeping the entrance in sight. Keeping my ability to provide security for any follow-on force. I ducked around the edge and saw six men in castle security uniforms dragging two trunks, two other men on the floor, both with their necks bent at unnatural angles. Behind a pillar next to the wall were the Israelis, trapped in the hallway.

A man advanced, pistol held with both hands, blasting away at the pillar they were hiding behind. Closing in close enough to ensure no escape. I reacted without thought, springing up and racing into the hall.

The man saw me coming and rotated his weapon toward me, causing me to instinctively slide low on the marble, regretting my choice. Before he could squeeze the trigger, Aaron leapt from behind his cover, snatching the man's gun arm and rotating it in a circle like a pretzel. The bone snapped, causing the man to scream, and Aaron flipped him on his back and hammered his face with a straight punch. The other men started firing and Aaron flopped back behind the pillar.

I scrambled in beside him and said, "What the hell is going on? There's a damn army here."

He said, "I don't know. We saw the dead guys in the hallway, then the door burst open before we could retreat and those assholes came out shooting. They're getting away with the Torah."

I peeked around the pillar, drawing rounds from the remaining men and snapped back. I said, "It's gone. Let's get the fuck out of here."

Shoshana said, "That isn't happening. No way."

I heard a guy shouting orders, and it wasn't in Polish. It was some weird language that I didn't immediately recognize. Shoshana did, though. She listened to the commands being given, and glared at Aaron with fire. She said, "We're *not* leaving without the Torah."

Before I could reason with her, she sprang up, running toward the men in a zigzag pattern, the hallway stretching out in a funnel of death.

One trunk was being dragged into an elevator, the other right behind it. Aaron shouted at her to stop, and the men began shooting. Shoshana was miraculously missed with the first salvo. She realized her stupidity and slammed behind the next pillar in the hallway, this one much closer to the enemy, the angle leaving her dangerously exposed.

Aaron grabbed the pistol from the man he'd killed and rolled into the open on his chest, blazing away at the group and drawing their fire off Shoshana.

Aaron got off four rounds, dropping one man, but then he was hit, causing a sharp scream. I leapt out and grabbed his leg, pulling him back behind the cover of the pillar and seeing blood on his shoulder.

Jesus Christ.

This entire mission had gone to complete shit.

I grabbed the pistol from his hand, checked the chamber for a round, then rotated around the pillar. I shouted, "Shoshana! Back here. I'll cover."

I pumped two rounds down the hallway, hitting one man in the gut, and then my weapon locked open, the magazine empty. The man I'd hit fell into the elevator and the other men slapped against the wall, then realized I was empty. I dove back behind the pillar as they returned fire my way. The elevator doors closed, and two men remained. They saw their opening and charged Shoshana, trying to get an angle around her pillar.

I heard a noise behind me, and whirled, ready to kill. Jennifer appeared, sliding down the wall at a rapid pace. Ignoring my order to get the hell out at the first sign of trouble.

I locked eyes with her and shouted, "You got Aaron!"

Nothing more.

The two men down the hall closed within striking distance, and Shoshana had a choice: die curled in a ball, or attack. She chose the latter.

She leapt on the closest man like a lion on a gazelle. As weak as his firearms skills were, his hand-to-hand ability was far worse. He was no match for her. The second man danced around the two, frantically looking for a shot, but unsure if he could hit whom he needed to.

Giving me time enough to reach him.

19

★★★

He heard me coming at the last second and rotated with his weapon. I'd never had the chance to use a superman punch, feeling such a thing was ridiculous, but it worked here. I launched myself in the air and cocked my arm. I saw the barrel turn and my fist exploded out with over two hundred pounds of muscle and pure adrenaline behind it. His head snapped back like it had been hit with a cinder block, and he dropped.

I landed on his body, got my footing, then turned to the other fight. Shoshana had her man on the ground, legs wrapped around his waist and his head trapped in her arms. I leapt up to help her, and she jerked harshly. I heard the *snap*, his body going limp, giving up everything in a final tribute to her prowess.

I grabbed her shoulder, and she whirled, swinging a fist. I slapped it aside and said, "It's me! Stop it, it's me!"

At that point, Shoshana did something weird. She pulled up the dead man's sleeve, exposing a tattoo, then cursed. She stood, enraged, and said, "We need to get the Torah from those fucks."

I said, "Aaron's hit. Let's get out of here."

The words were like dropping ice in boiling water, cutting her anger. She sprang upright and said, "What? Where?"

I turned back to the hallway, pointing at Jennifer putting pressure on Aaron's wound. Shoshana gasped and started to move toward them when the second elevator dinged. The doors opened and two men spilled out, within a foot of us. Both hesitant and confused.

Shoshana went into combat mode, snatching the pistol from the unconscious man at her feet and smashing the closest guy in the skull with the barrel. He staggered into the wall, holding his head, and she sprang back for a shot. The second man jumped like he'd been hit with an electric current, and she began to squeeze. In the span of a microsecond, I realized they held no weapons.

They're the real castle security.

I slapped her gun arm and the round went harmlessly over their heads. I spun her away, then lashed out with my boot, catching the first guy full on in the face as he was crouched over in pain, snapping his head back into the wall and laying him out. The second had his radio up, screaming into it. I swept his legs out from under him, then hammered his temple. His body went limp.

I checked that they were both breathing, then turned to Shoshana. "Get ahold of yourself. These men aren't the bad guys. No killing."

She looked like she wanted to gut me, and I saw the third elevator rising, one floor away.

Holy shit.

Jennifer had Aaron on his feet, and he appeared to be okay. I shouted, "Jennifer, can you get him down?"

Aaron's arm around her shoulders, staggering the way we'd come, she said, "Yeah. If you keep them off me."

I heard the elevator ding and looked at Shoshana. There was only one way Jennifer could get him out, and that was if we were the ones being chased.

I said, "We need to be the rabbit."

She understood and nodded. The doors opened and two more unarmed men spilled out. I waved my arms and shouted, then took off running, Shoshana right behind me. They followed, yelling into a radio.

We fled down the hallway, then hit the staircase, sprinting upward. We took two turns, then exploded out onto another ornate floor, the men trying hard to reach us. Thank God they were old and out of shape. I started to go right and Shoshana grabbed my arm, saying, "Left. We go left."

I followed her, hearing the men pounding up the stairs. I said, "What are we doing now?"

She said, "Follow me. We need to do some cat and mouse, but I know how to get out of here."

We ran down yet another huge hallway, then darted into a small room with a shallow stairwell. Literally, a closet with a three-foot-wide stairwell leading up. She started climbing and I said, "How did you know about this?"

"I memorized the floor plan. Shush and follow."

I did.

We entered a balcony overlooking some sort of amphitheater and she cut right, opening a small door that looked more like an access panel. We crawled through and I found we'd returned to the main hallways of the castle, but I'll be damned if I knew on what floor. She ran down the marble until she reached a bookshelf, then stopped, breathing heavily.

She said, "If they catch Aaron because you made me flee, I'll kill you."

I said, "If they put Jennifer in jail because we helped you with this stupid plan, I'll beat you to it."

She looked up at me, and I felt the weird glow. She pulled the book-shelf out, exposing an unfinished shaft leading down, ironworks and studs from years ago threaded into the rock. I was astounded. I said, "Where does this go?"

"It's an old elevator shaft built by the Nazis. Never finished. It goes into the tunnels of Project Riese. We'll escape below the castle."

I said, "That's pure magic. I'll never question you again."

She looked at me with a mixture of sadness and pride and said, "You should have questioned. I was wrong about this one. Completely wrong."

I said, "We don't have time for self-pity. Get your ass in there."

She shimmied onto the iron and began climbing down. I followed, pulling the bookshelf back as far as I could, but forced to leave a gap. I heard men shouting in the hallway and continued down, turning on my headlamp to see, but afraid they'd catch the glow. We sank lower and lower, slowly picking our way down and hearing the shouting from above, but nobody checked behind the bookshelf.

After ten minutes of climbing, we hit the bottom, a rough square with a placard outside it, describing why the shaft had been built. Shoshana held a finger to her lips, then exited, going left into a tunnel underneath the castle. We walked for about forty meters, then hit a junction with an unlocked iron gate. She opened it, and we were now in a much bigger tunnel, with placards every ten feet and pictures hanging on the wall.

She said, "We're back in the museum. This exits on the south side."

I said, "You are a damn genius."

She said, "Not yet. We aren't out."

20

★ ★ ★

She jogged down the tunnel, her headlamp bouncing, and I followed. We reached an oaken door and she hesitated, putting her ear to it. Then she opened it. I felt a breeze and a spattering of rain, and we were out. We exited into a courtyard of groomed landscaping and fountains, two floors below the entrance. The bracing rain hit us, and I realized we were on the opposite side of the castle. We'd entered on the north side, but were now on the south side. Above, we saw flashlights bouncing back and forth in the entrance courtyard. I pulled off my balaclava, enjoying the rain against my face. She did the same. I said, "Where do we go from here?"

"On this path. We can cut underneath the main courtyard and get out."

She started to move, but I pulled her up short, saying, "You sure? You're not just guessing? We're about to expose ourselves."

She said, "I'm sure. Mission prep. You didn't get the same, but we've been planning for months. In the end, it did no good."

I said, "Yeah, it did. Don't worry about that damn Torah. You were right. They were coming for it. Nothing we could do about that."

She started moving, saying, "I'm not worried about the Torah."

Flinching at every shout we heard, we jogged up the path, the castle courtyard above us. The path turned north, running into a tunnel that stretched underneath. We went through it and found ourselves back on the north side, on the same road that led to the hotel. I paused, staring down the blacktop. The van that had been there before was gone, and I held no illusions as to why.

We took a quick look around, then sprinted up the road, entering the sweet embrace of the lights of our hotel. We went to the parking area, and I saw that our car was gone.

Shoshana cursed, and I said, "That's good news. Jennifer will take care of him."

She said, "If she didn't leave him for dead and run to save herself."

I said nothing, standing in the drizzle, waiting on the apology. It came.

She sighed, then leaned into me and said, "Sorry. I know Jennifer would never do that. I'm . . . just worried about him. He's . . . someone . . . that . . . that . . ."

Having never seen her express emotion, I was unsure what to do with the little demon. I wrapped my arms around her and said, "Yeah, you talk about as well as I do. Look, he can't be hurt too badly or he couldn't have gotten down the ladder. And we know he did, because the car is gone. Thank God you guys kept a room. Let's get off the street and give them a call."

It was a risk, but not much of one. They'd never think that whoever had hit the castle would be staying in the hotel connected to it.

The comment brought her up short, giving her a shot of confidence. She broke from my embrace and raced up the stairs, jamming her hand in a pocket for the key, and I realized she'd read into what I'd said.

She exploded in, finding the room empty.

She threw the key to the ground and looked at me. I said, "I told you to give them a call, not expect to find them here. Come on. I taught Jennifer. I'm sure she's getting him med care right now."

She dialed, and Aaron's phone went to voice mail. I tried Jennifer and got the same. I said, "Look, maybe they're at a hospital. They'll call back. The car's gone. Someone with a key took it, which means Aaron. I'm not worried about Jennifer. I trained her. I know she's okay."

She looked at me with venom, thinking my only concern was Jennifer's welfare. I said, "That's not what I meant and you know it. Jesus. I can't sleep here wondering if you're going to kill me. And I'm really tired."

She sat still for a moment, then said, "You're sure he's okay?"

"You're asking me? With your psychic mumbo jumbo?"

She flopped onto the bed, the mattress sagging under her.

I went to the minibar and pulled out a beer. I said, "Yeah, he's okay. My ESP is telling me he's with Jennifer."

I saw her anger rising at my sarcasm. She said, "My actions got Aaron shot."

"Stop that. You were trying to accomplish the mission. Although I'll say you might want to take a hard look at doing things that are suicidal, regardless of what your Spidey-sense, or Hanukkah-sense, or whatever you call it is telling you."

I changed the subject. "What was up with the guy you slammed? The one with the tattoo?"

She evaded, saying, "Nothing. I just recognized the tattoo from Israel. I was surprised to see it."

I said, "They were speaking Hebrew, weren't they? And you recognized who was giving the orders. I saw you. Tell me I'm making that up."

She said, "No, he was speaking Yiddish. I'm not going to talk about it."

I let it go. She glanced around the room and said, "There's only a queen-size mattress. You sleeping on the couch?"

I chuckled and said, "Hell no. You can squeeze your ass over as far as you want, but I'm sleeping in a bed after all this."

A scary little grin slipped out, and she said, "I knew you were sweet on me."

She stretched out and slapped the mattress, saying, "Come on. Let's sleep." Then gave me a look straight from Linda Blair in *The Exorcist*.

I said, "That's okay. I see your point. I'll take the couch."

21
★★★

Kurt Hale threw his parking pass on the dash, then saw the president's national security advisor and the vice president leave the West Wing of the White House and speed-walk toward the Old Executive Office Building, followed by a scrum of advisors all working a BlackBerry or other electronic device.

He looked at George Wolffe and said, "I don't think we're on the agenda anymore."

"What's your guess? The attack in Belarus?"

"Yeah. Unless we've had another Benghazi somewhere that we haven't heard about."

With the Taskforce on stand-down, it had been deemed unnecessary to bring the entire Oversight Council together for simple updates that had no operational ramifications. Kurt had taken to providing President Warren with a weekly update on the ongoing fallout in Greece, and the potential exposure from the investigation of Secretary Billings's death. This week, President Warren was overseas at a G8 conference, so the reporting had been delegated to Alexander Palmer, the national security advisor, and Kurt had good news. Only now it looked like he wouldn't get to deliver it.

Kurt said, "Come on. Let's hit him up before they get inside."

They broke into a jog and caught up with the back of the pack, then circled around to the front. Palmer saw the arrival and smiled. "I tried to catch you before you left to come over here. Sorry. Our meeting's been postponed."

Kurt said, "Yeah, I gathered that, sir. It would have been an easy one anyway." Out of formality, Kurt nodded at Vice President Hannister, saying, "Sir."

Hannister said, "Good to see you, Kurt. I hope it was a positive development."

Kurt glanced back at the trailing advisors, none of whom were read on to Project Prometheus, and was pleased to see them all self-absorbed in digital land.

He said, "Yes, it is. The Greeks have busted up a mafia cell responsible for forging the passport the suicide bomber had on him. They're wrapping up their investigation, leaving all the loose threads alone. They want to put it past them, and have tied it up in a neat bow of Greek antigovernment jerks leveraging an Islamic lunatic. As long as we don't push, it's over."

Palmer said, "Billings was the secretary of state. How can we not push without looking like we're hiding something?"

Kurt said, "Come on, sir. There's pushing, and then there's *pushing*, with threats behind it for enforcement. Sure, have State proclaim the relentless search for the truth, or whatever they want, but follow it with BS about trust in the Greek government. Then let it die."

They reached the steps of the Old Executive Office Building and Palmer said, "It does sound good, but we'll have talk about this later. Sorry."

"I'm available at any time."

Vice President Hannister said, "Why don't you two come on up? Sit in the back. I might want your opinion, off the record, when it's over."

Kurt looked at George, then said, "By all means. What's this about?"

"Video teleconference with President Warren. There was a terrorist attack in Belarus last night, against Russian aircraft stationed there, and Putin is going nuts. He didn't show at the G8 conference because of it."

They trotted up the stairs, then continued speed-walking down the marble hallway until they reached an NSC conference room, a line of people trying to get in but held up by the fact that they each had to surrender all electronic devices.

Kurt looked at the size of the group and whispered to George, "As much as I bitch about the Oversight Council, can you imagine trying to get anything done with this giant beast?"

George chuckled and said, "Stick behind Hannister. He's not waiting."

Sure enough, like Moses parting the Red Sea, the lower-level staffers stepped left and right, and the royalty of the national security advisor and vice president strode right up. Kurt and George followed, blending in with the other ass-kissers and coffee-grabbers of the personal staff.

They entered a conference room dominated by a long oval table, each seat taken by the members of the president's national security team. Secretary of defense, chairman of the Joint Chiefs of Staff, director of national intelligence, attorney general, and a host of others. In the secretary of state's position was some unknown place sitter. In the back were rows of standard metal chairs, filled with numerous aides and lesser individuals.

Kurt and George filed through to the back, Kurt saying, "No wonder nobody can keep a secret in this town. Might as well let everyone in with their cell phones on speaker, dialed in to *The Washington Post*."

They sat for about fifteen minutes, staring at the blank screen in the front of the room, everyone buzzing in small group discussions. Eventually, the screen flickered, then cleared, showing President Warren in another room full of people, making Kurt chuckle.

Alexander Palmer said, "You have us, sir?"

"Yes. Everyone there?"

"Everyone I could get on short notice. The deputy secretary of state is in Honduras on that global engagement deal. We have the undersecretary for political affairs on this end in her place."

"Well, bring me up to speed. Is this a crisis, or just a tempest in a teapot?"

"Yes, sir, I'm turning it over to General Durham."

The chairman of the Joint Chiefs stood up and said, "Sir, as you know, Russia is in a start and stop phase of building an airbase in Belarus. In between they've placed Su-27 Flanker squadrons at two locations in Belarus."

The screen split and a map appeared next to the president's face, showing the country of Belarus marked with two blue marbles: one southwest of Minsk, the capital, and one northeast.

"These aircraft are comparable to our own F-15s, and the deployments are a direct result of our reaction to the crisis in Ukraine. Last night at around 0200 local time, 1900 East Coast time, the squadron in Baranovichi was attacked."

The marble to the southwest turned red.

"We cannot confirm casualties, but from satellite imagery, we know that at least two aircraft were destroyed. Russia is proclaiming it a terrorist attack, and has mobilized forces on the border, demanding that Belarus let them in. Basically, they're saying that Belarus can't—or won't—protect the airfields, and that Russia will do so, with or without permission."

President Warren said, "From what I'm hearing, Putin's claiming Chechen terrorists."

General Durham turned to the director of national intelligence and said, "John?"

The DNI said, "Sir, I'll be honest. Given the closed nature of Belarus and our lack of penetration, everything I'm about to say is extremely rough."

"Have we talked to the embassy? The station there?"

"Yes sir, but calling it an embassy is stretching things. It's really only a consulate. The Belarusians forced us to chop the embassy by more than half nearly a decade ago, and since then they've whittled away at the numbers we could station there. We don't even have an ambassador, which is to say, the station can talk a lot about the politics of the next Belarusian presidential election and the dynamics of their relationsip with Russia, but has no ability to penetrate a tactical attack on the spur of the moment. We have little real-world intelligence."

The DNI waited on an admonishment, but all the president said was, "Go on."

"You are correct that Russia is blaming Chechen terrorism, and to back that up, there was a message claiming credit on an Islamic website coming out of Dagestan. In addition, they say they've found weapons with biometrics—fingerprints—of known Chechen insurgent figures."

"But?"

"Well, the claim of credit was removed within hours and followed up explicitly with a denouncement of the claim. They're now saying they *didn't* do it. And they're saying it through a recording of the man whose fingerprints are allegedly on the firearms found at the base."

"Jesus. Can I get a simple answer here?"

22
★★★

Jennifer and I came back to Aaron's room bringing a present of beef jerky from a market in Wroclaw. She didn't think Aaron would want it, but that was ridiculous. Any man on earth would appreciate beef jerky. She'd wanted to bring him some candy-ass pastry.

I opened the door and saw Shoshana tending to Aaron like a child taking care of a puppy. Never mind that Aaron was pretty much good to go.

I said, "How's Iron Man doing?"

He grinned sheepishly and said, "I can't complain." He flicked his head to Shoshana and said, "She's working hard for something."

I said, "Yeah. Something. Stay away from that. Still waiting on the mighty Mossad for a report?"

He said, "I spoke with them. I'd like to talk alone. Can we do that?"

I expected that answer, given what had transpired. I held up my bag and said, "Yeah. We brought some jerky. I'm sure that's wolfsbane to females."

Shoshana stood up and said, "Jennifer, you want to go shop the old town?"

Standing by the door, Jennifer said, "Shop for what? I don't think they sell silenced weapons here."

Shoshana bounced up and said, "No, no. I really want to shop. Let's go look at wigs."

"Wigs? Are you serious?"

Shoshana's face faltered, and I realized she had no idea what "shopping" with women meant. Whenever she needed something, she just went out and bought it. She'd never gone shopping solely for the experience, and she was just guessing, probably from watching reruns of *I Love Lucy*. She glanced at me, like I had an answer for her, but then Jennifer pulled us all out of the well. She said, "Come on, Carrie. I'll take you out. Let the menfolk do what they do."

Shoshana beamed and said, "I'd like that. Let's go buy stuff. Just like you do with Pike."

Jennifer actually laughed at that, and Shoshana looked confused again, like some Vulcan trying hard to fit in with the humans. Jennifer said, "If you want to go shopping with me like I do with Pike, that'll be a short trip."

She said, "You guys don't go shopping together? Like I see in American movies?"

Jennifer looked at me for help. I said, "Yes, we do. I just don't enjoy it. You'll be shopping with her exactly like me."

Shoshana slid her gaze to me, and I saw she was really trying. I said, "Jesus, woman. I get it. You want me to have some secret talk with Aaron. Get out of here. I don't need ESP to see that."

Shoshana said, "Nephilim, you were right about Aaron last night. Again. I'm glad you were there."

I said, "I'm happy I was, but don't put some mystical stock in it. We were just lucky he was okay."

She said, "It wasn't luck. When my phone rang this morning, I knew why."

We'd woken up at the crack of dawn with both phones buzzing at the same time. Shoshana had answered hers and I'd answered mine. Both said the same thing: Aaron was okay, and in the hands of a veterinarian in Wroclaw. I'd laughed at that. *The best the Mossad can do is a vet?*

He had an in-and-out wound to his trapezius, nothing but tissue damage. One inch to the right, and he'd have been missing some lung. He'd coordinated his own treatment, talking to some handler in Mossad, then giving Jennifer instructions to a safe house.

We learned that he'd made Jennifer turn off their cell phones, un-sure what our status was and knowing that if we'd been captured, their phones were vulnerable to being tracked due to our association.

Smart tradecraft, even if it had driven Shoshana nuts.

We'd checked out of the hotel like anyone else, and Jennifer had picked us up amid a bunch of flashing police lights. We'd acted as-tounded at the activity, and then left.

On the way, Jennifer told us of her trials getting Aaron down the ladder. She'd left it in place, and was worried about that. I laughed and said it would only lead to more confusion. She asked us about our own escape, and, after some back and forth war stories, we ended up at my major question: What the hell, exactly, had happened?

I knew we'd been suckered beginning with the first invitation. We'd done what they'd asked, and had been met with subterfuge at every turn. Yeah, Shoshana had "predicted" that someone was going to steal the goods, but she never said a damn thing about them speaking Yiddish. And then she'd recognized a tattoo from Israel. It stunk to high heaven.

Shoshana remained mute in the car, refusing to answer my ques-tions. I became irate, but she only doubled down, ignoring me com-pletely. I gave up, waiting on Aaron.

It had been an uncomfortable forty minutes.

We met Aaron at the same hotel we'd left the day before, wearing a bandage and a hotel bathrobe. He opened the door like a bank rob-ber, peeking behind us as if we were hiding a SWAT team. I barged in and demanded answers.

And he gave them, holding nothing back.

It turned out I was only half right.

Yeah, they'd tricked us into coming over, but that was the extent of it, and I already knew that. They truly had no idea someone was hunting the plunder until Shoshana had seen the man in the room.

Or that the person doing the hunting was a former Mossad agent.

Unlike Shoshana, Aaron had opened up completely. The men who'd taken the artifacts were, in fact, from Israel. The individual shouting the orders had once been a Mossad agent named Mikhail, and he'd been let go in a manner that was less than civil. Apparently, he'd used his Mossad title to fleece the organization at every turn, padding travel vouchers and using his overseas posting to funnel back electronics and other goods for profit on the black market. Not unlike some bad apples in our own defense and intelligence architecture.

Shoshana had recognized his voice because she'd worked with him on an operation, and had been the one to turn him in. She was, to say the least, not his favorite person, and the feeling was returned in spades, which explained her lunatic stunt in the castle.

After being let go, Mikhail had been rumored to have started selling his skills to the highest bidder, and had fallen in with a cabal of Russian Jews, earning money off the skin of others, regardless of their affiliation with Israel. The tattoo Shoshana had seen was for an organized crime faction affiliated with a much bigger Russian group, one of the largest in the world.

The totality of the information had caused Aaron to send in a flash message to Mossad—something completely unwarranted given the lack of lives in the balance—but Aaron felt it necessary. He asked us to remain for another day, and, given that we had nothing else going on, Jennifer and I agreed.

In the interest of privacy, we left them alone in the room to wait on a Mossad response. Jennifer and I wandered around the old town, where I found out that Wroclaw had better beef jerky than Texas, which was no mean feat.

We'd eventually run out of things to look at and returned.

With Shoshana's insistence that she go shopping with Jennifer, I knew we were about to be asked another favor.

I just wasn't sure I wanted to hear what it was.

23

★ ★ ★

After the president's outburst, Kurt Hale was glad to be in the cheap seats instead of at the adult table. The room remained silent for a couple of ticks, until President Warren said, "Well, is everything really fifty-fifty, or do we have any analysis that matters?"

Finally, the director of national intelligence said, "Sir, there is no clear-cut answer in this thing. On who is responsible for the attack, I hate to say this, but it's a coin toss. There's no way to verify that the recording denouncing the attack is actually from the warlord in question, but it's equally impossible to verify the fingerprints on the weapons in the first place. It's a he-said, she-said situation right now."

"Except there *was* an attack. We know that, right?"

"Yes. There most definitely was an attack. The Russians are claiming twelve dead and four aircraft destroyed. We have no idea about the dead, and can only confirm two aircraft."

General Durham said, "Sir, it's my opinion that it's staged. It's a way for Putin to take over Belarus."

At the words, Kurt snapped his head to the chairman. Everyone shuffled in their seats, shocked at the conjecture.

President Warren said, "You're telling me that Putin blew up his *own* aircraft so he'd have an excuse to invade Belarus?"

Durham said, "I know that sounds outlandish, but there is precedent for this kind of behavior, starting with the little green men who took over the Crimean peninsula. He claimed forever that the Russian military had nothing to do with Ukraine, and it was a spontaneous uprising, but now admits he had boots on the ground. There is also strong suspicion that his own internal security organization blew up the apartment buildings in '94 as a way to invade Chechnya."

The DNI said, "We could never conclusively prove those assertions one way or the other."

The secretary of defense said, "But there's more. Right now, we're tracking major movement to the border with Belarus. Movement that would have been impossible if they hadn't had prewarning to go. At best, they'd be rolling in two or three days."

President Warren said, "But why? Belarus is dependent on Russia for energy. If Putin turned off the tap, their entire economy would collapse. He wouldn't need to go to the trouble. Besides, they're allies."

"They *are* allies, but Russia has always looked at Belarus as a part of itself. Belarus has always been leery of the relationship because of that. The new Russian airbase is a good example. One minute, they've agreed to have it built, the next minute, Belarus tells them to pack sand. As for the energy, yes, you are correct, but if Putin did that, he would be the bad guy. He would be seen on the world stage as a bully causing suffering, and it would be a slow process, with the world interfering at every step. This allows him to act in self-defense, responding to an act of terrorism. And he'll point to our actions as precedent."

General Durham said, "There's one other thing. Three years ago, Russia and Belarus engaged in a massive war game called Zapad 2013. The scenario revolved around Russia helping Belarus oust an 'illegal military formation' on Belarusian soil—terrorists. The exercise involved a hundred and fifty thousand troops and trained everywhere from Kaliningrad on the Baltic Sea, through Belarus, and into Russia. Those same troops are the ones being mobilized."

"So you're saying that they're running a play that's already been rehearsed? That the exercise was just a warm-up?"

"Yes, sir. If you look at the military bases they need to 'protect,' they surround Minsk. Take into account they'll also want to protect their radar station on the border with Lithuania, and they'll have the country."

President Warren rubbed his face and said, "Okay, big question: Why do we care?"

General Durham said, "Sir, Belarus isn't the only issue. We have to consider the Baltic states. Putin is taking advantage of our focus on Syria and the Middle East. He's trying to rebuild his empire, one piece at a time."

"This sounds like the old domino theory from Vietnam. I should intervene in Belarus to prevent the rest of the states from falling?"

"Sir, first things first: We can't prevent the others from falling. We've withdrawn almost all of our forces from Europe, and most of the new countries joined NATO not because they could help the alliance, but because NATO could protect them. If Putin wants the Baltic states, he's going to get them. Hell, if he wants Poland, the Czech Republic, and Slovakia, he's getting them, too. They don't have the forces to prevent it, and we'll be too slow to stop it."

President Warren leaned back in his chair and said, "I'm assuming you're saying this from some statistical viewpoint and not just from personal emotion about Putin's intentions."

General Durham glanced at the SECDEF and got a nod. He said, "Yes, sir. Unfortunately, I am. We've run close to a dozen tabletop war games, with a bunch of different variables, and it doesn't matter how we slice it: We can't defeat simple time and distance. The same oceans that protect us prevent us from getting there with enough combat power to stop him. If he's emboldened—if we let him walk into Belarus—we might live to regret it. We might be left with the choice of a hard fight to evict him from NATO member countries, or letting it stand in a new world order."

The president took that in and said, "State, what do you think?"

Kurt watched the poor undersecretary for political affairs squirm in her seat. When she spoke, it was absolutely Orwellian, "Sir, we believe that such fears may be unfounded at this stage, but may be proven correct at a later date with further evidence. It's too early to tell if Putin is simply responding to a terrorist attack much like we would, or if he has a more ambitious agenda."

President Warren took a breath and said, "Thank you for that."

Kurt realized, as much as he had despised Secretary Billings, the lack of a secretary of state with experience was hurting the discussion.

President Warren said, "Mark? What's your call?"

The secretary of defense said, "Waiting on the evidence means waiting on him to invade. Make no mistake, he wants a new world order."

The undersecretary for political affairs blushed at the slap. The SECDEF continued, "He actually wants an *old* world order, and our next steps will either enhance his ability to get it, or give him pause. That's my call."

President Warren nodded and said, "Okay, okay. Looks like the G8 summit's a bust. Ms. Undersecretary for Political Affairs, what's your name?"

"Elizabeth, sir. Or just Beth."

"Okay, Beth. I need you to engage the State Department. Not sure how you ended up in the hot seat, but you now have the full weight and confidence of the president of the United States."

Showing absolutely none of the confidence he professed, she said, "Yes, sir. What would you like?"

"I'd like you to get me to Russia. I'd like a meeting with President Putin, so I can personally tell him to back off before we go to guns."

24

★★★

Shoshana grabbed the purse she'd purchased in Georgetown and slung it over her shoulder, attempting to mimic Jennifer. Honestly, it was humorous watching her trying so hard to act normal when I knew as soon as she left the room, she'd be scanning for threats. She was incapable of leaving the red zone of awareness.

Jennifer said, "Let's go see if we can find a wig. Or maybe an apron for working in the kitchen."

Shoshana nodded, not even getting the joke. Jennifer shook her head and I said, "You've got your work cut out for you."

The door closed and I turned to Aaron, saying, "Okay, secret agent man, what's up?"

Behind him the television was tuned to a breaking news story from the BBC. Before he could answer, I pointed and said, "What's going on?"

He glanced at the TV and said, "Terrorist strike in Belarus. They hit Russian assets, and Putin's starting to rattle sabers."

I watched for a second, then lost interest. If it were like every other news story on terrorism, whatever they were reporting right now would be proven false later. Better to just wait until the smoke cleared. I sat down and said, "Let's have it."

Aaron rotated to me, flinching a little bit from his wound. I said, "You sure you're okay?"

"Yes. It'll hurt for a while, but I'm fine. I've been shot before, but this does bring up an interesting dilemma for me."

"What?"

"My employer wants me to pursue. They want the Torah. Unfortunately, I would be less than the ideal candidate because of my injuries. And Shoshana is burned."

"We had on balaclavas last night. Nobody recognized us."

"I was a bit circumspect with regard to Mikhail and Shoshana, out of deference to her. Their relationship is, to put it mildly, a little bit more than a work disagreement."

"Which means?"

He said, "Can I trust you to be discreet?"

"Yes, of course. Come on. This isn't the sixties, with me sipping martinis and playing baccarat. Your spies are the ones that always steal from us. What?"

"First, you need to know I will not put Shoshana in a position where her . . . shall we say, less stellar emotions come into play. That happened last night, and I don't want it to happen again." He paused, then, as if it was the great reveal, he said, "She is special to me."

I laughed and said, "I got that. I know."

He looked at me, and I realized I'd missed his point. He said, "You told me a story about Bosnia once. Where Jennifer risked all to save you when she was but a neophyte. My story is different. Shoshana was used by our intelligence services to kill, and she was good at her trade. She was given to me as a castaway. We did a mission once, in South America. We were tracking a suspected Nazi camp guard from Auschwitz, and she was a handful."

He shook his head and said, "Long story short, she didn't care about anything but the mission. We got into some serious trouble, and I should be dead. But I wasn't because of her. She dragged me through miles of jungle because, in her words, she 'saw something in me.' And now I'm alive. I owe her my life, and I will protect her because of it."

I nodded, realizing I was hearing something that had never been spoken. I said, "Okay, I'm with you. I like her, too."

He laughed and said, "You and she are connected in a way that I can't explain. And neither can she. Did I tell you it was her idea to bring you in?"

I shook my head.

He said, "Well, she did, but I held something back about the man in the castle. She wasn't on a single mission with him. He was her team leader, and he was a devil. His chosen form of catching terrorists was setting them up with her. She slept with them, and he killed them at their most vulnerable. You know about her ability to read people, right?"

I leaned back and held up a hand, saying, "Yeah, yeah. She's psychic."

He chuckled and said, "I won't push, because I know you believe. Yes, she can read a person's heart. And Mikhail killed a man that she was convinced was innocent. He covered it up, and it was easy to do. The target was Palestinian. The same problem happened again, on a different target, and she refused. She broke up the operation, and then, when he tried to burn her for it, calling her a traitor, she spilled everything she knew about his side income. It ended badly, for both of them. He was booted from the Mossad, and she was permanently twisted, losing the ability to trust."

He shook his head and said, "Honestly, she was probably twisted before then, after the way they used her."

I didn't know what to say to that, so I let it ride, waiting.

He said, "She's damaged, but she's come far from those days. She used to be an absolute killer, devoid of emotion." He paused for a moment, then said, "Now she's still a killer, but she's looking for something else. Beginning to believe she can have something else. I don't want her to backslide, and Mikhail will cause it. She hates him to the core of her being. I cannot have her involved in the operation I've been directed to do. She simply can't accomplish it."

I took that in, then said, "Which is what, exactly?"

"I told you. They want us to retrieve the Torah. And I could use your help to do that."

I snapped a leg out, kicking the table. "Bullshit. That fucking Torah may have been something to send you two *contractors* after, in a backwater way, but no way are they pursuing it that strongly. If it's so big, why not send in an active-duty team? Why keep you guys on a string? Quit fucking with me. Or I'm done."

Aaron remained still at my outburst. I knew him to be an honest man, and I trusted him, so I waited instead of storming out of the room.

He said, "Okay. I'm not exactly sure what they want. They're using the Torah as an excuse for my mission, but it *is* odd. My opinion? They want to keep tabs on Mikhail without devoting resources. Without risking anyone."

"You mean without risking anyone from Israel. Because risking Grolier Recovery Services is perfectly fine."

He smiled and said, "Yes. That's what I mean. But there's something else that might interest the United States. The man in charge of the operation is a Russian Jew named Simon Migunov, and he's very, very powerful. He's one of the most powerful organized crime bosses in the entire world, and he's on your FBI's Ten Most Wanted list."

"I'm not in the FBI. I don't do arrests."

He stood and went to the minibar, pulling out a water bottle. He said, "I very well know your skills. Making arrests certainly isn't one of them, but manhunting is, and if I'm to continue with my employer, I have to accept this mission. I can't accept without help. I'm asking you for that. Warts and all."

"Warts and all? Really? You're asking me to act on behalf of the Israeli government as an American citizen. Christ, I'm not even Jewish."

"I'm not asking out of religion or nationality. I'm asking out of friendship. Isn't that deeper than the other two?"

"Friendship? Bullshit. You're asking because you can't do it *without* my help. You've played me from the beginning."

He took a sip of water, then locked eyes with me. "Yes, I did, because I knew you wouldn't do it otherwise, but I also knew you wanted to. We are not that different. We live for the mission, but we want to believe. Want to sleep at night knowing that what we did was for the greater good. Yes, I tricked you, but I did so with your full knowledge."

He set the bottle on the counter and with his back to me he said, "Look, if I don't do this, I'll lose future contracts, and unlike you, I can't go flitting off to some archaeological dig to pay the bills, but it's about more than money."

He turned and said, "You love Jennifer, do you not?"

The question was abrupt, and rude. Like a shot of water thrown in my face. Truthfully, while I had an answer, I wasn't willing to voice it.

He saw the emotion crawl across my face and, with a look of understanding, said, "I don't expect a response. Your partner, Jennifer, knows right from wrong. Shoshana is still learning. She studies you and Jennifer not as a joke. She really thinks it's helping. I won't disclose our conversations, but rest assured, I'm not asking for my *business*. I'm asking for *her*. She looks up to you two unlike anything I've ever seen."

I didn't want to hear those words. It was unfair.

I said, "Okay, okay. Even if I said yes, we don't have enough men. You don't even have a start point."

He became energized at my halfhearted pushback. "Yes, I do. Simon is in the capital of Slovakia right now. We have his address. We believe he's planning on selling the artifacts within a week. All we need to do is interdict the shipment. The gold is a side note. They want the Torah. And yes, they probably want to know what the hell Mikhail and Simon are up to. The two together are not good for the Israeli image, so to speak. We get the Torah back, and report what we've seen. That's all. An expendable operation, at the end of the day."

"Expendable. Man, I love hearing that word."

"Look, we'll have full support of the Mossad. I can get technical kit, weapons, and intelligence support. We won't be alone."

I said, "No, we won't, because I'm not doing this without sanction from my higher. Let me get permission to get Knuckles over here. Get him in the game."

He held up a hand and said, "Wait. I talked to you with discretion. No way can I have you bring this up to your command."

I said, "My command no longer exists. Let me talk to my boss. He's a good man. I won't give out specifics. I'll just ask for Knuckles. Tell him I'm working with you—he knows you, he's the one that gave you the medals for Brazil—and tell him I'm working something important. Let me get a blessing from him, and I'll be a go."

"How on earth are you going to get his blessing without telling him what you're doing?"

I said, "The guy is on the FBI's Ten Most Wanted list. That'll hold some weight."

Aaron shook his head and said, "No, it won't. If it did, they'd have dedicated assets to him much earlier. He's not hard to find."

I smiled and said, "You're exactly right, but we have one other ace in hand."

I pointed at the television, the newscaster talking about mobilizing Russian forces. "If I were to guess, Kurt's probably begging for a way to get someone close to that shit."

25

★★★

Simon took a sip of wine and said, "Fabulous view, don't you agree?" Never wanting to put his back to a door, Mikhail had to crane his neck around, catching the sparkling lights of the Bratislava Castle reflecting off the Danube River five stories below.

The restaurant was situated in the middle of a bridge that spanned the river. Slapped high above on iron girders like the Seattle Space Needle, the eating area was a saucer-shaped capsule with three hundred sixty–degree glass views. It was called, appropriately enough, the UFO restaurant.

Mikhail said, "Yes, it's beautiful, but I'd rather not discuss the view."

Simon grinned and said, "So it wasn't the easy operation you envisioned."

"Someone else came for the gold. And it can only be the Israelis."

"How do you know?"

"I don't. They got away, and they were wearing hoods. I never heard them speak. But the coincidence with the visit earlier for the Torah is too stark."

"What is the fallout from the police?"

Mikhail shrugged and said, "They're treating it like a break-in for art. They don't want anyone to know that they lied about the train, so it's not even being mentioned. The official story is the robbery was interrupted, and nothing was taken."

Simon laughed and said, "You really have to love the duplicity of governments. Makes it easy. You have the trunks here?"

"Yes, although I'm not sure why you chose Bratislava."

"The Albanians run things here. I couldn't go anywhere connected to my old haunts. I'd last five seconds. You saw the news. Belarus is in play, which means I'm no longer needed. No, it's safer here than Moscow."

"You don't think Putin can find you here?"

"Oh, he can find me. I'm sure he's already looking, but it's a reach and he has his hands full right now. Once he's committed to a full-fledged war, I'll be safe forever. Where are the goods?"

"I have a contact here. Runs a diamond wholesaler, right down this bridge in the pedestrian shopping area. He's got enough safe capacity to ensure protection."

"Pedestrian area? The part of town locked down for vehicles? Can you get a car in there? I don't want to walk up the street dragging a suitcase."

"Don't worry about it. He's got an armored truck that he uses. He has passes to enter the area. You just tell me where it needs to go and when. I'll do the rest."

Simon did so, passing him a card with an address and saying, "I'm sure the content will be complete, correct? Not that I'm questioning."

Mikhail said, "Yeah. It's complete, with the exception of the Torah. I've taken that as payment."

"Good enough. But I can get that brokered as well, if you'd like. I can get you a great price."

"I told you, I have a buyer in Austria. I've already shipped it there. It's waiting on me and my buyer."

"Fine, but I have a few more tasks for you to earn the right to sell it."

"What now? Your Russian lunatics from the Night Wolves are already in Ukraine. Fire and forget."

"I need to guarantee NATO loses their minds. Swiftly. This strike may be enough, but I need to be sure. I'm in contact with a man from Russia. He's been trying to sell radioactive material in Moldova to various Islamic groups and had his little operation broken up by the authorities. He escaped, and now he's desperate. He knows he's holding something that's hot as hell—pardon the pun—and growing more and more worthless. I want you to buy it from him."

"Plutonium? Is that it? What crazy idea do you have now? A dirty bomb?"

Simon smiled and said, "Yes. Well, it's actually a small bit of uranium, and it will cause enough panic to overcome any restraint from NATO. Especially when we leave evidence that a former security agent from Russia sold it to the Night Wolves. Of course, Kirill doesn't need to be privy to that little bit of information."

The waiter arrived and Mikhail waved him away, leaning over the table when the man had moved beyond earshot. "Simon, you have lost your fucking mind if you think I'm going to be involved in setting off a dirty bomb on the European continent."

Simon glanced around at the outburst, then leaned forward with some heat of his own. "Sit back. *Now.* You forget where you come from. *I'm* the one who picked you up when nobody wanted you. I'm the one who made you in this business. I'm the reason you aren't eating out of a garbage can when everyone else said you were a thief. Nobody would hire you after you were let go. *I* did."

Simon sat back, his expression relaxing, and took a sip of wine. He glanced around the room. Nobody was paying any attention to them. He said, "This purchase isn't a real dirty bomb. I'm not asking you to kill massive amounts of people. He's got so little of it, it won't do anything but trigger the radiac meters and cause massive panic. Something to guarantee I won't have to worry about President Putin tracking me down. I need you to get it from him and deliver it to the Night Wolves. And *then* we'll be done."

Mikhail took that in, understanding the power Simon held and the veiled threats of pushing back. Even as a hunted man, he was still the alpha wolf. Mikhail said, "What will they do with it?"

"They'll take it to Poland. A final attack against NATO interests. It'll pollute nothing more than some American aircraft. But it'll be enough."

"You don't need to do this. The next attack will be enough."

"Maybe. Maybe not. I want to be prepared. You still have contact with Kirill?"

"Yes. I still have his number. If he isn't dead."

"He's not. He's a survivor, and has been forever. Where is he?"

"Shit, who knows? If I had to guess, just watch the television. The next big news story will be a Western Tornado or Falcon blown out of the sky."

26

★★★

Kirill snatched the binoculars and said, "Christ, man. Is it a Buk launcher or not? That's the only question."

Oleg said, "It's a Buk, but it doesn't have the Snow Drift radar array vehicle. I can't shoot a plane without the radar assembly that controls it. It's just a missile launcher. We can't identify and hit what we want without the radar."

Kirill said, "Bullshit. How was that plane shot down earlier? The civilian aircraft?"

Oleg sighed and said, "Each launcher has an internal radar that can be used for targeting, but it's imprecise. It can guide the missile, but can't identify the target. You want to blow another civilian aircraft out of the air? We need to find a group of launchers with the control vehicle. The Snow Drift radar. It's something that can precisely define friend or foe. Something that will prevent us from killing another damn plane full of civilians."

Kirill dropped the binos and said, "We can't keep driving around the countryside. We have to kill a NATO aircraft, period. Is there some other way to do it?"

Oleg, looking a little sick, said, "Maybe. They fly overhead all the time, but they don't fly alone. If the radar shows a group of planes, odds are it's a NATO flight. Civilian aircraft don't fly in formation."

Kirill said, "Perfect. Boys, get your coats on."

The men put on the trappings of the Russian air force and Oleg said, "What are we going to do if they don't believe we're Russian military? How are we going to get them to allow us in the Buk?"

Kirill pressed the gas pedal and said, "They aren't going to question anything. Because they'll be dead."

They bounced down the rutted dirt road, clearing the tree line and entering the field, the Buk M1 launcher system sitting idle, four missiles aimed at the sky, the cab pointed at a gap in the trees for rapid escape once the missiles were fired.

They closed within a hundred meters and saw no sign of life. Oleg said, "Maybe it's empty." No sooner had the words come out of his mouth when a bearded man wearing a ragtag uniform exited the Buk with an AK-47. He held it at the ready, not threatening, but definitely not slung.

Kirill stopped the vehicle twenty feet away, then exited. Speaking Russian he said, "Evening, comrade. How goes it?"

The man said, "Fine." He pointed the AK and said, "Who the fuck are you?"

"Nobody of consequence." Kirill held his own AKM in a nonthreatening manner as the rest of his men exited the vehicle. He continued, "We, of course, were never here. We're simply checking the maintenance of the launchers in your area."

The man smiled and said, "We haven't had anyone in this sector in weeks, and even then, I've never seen anyone wearing Russian uniforms."

Having fought inside Crimea as a "volunteer," Kirill knew all too well how the Russians operated, so much so that he suspected some of his Night Wolves compatriots during that time were, in fact, Spetsnaz—Russian Special Forces. He'd fought with the men whom the press would later label the "Little Green Men"—Russian specialists in the dark arts who eschewed wearing a uniform to project the image of a spontaneous uprising. In this case, wearing a uniform was necessary to defuse the rebels manning the Buk, even if it looked odd.

Kirill said, "Times are changing. Especially here, where the revolution is complete."

The launcher was parked in the Donetsk Oblast, the heart of the so-called spontaneous uprising, and Kirill knew the man would believe what he said. There was no longer any fighting here, the terrain solidly held by pro-Russian separatists. The man turned to the vehicle and shouted. Two other men exited, one wearing a leather helmet and headset, both looking at the crew of Russian air force in confusion.

Kirill said, "What are your mission parameters?"

The man with the helmet said, "We wait. We've been waiting forever, since the ceasefire. If they bomb us, we'll get a call, and we'll defend against it."

"How do you know the launcher will work? You have no radar array."

"It works. We track aircraft all day long."

Kirill said, "Good, good. All for the motherland, right?"

The helmet smiled, and Kirill shot all three, stitching them from the hip, his AKM held low, emptying an entire magazine.

The men with him were startled by the fire, jerking back at the explosion of rounds. As quickly as it had started, it was over. The silence stretched out, Kirill's weapon smoking.

Oleg was the first to recover. He said, "What the fuck are you thinking?"

"Get inside. Start working the launcher. Find us a target."

Oleg stomped in front of him, waving his arms at the carnage. "Was this necessary? Did you have to kill them? They're us, for God's sake. They're with us."

Kirill changed magazines and raised the barrel. He said, "Get inside."

Oleg stood still for a moment, then turned toward the launcher. Misha went to the dead men and began going through their pockets, looking for loot. He was followed by the other two, until Kirill said, "Leave them alone. This wasn't for profit."

They backed off, like puppies scolded for chewing a shoe. From inside the launcher, Oleg shouted, "I have something."

Kirill rushed forward, looking into the cramped cockpit of the Buk. He saw nothing but green screens and switches. He said, "What?"

Oleg pointed at a round radar display, saying, "Three aircraft flying together. They have to be a NATO patrol."

"Are you sure?"

"Well, they're flying much higher than a civilian aircraft. They're at 41,000 feet. And they're flying together."

"Can you reach them?"

"Oh yeah. This system was designed with the SR-71 in mind, the American spy plane. It can go as high as 70,000 feet. To the edge of space at twice the speed of sound."

Kirill nodded, seeing the small blips on the screen, realizing each represented a human flying an aircraft that was about to be obliterated. He said, "Can they defeat the missiles?"

"Maybe. Maybe they can defeat one. But they can't defeat all four. The missiles don't have to hit. All they have to do is get close. They explode when in proximity, throwing out shrapnel, and those planes don't have enough defenses to stop all of them if we fire in sequence."

Kirill said, "And we only need to hit one. Fire."

"I have to have help. Swiftly, because they're moving at top speed. Once I painted them, they knew they were being tracked."

Kirill yelled outside for Misha, and within two minutes, Oleg had instructed him on the sequence required. Both looked at Kirill. He said again, "Fire. Kill those bastards."

Oleg initiated the warm-up of the missiles, selecting the middle dash and locking the target. He shouted at Misha, and the man began flipping switches and punching buttons, synchronizing the radar with the missiles. Oleg heard a beep, telling him that the missiles had the information, and his hand hovered for one second before stabbing a large red button.

The tractor shook with sound and fury, and a scream pierced the air.

Kirill turned to leap out and Oleg grabbed his arm, saying, "No! Whoever it is was caught in the blast of the missile. Wait."

Three seconds later, the second missile left. Three more, and another one launched. Twelve seconds after Oleg had pressed the button, the final missile shot into space.

Kirill jumped outside and saw one of his men at the rear of the vehicle, burned beyond recognition, his arms locked in a rictus crucifixion. Another, Alik, was farther away, in the front of the vehicle, crouched down with his hands on his ears.

Kirill looked upward, seeing the contrails of the four missiles stretching out into the bright blue sky, like the most expensive fireworks on earth. He saw a pulse of light, then two more.

He whispered, "For the motherland."

27

★★★

Kurt Hale watched Vice President Hannister go through his document line by line. He glanced at George Wolffe, who only shrugged—*too late now.*

It was the official roll-up of the Greece investigation, encapsulating the fact that the Taskforce was in the clear and could begin operating again—along with a little bit of information he'd hoped would be overlooked. Back when it was only the national security advisor reading it.

With the flashpoint of Belarus, he'd known that Alexander Palmer would be preoccupied, and that he'd take the report and file it with a hundred others from a thousand different feeds that just weren't that important right now. Information he had to take in, but that really belonged in yesterday's news cycle. Because of the classification of Project Prometheus, all reports were delivered on hard copy, so Kurt had delivered the final one himself.

He expected to drop it off, maybe have a word or two, and be on his way. And that would have happened, if Vice President Hannister hadn't appeared in Palmer's office, just down the corridor from the Oval Office.

He'd popped in, getting halfway through a question before he'd noticed Kurt, and had paused. He'd asked what they were doing in the White House, as if Kurt and George were supposed to be operational somewhere. Kurt told him, and he'd asked for the report. Palmer had given it to him, and the vice president had asked all in the room to follow him to his office down the hall.

Now Kurt and George waited on him to finish, with Alexander Palmer fidgeting on the opposite couch, wanting to get back to work.

Kurt understood why. Palmer was President Warren's right-hand man. Every president had a different take on who was influential in their administration, with some leaning on their chief of staff and others looking to their vice president. President Warren listened to Alexander Palmer, and with Russia threatening to upset the current world order, Palmer had little time to waste.

As much as he wanted to tell Hannister he had to leave, he couldn't. Hannister was, at the end of the day, the vice president. Even if he was completely out of his depth.

Hannister had been put on the ticket for domestic reasons. A former professor of economics at Brown, he was an expert at a plethora of things that mattered little when the guns began to fire. An analytical man who would be happy studying unemployment figures and taxation rates for decades, but when it came to national security, he was lost. And he would be the first to say so. But the man was scary smart, and could digest prodigious amounts of information. Which meant he'd probably find the hidden Easter egg Kurt had hoped Palmer would miss. But then again, maybe he'd get lucky.

Hannister did not.

He looked up from the report and said, "You sent a Taskforce member over to Slovakia?"

Palmer quit fidgeting, looking at Kurt.

Shit. Here we go.

Kurt said, "Well, yes and no. Currently, there is no Taskforce, and Knuckles—the man you're seeing there—was asked to help out Pike on a Grolier Recovery Services operation. He just asked if he could take some leave and help, because I require the men to get permission for accountability purposes. I put it in the report because, yes, he's gone, but it's not Project Prometheus. I was just covering the bases, making sure everyone is informed."

Palmer said, "Wait, wait, what the hell is Pike doing? That's never been reported."

Kurt said, "Pike's a civilian. When you put the Taskforce on ice, I couldn't tell him not to make a living. What he's doing is completely outside the scope of Prometheus. Knuckles is active duty. I felt it prudent to inform you."

Hannister said, "Does this have anything to do with Belarus?"

Kurt said, "Of course not. Jesus, come on, sir, I wouldn't do something like that."

Palmer said, "Why Slovakia? What's going on?"

"They were hired to recover an ancient Torah taken by the Nazis in World War Two. It's right up the GRS playbook. They've got a handle on it, but needed some extra eyes. That's all. Knuckles was sitting around here waiting on you guys to make a decision. He asked if he could go help, and I said yes."

Hannister said, "Because you feel so strongly about recovering this Torah?"

Kurt said nothing, looking at George. Trying to find an answer that made sense in the room. George provided it.

"No, sir. Because Kurt feels strongly about the problems occurring overseas."

George turned from the vice president to Palmer and said, "You've frozen the Taskforce out of everything, and yet the world continues turning. Kurt just wanted to place some eyes in the region. In case."

"In case of what?"

"In case they can be useful."

"You can't do that without Oversight Council approval! Jesus, you're freelancing Taskforce assets."

Kurt said, "Freelancing 'assets'? Listen to what you're saying. Knuckles is a man. Pike is a man. They aren't 'assets,' and they aren't doing anything on behalf of the Taskforce. They're doing their own thing, but they may be useful over there."

Palmer started to say something else, but was cut off by Hannister raising a hand. He said, "You sent them, and I trust that. That's not why I asked you to come in here. Can I ask you a question, away from my position as vice president? Man to man?"

Nobody said a word. Kurt wondered where the line of questioning was going. He nodded.

Hannister said, "President Warren bounces things off you from time to time, doesn't he? Outside the Oversight Council? I've seen you and him alone."

The statement was true, but it had never been formally articulated by anyone. Kurt had a unique relationship with President Warren, having come up with the idea of the Taskforce to begin with, and convincing the then presidential candidate that it was a necessary thing. Outside the political system, even outside the politics of the military, President Warren had taken to asking Kurt for his unvarnished views. In truth, Kurt had never been comfortable with the relationship.

Not sure what to say, Kurt simply responded, "He's asked my opinion once or twice, yes. Just as I'm sure you ask others who aren't officially part of your staff."

"President Warren is flying to Moscow as we speak. Is something going on that I need to be aware of?"

"No. Absolutely not. Please. We live in a world of secrets, but let's not make this into something it's not. I'm not running any operations off the books, away from the Oversight Council."

Hannister took that in, then said, "Okay. Can I ask your opinion? Get your unbiased view, away from the politics?"

Kurt looked at George, now in unfamiliar territory and not liking the terrain. He said, "Sure. Of course, sir."

Before the question could be asked, the vice president's phone rang. He looked at the digital display and Kurt saw his eyes widen slightly. He picked it up.

After saying hello, Kurt heard two sentences: "What? Are you sure?" The vice president listened for close to a minute, then said, "Who did it?"

He hung up the phone, staring at the wall in disbelief. After a few moments of uncomfortable silence, Alexander Palmer said, "Sir?"

The word snapped Hannister out of his daze. He looked at the men on the couches and said, "Air Force One was just blown out of the sky."

He took a breath and said, "President Warren is dead."

28
★★★

I heard Knuckles break squelch and stopped talking, hoping we were now in play. We were not.

"No change. I say again, no change."

I clicked the little microreceiver of my radio, courtesy of the Mossad, and said, "Roger all."

It was a dinky thing that looked to me like it had been made by a division of Kenner Toys using Easy-Bake Oven parts, but it seemed to work. I would have preferred a Taskforce kit, but beggars can't be choosers, and I certainly wasn't going to complain with Shoshana in my car. When she'd given the equipment to my team, she seemed to think it was the equivalent of a Maxwell Smart shoe phone.

Knuckles said, "Are we sure this information is accurate? I mean, I've been out here all morning. Maybe I should be getting back home."

Shoshana scowled at the words, a little bit of the dark angel coming out. She didn't take criticism very well. She started to click onto the net and I held up a finger, saying, "Mossad says it's accurate, and you heard Kurt. We stay."

Between the time Knuckles had taken off from the United States and the time he landed in Europe, the world had become a different place. While he was in the air, the leader of the most powerful country on earth had been killed, and the fragile status quo between East and West was on the verge of crumbling completely, leaving crushed bones and scorched earth in its wake.

As Archduke Ferdinand could tell you, war has a logic all its own, and it was rarely sane.

Jennifer and I, naturally, had been rocked by the news story, spending three hours in front of the television, but very little was publicly known other than the fact that Air Force One had crashed while flying to Moscow. Conspiracy theories abounded, with leaked stories supposedly from F-16 pilots saying missiles had been fired. Ukrainian nationalists blamed Russia, and Russia itself spewed forth a spasm of propaganda denouncing such statements.

The crash site was near Luhansk, Ukraine, close to the Russian border and firmly in rebel-held territory. For its part, the rebel command had immediately cordoned off the area but were refusing admittance to anyone—Russia, Ukraine, United States, or NATO. The decision seemed to stem out of confusion more than anything else, but it wasn't being perceived that way by the media.

It had taken some effort, and a million redials, until I eventually got Kurt on the line and asked if I needed to come home. I was spoiling for a fight, asking for what wasn't being said in the open press. What was the Taskforce seeing? He had very little time to give me any inside skinny. All he did was tell me to stay. I argued with him, but the Taskforce was still on stand-down. He had no way to get any forces into the European continent, and I was conveniently located right near the epicenter. It would do him no good to fly me home only to fly me back. He wanted me as a hedge, so much so that he'd ordered Knuckles to remain with me as well. Against orders, he'd established a Taskforce duty desk manned 24/7, and had directed me to check in with them daily, in his words, "Just in case." I'd asked him if creating the cell was smart, given the stand-down, and he'd cryptically replied, "I have the ear of those who matter. It'll be okay."

Knuckles had landed, and in between taxiing to the gate and exiting the aircraft, he'd learned what had happened. He had immediately set about buying a ticket back home, convinced he was going to miss out on a deployment somewhere, until I'd relayed Kurt's orders. He obeyed, but sure didn't like it.

He came over the radio again, saying, "How do we know these pictures are accurate? Who's vetting this stuff?"

Shoshana scowled again, saying off the radio, "I need to finish showing you how to use the camera. Tell him to shut up."

I chuckled and clicked the microphone. "Shoshana says shut up and continue the mission. I have to learn to work some tech kit."

"Tell that devil she can get her own ass out here. Oh, wait, she's worthless for this mission. I forgot."

That was enough. She clicked on and said, "The information is straight from Mossad. It is more accurate than anything you would get from your government, and much better than the stick-figure pictures you had me use in Jordan."

I waited on a response, but didn't hear one. Knuckles wouldn't admit it, but he was afraid of her. And honestly, she was right. While Jennifer and I had been glued to the television in Poland, Aaron had met a contact somewhere secret and had been given the location of the safe house, blueprints, and very clear photos of Mikhail Jolson and Simon Migunov. Both were Israeli citizens—with Simon having dual citizenship in Russia—and one had worked with the Mossad, so it had been an easy task to get biometric data.

Knuckles's comment about the photos was a little harsh, because they were exponentially better than the ones we usually had for positive ID: some grainy picture of a terrorist with a beard, half-turned away from the camera, and the photo looking like it had been taken in 1960.

When Aaron returned with the information, he'd seemed surprised we were still in Wroclaw. I'd told him we were his for the time being, but we might be called away at any moment. He'd known that was the best assurance he'd get, and we'd set out for Bratislava, passing through the Czech Republic, then swinging through Vienna, Austria, to pick up Knuckles. The total trip took a little over six hours, once again mildly surprising me that we could travel through so many different countries in less time than it took to drive across the state of Texas.

We'd arrived in the early evening and immediately conducted a reconnaissance of the safe house Simon was supposedly using, formulating a surveillance plan for the following day. I wasn't sure what to expect, but while the opulence of the place wasn't a surprise, the location sure was.

A three-story building made of modern steel and glass set on the side of a hill overlooking the city, it fit the profile for a man who supposedly ran one of the largest organized crime syndicates in the world, but the neighbors next door were not who I would have expected from a master criminal. He had plopped himself right in the middle of some of the tightest security in Slovakia.

The house was situated in rich-man's land, so to speak, and sprinkled in among the neighborhood were the mansions of diplomats and elites of other countries, all bristling with cameras. About a half mile away was the home of the US chief of mission, right where I wanted to set up. Located just around a bend on the winding road that led past the target, it would have been the perfect spot for me to wait, but the surveillance cameras on the building bulged out like warts on a frog and forced me to edge closer than I wanted.

Jennifer and Aaron were parked on the same road, but on the other side of the target house, effectively preventing anyone from leaving without getting picked up by one of us. We had two cars each, depending on who left first. If it was Simon, then Aaron and Shoshana would take the follow. If it was Mikhail, it would be Jennifer and me. Knuckles was in the center, acting as the trigger for any activity.

In our haste to complete the reconnaissance and get established, we hadn't had time to learn the special tech kit the Mossad had provided, so Aaron was in the car with Jennifer showing her the ropes, and I had the little demon with me. Shoshana was getting antsy to get back to her car, and wanted to finish my instructions before someone began stirring in the house.

When Knuckles didn't come back on with a witty retort to her comment about the photo, she said, "Okay, look here, Nephilim. The key thing is to make sure the autofocus is on the face. It's got to be clear. If the lens focuses on bricks or trees behind or in front, we get nothing."

In truth, while we had a box built on the target, we weren't sure if we were going to penetrate the house or some other establishment, so we'd opted to develop the situation by following either Mikhail or Simon. To help, the Mossad had provided something I'd never seen before, and I had to admit it was pretty ingenious: a remote lipreader. Something that really was straight out of *Get Smart.*

Basically, it was nothing more than a very small, very powerful lens that could be hidden in clothing. A cable from the lens went to a small tablet with a seven-inch screen, where the camera software resided. You manipulated the zoom of the lens through the tablet, focusing on the faces of whoever was having a conversation, and then hit record.

Software in the tablet translated the movements of the lips into words, or so the Israelis said. Internally, I figured it would work, since teaching someone to read lips couldn't be any more difficult than programming a computer to do the same. It was a pretty unique twist on facial recognition software, and eliminated the problems of distance or ambient noise encountered with acoustic microphones—like being separated from the target through glass—but it did have the one drawback that you had to see the subject's face.

I said, "Can this thing recognize different languages? Lipreading is going to be based on the language they're speaking."

"No. Well, yes, but not mobile. You have to set it to a language. It's set for Yiddish right now, for a real-time read. If it encounters another language, we just need to ship the digits back to headquarters and they can manipulate the algorithm."

"What does Mikhail speak?"

"Hebrew, English, Yiddish, Russian, Spanish, and German."

"Jesus. He speaks all those languages?"

"Yes. He is very smart."

She spat the words out as if they were causing her mouth to burn. I didn't want her to get all fired up, so I changed the subject. "Seems simple enough. How much memory?"

"Enough for thirty minutes of filming. But don't try stopping and starting to conserve space. It'll just screw up the algorithm as the computer tries to make sense of what is being said."

"What's the other box for?"

At her feet was a small Pelican case of about ten inches. She said, "It's part of the system, but it's not something we'll use here. I don't have time to train you on that."

I didn't press. Instead, I said, "Let me test it on you."

"I don't speak Yiddish."

My mouth dropped and she laughed, saying, "You are so gullible. We're too close together for it to work, I think."

"Let's try." I pulled back as far as I could, then got a focus on her lips. I said, "Okay," and hit record. She spoke a couple of sentences, then quit. I stopped the recording, letting the computer do its little dance, and then, like magic, the video played with what looked like closed captioning from a television sports show.

I'm sorry about what happened to your president. I hope you and Jexxxixer can stay and help, but I suppose that is selfish. You'll be called to fight but I wish you wouldn't. Too much death. I don't want to fight anymore.

I noticed that it hadn't recognized Jennifer's name as a word, then saw what she'd said. I glanced up, a little embarrassed, as if I'd heard a secret I wasn't supposed to.

She said, "Did it work?"

"Uhh . . . yes."

She had a bemused smile on her face and said, "It's true."

"We aren't going anywhere anytime soon. If I had to bet, my government's probably too busy fighting themselves right now."

29
★★★

It was closing in on three in the morning, and Philip Hannister still had not taken a seat behind the Resolute desk inside the Oval Office, preferring to pace or use the couches as he had as vice president.

In a hurried ceremony reminiscent of President Johnson's in 1963, Hannister had been sworn in to the highest office in the land with zero pomp and circumstance. Unlike President Johnson, he was immediately confronted with debilitating decisions that could lead to total war. An analogy with Johnson would only be accurate if JFK had been assassinated during the middle of the Cuban Missile Crisis.

Kurt Hale had been with him since that first awful phone call, and Hannister seemed to want it that way, using him as a touchstone to President Warren, as if Kurt was the only man he trusted in the room. At first, Kurt had tried to break contact and return to his comfortable world of covert action, but Hannister had insisted that he remain, and so he'd sat in the back while the initial investigation occurred, barely uttering a word. Now, after hearing some of the crazy ideas being spouted by the supposed experts in world affairs, he was more than willing to provide advice and assistance.

Hannister was preparing to address his national security team for the first time, and he seemed lost. Kurt wanted to provide what strength he could, feeling an oppressive, unwarranted responsibility for the future of the country. He couldn't imagine what was going through President Hannister's mind.

Looking out the window at the darkness, Hannister said, "They're going to tell me to go to war."

"Sir, if Putin did this—even by omission—it's unavoidable. War was *his* choice, and he needs to be crushed for that . . ."

Kurt let his voice trail off, not finishing the other side of the coin. Not wanting to be the advisor Hannister believed he was. Craving the safe lane he'd been in for his entire military career, where he simply executed policy, not determined it.

Hannister turned and said, "But?"

Kurt took a breath and let it out, taking the first step into terrain he despised. A world of spin and half statements designed to make the masses happy, but having little to do with true security.

He was now in the game, whether he wished it or not.

He said, "But we don't *know* Putin did it. You don't want to start World War Three based on faulty assumptions. You don't want President Warren to be the catalyst for a war that could have been avoided."

"I also don't want to be the president who did nothing while Putin rolls into Belarus, Poland, and the Baltic states. And the drumbeat for war in Congress is going to be almost unstoppable."

"Fuck the politics." Hannister's head whipped around at the curse word. "Sorry, sir, but having the legacy of possibly destroying the earth as we know it is what you're looking at. Ignore what the damn politicians say. You're the *president* now. Not a member of a political party."

Hannister took in the words and nodded. He put on his coat, saying, "Let's go see the national security team."

Surprised, Kurt said, "You want me in there?"

"Yes, if you don't mind."

"No, no, that's fine. Nobody's going to listen to me, so before we go in, remember that every action has consequences, and what we do could be a self-fulfilling prophecy."

"What do you mean?"

"You worry about Russia and the Baltic states, and rightly so, but play it from both sides: If Putin *didn't* have anything to do with this assassination, but he assumes that we *believe* he did, he'll be watching our response. Right now, he's not in Belarus, but if we react like we're going to war, he'll do what he thinks he must to protect himself. In other words, we might drive him into Belarus. And then into the Baltic states. This game isn't one-sided."

Hannister sighed, the weight of his decisions hitting home. He said, "Let's go see what they have to say."

The White House situation room was in chaos. Empty coffee mugs, trays of half-eaten finger sandwiches, and reams of reports that nobody was reading were scattered around. Instead, Kurt could hear the president's national security team shouting at each other from the open door.

Spittle flying from his face, the chairman of the Joint Chiefs said, "Christ almighty, I cannot believe you people at State are still holding out for more evidence. We have the reports from the escort pilots. They were attacked by a Russian missile system. You think we're really going to find a broken ball bearing at the crash site that led to the downing?"

Beth, the beleaguered place holder for the deceased secretary of state, held her ground. "I don't know what we're going to find, and neither do you."

"Putin wanted into Belarus, and President Warren was going to tell him to back off. He was the only thing stopping that maniac. Now he's dealing with President Hannister. Which one works out best for him?"

President Hannister entered the room at those words, staring full on at General Durham. The CJCS, caught short, stammered, "Sir . . . that's not how I meant it. . . ."

Hannister waited a beat, not uttering a word. When he was sure that the rest of the room was focused on him, he said, "Well, how *did* you mean it?"

"Putin's trying to retake what the Soviets lost back when he was a nobody KGB agent, and killing President Warren helps him in that goal precisely because of the chaos left behind."

Hannister turned to the director of national intelligence. "What are we seeing in Belarus?"

"He hasn't entered yet. Russia has stopped all movement to the border, but they're still saying they're going in, and all intercepts we have point in that direction."

General Durham said, "He's going to cover this up as some sort of misfire, then he's rolling in. If we don't get on war footing right now, we'll be too late."

"But if I do, I might push him into undertaking exactly what we don't want."

General Durham took a controlled breath and said, "Sir, you can what-if this to death, looking for the easy out, but the bottom line is that we're an ocean away. We have to start mobilizing *now*. We've already wasted the entire day."

Alexander Palmer said, "What about options short of full-scale war?"

Hannister said, "Such as?"

Palmer turned to the secretary of defense and said, "Can't we surgically retaliate?"

"You mean kill Putin with a missile?"

"Well, yeah. Tit for tat."

"Yes, we could do that. It won't be a drone strike. It'll be more like a dozen Tomahawk cruise missiles, but it can be done."

General Durham looked at Hannister and said, "Sir, you'd have to rescind executive order 12333, because it forbids assassinations."

Kurt finally spoke. "Have you people lost your minds? You're actually talking about assassinating a head of state? And you think that'll stop a war?"

General Durham said, "Who the hell are you?"

The few in the room who were read on to the Taskforce shifted uncomfortably. Hannister spoke. "He's my advisor. And he asked a good question."

Palmer said, "Well, maybe we don't kill him, but react with enough force to show him we mean business."

Hannister said, "So we shower him with cruise missiles and you think he'll simply back off? Or will he be driven to go to war by a population that's incensed we just attacked them?"

General Durham said, "Christ, sir, he *murdered* our president! That's the attack we should be talking about. Our entire country is screaming for blood. We have to do *something*."

Hannister said, "I agree, but that something had better not end with him or us crossing a nuclear threshold. I've found that pride is viewed as much more important *before* an action than after. After, it's usually seen as a mistake."

He tapped his fingers on the table then said, "Go ahead and mobilize. Do whatever you need to prepare to defend NATO."

Durham said, "Yes, sir."

"But *only* mobilize. Nobody crosses the Rubicon until I give the word. Is that understood?"

The secretary of defense nodded, saying, "Yes, sir, of course. What about the crash site? Right now they're still saying we can't get in."

With a steel Kurt hadn't heard before, Hannister said, "We're moving to the crash site whether they like it or not. Immediately. Who can do that? And don't tell me it'll take forty-eight hours to figure it out."

"Sir, we have units deployed to the Black Sea Rotation Force in Bulgaria. Right now we have a contingent of the 2nd Marine Division training in Latvia. They have armor. They can do it."

"Get them rolling, and this is from me: Nobody will stand in the way of us getting to the crash site. Nobody."

For the first time, General Durham smiled. President Hannister caught the look and said, "But that is the *only* offensive action right now. Is that understood?"

Chastened, General Durham said, "Yes, sir."

Hannister took a slow look around the table, then said, "Do not forget who the commander in chief is in this room. I will defend this nation if warranted, but I'm not going to war just to do *something*."

He left the room without another word, Kurt stepping quickly to catch up. Kurt said, "That was pretty good, sir."

Retracing his steps to his office, Hannister said, "You really think so? Because I felt completely out of my depth."

Kurt chuckled and said, "Yeah. You laid down enough priorities, but more important, you took control. That'll be crucial in the future."

They passed the Oval Office and Kurt did a double take. "Sir?"

Hannister saw what he'd done and smiled. "I guess I still want to be vice president."

He stopped and said, "You should go home and get some sleep. I might need you tomorrow. I appreciate you stepping in back there. It seems we're not as smart at the executive level as we appear."

Kurt smiled and said, "It's not that hard, sir. When I was a brand-new second lieutenant, my commander told me something that's served me well in many ambiguous situations. He said, 'I know you don't have a clue what you're doing, and you'll have to listen to others for advice, but remember, at the end of the day, if you don't think it's right, it's probably not.' Sure as shit, he was correct. Many a time I've been in a room where the smartest guy was advocating something stupid. They mean well, but that's why you have the hat that says 'commander in chief' and they don't."

Hannister nodded and said, "Unfortunately, being right might not matter here. Forget proving Russia was behind it. I fear we must prove they positively *weren't* involved. Anything less than that—any ambivalence or loose threads—and we're going to war."

30

★ ★ ★

With one phone call from the situation room, an invisible tidal wave was set in motion. A massive beast built for the Cold War, but rusting from continuous deployments to hot spots around the world, the US Department of Defense began the impossible task of preparing for World War III.

In the Pentagon, poor colonels and majors flailed about, trying to reorient on a threat they hadn't studied in twenty years—and, for some of the up-and-comers who'd been promoted below the zone, never. Raised on combat in Afghanistan and Iraq, they began studying OPLANS that hadn't been dusted off since 1989. The Fulda Gap of old West Germany was switched for the Suwalki Gap of Poland, a small sliver of terrain that connected Belarus to the Russian enclave of Kaliningrad. Orders were sent, some that made no sense, and the beast began to awaken. Nobody inside the puzzle palace knew where it would lead, but all knew it was serious business.

At Fort Bragg, home of the acclaimed 82nd Airborne, the duty officer of the 18th Airborne Corps received a flash message. The first real-world one he'd ever seen. He had the duty NCO read it to make sure he wasn't about to make a mistake in waking up the entire chain of command. He was not. He immediately pulled down his duty book and began working the specific instructions included within. Down the road, the duty officer for the DRF Alert Battalion of the 82nd Airborne picked up the phone, sure the message was a mistake. They had no emergency deployment readiness exercises planned, he was positive, as it was a special requirement for young duty officers to penetrate the higher headquarters like Soviet spies.

Any lieutenant taking on the mantle of duty officer immediately leveraged what was known as the E-4 Mafia—enlisted drivers, cooks, aides, and anyone else—to determine what was in store on his watch. No lieutenant wanted to be caught short with an EDRE while acting as the duty officer, and any EDRE that came down—supposedly a complete surprise—never were to the men filling the billet. This one was. He initiated the procedures, noticing that it wasn't just the DRF-1 Battalion, but the entire brigade. In fact, the DRB-2 Brigade was being alerted as well. And it sank home. This wasn't an exercise.

There was very little in Minot, North Dakota, that would interest any enemy of the United States, with the exception of the two legs of the nuclear triad that were located on the windswept prairie. One, the 5th Bomb Wing, comprised the anachronistic B-52 Stratofortress. Anachronistic in name only. Since its creation, the mighty B-52 had been written off time and time again, and yet it was still the most potent weapon in the US Air Force. Used in both Afghanistan and Iraq, the aging airframes had outlived just about any other aircraft, with the last B-52 rolling off the line in the 1960s. At the heart of their creation was the unimaginable: nuclear war.

When the missiles began to fly, one of the enemy goals was to prevent the 5th from leaving the ground with their deadly payload, and because of it, the Air Force had developed Minimum Interval Takeoff procedures, or MITO, where the entire trundling beast would elephant walk to the flight line and take off at intervals that were so close they were nearly suicidal, all in an effort to get the fleet into the air before Armageddon struck. At the height of the Cold War, the wing had been tested over and over again, proving that if the worst occurred, they could be airborne with their payload before the holocaust destroyed the base. But it had never happened for real, until tonight. In one of the many miscommunications from a system decayed from constant small wars, the 5th Bomb Wing duty officer read the worst message he had ever seen. Missiles were inbound, and he had to initiate a real-world MITO. For a unit that had long ago forgotten about the nuclear threat.

At Fort Hood, Texas, the alert went a different way. It wasn't the warfighter jerked out of bed at four in the morning. It was the logistician and mechanic. Home of the 1st Cavalry Division, its heart was armor. Its soul was heavy steel and uncompromising firepower. Something that couldn't be deployed in the amount of time necessary, but, having foreseen that very dilemma during the Cold War, giant stockpiles of equipment had been stored in what was then West Germany and other countries, waiting—as they said back in the day—for the balloon to go up. For the first time in history, it now had, and the first into the fight would be the men and women who would break out the stockpiles of the weapons of war. M1A1 Abrams tanks and M2 Bradley fighting vehicles that had been stored for decades, the initial deployment would be spent clearing out the dry rot and getting them mission capable from a warehouse that nobody thought would be utilized after the wall fell. At Fort Hood, the command would spend its brief amount of time perfecting the skills on the combat systems they owned, using the sprawling terrain of Texas, preparing for a war in Europe with equipment they had never seen. They would fall in on war stocks that had rarely been used, and most certainly not to the extent that was being contemplated here. The REFORGER exercises were a thing of the past, the last having taken place in 1993, when

NATO habitually tested its muscle against the Warsaw Pact. When the Warsaw Pact disintegrated, so did the exercises. Except now, RE-FORGER was happening for real.

In any mobilization of this size, the scope itself took on a special meaning. President Hannister may have ordered nobody to cross the Rubicon, but there has always been a critical mass in war. Whenever enough forces were deployed, regardless of the reason, the question of defense or offense became moot. The units themselves, commanded by well-meaning men and women who only wanted to ensure survival in a fight, became a driving force in the fight itself.

The planning and training for the eventual clash became a precursor, like leading a racehorse to the stall, with everyone from the lowliest lieutenant to the division commander pressing for the order to attack, all knowing what happens when the gate opens.

President Hannister didn't understand the complexities of the deployment, but Colonel Kurt Hale should have realized that the Rubicon had been crossed when the president issued the order for mobilization.

It would be very, very hard to put the horse back in the barn after it had been primed for a race. When fully formed on the European continent, it would want to run, as it had been trained to do, and the men in the saddles would advocate for the gate to open. Begging to be let go.

The opposition understood this, watching warily and matching the mobilization step for step.

Sitting in his estate in Slovakia, Simon Migunov saw none of this, but he was about to accomplish his end goal: slaughtering untold hundreds of thousands so he could walk free.

31

★ ★ ★

I looked at the screen again, seeing the words from the translation on the small tablet and wondering if I was about to step onto thin ice. I decided it was worth it. I said, "What do you mean, you don't want to fight anymore? Are you talking about not fighting with me? Because I'd love that, trust me."

Shoshana floated her weird glow on me and I realized I didn't want to go where we were headed. But it was too late. She said, "No. I don't want to fight, period. I want what you have. I want to do something like you do with Jennifer. Where I can use my skills for something else."

"With who?"

She dropped her eyes and put her hand on the door handle, saying, "I need to get out of here before you guys get committed."

I grabbed her arm, preventing the door from swinging open. I said, "Hey, come on. Nobody's here with us. You want to start a business doing something else? Away from Aaron? Does he know?"

She looked up at me, and I saw I'd missed the entire thing. She wanted *Aaron* to leave their life, with her. And she had no idea how to make that happen.

She quit pushing the door and said, "You and Jennifer have found something together. I yearn for the same thing. I don't want to kill people anymore. I crave a normal life."

I wanted to tell her the truth, because I knew who she was, but I couldn't. I settled for reality. "Do you even know what normal is? Trust me, for people like you and me, it's not that great. You'll be sick of it in a month."

She closed the door and sat for a second, not saying a word. And I realized she'd picked me for the camera instruction for a reason. She wanted to talk, and of all the people she'd ever met, I was the one who was most like her.

She thought for a moment, then shook her head violently, saying, "No, no, no. I don't want to hear that. I've watched you two. You and Jennifer are connected like Aaron and me. I see it. I feel it. I want to do something like that. I want to be happy."

I said, "You're not now?"

She leaned her head back and said, "I'm not sure. I'm not sure I even know what happiness is." She looked at me and said, "Am I happy? Is this it?"

I chose my words carefully. At the end of the day, I really did care for her, and I didn't want her to feel the pain I had felt in the past. "Look, you have a particular set of skills, and they're useful, but you don't need to toss them away because of what happened to you. You can still use them for good. With Aaron."

She said, "This mission is good, but good missions are few and far between. That asshole we're chasing, Mikhail, is an example of that. He and all the others wanted my skill at killing, but not my skill at preventing death. Aaron is the only one who saw beyond what I had become. I know what I am, and it's evil."

Shoshana was about the most lethal killing machine I'd ever met, yet she was analyzing herself in a way I never could have. And she did deserve happiness, but she'd never have it, as long as she didn't understand the skills she owned were God-given, and were neither good nor bad. They were just skills. Some people could sink a basketball from forty feet time after time. Some could survive in chaos, completing the mission no matter the obstacles. Different abilities, but still, just skills.

The conversation triggered a realization for me. Something from a ridiculous movie I'd watched as a young man. I said, "You're the Pumpkin King. I can't believe I haven't seen that before."

She looked at me with suspicion and said, "What is that? Some American insult?"

"No, no. It's from an American animated film called *The Nightmare Before Christmas*. The Pumpkin King is in charge of Halloween, but wants to be Santa Claus. He wants to be in charge of Christmas, but he's a badass. That's you."

Confused, she said, "So what's that mean? I can't change?"

I realized I was saying exactly that. "No. Wait. In the movie, the Pumpkin King is a good person. He's just trapped in his world. He realizes he can change his world without taking someone else's. That's all I meant."

She looked at me with slitted eyes and I said, "Shit. I don't know what I meant. I do know that you have skills that are good. That you *use* for good. You shouldn't toss them aside. Using them doesn't make you evil. Only the outcome is potentially bad, and *you* determine that. Like what we're doing here."

"I don't want to kill anymore. And I'm not. No matter what this mission brings. I'm done killing."

I said, "You can't call that. We might get into a situation where it's inevitable. You *know* that."

She looked at me with conviction and said, "No. I'm *not* the Pumpkin King. I want to be something else. I won't use my skills for death anymore."

I had no idea where the little demon was going with this. It was the strangest epiphany I'd ever witnessed, and I was wondering why she was telling me and not Aaron.

She shifted tack yet again and said, "Do you love Jennifer?"

That caused a small explosion of air from my lungs. "What the fuck? Are you kidding me with this? Why do you Israelis always ask that?"

"It's a serious question."

"Do you love Aaron?"

She said, "Yes. I do. He doesn't know it, but I do, and I want to be his Jennifer."

I leaned my skull on the headrest, buying time, then said, "Well, maybe you should tell him, dumbass. You can't be Jennifer and keep that shit bottled up."

She said, "I don't want to be the Pumpkin King."

The words were so sad I had no answer. Like a handicapped child dreaming of playing in the NFL, she would never be Jennifer. Ever.

Our earpieces squelched and I heard Knuckles say, "Got movement in the foyer. It's Mikhail."

Shoshana opened the door to leave and said, "Maybe you should tell Jennifer how you feel. She would appreciate it as well."

She exited the car slowly, then turned and looked at me in her weird way. I felt the spear of her gaze and wondered how much of the exchange had been me helping her. The conversation left two competing thought streams going through my mind, but only one required my immediate attention.

"What do you have?"

"Mikhail's talking to Simon. Got them both, and Mikhail's about to leave. Looks like they're shouting at each other."

The call made me wish we'd equipped Knuckles with a lipreading camera, but he was hidden on a bench in some sort of memorial park and couldn't get close enough for it to matter.

Hearing the radio, half out of the vehicle, Shoshana turned around, now all business. She said, "You good?"

"Yeah. Get staged in your car. Bet you dinner it'll be me leaving."

She said, "Nope. I got a feeling I'll be doing the surveillance on this one."

She exited the vehicle and I tossed the Pelican case housing the extra equipment in the rear, under a blanket. Knuckles came back. "We got a problem. Mikhail just left the house, but he didn't go to a car. He's crossing the street and headed right at me. On foot."

Shit.

"Intentions?"

"He's walking into the memorial. Pike, it's wide-open in here. If he gets up top and conducts a meeting, you aren't getting close."

I knew what he meant from my recce the day before. Just across the street from the target house was a memorial park for the fallen Russian soldiers who had liberated Bratislava during World War II. Built on a hill, it was crisscrossed with paths and benches, with a monument at the crest, a forty-foot obelisk on top of a pillared square of granite. All told, the park was probably ten acres of open terrain. A perfect spot to conduct a meeting because it would require absolutely no countersurveillance. Anybody trying to penetrate would be spotted. Jennifer and I could wander through once or twice, since there were others in the park, but no way would we be able to focus on a meeting for any length of time.

I said, "What's your recommendation?"

"Forget it. I'll remain in place and pick him up again when he leaves. You won't get any useful intel if you attempt a penetration, and if you get burned here, you're no good for anything else."

I started to respond when my door swung open and Shoshana climbed in like she was being chased. She frantically looked around and said, "Where is the Pelican case?"

I pointed to the backseat. She grabbed the case and ripped it open. She pulled out a tan box connected to a thick computer tablet by a wire. She opened the box. Inside were what looked like a toy helicopter, maybe six or seven inches long, and a folding joystick.

"What the hell is that?"

"Something from *Get Smart.*"

She grinned at me, and I thought, *How in the hell did she know?*

32

★★★

Shoshana began breaking out the separate components, saying, "Give me your computer, quickly."

I handed her the tablet we had tested earlier, asking, "What is it?"

She said, "It's the other part of the system," and she called Aaron, speaking in rushed Hebrew. She took the tablet, then manipulated it until it was slaved to the control unit. I asked, "Bluetooth?"

She handed me the toy copter and said, "Yes. Hold this out the window in the palm of your hand."

I did so, and its rotors began turning, startling me with a little hurricane force of wind. It took off, a giant bumblebee flying into the air. In seconds, it was out of sight.

I turned to her, watching her manipulate the joystick, and saw what the bird saw, the land being eaten up as it flew toward the memorial park. The detail was impressive for such a small drone. Embarrassingly enough, I'd seen nothing like it in all my time working with James Bond stuff. *Taskforce R&D guys are getting an ass-chewing over this.*

"Did your command invent that?"

"No. It's called a Black Hornet, and it's made in Norway. We just modified it to work with the lipreader software. The original has both a thermal camera and a normal one. We ditched those because we needed a better lens and had no need for thermal."

Knuckles came on. "What's the call?"

"Stand by. . . . Shoshana is working some magic."

"What's that mean?"

I glanced at the screen and saw a bird's-eye view of Knuckles sitting on a bench. I said, "Looking at you now. Which way did he go?"

He glanced around, seeing nothing, then said, "Straight up the stairs. He didn't deviate. I think he's headed to the monument on the top."

To Shoshana, I said, "Will you break link? How much distance can you get?"

"Over a kilometer. We're good on that. Time is the killer. I only have twenty-five minutes of flight time."

Knuckles fell from view as the drone went higher into the air, focusing on the monument. Shoshana did a slow circle around it, then said, "There he is. And he's with someone."

She zoomed the lens and I recognized Mikhail, standing just inside the overhang of the monument. A pillar stood between the drone and whomever he was talking with. Shoshana slid the drone sideways and the second man came into view, a burly guy with a two-toned face, the upper tanned, the lower white. It took a second to realize why. *He just shaved off a beard.*

Shoshana said, "Are you getting feed?"

I looked at my tablet and said, "Yes."

"Hit record."

I did so, and the computer began working its algorithms as it took in what the two men were saying. I could see the gestures the men made, but wouldn't get a readout until we were through. The burly guy looked agitated, and Mikhail was matching his temper. Whatever was going on, with Knuckles's report about an argument with Simon and now this, something clearly wasn't going right for them.

The meeting lasted a little less than ten minutes, and ended with Mikhail handing the other man a slip of paper, then clapping him on the back. When they separated, Mikhail retraced his steps and the other man went in the opposite direction, leaving the park from another exit. We stayed on Mikhail.

I stopped the recording and keyed the radio, "Knuckles, Koko, meeting's over. Mikhail's headed back your way."

"How are you seeing that?"

"I told you. Shoshana magic."

Jennifer came on, apparently not appreciating my jokes. "Knuckles, this is Koko. The Israelis have a drone."

Knuckles said, "So I'm free to go? I'd prefer he didn't see me twice."

"No. We'll track him, but we only have about ten minutes of flying time left. I don't want to lose eyes-on because our technology failed."

Jennifer said, "Aaron has one over here as well. We can launch it when you run low."

I thought about that for a second, and then decided against it. "Good idea, but Knuckles stays. We have no way to recharge these things in the car, and we might need yours later."

I got a roger from the team, and said to Shoshana, "Where is he?"

"Coming down the steps now. He'll be in view of Knuckles in seconds."

And sure enough, Knuckles said, "I have eyes-on. He's walking back to the house," then, "Break—break, Simon just exited the building. Moving to the Beemer parked out front."

Shoshana worked the drone and, off the net, said, "Get ready to record. They're going to talk."

Sure enough, Mikhail shouted from across the street, then jogged toward Simon. Shoshana waited until Mikhail linked up before zooming in on their faces. She said, "Hit it," and I did.

The conversation was brief, but the image was crystal clear. If we didn't get a recording out of this, it was the software's fault, not the camera angle.

The two men shook hands, then Simon opened his car door. I punched the tablet to stop the recording and initiated the translation software, saying, "Get that drone back here. You've got Simon when he leaves."

Looking at her tablet, she said, "Mikhail is moving to a car as well. We're both going into motion."

I called it out to the other teams, telling Knuckles the bird was off and to give a time and direction when the two targets departed. I said, "We need to get that drone back. We're about to move."

I saw something hit the hood and she said, "It's here."

My tablet vibrated, telling me the computer had done its work, and the meeting on the hill began to play on the screen. Unfortunately, it was absolute gobbledygook, like the tablet was giving us what Charlie Brown's cartoon teacher said. "What the hell is this thing doing?"

She took it and said, "Wrong language. They weren't speaking Yiddish."

"That's just great. What good was any of that, then?"

She began to fast-forward the video, saying, "We send it back if we need to. We have a whole day of surveillance in front of us. Might not have anything to do with the Torah anyway."

She reached the meeting with Simon and hit play. Miraculously, the short conversation appeared correctly. Shoshana said, "Speaking Yiddish now."

Mikhail: *He wasn't too happy with the additional mission. He seems to think the last one is clearly enough. He's shook up about what he did.*

Simon: *He fucking should be. I couldn't have asked for a better target, but he's a dead man walking now. He just doesn't realize it. Will he continue? What do you think?*

Mikhail: *I gave him instructions for a meeting in Poland. I think he'll be there. I gave him a lot of cheering about how proud the motherland was of him. I'll do your meet first, get the stuff, then go meet him. After that, we're done, no offense.*

Simon: *I understand. But we still have the business here, yes?*

Mikhail: *Headed to meet my diamond guy now. I'll set up the transfer of the gold for tomorrow. You should have it by tomorrow afternoon. Minus my payment, of course.*

Simon: *Of course. And now I'll get to spend my earnings.*

Mikhail: *I don't know about that. The firestorm you're stirring up may protect you from Putin, but it won't from the devastation of another world war. You should take a look at the pictures of Warsaw from the forties, then try to figure out where you'd spend your gold in that destruction.*

Simon: *Let me worry about that. The Americans will quit if there is a coup. I know them. They aren't the Nazis.*

Mikhail: *You sure? You see the news? They aren't fucking around, and both of those guys have nukes.*

Simon turned to his car and the conversation on the video ended. I said, "What the hell was that all about? What's the US doing?"

Shoshana opened the door to go to her car and said, "I don't know, but that first meeting is irrelevant. Mikhail just said he's going to discuss the transfer of the gold. The next one is key—and that's you. Don't worry about the United States right now. They aren't going to start World War Three in the next few hours."

I tapped the screen and said, "I don't know about that. People seem to forget that kindly Uncle Sam also has brass knuckles."

Knuckles came on, saying, "Simon to the north—Aaron, that's you. Mikhail to the south. Pike, you'll have him in two minutes."

Shoshana said, "We'll talk about it at the hotel tonight," then closed the door, starting her coordination with Aaron for their follow and leaving me wondering what was occurring one country away.

33
★ ★ ★

The rolling metal coffin hit a particularly nasty pothole, and Felix Byrd slammed his head against the steel. Ordinarily, this would have caused serious pain, but this time, his skull was protected by an old-school Kevlar helmet. He glanced around to see if anyone else in the LAV had noticed, but if they had, they gave no indication that it was something to laugh at.

Bouncing around inside the armored LAV, Felix desperately tried to make his body movements match the rhythms of the vehicle, feeling nothing like the calm of the young men to his left and right. Some were actually sleeping, a feat he would later describe as surreal.

A senior member of the United States National Transportation Safety Board, he and two others had been flown over to Europe to inspect the crash of Air Force One.

At first, Felix had been incensed that there would only be three inspectors, knowing that many more would be required. He'd demanded a full team, complete with forensic capability, and had been rebuffed. He'd assumed it was because of some idiotic budget thing, right up until he'd met his ride to the site: a platoon of armored vehicles from the Marine Corps 2nd Light Armored Reconnaissance Battalion. Detailed to the Black Sea Rotational Force, they'd been training security forces in Latvia when they'd gotten the call, and Felix began to understand the reason for the size of his team. Security of the force had taken a backseat to the inspection itself.

Felix had been to many, many different crash sites, but never wearing body armor, and he should have known that no budget restrictions on earth would prevent a full investigation of the murder of the president of the United States and the destruction of the United States's flagship aircraft. He was dealing with restrictions that no money could overcome. Only the young men to his left and right could do that, and the thought scared Felix to death.

The Ukrainian government had given them permission to travel to the crash, but all understood that the proclamation was nothing but hollow words once they reached the east. The initial penetration across the border had been fine, but the rebels held the east, and they maintained that nobody was to enter "their" area—Kiev and its Western puppets be damned. A test was coming one way or another.

First Lieutenant Dane Raintree understood this better than the three NTSB members in the back. Unlike most of the junior officers in his battalion, he had experience in combat, and knew that this had the chance of becoming a shooting war. Something different from Afghanistan and Iraq. A real, holy-shit slugfest.

He was the executive officer for his company, and had heard the deliberations during the war-gaming sessions. When the mission had come down the brass had worried extensively about a show of force that would cause the very thing they didn't want: a fight to the death. They'd settled on a single platoon for the mission, but in so doing, they were placing the future of national security in the hands of a second lieutenant who had no experience at all. Luckily, the commander of first platoon had just rotated home for a death in the family, leaving a slot open. A command billet that needed to be filled. And Raintree was chosen, both because of his proven intellect and because he'd been the last platoon leader of that unit and had served with them in combat. He knew the men, and he had the experience to—in the words of his battalion commander—not do something stupid.

He'd been told that he was to reach the crash site and secure it, period. The unspoken command was that he would fight his way through, if necessary. Which caused him no small amount of angst.

He had over thirty men's lives in his hands, and only the assurances from his commander that whatever he did would be justified. He'd seen how that played out in Afghanistan, but his commander had provided ample firepower for a fight nonetheless.

In addition to the four LAVs with their Bushmaster 25mm chain guns—weapons that could shred anything short of a tank—he was being tracked by not one, but two armed Predators and a flight of A-10 Thunderbolt II aircraft. He knew he could handle anything the rebels had. He just wasn't sure he could handle the fallout, if push came to shove. He wondered if his commander had the clout to protect him.

They bounced down the highway, running straight east, now deep into the Luhansk Oblast—rebel-controlled territory—when he received a call from his platoon sergeant, the same one he'd served with, before he'd become the executive officer. A man he trusted explicitly. Riding in the lead LAV, running point into Ukraine against established doctrine, his gunny knew how dangerous the mission was—not in individual gunfights per se, but in how those gunfights could escalate into a lot of dead Marines who had yet to deploy to Europe.

"Wolfpack one-six, this is Wolfpack one-seven. I got a checkpoint ahead."

The entire convoy slowed at the call. Raintree started working the video feeds from the Predators overhead and saw a makeshift barricade with men left and right, all holding small arms. No anti-armor capability. The convoy jagged to a stop, a bull looking at the cape, wondering.

Raintree said, "I see no anti-armor. What do you have?"

"Same. But they don't need it. We pull up, Lord knows what will happen. We can't talk to them without exposing ourselves."

Meaning, some backwoods asshole from Ukraine could take it upon himself to shoot. They were secure inside the steel of the LAV, but they couldn't get past the checkpoint without talking. They had the permission of the Ukrainian government to be here, but that mattered little in Luhansk.

Raintree felt the pressure, felt the same debilitating choices of many Marines before him, about to make a decision that could alter the course of his nation. But he had his orders, and he had a dead president beyond. Truthfully, he was sick of being pushed around. Tired of cowering to a bunch of inbred rebels just because they believed America wouldn't unleash its power.

Fuck that.

"Wolfpack one-seven, ignore them. Continue forward."

"Sir, I can't ignore them. They've blocked the road."

"Are you saying you can't get through the roadblock with a LAV?"

"Well, no . . . just that it's . . . it's going to make a statement."

Raintree smiled and said, "Then let's make a statement."

And so thirty tons of steel blew through the first checkpoint as if it didn't exist, ripping across the raggedy-assed barricade like a chainsaw, all inside hearing the desultory fire of the small arms pinging off the vehicle's armor as if that had a hope of stopping the juggernaut that was America.

They rolled forward for another thirty kilometers before they reached the next checkpoint, this one apparently positioned specifically to prevent their advance. The Predator feed showed an antiarmor ambush, with defense in depth using weapons designed to puncture the steel of the LAV. Someone had been calling ahead. Raintree slowed the convoy to a stop. It was decision time for a person higher than him.

He called on the satellite radio, explaining what he had to his front to a man monitoring the command net, honestly believing he would be told to turn around.

He waited. And waited. Then heard the voice of his commander saying the last thing he expected.

"This is Wolfpack one-six actual. Eliminate the threat. Continue the mission."

His mouth dropped open. He looked back at the men in the LAV, and they saw on his face that something different was happening here. No questions from higher about collateral damage. No discussions regarding civilians or other blowback. No back-and-forth like they'd experienced in Afghanistan, even as the rounds were firing.

He said, "Sir? Say again?"

"Wolfpack one-six, this is straight from the commander in chief. Eliminate the threat."

A savage smile spread across his face at the words. The most powerful man in the United States had his back, allowing him to be a Marine. "Roger all."

High above them, floating like bloated castoffs from an experiment, were two A-10 close air support aircraft. Built during the Cold War, they were created for one purpose: killing Soviet tanks. Neither sleek fighter nor long-range nuclear bomber, they were bastard children for a fight that had never happened. The Air Force had tried repeatedly to kill them, preferring to spend the money on more expensive next-generation fighters and bombers, but outcry from the men on the ground had stymied them at every turn.

A titanium bathtub built around a 30mm rotary cannon that fired depleted uranium shells, it could shred any armor in existence, and it was built to fly low and slow, slugging it out right above the ground— and survive. Affectionately called the Warthog, it lived up to its nickname, both in appearance and in capability. It was ugly and ferocious. Designed for tank battles on the plains of Europe, it had proven just as adept at close air support in Afghanistan and Iraq.

Every other airframe in the US Air Force was dedicated to a mission that defined that service's reason for existence, be it air superiority or counterforce nuclear targeting. No other platform was dedicated to the man on the ground, and no other was as loved by the grunt.

The two aircraft circled lazily in a cloudless sky, as if they were executing a waiting maneuver for an airshow. Tracking back and forth, they showed no indication of the death they held.

For the first time since their initial radio check, Raintree called them. "Joker, Joker, this is Wolfpack one-six. Got a problem in front of me."

"Wolfpack, this is Joker, I got 'em. What do you want me to do?"

"Eliminate the threat."

Raintree expected some questions, or at least an exclamation of surprise. What he got was a voice with all the emotion of a man talking about taking out the garbage. "Roger that. Understand take out the threat. Hold your position. Coming in north to south."

Raintree said, "Roger all. Smoke those assholes."

The two birds rolled out into an attack run perpendicular to the travel of the convoy, lining up their targets in a neat row. Less than a hundred meters off the deck, they unleashed the guns. Sounding like God was ripping a giant piece of canvas, the rotating cannon devastated the earth, shredding man and machine alike, the screams lost in the noise of the destruction.

The men on the ground, of course, couldn't pinpoint the difference when the aircraft went from lazily tracing arcs in the sky to turning into a killing machine. They couldn't be faulted for that. They had no way of knowing that American policy had had a seismic shift from just a day before. Having learned from past US actions, they believed that the threat of violence alone was enough to stop the convoy from advancing. They didn't understand they were in danger until the awful sound of the guns ripped them apart, teaching a final lesson in global politics.

The convoy began rolling again, and after that display, nobody came close to them. The word spread swiftly—try to stop the Americans, and you will be slaughtered. For once, the United States was serious. Further checkpoints were dismantled, with rebel formations fading into the wood line, none wanting to face the firepower that the small platoon held in the palm of their hand.

Lieutenant Raintree reached the crash site an hour later, a desolate gouge in the earth two football fields long, the terrain littered with rubble from the aircraft, brightly colored bits of cloth flapping amid burned steel. He positioned his men into a security formation around the site as best he could, telling Felix his team had six hours.

He called a SITREP to his higher, then sagged in his seat, happy they'd had no fight he couldn't handle. He glanced in the rear and saw the empty body bags, reminding him of the reason he'd come. The crash investigation was important, but it wasn't the primary mission. He keyed the radio and deployed the body recovery team. Their task was to retrieve the mortal remains of the president of the United States. He remained in constant contact with the other LAVs and the airpower overhead, thinking of nothing but the security of his men, spending a nerve-racking six hours on the ground deep in hostile territory.

He was but a small fish in a big pond, and he didn't realize that Russia had taken notice of his actions. Had seen the willingness to use force.

34
★★★

I watched Jennifer crunch through the peanuts on the table, patiently waiting for the Israelis to show up. She caught me looking and said, "What? They're part of the room package. You can get a sandwich if you want."

I laughed and said, "You getting points off this room, too?"

We were currently in the business lounge of our hotel, chowing down on free peanuts and beer. After our horrendous flight over, with both of us stuck in the middle of the airplane for what seemed like an eternity, Jennifer had become obsessed with frequent flyer miles, continually locating any hotel that would give her points toward her elusive goal of having enough to get upgraded on our next flight. Which was why we were staying at the Grand River Hotel on River Park, right next to the Danube.

She grinned and said, "You won't think it's funny when I go home in style."

I saw the door to the lounge open, and Knuckles came in, freshly scrubbed from a shower. He went straight to the bar and pulled a Stella, then sauntered over.

"Nice lounge. How much extra did this cost?"

I just shook my head. Jennifer said, "It's not 'extra.' It's part of the package I found."

"Are the Israelis fronting the cost for this?"

She slid her eyes sideways, reaching for more peanuts. "Well . . . no. I had to upgrade. But it's going to be worth it."

He looked at me and I rolled my eyes. Knuckles asked, "You have your own room?" She nodded. "You spent the night in it yet?" I saw a tiny tinge of red in her face, and knew why. Outside of storing her suitcase, her room hadn't been used at all. He said, "That's what I figured. If you're going to sleep in Pike's room, why don't you cancel yours and then get the Israelis to pay for the upgrade? It'll probably be cheaper for them."

Surprised that he hadn't used the revelation to poke fun at her, she considered the suggestion and said, "That's a great idea! Pike, you'll need to cancel *your* reservation. If I do, I'll lose all my points."

"No way. Not doing it."

"Why? We aren't on a Taskforce operation. We don't need to worry about the fraternization issue. Who cares what the Israelis think?"

She was really getting fired up about the idea, running through her head how she was going to get points *and* come in cheaper. I said, "So I have to sacrifice to get you upgraded to business class?"

She popped a peanut in her mouth and said, "That's not the way to look at it. We're saving Grolier Recovery Services money. It's business."

Knuckles laughed and said, "Sort of like saving money on a new pair of shoes you don't need because they're on sale."

She ignored him, saying, "I'll cancel your damn reservation. Just move your stuff to my room."

I said, "Or what?"

She arched an eyebrow and said, "Or nothing. Just that that's where I'll be sleeping from now on. By myself, if that's what your stubborn brain wishes."

Knuckles gave a low whistle and said, "Game. Set. Match. Shoshana should have been here for that expert display of relationship manipulation."

Sweet as can be, Jennifer said, "I don't know what you're talking about. As the financial person for GRS, I can't justify renting a room that's not being used."

I waved my hand, cutting the conversation short and saying, "Where are Shoshana and Aaron, anyway? All they had to do was check out the delivery vehicle."

"Don't know. Maybe they ran into an issue. It *is* an armored car service, after all."

Aaron and Shoshana had tracked Simon all over town, where he did nothing of interest. He eventually ended up at a concert in the Slovak Radio Building, a monstrous inverted pyramid from the old Soviet days that now hosted symphony orchestras. They'd stayed there, eyes on Simon, until we'd called with our information, which caused a change of mission.

I'd begun following Mikhail as soon as he'd passed. Jennifer fell in behind, picking up Knuckles on the way, and we'd begun a loose track.

He'd driven down the winding roads, taking lefts and rights, and making me wonder if he was running a surveillance detection route. It was hard to tell, because the roads themselves were really just narrow lanes, and he could plausibly be using his knowledge of shortcuts to get down the hillside. Which is exactly what a good surveillance detection route would look like. Forget about all that Hollywood stuff of running red lights or sharp U-turns; a good route looked normal, where the target could pick you out without you even realizing he'd done it.

If he were running one here, he would be checking to see if any cars stuck with him over time and distance. As I had no idea one way or the other, I'd chosen discretion, and backed off after two turns, letting Jennifer pick up the follow.

I'd paralleled on a side street, keeping track with Jennifer's calls, and Mikhail had finally entered a four-lane main thoroughfare, with a tram for public transportation in the center. Jennifer pulled off him and I intercepted, still having no idea if he was practicing tradecraft or just driving. He hit the Danube and went right, returning to the spaghetti streets. Jennifer and I flip-flopped back and forth, trying to remain inconspicuous, until he rolled up to a large outdoor promenade, making a sharp right and disappearing into an underground garage.

Trouble. If he were smart, he'd just sit and watch for a few minutes, tagging everyone who entered. On the other hand, if we waited until we were sure he wasn't watching anymore, we'd lose him as he exited on foot.

I quickly glanced around, seeing no parking whatsoever on the surface. Which stood to reason, since they'd built a damn underground garage.

Jennifer came on. "Pike, Knuckles is working his tablet. That garage is a hundred meters from the US Embassy."

She said it like it was a threat, but that, I was sure, was a coincidence. I said, "Not worried about it. Can Knuckles see foot exits from the garage on the map?"

Knuckles came on. "Yeah, I can. The entrance ramp is new construction. Apparently, the US government made them move the entire entrance to the garage after 9/11. It used to be directly in front of the embassy. Now, all exits near the embassy are blocked. There's only the main auto entrance where you are, and a foot exit on the other side of the promenade."

I glanced across, seeing restaurants and outdoor cafés with people out enjoying the sunshine. "Koko, stage up behind me, but don't enter the garage. Knuckles, go foxtrot and get eyes on that exit. If you see our target, give me a call. We'll park and meet you. Keep him in sight, but don't get too close. He might recognize you from the memorial."

I heard "Roger all," then saw Jennifer come up behind me in the small circle. I watched Knuckles exit and walk across the promenade, sticking close to a woman pushing a pram. I figured we had about fifteen minutes before someone hassled us to park.

He got in position and Jennifer came through my radio. "You know why this park is famous?"

Knuckles said, "I know someone who's going to tell us."

"Yes. You could use the history. This is where the Velvet Revolution began in the Slovakian part of Czechoslovakia. Prague got all the news, but the same thing happened here. In fact, the first demonstration was right here, led by students in 1989. In just fifteen days, the communist government of Czechoslovakia ceased to exist."

I looked in my rearview mirror and saw Jennifer staring at me through the windshield, an impish grin on her face, always proud to teach us knuckle draggers a thing or two about how small events can have big impacts. I winked at her in the mirror, and the grin turned into a smile.

I was blessed with her as a partner—both professionally and personally—and it was a miracle she put up with my BS. Then again, Jennifer recognized that all my bluster was just that: BS. She knew where I stood with her.

At least, I thought she did. I remembered what Shoshana had said to me, and wondered if I should work harder to show Jennifer how much she meant to me. I mean, surely she could figure that out on her own. I didn't have to put it on a whiteboard or anything, did I?

Knuckles interrupted my juvenile, eighth-grade thoughts, saying, "Got him. He's moving west, just strolling. You're free to park."

I put the car in drive and rolled down into the garage, finding the first place I could. I watched Jennifer park behind me and waited on her. She reached me and we began speed-walking up the staircase that led to the exit Knuckles was watching. I said, "You think you're good for this?"

"Yeah. I think we're both good. Knuckles is the risk. He was in the memorial, so there's a chance he'll be burned."

We reached the top and I said, "Let's get him out of play. Ready to go on a date?"

She said, "Yeah, like that'll happen anytime soon."

What's that mean?

35

★★★

She slid her hand into mine before I could respond, completely focused on the mission, her comment just slipping out like a person bitching about their dog tearing up the lawn. Aggravating, but something that must be endured. She said, "Your camera ready to go?"

I checked a pouch inside my knapsack, glad to be back on the mission, and said, "Yep, tablet's ready to record."

We broke the plane of the door and I called Knuckles. "Give us a lock-on."

"Headed into the pedestrian area. Go right from the exit, cross the promenade, and take your first left. He's walking straight up the street, like he's got a destination."

"Street name?"

"Rybarska Brana. Or something like that."

"Got it. Headed that way."

We walked down a narrow brick road with shops left and right, the buildings fronting the lane three stories tall. A really quaint area of town full of local craftsmen and cafés, every so often it had metal sculptures of men going about their day, the most famous being a worker made of brass climbing out of a manhole cover. The lane was spotlessly clean, and possibly older than anything in our own country. It could have been a Disneyland set, if the actors at Disneyland were actually making a living instead of pretending.

We walked up the street hand in hand, just a couple out enjoying the weather. Within two minutes, Knuckles came on. "He just went into a pub called the Dubliner. Straight up the street on the left side.

If you're on the road, you got about a hundred meters, maybe less. You'll pass a square on the right, and then it's just ahead. I'm off."

I said, "Roger all. Keep eyes on the front. We got it."

We walked past the square, a church on the other side, then a couple of different pubs before seeing a green awning proclaiming an authentic Irish bar. Had to be it. I saw Knuckles on a bench down the way and said, "This it?"

He said, "Yep. He's been in for about a minute."

"Got it. Keep your position. He leaves, and we're staying. Don't follow unless I call. Just track a direction."

"Roger all. You look cute holding hands, by the way. Takes the edge off your Cro-Magnon ass."

Jennifer opened the door and I said, "Thanks, hippie. Sometimes I can pull off the date mission."

Jennifer smirked and said, "No, you can't. But I'd rather pretend with you than him."

She said it off the radio, but my microphone picked it up. Knuckles said, "What was that? What did she say? She's got to be kidding after the Caymans."

I didn't respond, searching inside for our target. The pub was crowded even this early in the day, but I found him with his back against the wall, by himself, staring at us. No doubt, we were burned for any other surveillance today, but we were good to go here, for this one shot. Jennifer caught his glare and kissed me on the cheek, diffusing the situation.

The bar was stacked with a rack of local men, no Eurotrash among them. They saw us approach, but recognized immediately that we weren't from there. Something I'd seen the world over. Locals could smell strangers like they were farting propane. Even so, they were friendly.

There was only one stool available, which I gave to Jennifer. She sat and ordered a couple of rum and Cokes—getting a look of confusion at first—and I waited for the bartender to leave. Wasn't my fault he rarely served pirates. When it was clear, I leaned into Jennifer's ear as if I were whispering. Which, I suppose I was. "How in the hell are we going to get a facial of that guy from here?"

She laughed like I was a witty guy and said, "Corner of the bar behind you. Two stools with the patrons leaving. We should move. I take one side, you take the other. We'll have crossing fields of fire for the camera."

She then pointed in an exaggerated way. I turned and looked, seeing the bar take a right-angle right next to where the servers picked up drinks, the two people standing to leave. She was right. I nodded and we moved, studiously ignoring Mikhail.

We sat down almost across from each other and I said, "You got Mikhail. I'll get whoever shows."

She said, "Yep," and surreptitiously manipulated the camera in her blouse, focusing on him. She pulled out the tablet like she was checking her mail, and we waited.

But not for long.

An older gentleman arrived, wearing a tie and a tweed coat, with a trimmed goatee that made him look more like a merchant than a gangster. He shook Mikhail's hand and sat across from him, his back to the door and his face looking straight at me. I glanced at Jennifer and she nodded. I reached into my backpack and hit record. Jennifer did the same, as if she were surfing the web.

The two men spoke for about twenty minutes, then shook hands and left. We made no attempt to follow, knowing we'd risked it all on this meeting. If Mikhail saw us on the street again today, he'd know he was under surveillance. We'd need to wait a few days to let the heat state die down before we could be used against him again. That didn't mean I couldn't employ Knuckles on the new man.

I called him, giving a description and telling him to ignore Mikhail and pick up the new guy. He did so, and we let the computer's algorithm do its work. When it was done, I held my breath, hoping Mikhail was speaking Yiddish instead of one of the other five languages he knew.

Jennifer's tablet cleared before mine, and she said, "It's coming in clean."

Two seconds later, my tablet began playing, and whole words scrolled across the bottom of the video instead of gobbledygook, causing me to smile. When both were complete, we had just about everything we needed for the transfer.

It took a little back-and-forth, as each tablet only had one side of the conversation, but it was easy enough to decipher: The elderly gentleman was a diamond wholesaler, and the transfer was happening at his shop tomorrow morning. An armored car would pull up, the gold—and presumably the Torah—would be loaded, then the armored transport would deliver the goods to a waiting eighteen-wheeler out of town, on the highway to Austria. Which meant we had to hit the diamond place tonight.

I called Knuckles and found out the man had walked straight back to his office. It was literally around the block, on a street called Venturska. We linked up with Knuckles and determined in sixty seconds that a hit here was out of the question. The diamond wholesaler was off the street, through a tunnel in a building that led into a courtyard like a mini-Paris-type thing. And it was definitely wired for defense, with cameras and alarms all over the place. To make matters worse, the entire area we were in was restricted to pedestrians. The only vehicles allowed in had special permits. We could probably get away with bringing a car, but the risks of getting pulled over far outweighed the usefulness. To make matters worse, some of the narrow roads had ornate wrought-iron poles set into the cobblestones, blocking entrances. We'd be trying to escape from a veritable bear trap, with very few ways in and out, and even if we did, the vehicle would be on a thousand different surveillance cameras, which meant compromise after the fact.

That left the armored car itself. The very thing that hampered us from using a vehicle actually enhanced our ability to interdict one. It would have the special permits, but would also have to follow the rules of the city, using only those narrow lanes that weren't blocked. In effect, it would be canalized, and we could be waiting. Which is what caused Aaron and Shoshana's change of mission off Simon. I called them and redirected their effort to the armored car business, getting all the information we could on the vehicle to plan an assault.

We'd completed a recce of the area, determining where the armored car would have to go, along with assault options, and had come back to the hotel with the waning light of the sun flickering off the Danube. I figured it would have taken us twice as long to do our side of the mission versus the one I'd given the Israelis, but apparently, that wasn't so. Jennifer and I had been waiting for damn near thirty minutes, long enough for Knuckles to return to his room for a shower and for Jennifer to order some finger foods.

36
★★★

Jennifer popped another peanut and looked at her phone. She said, "Text from Shoshana. They're on the way back. They got a complete dump, and she ended with something for you."

"What?"

"She says, 'Tell Pike we emplaced some more Shoshana magic.'"

Knuckles said, "What does that mean?"

I said, "How the hell would I know? She's crazy. I just hope Aaron sent that other translation back to the Mossad."

Knuckles said, "You mentioned that before. Why? We got the transfer information."

"That conversation with Mikhail and Simon was in Yiddish. We got the translation, and it was strange. They weren't talking about gold. They were talking about geopolitical stuff."

I pointed at the TV, tuned to the BBC and discussing the ongoing tensions growing between East and West, the screen showing stock footage of US Marines disembarking from a light armored vehicle. "Mikhail and Simon were talking about what's going on in Ukraine. I don't know, I just got a feeling here. It's important. Much, much more important than this damn Torah."

Jennifer started to give a smart-aleck reply, then saw the look on my face. One she'd seen before, when the Taskforce hadn't cooperated with what I wanted, and I'd been proven right in the end. She nodded and said, "He'll send it, if you ask."

As if on cue, her phone vibrated. She texted a message back while saying, "They're here. On the way up."

I said, "About damn time."

Three minutes later Aaron came through the door, Shoshana behind him, dressed in the clothes she'd purchased with Jennifer in Wroclaw. She looked almost normal. Aaron said, "How are we allowed to use this place? I didn't think the lounge was included with the rooms."

I said, "Jennifer did it. We're paying."

Jennifer cut in, saying, "No, that's not true. We needed a place to plan, and I'm canceling Pike's room. He's moving in with me. All in all, it saves you guys money."

Shoshana looked suspicious. She said, "Pike sleeps in your room so we can use this one? He is willing to sacrifice that way? Why?"

I said, "I'm not 'sacrificing,' because I'm not sleeping in her room. Jennifer's trying to get a first-class upgrade. That's all. Talk to her about this."

Jennifer slitted her eyes at me, and I started to backpedal. Shoshana, having no idea about anything between man and woman, said, "Wait, she sleeps in your room now, right? But you won't sleep in her room? Is this how your relationship works? You feel insulted by her demands, but it's okay if you do the same?"

I felt like my head was going to explode. "No, damn it. It's just stupid. I shouldn't have to move rooms. . . . Jesus. Forget about the rooms. Let's talk about the mission."

I saw Jennifer glowering, but pressed ahead. "We've got a pretty good plan of attack tomorrow, with a way to isolate the car, but we need your intelligence to see if it's even worth it. What did you find?"

We talked for the next few minutes, comparing notes. Knuckles asked specific questions about the car itself, which would be the hardest thing to penetrate. Cracking an armored car was analogous to cracking a safe, with each having a unique vulnerability, and we needed to know for sure that we were leveraging the right one. Armored cars were made precisely to prevent penetration, and standing on the street after stopping the vehicle, with our asses in the wind, wasn't the time to figure out that our plan had no chance of success.

In the end, Knuckles was satisfied we could crack it—and he was the expert on that sort of thing, having done an actual armored car heist in Bulgaria for a Taskforce operation that was dicey, to say the least. He'd assaulted in the street much like we were going to do here, and this car had the same vulnerability that he'd leveraged before.

His assault was a violent encounter that had looked random, with heads getting smacked and people screaming, but that was all just show for the cover. It had been executed with a precision few men could achieve, least of all a random criminal element, and all that had been predicated on Knuckles's research into the target.

We kicked around a few isolation contingencies and different ways to stop the vehicle, eventually ending up with a plan—although I thought it was a little Machiavellian. It would get the job done, provided the men inside decided to quit. If they didn't, we'd be left outside turning red in the face, because there was no way I was going through with the bluff.

Our getaway after became the focus, and I'd detailed Jennifer to rent some mopeds first thing in the morning. Cars couldn't traverse willy-nilly, but mopeds sure as hell could, and we'd only be carrying the Torah. We looked one more time at the map, pulling up street view, and I said, "This might actually work."

Shoshana said, "Of course it will, with your help."

I nodded and said, "I want something in return."

"What?"

"I want that recording we made this morning." I turned to Aaron. "Did you send it?"

Aaron said, "No, I didn't. And now I don't have to. We have the mission. Whatever those guys were talking about, it's irrelevant."

I said, "It's not irrelevant. It's important. What those two were discussing is much more important than some Torah. I'm sure of it."

"Pike, I don't own Mossad assets. We have what we need. The rest is just extraneous intel. Smoke and mirrors that have nothing to do with the mission. I can't ask them to use their cell to translate. They're busy with other, more pressing taskings."

"You mean you won't because you don't want to lose the next contract by being a pest."

He leaned back, looked at Shoshana, then said, "Yes, that's true. I'm not a member anymore. I have to make a living now. I can't order people. I can only beg, and that has to be tied to the mission. When the translation comes out, it won't be anything we don't already know, and it will hurt my company."

I kicked the table and said, "I don't give a shit. I'm asking. Not as a friend in a company, but as a compatriot, regardless of where we're from. This is *important*."

"Why?"

I leaned back and said, "I don't know why. It just is."

Shoshana was giving me her weird glow, only this time it was with a twist of understanding. She got it, and I was glad to have her on my side.

She said, "He feels something. He sees what's going on."

That wasn't what I expected. I didn't need all her goofy mind-reading shit. I said, "Hey, don't go all psychic on me. I just think it's critical because of what they said. They were talking about Putin, and they mentioned a target."

She said nothing for a moment, and I looked at Aaron. He was waiting on her. Waiting on a decision, which is something I'd never seen before.

Shoshana said, "You ever wonder why you're so lucky? Why you're my lucky talisman?"

Exasperated, I said, "It's not luck. It's planning. Come on, all I'm asking is that you send the recording back to see what they said."

Shoshana glanced at Jennifer, then gave me a little secret smile.

"Yes. You are right. It's not luck. You are like me. You see things that others don't. You don't understand it, but it's true."

Enough. No way was I going to pretend to be some psycho like her. I said, "What the hell are you talking about?"

She turned to Aaron. "Do it. Send it to Mossad."

Aaron looked conflicted, caught between us in the lounge and his masters at home. He said, "Shoshana, I would love to, but if I do, we'll be billed. They'll charge some stupid amount just to punish me when it proves unnecessary. They might even charge enough to cover the profit of this trip, absolving them from paying us."

Knuckles said, "So I guess the Jewish stereotype is a little true."

Aaron glared at him, and Shoshana said, "Aaron, if you want to sleep with me, you'll do it."

The room went completely silent, each of us trying to ascertain if we'd heard her correctly. She felt the stillness, growing agitated. She finally said, "What? Isn't that what you do in a relationship?" She turned to Jennifer, her face blossoming red for the first time I'd ever seen. She was embarrassed and realized she'd made an enormous mistake. "Isn't that what you do with Pike?"

Jennifer said, "Uhhh . . . no. You and I need to talk. For real."

She said, "But you wanted him to move rooms. . . ."

Completely flustered, Aaron said, "I'll send it, I'll send it. But it had better be worth the cost."

Wanting to get out of the lounge, afraid of what the little demon would do if she thought we were making fun of her, I said, "It's worth it. Trust me."

Knuckles stood up and said, "Well, this has got to be the strangest mission planning I've ever done. See you in the morning."

He stood to exit and Jennifer said, "Hang on, I'll go with you."

The door swung closed, leaving me with the Israelis. I said, "Look, if they go all stupid on you, I'll pay for the translation."

Aaron said, "Not necessary. If you feel it's that important, I'll send it. I'll worry about the fallout later."

I said, "It is. But if I were you, I'd worry about what happens when I leave this room."

He glanced at Shoshana. She'd recovered from her previous comment, but still looked chagrined. Like she'd farted on a first date, which, I suppose, is pretty much what she'd done. I tossed her a bone.

"We need to get some sleep. Long day tomorrow." I looked her in the eye and said, "And I've still got to move my luggage."

She grinned at the words, understanding that in the end, Jennifer had won, and therefore, so could she.

Not wanting to be left alone with her, Aaron said, "What makes you think that recording is anything other than another criminal act?"

I said, "What Mikhail said about a target. I think he was talking about the president, and I have a feeling that my government is about to go to war for the wrong reasons."

Shoshana nodded solemnly, as if she understood. Aaron simply stared at me, wishing me to remain.

I pitied him.

37
★★★

Looking in the distance, President Hannister could just make out the C-17 Globemaster, a small pinprick in the blue sky. He glanced at the honor guard to his right and saw them imperceptibly straighten. This was the one.

The aircraft rapidly grew in size, until Hannister could make out the windows of the cockpit and the landing gear underneath. It seemed to slow in the air, gracefully approaching the runway of Dover Air Force Base, then touched down with a puff of smoke off the tires.

The plane rapidly taxied to their location, all other operations halted for this one flight, and wheeled around until its tail was facing the procession. The ramp began to lower, moving at a pace that lent dignity to the affair. Before it touched the ground Hannister could see five flag-draped containers. He heard someone sniffle, and saw Chelsea Warren, Peyton Warren's daughter, pushing a handkerchief to her face. Peyton's son, Chad, was stoic.

There had been some consternation on how the return would be handled, with the staff discussing how best to depict the event for the press, but Libby Warren, President Warren's widow, had cut it short, saying the return would be handled exactly like every soldier who had come before. In her words, "He died in war, and he'll be treated with the same respect. No giant processional. No horses or bugles or twenty-one-gun salutes. No parades or speeches. Whatever the soldier gets is what he gets."

And so they stood at attention on the greasy Dover tarmac, the sky blindingly bright, the wind whipping the dress hems and pant legs of the procession, watching the ramp lower.

When it was finished, Hannister could see five men in uniform, one behind each casket. The honor guard began to march, brightly colored in the uniforms of each service, trooping up the ramp in a platoon-size formation. They broke ranks and positioned themselves in a practiced motion, three men to a side, one at the head of each casket. Hannister could faintly hear the commands in the wind, and all five caskets rose; then, one by one, began the train to the waiting transfer vans, passing by the families who had gathered to pay respect.

The uniformed men to his left and right began to salute, and he followed suit, wishing he'd had the time for someone to show him how to do it correctly.

President Warren came by first, followed by the remains of only four of his staff—the few who could be found and positively identified in the time allotted at the crash site.

A second flight was scheduled later that day, bringing home the remains of between twelve and eighteen people. Those remains would get the same dignified return, but they would be moved to the mortuary for forensic analysis to determine who they actually belonged to.

The train of the dead passed by, the only noise the clicking of shoes on the asphalt, and one by one the caskets were loaded into a US Air Force transport vehicle, just like every other soldier who had made this same sad trip. The salutes were dropped, and the vehicle drove away. The procession began to break up, the families of the staffers moving to the mortuary on foot, the presidential family standing still, unsure of what to do next.

President Hannister went to Libby and said some words, then shook the hand of Chad and kissed Chelsea on the cheek. And that was it.

Within seven minutes he was inside Marine One, flying back to the

White House, flanked on all sides by members of his national security team, all of whom had been working nonstop.

Hannister said, "Anything new?"

Alexander Palmer said, "It was a rocket. Positively confirmed by the NTSB team. Air Force One was attacked."

Hannister looked out the window, the ground falling away as they rose, and muttered, "Christ," then said, "They found the black boxes? What do you mean, 'positively'?"

"Yes, sir, along with other evidence. What they found is irrefutable."

"Where did the missile come from?"

General Durham said, "We've gone over all the satellite footage and have a heat source inside Ukraine at the time of the incident."

"So it didn't come from Russian soil?"

"No, but it was most definitely a Russian-made missile system. We believe it was a Buk, the same system that brought down the Malaysian airliner."

"So this could be a mistake? Or do we believe it's deliberate?"

The director of national intelligence said, "Sir, the heat signature is inside rebel-controlled territory, which is to say, it's pretty much in Russian territory. They don't do anything without approval."

Hannister turned to him and spoke slowly. "Be clear on what you're saying. Very, very clear. Is it your assessment that Russia deliberately attacked and killed the president of the United States?"

"Sir, Russia has been on the leading edge of Ukraine and Crimea from the beginning. Every single event that has transpired there has been at the behest of Putin. Make no mistake, when he wanted a 'spontaneous' uprising, he got it. The fact is that the rebels wouldn't even have the Buk system if it weren't for Russia, and they surely wouldn't have the training to use it by themselves."

"You didn't answer my question. It's a simple yes or no. Is the intelligence community telling me this is a slam dunk? Because if they are, the end state is going to be the same as last time."

The DNI paused, not wanting to use the words his predecessor had used in the run-up to invading Iraq, telling the administration that the existence of Saddam Hussein's WMD was a "slam dunk." He finally said, "Nothing is one hundred percent, but knowing what we do about the state of play in the rebel-held territories, it would be impossible for them to fire missiles without being ordered to by the Russians."

"Then how did the Malaysian airliner get shot down? Are you saying Russia ordered that as well?"

"No, not at all, but that is the exception that proves the rule. The Malaysian airline was a mistake that cost Russia and the rebels greatly on the world stage, and because of it, Russia gained complete control of all the systems they had given to the rebels. Precisely to prevent another accidental shooting. If a shooting occurs now, it's deliberate."

Hannister turned to the State Department's undersecretary for political affairs—now a de facto secretary of state, and said, "What's Putin saying? Have you talked to their foreign minister?"

"Yes, sir. They're not disputing the missile launch, but are claiming a terrorist attack. They're blaming Ukrainian nationalists, a group called the Crimean Tatars. They were pushed out of the peninsula after the annexation, and are the ones we believe exploded the power grid going into the Crimean peninsula a year ago. Russia is actually using the attack as a way to leverage support against them."

"So you're with the DNI? You think Russia's behind the death of President Warren?"

"No. Not completely." She pulled out a tablet and said, "The foreign minister sent these photos. Of course, there's no way to tell if they're staged or when or where they were taken, but he is adamant that this is the Buk that launched the missiles."

She flicked through a few applications, then brought up a stark picture: a Buk missile launcher with no missiles mounted. In the foreground were three dead men, splayed on the ground as if they'd been executed, blood running over rebel uniforms.

Beth said, "The foreign minister says these were the rebels manning the launcher, and that someone killed them and took it over."

Hannister used his finger to tap the screen on a black blob, saying, "What's that?"

"A human. Someone who was caught in the backblast and literally cooked."

Hannister said nothing, letting the picture sink in, truthfully wanting a solution to appear. Anything to tell him what to do next.

General Durham said, "Sir, I told you this is exactly what Putin would do. Claim a misfire, then storm into Belarus. From there, he's one more false crisis away from the Baltic states. Make no mistake, he's going to play you. He doesn't want a war, and is convinced he doesn't need one. All he needs is plausible deniability, and one crisis after another. He's going to walk all over us."

"Where do we stand with deployments?"

"Not nearly as good as we should be. I've got one brigade of the 82nd in Poland, and another on the way. I have about fifty percent mission capable on war stocks for the 1st Cavalry Division to fall in on—they needed a helluva lot more work than we expected—so I can't do anything with that for at least another week. The problem is our ongoing commitments. Iraq and Afghanistan have sucked us dry. Both the 173rd Airborne out of Italy and the 2nd Cav out of Germany are committed in another theater. At this moment, I've got a battalion of Rangers, the Marine Corps Black Sea Rotational Force, and a Stryker Brigade out of Fort Carson. I can cobble together a fighting force, but it's nowhere near what the Russians can bring to bear. The one bright side is airpower. We can absolutely annihilate anything that flies over Europe, which will give us an edge on the ground. Bottom line: I can fight right now, but if you want to seize terrain, I need another month."

Hannister nodded at Alexander Palmer, wishing mightily he'd brought Kurt Hale with him. "What do you think?"

"Well, I'm not as bullish as the chairman on culpability, but it does look pretty incriminating."

"Who's analyzed these pictures? I'm sure someone has."

The DNI said, "We did, in fact, analyze them. The Buk in the picture has been seen before in Ukraine. It's included in some other images we have, and has enough identifying characteristics that we can confirm the specific launcher, so we know it's an actual rebel Buk and not staged. The rebel uniforms are accurate, as is the terrain surrounding the Buk. It is most likely a complete charade for our benefit, but we can't prove it through the imagery. There is nothing we can find where we could say, 'Nice try. Why is X in this photo?' It's as real as we can prove, but that doesn't *disprove* a setup. Remember, the Russians are expert at this sort of thing."

Hannister said, "Except for the burned guy. That's a bit much."

Beth from State said, "Yes, yes. I was saying that exact same thing. Why put a burned guy in the picture? The dead rebels are enough to prove what they wanted. It's just random enough to . . . to . . . be real."

General Durham said, "Awww, bullshit. Look, sir, NATO is spinning up over this, and individual countries are starting to rattle individual sabers. We need to get on top of it. Show leadership, or we're going to have leadership stripped from us, just like what happened in Libya. You can't lead from behind here. You have to *lead*."

38

★★★

Hannister bristled at the words, saying, "And just what does that mean? Is your sole view of leadership nothing more than wielding a hammer?"

General Durham took a breath. With over thirty-seven years of service, he'd seen the good and the bad, and he was convinced he was seeing the latter now. He said, "Sir, you're about to cause World War Three because you're dithering. You want to fire me, then go ahead, but President Warren nominated me because I don't dance. I tell it like it is. If we don't take charge of this, mark my words, it will grow out of our control."

When Hannister didn't respond, he said, "For Christ's sake! They killed our president! Surely on a personal level that means something."

The outburst from General Durham was like a slap in the face. Hannister leaned forward, speaking so low that what he said was lost by the noise of the helicopter to those on the outer ring of seats.

"General Durham, I appreciate your advice, and I realize I have never served in the military, but if you question my commitment to bringing President Warren's killers to justice again, I won't fire you. I'll rip out your fucking heart."

Durham looked stunned, having never seen Hannister show any emotion whatsoever, least of all a penchant for violence. He slowly nodded, and Hannister said, "I will pretend you never said those words, and I will expect absolute loyalty and the same unvarnished truth you gave President Warren. Is that understood?"

"Yes, sir. I . . ."

Hannister cut him off with the wave of a hand. Returning to his usual calm, analytical self, he said, "Water under the bridge. What do you recommend now? What's Russia doing?"

"They're staging on the border of Belarus. At least two divisions, with others mobilizing. The death of the president has caused a pause in their plans, but they're on the verge of invading. Nothing we can do about that, and they know it. They're going in."

"What's Belarus saying?"

Beth said, "They're vacillating. One minute they denounce the Russian posturing over the supposed terrorist attack at their airbase, the next minute they're talking about their close ties with the Russian people and insinuating they'll invite them in. President Warren's death has caused chaos. They're not sure what to do."

"Because they see us as a threat?"

"Yes."

General Durham said, "It's irrelevant what they 'see.' *Russia* is the threat, and Putin is playing us like a fiddle. Sir, I'm telling you, there is no walking this back. No matter what we do, Russia is going in. They'll just change the language of why. Whether it's a terrorist attack against their interests, or shoring up an ally against our 'provocation,' Putin is getting what he wants."

"So what do you recommend we do?"

"Show strength. Show him we mean business. Show our NATO allies that we are serious."

"But that's a fine line. If we project too much strength, we get exactly what we don't want. Total war."

"Sir, Putin killed our president. Putin engineered this. We are just reacting, and we can do exactly like he envisioned we would, giving him a fait accompli, or we can stop him."

"And what if he didn't?"

"Didn't what?"

"Didn't kill Peyton Warren? What if he's sitting in his country right now freaking out over the death? What if he's only reacting to us?"

General Durham sat back and rubbed his face, then said, "Sir, we can only use the evidence we have, and it's pretty conclusive. I don't want to go to war any more than you do, but I think I need to make clear what's at stake here: a complete restructuring of the world order. We don't push now, and Putin will use that opportunity to invade the Baltics. At that point he'll have triggered a NATO response, which we will no longer control. You worry about World War Three, but sitting and doing nothing will guarantee it."

Hannister closed his eyes and leaned back, the vibration of the helicopter soothing. Everyone else waited for a response. When one wasn't forthcoming, Alexander Palmer said, "Sir?"

Hannister opened his eyes. "Okay. Okay. Let's make a statement, but the statement is predicated on the death of our president."

General Durham nodded and said, "What do you want?"

"You said you had enough forces to hold, right? Enough to show we mean business?"

"Yes, sir."

"Get them to the crash site. No more tentative in-and-out stuff with only a few vehicles. Roll in with all the firepower we need. The reason will be body recovery. Finding the men and women we couldn't from the first incursion. Also, drive forward to the launch site with whatever we need. Tell the world that we're just trying to figure out what happened. We show we mean business, and it's all under the cloak of humanitarian reasons. No use of NATO at all."

Durham nodded and said, "Do we?"

"Do we what?"

"Do we mean business? If someone tries to stop us, do we back off, or press forward?"

Hannister considered what the chairman had asked, realizing it was easier to utter the words than to actually put someone in danger.

"Can we press forward without jeopardizing lives? I'm sorry for the question, I honestly don't know."

"Sir, the use of force will always jeopardize lives, but if we do it right, the lives won't be on our side. If Russia stays out, we can deal with anything. If they decide to intervene . . ."

He left the rest unsaid. Hannister turned to his newly minted acting secretary of state and said, "Beth, notify them. Tell Russia we're going in, and nobody is to stop us. Warn them."

Looking slightly ill, she nodded. Hannister turned to Alexander Palmer and said, "Is this right? Are we doing right?"

Palmer said, "I can't see how anyone could fault you for that decision."

Hannister barked a false laugh, then said, "Nobody will fault me today, but history might very well tomorrow. If we still have someone recording it."

And so the horses were led to the stall, confident in the sprint they were about to run. Happy to be let free on a course that was dictated by rails built by adults in the international community, they thought it would be a straight race around the track, flexing their muscles and pulling at the bit with little risk, not realizing that the dirt they were about to chew had no rails dictating the path. Others were hell-bent on destroying them, and one man's machinations would allow the horses to run free, out of control of their riders, bringing with them a destruction unseen in the history of the earth.

As Marine One set down onto the White House grounds, a single person held the key, and he didn't even realize it. Kurt Hale sat in front of his office computer, reading a message from a man he no longer controlled. A warrior that nobody in the upper echelons of the government trusted, but one who Kurt believed in without question.

Pike Logan had sent him a back-channel message outside of the normal Taskforce communication, directly to him, and it was simple.

Don't do anything stupid. What's going on over here is not what it seems. Give me time. Report later.

Kurt rubbed his eyes, the lack of sleep making his eyelids feel like sandpaper. He shut down the computer, wondering what Pike had found.

39
★★★

Even in the summer, the early morning air in Bratislava was crisp, around fifty-five degrees, which made hiding our weapons that much easier because of the jackets we wore to ward off the chill. We'd been in place behind a giant church called Saint Martin's Cathedral since eight A.M., and while the sun was up, the church itself blocked the rays, leaving us in the cold shadow.

After an extensive reconnaissance, we'd decided that this was the route the armored car would take, as the back of the church held a little courtyard with an exit onto a four-lane highway that crossed the Danube, the river less than two hundred meters away. From the diamond wholesaler, there were only a few routes out of the narrow cobblestone city center, and most took you deeper in before letting you exit. One route was shorter, but it ended up at the promenade with the underground garage, which meant more spaghetti roads before getting to the bridge that crossed the Danube. The driver of the car would not want to traverse all that. He'd want to get out of the canalized lanes and onto a high-speed avenue of approach as soon as possible, which meant he'd go north on Venturska, then west on Prepostska—a very narrow lane barely wide enough for a car to pass—before heading south again toward the church on Kapitolska, basically making a short box to get to the four-lane. He'd turn off of Kapitolska into this courtyard, then drive right through.

Or so he thought.

We had a tiny force to deal with the issue of stopping a veritable tank, which had required no small amount of preplanning. I needed every man because we had very little time to accomplish the tasks involved, and they were formidable.

One, we had to stop the vehicle, and it was built specifically to keep moving, with bulletproof glass, an armored engine, run-flat tires, and enough torque to climb out of a sinkhole. Two, once stopped, we had to penetrate the carriage. The bulletproof glass and door armor would protect the two driving, but our concern was the two men in the back. We had to get them to voluntarily open the doors, or it would take us blowtorches and over thirty minutes to hack our way in. Which brought up point three: We had little time to do all this and escape without compromise. We couldn't waste a second. We had to hit, get them to give up, then flee on our mopeds before the inevitable police response.

Mossad had provided the method of stopping the vehicle in the form of small limpet mines mated to a magnet—something they'd perfected in their elimination of Iran's nuclear scientists. They were designed to separate the tire from the wheel and render the run-flats useless. With Knuckles's information, and a short trip to a hardware store and a gas station, we had what we needed to penetrate the carriage. All we required now was to have early warning for the assault, and this was where we ran into trouble.

We simply didn't have enough manpower to spare someone at the diamond wholesaler for a trigger to alert both a tire team, then the assault force. Or so I'd thought. Then I'd learned what Shoshana's comment of "magic" to Jennifer meant. The Mossad had beat out Taskforce R&D yet again.

Apparently, there was such a thing as a "selfie drone," where the user wore a tracking device on a wrist and the drone followed just above, getting video. Biking, kayaking, snowboarding, you could get a Michael Bay–like view just by launching the drone in the air and then doing whatever activity you planned. Once launched, the drone would follow you like an obedient beagle.

The Mossad had taken that concept and refined it, and Aaron had emplaced it last night on their reconnaissance. Our target had a drone sitting on the roof, waiting to be alerted. Just a little over a hand's width in size and mated to a tracking device, it would hover out of view of the rear mirrors and give us a literal real-time show as it drove forward. Better than any stationary man guessing at approach. The problem was that it could be launched only once, which required eyes-on to see the vehicle actually show up.

At five after nine, Knuckles had called, saying the vehicle was in place, and begun walking back toward us on the path the truck would take, returning in time to help with the assault. Shoshana and Jennifer were on the narrow lane of Prepostska, standing by with what I called their little sticky bombs. For our part, Aaron and I were getting cold in the shadow of the church, two cylinders from the hardware store next to us, waiting on the endgame.

I felt the adrenaline kick in with Knuckles's call, but I knew we had some time. They still had to load the vehicle, and that would take at least ten minutes.

Aaron said, "I hope this thing works. Maybe we should have left Knuckles."

What the hell? I said, "We need him. One man on each side, one in the front to control the cab. We can't take down this truck with only two. It's why I agreed after hearing about the drone. What's got you spooked now?"

"The drone is activated by motion. I've sent it the instructions, so the next motion will cause it to launch, but sometimes the motion isn't jarring enough. The vehicle can leave and it doesn't realize it's moving."

"Jesus. Are you serious?"

He played with the tablet and said, "No. Just me venting. It'll work out." He smiled and said, "You know how it is. Always worrying at the last minute."

I did. I said, "Okay. If the truck shows up without warning, we just let it go. Fall back and reassess."

He said, "I don't think that'll happen. It'll pass Jennifer and Shoshana, and even if they can't emplace the tire disruptors, we'll know."

I said, "True, but we'll have no way of stopping it."

"Shoshana will figure that out. Trust me."

He was probably right, which brought up another question, because I was dying to know. I asked, "What happened after I left last night?"

He said, "What do you mean?" Like I was asking if he'd had trouble with his mattress.

"What do *you* mean, 'what do I mean'? What happened with Shoshana?"

He became flustered and said, "Nothing. I'm not sure what you're asking. We planned the mission." As if none of the awkwardness of last night had occurred. I said, "Okay, okay. Got it."

He said, "Got what? I'm telling the truth. We talked about contingencies, then went to bed."

"Together?"

He started to work the tablet and said, "Got motion. Bird's in the air." I thought that was possibly the worst time ever for a mission to start, but leaned over, seeing the feed.

The drone was right above the roof of the car, tracking it like a long shot from a heist movie. The vehicle turned onto Venturska, moving north. It was following our predicted path, and we were in play. I alerted the tire team.

Knuckles came into the courtyard, saying, "Girls are set. No pedestrian traffic. Good to go."

I said, "Let's hope your plan works out."

He said, "It will. Nobody wants to be burned alive protecting someone else's money."

I tossed him the detonator for the sticky bombs, saying, "Aaron, you got the call. You have control."

Staring at the screen, he said, "Got it. Car is making the turn onto Prepostska."

We both leaned into the screen, seeing the small lane almost bulbous with the fish-eye lens. The car advanced, and I watched Shoshana and Jennifer walk up the middle of the street, then break apart, going left and right, ostensibly giving the lumbering beast of a vehicle access on the narrow lane. The cab drew abreast, and both knelt down, slapping the magnets onto the slow-rolling wheels.

Point of no return.

The armored behemoth turned onto Kapitulska and was approximately thirty seconds away. I glanced around the courtyard, seeing the traffic on the four-lane thoroughfare and a couple walking down the sidewalk. They'd be out of view of the kill zone before the target entered. We were good.

I pulled out my balaclava and said, "Time to play robber."

Knuckles and Aaron did the same, cloaking their faces in black nylon. Knuckles withdrew a Browning Hi-Power from his back waistband and held it low by his legs. I reached for the cylinder to my right, a pesticide sprayer we'd purchased at a hardware store, now pumped full of unleaded gasoline. Aaron rose and set the tablet aside, saying, "Ten seconds."

He picked up his own pesticide sprayer.

I saw the vehicle nose into the courtyard, moving at about ten miles an hour. The driver saw our covered heads and hit the gas, but the weight of the armor prevented a rapid response. It huffed, a puff of smoke coming from the tailpipe, then lurched forward, racing for the exit.

Knuckles hit the detonator and two pops erupted, sounding no louder than the backfire of a car. I saw the front wheel on my side shred, and the entire front end sink into the pavement, the tires now useless and the car driving on the rims. Sparks flew, and Knuckles stepped to the front of the vehicle, brandishing his pistol. The vehicle ground to a stop. Knuckles pointed the weapon at the driver, and he raised his arms, then realized he was protected by glass that no pistol could penetrate. He locked the doors and began talking into a radio. Alerting the police and starting our clock.

Aaron and I raced out, him on the near side and me on the far. The vehicle was built with three weapons ports on each side, two low and one high, nothing more than little tubes that would allow a person on the inside to jam a rifle barrel through it and begin firing, like an old archer's slit in medieval castles. From Aaron's reconnaissance, we knew they had no assault weapons to use—only pistols—but the model they'd purchased had the weapons ports. Which meant we could introduce something to the inside.

I jammed the nozzle of my pesticide sprayer into the high port and pressed the lever, jetting the inside with pure gasoline. Aaron did the same on the far side. I heard the men cursing and screaming on the inside, but kept the lever depressed. When the air in the canister ran low, I pulled it out, pumped it up again, then repeated the spraying, getting more cursing. When my tank was expended, I ran around to Aaron's side.

"You done?"

"Yeah. Two loads."

I looked up the street, seeing Shoshana and Jennifer pulling security, blocking the road to prevent anyone from entering. I said, "Showtime. Let's hope they don't push us."

I walked around to the front, seeing Knuckles standing stoically with his pistol raised, the cars behind him on the four-lane road obliviously passing by. I went to the cab and tapped on the window. The driver jumped, then looked at me.

I said, "Tell the men in the back to open up."

40
★ ★ ★

The driver shook his head, his eyes wide with fear. I said, "Yes. Do it. Please. Ask them what they're smelling."

He spoke into a hand-mic, gesturing wildly in a manner the men in back couldn't see. He listened to them scream about something, then turned back to me, saying nothing. I held up an extended-reach lighter, like you'd use to start a charcoal grill.

I squeezed the trigger, letting the flame leap out. I said, "That door is going to be opened by the explosion of the gas vapor in the back. Unfortunately, your men will also be roasted. They can't stop it. All I have to do is stick this into a weapons port and press the trigger. The doors open. And your men die."

That was complete bullshit, of course, with the exception of his men roasting. If it were possible, his eyes grew wider.

I said, "Ten seconds. Starting now."

He yelled into the outside radio channel, trying hard to get help, but the universe was not on his side. I said, "Time's up," and turned away, praying.

He switched channels to the back and began yelling at them. I walked out of sight, Knuckles taking a position to the rear.

Nothing happened.

I jammed in the extended lighter, letting them see the promise of death.

The locks on the doors began popping, the men inside screaming at us to stop. The doors swung open.

I ran around to the back, seeing Knuckles putting two men on the ground, his weapon held at the ready. He ripped off a key ring and tossed it to me, and I jumped into the back. Aaron followed, and we went through the keys until we hit the one unlocking the chests.

Inside were gold items worth millions of dollars—rings, watches, necklaces, bracelets, coins, you name it—but no Torah.

Aaron jumped up from the second chest and said, "Where is the Torah?"

Kneeling down, digging through the first chest, I just shook my head. He screamed outside, "Where is the Torah?" The men on the ground looked at him, confused. He leapt down and slapped the closest in the face. "The Torah? Where is it?"

The man clearly had no idea.

I heard the first whiff of a siren on the air and said, "We need to go."

"No!" He turned to the man and repeated the question. He got the same response. I said, "We *need* to go."

Without waiting on the answer, I jumped out, calling Jennifer on the radio. "Koko, exfil. Dry hole."

She said, "Dry hole?" Shoshana started moving toward me. I said, "Carrie, get your ass out of here."

Jennifer grabbed her arm, and they went to the mopeds they'd stashed. I turned back to the car and said, "Aaron?"

He nodded. Knuckles was already on his mighty steed, looking ridiculous, waiting on me. To Aaron, I said, "Sorry, man. It's not here and these guys don't know anything about it. They're just hired transport. We need to regroup. Drop the note and let's go."

Aaron nodded again, still struggling with the fact that we were leaving empty-handed. He stalked over to the man on the ground and laid an envelope on his back, then leaned into his ear, whispering, "You are delivering the last vestiges of dead men. The man you work for is stealing the heritage of those murdered by Nazis. Something I would think you would understand in this city."

The contents of the envelope described exactly what was contained in the chest, preventing the armored car from delivering its goods once the police arrived—and hopefully causing absolute chaos in the follow-on investigation. I mean, really, who hits an armored car and then leaves the juicy proceeds behind?

We kicked the mopeds into gear, and threaded our way out, retracing the steps the armored car had taken, then splitting up into ones and twos, using exits that were blocked to cars, running out of the rat maze of streets. An hour later, we were back in the hotel, the rental mopeds turned in. I entered the lobby alone and called Jennifer, saying, "Who're we waiting on?"

"You. Everyone else is here."

"In the lounge?"

"Yep. Come on up."

"Okay. On the way." I started to hang up and heard "Pike? You still there?"

"Yeah, what's up?"

"Shoshana is acting weird. She was asking me all kinds of questions while we waited on the truck. I don't know what's going on with her."

"She talked to me. I'll tell you about it later."

"Okay. Just wanted to give you a warning."

"About what?"

"I think she slept with Aaron."

Great. Can't wait to see this shitshow in action.

I exited on the business lounge floor, told the lady at the desk my room number—Jennifer's number—then wound to the back, finding the team sitting on the same couches we'd used to plan the mission. Shoshana was curled up next to Aaron like a cat. Aaron was studiously ignoring her, typing on a laptop. Jennifer and Knuckles were across from them, on another couch. Jennifer smiled at me, flicked her eyes at Shoshana, then raised her eyebrows, as if to say, *What's going on with her?*

I looked at the seating. I had the choice of sitting next to Shoshana or squeezing in beside Jennifer. Wasn't much of a decision.

I sat down, pushing Jennifer aside, and she pinched my hip with a hand, her curiosity about Shoshana getting the better of her. For his part, Knuckles just handed me a Stella, saying, "Win some, lose some." He couldn't care less what was going on with the Israelis.

To Aaron I said, "So, what's the story?"

He looked up from the computer and Shoshana uncoiled, just like a cat stretching, then leaned back, putting her weight on Aaron. He glared at her, and shifted left, then said, "Mossad thinks Mikhail has the Torah. From what we've gleaned, we think it's his payment for the mission."

I said, "That's not the story I'm talking about."

He said, "What do you mean?"

Shoshana looked at me, eyes bright, and said, "Are you making fun of me? Like Knuckles does with Jennifer?"

And it became clear. She *wanted* the attention. She wanted the feeling of being normal, not realizing that Knuckles making fun of my relationship with Jennifer was about as far from the ordinary world as possible. People in normal careers didn't have an issue with a simple relationship between a man and a woman, but she had never seen it.

Then it hit home why she could even claim that status. Jennifer was right. I said, "Holy shit. You guys are . . . are . . ."

Shoshana waited on me to say it. I couldn't. Jennifer had her hand to her mouth.

Aaron said, "Can we talk about the damn mission?"

Shoshana said, "You sound just like Pike. I've heard that a hundred times whenever anyone brings up Jennifer." She was happy as a clam, pretending that she'd become some twisted, alternate-universe version of Jennifer and me.

He glared at her, and Knuckles said, "This is borderline schizophrenic. Shoshana, you have some mean skills, but you are without a doubt the craziest person I've ever operated with."

And the real Shoshana finally returned, the dark angel flaring out at his attempt to puncture her fantasy. She locked eyes with Knuckles, the fake relaxation gone as if it were nothing more than a veneer of paint, her face now reflecting a penchant for violence that was all too real.

She hissed, "You know nothing about me. But if you'd like to learn, I'm willing to teach you."

I held up my hands and said, "Whoa, whoa, come on."

She leaned back into Aaron and said, "Get ahold of your teammate. He needs to learn some manners."

I locked eyes with her and said, "Okay. Everyone take a break. No more talking about shit that has nothing to do with the mission."

Her eyes on mine, she nodded slightly, letting the moment pass. I said, "Aaron, what do you have?"

"Nothing more than I told you. Mossad thinks Mikhail has a buyer in Vienna for the Torah, but we don't know where he is or, more important, where the Torah is."

"So we're done here? Time to go home and call it?"

"Looks that way, for the Torah mission, at least. I'd really like to shove that thing up his ass."

I saw Shoshana squeeze his hand, and knew it had nothing to do with her newfound attempts at a relationship. She despised Mikhail with a visceral hatred of a level that I had only seen once before, when it was me doing the hating. It was molten and dangerous, and she deserved to lance that boil, much like I had done.

I said, "Well, you want to chase him, we're still available."

Aaron glanced at Shoshana, then at me. I said, "What?"

Shoshana said, "I want you to find the Torah. I want you and Jennifer to help me destroy that . . . thing that possesses it." She flicked her head at Knuckles and said, "Maybe even with the man-whore. But

I won't ask you to do it. The Torah must wait. But maybe Mikhail won't have to."

"Why?"

Aaron said, "I received the translation from Mossad. They charged nothing, and are screaming for why I asked for it."

"Because?"

"Because it's not good. Shoshana thinks you're right, and so does the Mossad. Someone's pushing the United States and Russia into a war, and Mikhail is at the center of it."

I said, "You're kidding me."

Shoshana said, "No, he's not. You felt it, and it's true. You have the gift."

Jesus. Not this again. "What, exactly, does it say?"

"Too much to talk about. I'll give it to you, but when I do, you've got to protect how you received it. When you read it, you'll see that war is about to erupt in Europe."

I said, "I can do that, but I have to send it forward. You know that."

"I do. And so does the Mossad. It's scared them. They can't do anything, but . . ."

"But what?"

"They've . . . insinuated that we should help."

I said nothing, and he rapidly continued, "It's your call, of course, but, if the mighty United States could use our skills, we're here."

"Why?"

"Because a world war in Europe is definitely against Israeli interests. Nothing more."

I looked at Shoshana, and she said, "Because we believe in you, dummy. You helped us, and we want to help you. Aaron went out of his way to get approval. Don't try to read into this."

I broke into a grin, liking the statement. Liking Shoshana turning back into Shoshana. I knew she was the one who had convinced

Aaron, and it made all the difference. She was the Pumpkin King, even if she wouldn't admit it. But I saw my chance to tweak her. Finally.

I said, "Really? Did all this become clear before or *after* you closed the door to Aaron's room?"

I wasn't sure what to expect, but what I got would have rated as the last thing on the list. The fake emotion vanished, the pretense of projecting a relationship disappearing like smoke.

She put her hand on Aaron's, projecting a sincerity as clean as new-fallen snow. She said, "No, Nephilim. You are my brother, nothing more. You are not my touchstone."

Jennifer nodded her head in approval and said, "Maybe we don't need to talk after all."

41

★ ★ ★

President Hannister said, "Okay, Kurt, you got us here early. We only have fifteen minutes before the rest of the national security folks arrive. What's up?"

Kurt said, "I'd rather wait until the secretary of defense gets here. So I don't have to repeat myself."

Kerry Bostwick, the director of the CIA, pointed at Alexander Palmer and said, "National security advisor, SECDEF, me, the president. If I didn't know any better, I'd say you're bringing back the principals of the Oversight Council. All that's missing is the secretary of state."

Kurt said, "He's dead, and that's exactly what I'm doing. I have some information, but it's Taskforce. I need to get it in front of folks read on before the rest get here."

Palmer said, "The Oversight Council is defunct right now. Terrorism has taken a backseat to the problems in Europe." He turned to the president and said, "Sir, we don't have time for political games here. Kurt's obviously trying to get his unit back in play."

Then the full measure of what Kurt had said sank in. Palmer said, "And what the hell do you mean you have 'Taskforce information'? They're supposed to be inactive as well."

Kurt said, "It's not purely Taskforce, but it has everything to do with what's going on in Europe."

Before anyone could ask another question, Secretary of Defense Mark Oglethorpe entered the Oval Office. He said, "What's the fire? I've got an assault into fortress Europe to deal with."

President Hannister said, "Kurt?"

Kurt laid a slim manila folder on the table and said, "This is a report from the Mossad, gleaned by Pike Logan. Bottom line: A Russian Jew named Simon Migunov is manipulating events to force a war between Russia and NATO."

The group of men were speechless. President Hannister found his voice first. "You mean an individual man is about to cause World War Three? Not Russia? How?"

"A little of both, actually. Mossad believes the Belarus attack *was* instigated by Putin, using Simon as a cutout. Their assessment is he wanted to take Belarus as a fait accompli, but then President Warren was killed. According to the intercepts Pike got, the same team was responsible for both, and they *believe* they're working for Putin, but they're not. At least, not anymore. And they have another attack planned, location unknown."

"Why?"

"Simon's the head of a huge organized crime syndicate—he's also on our top ten FBI list. He was in jail for over a year based on the whim of Putin. We think he's using Putin's own assets to get him overthrown or destroyed. Maybe it's self-preservation. Maybe a vendetta. Maybe he's just crazy. We don't know why, but it's real."

Kerry had the file in his hand and had read the first sheet. "This transcript doesn't say any of that. It's one guy bitching about killing the president and how he was told it was NATO aircraft, and the other guy saying he did good and Putin would be proud. The first guy is agitated, wanting out of the whole thing. The second convinces him to continue—and I quote—'for the motherland.' Everything here shows it to be at Putin's hands."

He set the page down and said, "Where is Mossad getting what you say?"

Kurt said, "Actually, it's Pike. Read the second transcript. That's a man named Mikhail—an ex–Mossad operative—talking to Simon. It's compelling, and it's straight from Pike Logan."

Kerry did so, then said, "Jesus." Alexander Palmer took the pages, scanned them, and said, "There's no smoking gun here."

President Hannister said, "Kerry? What did you see?"

Kerry took the pages back and said, "One paragraph. Mikhail to Simon: *I don't know about that. The firestorm you're stirring up may protect you from Putin, but it won't from the devastation of another world war. You should take a look at the pictures of Warsaw from the forties, then try to figure out where you'd spend your gold in that destruction.*" He looked up and said, "Mikhail is not happy with the path they're taking, and it's clearly not the path Putin wants. It's not Putin's doing."

Hannister said, "But why? Why on earth would they want a war?"

Kerry said, "Because of the next sentence from Simon: *Let me worry about that. The Americans will quit if there is a coup. I know them. They aren't the Nazis.* Simon wants a coup, and he's using us to get it."

Palmer said, "This is ridiculous. Let's take it to NATO and get everyone to stand down. We're about to go to war over nothing."

The SECDEF said, "We can't just 'take it to NATO.' They're going nuts right now. Yeah, we have a big chair at the table, but Putin is moving into Belarus as we speak. Poland is mobilizing because of it, and the NATO rapid reaction force is deploying—a brigade under the command of Spain. We can't tell them to stand down. The threat is *real*. And we're bound to support them."

President Hannister said, "Russia is going into Belarus? When did that happen?"

"Sir, it's starting now. The president of Belarus chose sides. He picked Putin. He's invited him in. My guess is he'll start stacking up against the border of Lithuania and Poland, protecting his ability to get to the Kaliningrad Oblast and the Black Sea, and isolate the Baltic states. He's preparing for a fight."

"Jesus Christ."

Nobody said anything for a moment. Kurt took the silence as an opening. "Sir, if you read the transcript, it shows they have another attack planned. Whoever those guys are, they're following someone else's lead and are going to do what they're told. Right now, we're on a tripwire, and if that attack occurs, we're going to lose the ability to stop the forward momentum. We're going to war."

Hannister said, "Putin is already moving."

"He's moving because he's posturing. He doesn't want a war any more than we do. Only Simon wants the war. Putin's just getting ready for the punch, like a guy holding an arm over his face. We can't give anyone a reason to throw that punch."

Palmer said, "Sir, we need to call off the show of strength. This is getting out of control. We don't want a force in there if someone else lights the fuse. They'll be surrounded and massacred."

Hannister said, "Where do we stand with that?"

Oglethorpe said, "Sir, we can stop the assault, but we already have men on the ground. We conducted a HALO operation both at the airfield and the crash site. Pathfinder teams are on the ground right now, and their exfil platform is the follow-on force."

Hannister looked stricken. He said, "You only briefed me about this six hours ago. It's already in motion?"

"Sir, it was in motion once you gave me the word to execute."

Kurt exhaled and said, "So we're committed?"

Palmer said, "Wait, what's the plan? I thought you guys were going to drive in. This wasn't supposed to happen for another day, with our ability to pull out at any time. A simple show of force."

42

★★★

Mark Oglethorpe said, "No. I was given the mission to secure the crash site, and my team decided the easiest way was to project force directly to the area. Driving and waiting to get shot at was not the optimum solution."

"What does that mean?"

Oglethorpe turned to Palmer and said, "It means I briefed the president of the United States. Sorry if you were getting a latte."

Palmer turned to Hannister and said, "Sir . . . I can't help you if you don't include me."

Oglethorpe said, "He included you in the conversation on Marine One. When the decision was made."

Hannister said, "The Joint Chiefs had little time. Mark asked for a special session. He needed to get things moving, and they briefed me, because I had to get the state department to notify the Russians. I had no idea it would happen this quickly."

Palmer said, "You mean he briefed you on a plan that was *already* in motion. Getting permission after the fact." He turned to the secretary of defense and said, "Did you really use his lack of experience to get what you wanted? No way could you get someone on the ground that quickly *after* you got permission."

Oglethorpe leaned into Palmer and said, "I *had* my orders, and *you* agreed to them. I was just getting final approval for the plan. And yes, it was already in motion."

"So what's Russia going to do when NATO invades the Ukraine? Did you think of that?"

Oglethorpe said, "It's not about NATO. It's all about the crash site. Humanitarian show of force, remember? No ally fingerprints are on it at all. It's purely American, as the commander in chief ordered. NATO is aware, but not involved at all. And the Russians are being alerted that we're coming."

Kurt saw the fracture occurring in the command team of the United States. Hannister was unused to the power he wielded, and it was showing. Kurt knew he had to short-circuit the schism before it devolved into personality clashes. "Sir, you gave the command. We need to see it through. Who *was*," he looked at Palmer, "and who *wasn't* read on to the plan is irrelevant now. Let's deal with the facts."

Churlishly, Palmer said, "Okay, what *are* the facts?"

Oglethorpe said, "After analysis, securing the launch site for the missiles was deemed irrelevant. The launcher is gone, as are the bodies. That left the crash site. Trying to get armor there would telegraph our intentions and only allow the enemy to prepare, if they so desired. We decided a vertical envelopment was the way to go."

Palmer said, "What the hell does that mean?"

Kurt smiled, nodding at the secretary of defense. "Airborne operation. That's pretty ballsy."

Palmer said, "You're parachuting in? Why?"

"We can't sustain a force that far from friendly lines. We needed a lodgement. We found an airfield near Severodonetsk. It's been in and out of Ukrainian hands, but was close enough to the crash site to allow us to use it as a lily pad for further operations."

"So you're going to seize the airfield? And then what?"

"Simultaneously, we're going to seize the crash site. Two battalions of the 82nd Airborne are preparing to jump right now, but they only have light arms. Our orders were to make a statement, but not get anyone killed. So that requires firepower, which will be coming from the airfield twenty kilometers away instead of two thousand. The

Ranger's first battalion will seize the airfield, the 1st Stryker Brigade, 4th Infantry Division will flow in and reinforce the 82nd, and the heavy armor from the Marine's Black Sea Rotational Force will arrive overland in twenty-four hours in case anyone wants to test us."

Hannister addressed the secretary of defense, "Given this new information, should we hold off?"

Oglethorpe said, "Sir, as I said, I have pathfinder teams on the ground right now. They dropped out of an aircraft from thirty thousand feet. The only way back to us is with their feet. They can do it, but you're risking them being compromised on the move, and paraded on television. They'll be just as big of a catalyst as anything else."

Palmer said, "So you've committed us to a course of action we can't extract from? What were you thinking?"

Kurt had heard enough. "He's executing United States policy with the least projected casualties, as ordered by the commander in chief. I wasn't there, but I believe you were."

Palmer said nothing. Kurt continued, "Sir, what's happening at the crash site is fine, but we're putting our guys in a fire sack if something else triggers a fight. It was a good decision at the time, when we were dealing with just Russia, but now we're not."

Hannister looked slightly lost. "Okay, okay. I have to convene a national security meeting in five minutes. What do I say? What's the recommendation?"

Palmer said, "Call it off. Before we are further committed."

Oglethorpe bristled, but Kurt beat him to the punch. "We're *already* committed. Do you think the team on the ground's life is less valuable than the ones flowing in? Jesus. Listen to yourself."

He turned to the president and said, "You can't shut down the operation now, nor should you. That decision was correct. We need to show American resolve. This thing is in motion, and we need to manage it. Running now, based on what we know, will do nothing—because Putin doesn't have the same information. He'll see weakness, and so will our allies, especially after you've informed him we were coming."

Palmer said, "We're about to put thousands of soldiers in the heart of Russian defenses. We go to war because someone else triggers, and they're all dead. You want that?"

"No, of course not. We just need to mitigate the risk."

Hannister, grasping at any hope he could, said, "How? What can I possibly do? We have nothing but a *report* of an attack."

Kurt said, "We have more than that. We have Pike Logan."

Palmer's eyes popped open, and he raised a hand, about to go on a tirade. Kurt cut him off. "I asked for you men for a reason. The Oversight Council is defunct, but you were all members. Pike found the thread of the attack, and Pike can stop it. Let the Taskforce loose. Let me execute what it was designed for."

Hannister said nothing, looking at his circle of advisors, waiting on an opinion.

Kerry said, "Given the options, it certainly couldn't hurt. We go to war, I doubt anyone's going to give a shit about that lunatic running around."

Oglethorpe smiled and winked at Kurt. He said, "That lunatic usually ends up fixing things. My assault force is in the air. My vote is, let him loose."

Hannister said, "What do you need?"

"I need the Taskforce reinstated. I need command authority to execute an Omega operation. I *need* the ability to help you."

President Hannister said, "You have it."

Kurt smiled and said, "Thank you, sir. Gotta go. I have some work to do."

Kurt turned to leave, but Oglethorpe caught his arm. "I wasn't kidding about the force in the air. They'll hit the ground in less than two hours. And Palmer's right. They can handle anything thrown at them from the rebel side, but if Russia sees them as a threat . . . if something triggers a fight . . . they're all dead."

Kurt let a wolf smile slip out and said, "I understand. I wasn't kidding about Pike, either. You do what you do best. Leave the rest to him."

43
★★★

The MC-130 Combat Talon's nap-of-the-earth flight was making Private First Class Joe Meglan airsick, but he would literally rather kill himself than admit it to anyone. The flight wasn't that long, and he was sure he could hold his stomach in check until they landed.

The interior was blacked out, the only illumination coming from pinprick LEDs, giving just enough light for him to barely make out the men to his left and right. He rolled his head around, taking deep breaths, and saw movement across the hull of the aircraft, where he knew the battalion command team was seated.

Something was up.

The word traveled left and right from their position, flowing out like ripples in a pond. He wondered what rock had been thrown to stir up the ripples. The loadmaster crouched next to the last man on their side, then came over to his side, shouting in his squad leader's ear. The squad leader nodded, and leaned into Joe.

"Runway's fouled. We're jumping. Five hundred feet."

The words didn't make sense at first, because that wasn't the plan. Jumping was just a contingency that he'd been told had little chance of happening, even as he was rigging up into his parachute. The airport was supposed to be in Ukrainian hands. Friendly hands. If the runway was fouled, didn't that mean . . .

The squad leader smacked his MICH helmet and said, "Pass it down, dumbass. We don't have a lot of time."

He did so, his earlier airsickness completely forgotten as his sphincter tightened into a knot. A second thought entered his head: He was on the runway clearing team. If the runway was fouled, he was going to work, and he had no idea what that meant.

While an airfield seizure sounded pretty much like any other assault, it wasn't. Like a hostage rescue mission, it was an orchestra of violence with specific objectives that had to be accomplished in a minimum amount of time. The RCT—his platoon—was a unique element that trained and practiced to ensure that the runway was serviceable within thirty minutes of the first parachute splitting the sky.

While others jumped out with the job of clearing objectives or securing key points, his task was arguably the most critical. All the other efforts meant nothing if the planes couldn't land. If he failed, they'll have just attacked and held a worthless piece of terrain. Any infantry unit could do that. Successfully seizing an airfield entailed the airfield functioning when you were done.

Everyone in his squad and platoon had practiced the RCT procedures over and over, the command throwing every conceivable contingency at them. Bulldozers, railroad ties, Chevy station wagons, random debris, you name it. The team could hotwire just about anything in existence, and if they couldn't, they knew how to disable the clutch to push obstacles out of the way by brute force. Joe Meglan knew none of this. He'd finished Ranger Assessment and Selection only three weeks prior, just in time for a deployment to Afghanistan. That was what his platoon had focused on, and now he was about to jump into the black night, over Europe, and execute a maneuver he'd never rehearsed.

He was jerked out of his thoughts by the right-side troop door opening, the wind blasting into the hold, the night sky huge and close. His platoon sergeant began conducting safety checks of the frame, acting as the primary jumpmaster, and it hit home. *We're going to jump.*

The time passed swiftly, and before he knew it, the six-minute call was made, then the command to get ready, the familiar orders for the airborne operation bringing a sense of normalcy and calm. *This* was something he knew about. The command for outboard personnel was given, and he staggered upright under the load of his parachute and over a hundred pounds of gear slung between his legs.

The other commands followed, a monotony of calls until the final one, each like a comforting shout-out from a friend, Meglan following along with every other shooter on the plane. A familiar blanket reminding him he was just one bit on the cog of the finest light infantry force on God's green earth.

Hook up! . . . Check static lines! . . . Check equipment! . . . Sound off for equipment check!

The man to his rear slapped his thigh, screaming, *Okay!* And he did the same to his squad leader. The squad leader relayed to the jumpmaster, and they waited on the one-minute warning. His squad leader turned back, knowing Meglan was adrift. He shouted, "Just find the rally point, then listen to whoever's there. Monkey see, monkey do. It's easy. We'll handle the hard stuff."

Meglan nodded, relieved, then shouted, "Will this count as a combat jump?"

His squad leader laughed and turned around without answering, disappointing Meglan. In his mind, if he was jumping into the unknown, he deserved credit for it, and—while no Ranger would ever admit it—every one of them coveted the small mustard stain on their jump wings signifying a combat jump. This operation was a little half and half, though. No declaration of hostilities, and no firm knowledge if anything below was actually hostile.

The one-minute warning came and went, then the jumpmaster gave the final, electrifying command: *Stand in the door!*

And the snake of jumpers shuffled forward, Meglan second in the stick, mashed together like cattle in a car, his squad leader facing the open maw of the night. Meglan kept his eyes glued to the red light above the door, willing it to go green. This was the worst for him. The waiting. The adrenaline coursing through his body making him feel like he was going to explode. *Come on, come on, come ON.* And it did. He saw the light turn green, then heard "GO!", and his squad leader disappeared into the night.

He slapped his static line at the jumpmaster and forcefully exited, feeling the wind tear into him, counting out loud, "One thousand, two thousand, three thousand, four thousuuuuh—"

His groin was snatched upward, his canopy blossoming over his head, the silence now deafening.

He barely had time to check his airspace for other jumpers before he saw the ground rushing up. He dropped his ruck on its lowering line a second before it hit, then slammed into the ground, performing a pathetic landing fall.

He rapidly shucked his chute and put his M4 into operation, lowering his night observation goggles and scanning for the hordes of enemy he expected to find. He saw nothing but parachutes landing all around and Air Force combat controllers zipping left and right on minibikes that had been parachuted in, each with a predetermined mission that belied the chaos.

He derigged his ruck, threw it on his back, and began jogging to the rally point, located at the juncture where the taxiway met the actual runway.

He arrived to find his squad leader had beaten him there, and was relieved he wouldn't be working with a team he didn't even know. Four other members of the squad approached at the same time, and the squad leader said, "C Co and the command group have linked up with Ukrainian military in the terminal. They're coordinating for help in clearing the tarmac, but we're not waiting. Let's go. Straight down the runway. We're eating into our thirty."

From there, it became almost boring. As he had no specific skills to apply, he pulled security while the others hot-wired the vehicles sabotaging the runway, watching them drive away before leapfrogging to the next obstacle. Occasionally, he was ordered to help push a baggage cart out of the landing path, but it was feeling routine. Like an exercise.

And then he heard the sound of guns in the distance. Three hundred meters away, on the northern corner, someone was shooting. He heard the thump of a 203 grenade, saw tracers arcing into the sky. Then the AC-130 Spectre gunship lit up the night.

Appearing exactly like a hose spraying fire on the ground, the 20mm Gatling cannon began its destruction. Cycling six thousand rounds a minute, the one in six tracers looked like a continuous stream, the rounds coming out so fast that the human eye couldn't separate them. The pummeling began, and a giant fuel-air explosion at the receiving end whited out Meglan's NODs.

The entire squad froze what they were doing, looking in the distance.

Jesus Christ. What the fuck was that?

44
★★★

Meglan waited for his headset to explode, but no reporting came through. Whoever was fighting wasn't a part of his element, and they weren't on his net. The squad leader listened for a moment, having the privileged rank to hear both the internal and command nets. He said, "Roger all. Still clearing," then said to his team, "Come on. The longer we fuck around, the longer it'll take to get some firepower in here."

They raced down the runway toward the last airport tractor, a baggage cart hooked behind it and straddling the tarmac. Meglan's team leader said, "What's happening?"

"Somebody tried to penetrate the perimeter with a technical. B Co smoked them."

They reached the tractor and the squad leader said, "Meglan, a vehicle may have flanked them, avoiding a fight. There's too much motion around here for the AC to pinpoint friendly from enemy. Keep your eyes out. But for fuck's sake, discriminate. Last thing we need is for you to smoke a bunch of Ukrainian military coming out to help."

Meglan nodded, thinking, *How will I tell the difference?* He took a knee and faced down the tarmac, toward the north. The chaos still swirled, parachutes falling from the sky, everything painted an eerie green in his NODs. He caught movement, dimly, a hundred meters away. It was a truck, racing down the tarmac toward them. He shouted, "Contact. Vehicle inbound."

One of his teammates looked up and said, "It's the Ukrainians. Hold your fire."

"Why are their headlights off?"

His squad leader, furiously working to hotwire the tractor, failed to hear the discussion. He cursed at the man above him, "Get the damn light on here."

Meglan watched the truck approach, coming close enough to see camouflage uniforms in the cab. He kept his weapon on them, but waved his off-hand, trying to get them to see him with the lack of night vision. Trying to show he was a friendly.

He shouted, "It's still approaching."

Working on the stranded vehicle, nobody heard him. The tractor finally fired up, and the squad leader rose from under the footwell just as the pickup truck came within thirty feet. Meglan saw two people rise from the bed, bringing rifles to bear over the cab, aimed at his team.

Later, he would say it seemed to happen in slow motion, and that he was sure he wouldn't be quick enough. But he was.

He rose, his entire world coalescing on the green dot in his sight. He saw the men in the cab screaming, the muzzles beginning to flash, then felt the rounds popping by his head. He ignored it all, focusing on the little green dot, the center of his world. He began firing controlled pairs, just as he'd been drilled in RASP.

One—two, shift, one—two, shift to the driver, one—two, shift to the passenger, one—two. . . . he scanned for another target, and found none.

The vehicle rolled past them, one man hanging over the side, his finger still in the trigger guard, the AK-47 dragging along the ground.

Meglan tracked the truck with his rifle as it went past, looking for another threat and letting out his pent-up breath.

The quiet returned, and the squad leader started reporting the contact, telling the command team to get a friend-or-foe signal on the Ukrainians. They searched the truck, moving it off the tarmac, confirming it wasn't the Ukrainian military—and confirming Meglan's skills.

They returned to the tractor, the squad leader putting it into gear, saying, "Good shooting." Nothing more, but it meant the world to Meglan.

Meglan nodded, and the tractor rolled past him, off the runway, the squad leader shouting as it rolled by, "Looks like you got your combat jump."

They returned to the rally point, and the word had already spread. Meglan had killed four men with four controlled pairs, never missing, even as the men were shooting at him from a moving platform.

It should have been something to revel in, but the airborne assault was continuing, and he had a job to do, with his squad leader shouting at him to get off his ass and pick up security. He did so, and the platoon leader called runway clear.

The first of the Ranger follow-on force landed, a C-17 full of motocross bikes and RSOVs—a *Mad Max*–looking vehicle based on the Land Rover and bristling with guns. They drove off, reinforcing the perimeter, and the assault continued, with wave after wave landing.

They'd made their thirty minutes.

An hour later, the first C-17 with the Strykers from the 4th ID arrived, the eight-wheeled armored vehicles rolling off the ramp and into the night. The chaos subsided, and the airfield took on the characteristics of a peaceful one, with aircraft after aircraft landing and disgorging its cargo. The first Stryker company rallied up their armored vehicles and headed off into the night to link up with the 82nd Airborne. Meglan had no idea how that jump had gone, but assumed it was on track, as nobody appeared to be flustered.

He sat in the dark, covering his sector, thinking about the men he'd killed. Happy that he'd done so, but thinking nonetheless. Killing a man will do that.

He watched the armor rolling off one aircraft after another, and felt no further fear. If all they had were pickups with AKs, the enemy didn't stand a chance.

He gave not a thought to the divisions of tanks and artillery a mere forty-five kilometers away, across the Russian border.

But they were thinking about him.

45
★ ★ ★

Mikhail entered the spacious home to find Simon in the living room, two of his five bodyguards/manservants bringing luggage from the upstairs bedroom.

"You're leaving?"

"Of course. I'd be an idiot to remain."

"My man won't talk. He's already on the run. I have him in a safe house where the police won't find him."

"You sure of that? He'll give up his entire business for you? Or will he turn you in, playing the unsuspecting friend who was just helping out?"

"He won't turn me in, and even if he does, it won't lead to you."

"Did he know what was in the crate? Did you tell him?"

"No. Of course not. He thought he was helping with an official Mossad matter. He doesn't know I no longer work for them. He'll keep quiet for the State of Israel."

"But now he's learned it was gold from victims of the Holocaust. Something the State of Israel would never hide. What's his history? Do you even know?"

Mikhail hesitated, the thought having never occurred to him.

Simon continued, "What if he lost family during that time? What if he was personally affected? Is he sitting in that safe house wondering if his grandmother's wedding ring was in that crate? How long will he choose you over that?"

Mikhail nodded, saying, "Good point. I'll take care of it."

Simon said, "Money won't work for this. He might be a Jewish diamond merchant, but this will transcend anything money can buy."

"I said I'd take care of it. I won't be using money."

Simon nodded and said, "Don't leave any evidence on the body."

Mikhail said, "Unlike him, you forget where I used to work."

Simon smiled and said, "Any way to get other valuables from his building? At least get something out of this disaster?"

"No. I'm not going anywhere near that place ever again."

"So you are the only one who makes money out of this."

"Don't go there. The Torah was agreed upon before any of this happened. It's simply my fee."

"Yes. I paid you for a service, and that service didn't occur."

"Don't blame me for the loss. What else did you want? The Israeli team hit an armored car! If they were willing to do that, they would have been willing to do anything. I still can't believe they didn't take the crate themselves."

"It matters little that they left it alone. My gold is still lost."

"True, but don't forget, I'm the one headed to Poland to meet up with your uranium source. I'm the one setting those Night Wolves nutjobs loose."

"Yes, that is certainly worth something. How much can you get for the Torah?"

"I'm not sure. I have a buyer in Vienna, but we're still negotiating. Maybe fifty thousand euros. Maybe more."

Simon walked to the front door, saying, "A lot of money I'm paying for getting so little in return."

His security held open the door, and they walked into the front portico, the security men loading his luggage into a black Mercedes.

Mikhail said, "You're getting your damn war. You're getting Putin overthrown. I'd say the Torah's a damn bargain for all that."

Simon said, "I believe I deserve a little refund. A small insurance payout, if you will."

Mikhail said, "I suppose that's not a request, is it?"

Simon shook his head.

"What if I refuse to meet your contact instead?"

"Then I'd politely ask for the Torah right now. But you don't want to do that, do you?" The implied threat hung in the air, neither man voicing it.

Mikhail sighed and held up his hands. "Okay, okay. Look, the Torah is in Vienna. I don't have it here. I couldn't hand it over even if I wanted. We can haggle over the refund later. I'll call you when I get there and retrieve it."

"Conveniently, Vienna is exactly where I'm headed."

"I told you, I'd handle the diamond merchant. You don't have to leave now."

"Oh, yes, I do. Have you seen what the United States is doing? I need a buffer country between me and the fault line."

"I saw, but they're just recovering their dead."

"Right now, yes. But they won't be in a few days, will they?"

"No, I suppose not."

"When you go, I want you to take some security with you." He pointed at two of his men, saying, "Pavel and Adam will travel with you."

"Why?"

"Let's just say I don't trust my contact as much as I should. He wants the money, but he's also connected to the Russian machine."

"Great. Anything goes wrong with that meeting and it'll lower your refund."

Simon laughed and said, "I understand, but I don't doubt your skills. When do you leave?"

"Tonight. Taking a late train. I have to see a diamond merchant first."

Simon said, "Be sure and tell him I said hello."

46
★ ★ ★

Sitting in the same spot I'd been in a day before, I saw the front door open and keyed my mic. "Get ready. They're coming out." Jennifer came over the radio. "Drone's airborne. Be there in four seconds."

I watched my screen, trying to see if I could find the UAV in the air above the entrance. I could not. Off the radio, I said, "Those things are pretty good."

Shoshana said, "Yes, better than the junk from your agency."

I laughed and said, "Yeah, yeah, I have to admit, you guys have been on top of that lately."

For early warning, we'd parked a car with a simple lipstick camera hidden in the dash down the road from the front entrance of Simon's place, then had staged Jennifer and Aaron at their same location from earlier, ready to launch the drone. The lipreading software wasn't that critical this time, because all we were doing was building a target package, but it couldn't hurt to use it. I hoped to hit the place either late tonight or tomorrow. We had the floor plan of the target thanks to the Mossad, but we needed to see the security. A floor plan couldn't kill us.

Shoshana said, "I shouldn't be driving on the mission. You need me inside."

Staring at the lipstick camera feed, I said, "Someone's got to drive the vehicle. I have a team coming in. People I've worked with for a long time. Aaron is doing nothing but pulling security as well. Don't get all insulted here."

"Your team hasn't studied the floor plan. Your *team* hasn't even set foot on the continent yet."

"They'll be here soon enough. This target isn't designated a hostile force. I can't afford someone killing in there just because they want to."

"So you don't trust me."

I said, "*Aaron* doesn't trust you. Let it go."

"I told you I wouldn't kill again. I can disable anyone in that place without killing. I'm who you need."

"Yeah, yeah. I love the new Shoshana, right up until the old one shows up. You find Mikhail inside, and he's dead. I'm not stupid."

She got a funny look on her face and said, "I wouldn't kill him."

I said, "What did he do to you?"

She said, "Nothing. I don't want to talk about it."

"Come on. I'm your brother, remember? Nobody else is here. What happened?"

I saw sadness on her face, a deep, deep cut. She said, "He was the master. I was the slave. He nearly destroyed me."

What the hell does that mean?

She reminded me of a child soldier getting reintegrated back into society after the horrific acts he'd been forced to do. She needed a psychiatrist, not my analysis. I said, "Okay, well, I only want the Pumpkin King when I ask. Not when your emotion gets the better of you."

She smiled and said, "I told you, I'm not the Pumpkin King. I'll never be that."

Man, she can get under my skin. I said, "Yes, you will. If I ask for the Pumpkin King, I expect to get it. Do you understand what I'm saying? I can't have this peacenik shit here."

She looked as if she were depressed at my words. Sad for me. I exploded, "Look, I don't know what the hell is going on with you, but if I need your skills, I'm going to ask, and you'd better produce. Otherwise, you two straphangers can get on the first plane back to Israel. Is that understood?"

She said nothing.

I said, "Is that understood?"

She said, "Yes, Nephilim. If you need me, I will be there."

I exhaled and said, "What *is* going on with you?"

She said, "Nothing. Or maybe everything."

God almighty.

In retrospect, I should have cut her right then and there. But fate interrupted, as it always did.

Jennifer came through our radios, saying, "We have a problem. Simon's leaving the building with suitcases. They're talking on the front porch. I'll give you the feed as soon as it's done, but my bet is an assault will not happen tonight."

Shit.

I'd sent the original transcript from our surveillance to Kurt a day ago, not expecting much, and I'll be damned if my boss hadn't opened up the world to me. I knew what the message said, but had little hope—with the way politics worked in America—that it would have made a blip on the radar given the situation in Ukraine right now. I should have realized that even our dysfunctional government could discern the connections every once in a while.

The United States had launched a bold airborne operation to recover the dead from Air Force One, and in so doing, had put thousands of men within striking range of the great Russian bear.

NATO was going haywire, with rapid-reaction forces deploying to Poland, and because of it, Belarus had invited in Russian forces, who were currently streaming to the border near Kaliningrad. The Baltic states were trembling in their boots, scared to death that nobody in NATO was strong enough to prevent a takeover, should Russia so choose.

It had become a dangerous world that only needed one little spark.

Simon and Mikhail were hell-bent on providing it, for reasons still unknown, and I'd been given unusual leeway to disrupt whatever they were plotting. The remnants of the Oversight Council had agreed to give me blanket Omega authority—something that had never before happened. Ordinarily I had to specifically detail what I intended to do before I got approval to execute. This time, the only caveat was no DOA authority, which simply meant I couldn't just kill both of them with a sniper rifle.

I'd asked for three things: one, the rest of my team; two, the Rock Star bird with a complete package; and three, the initiation of Task-force reachback assets, such as our computer network operations cell and intelligence fusion center.

Kurt had readily agreed, but told me only two of my men were available. Apparently, the third, Brett Thorpe—a CIA paramilitary officer—had already been deployed to Europe with the CIA. They'd wasted no time with the Taskforce stand-down and had sucked him right up. The other two—Retro and Veep—were flying over on a specially configured Gulfstream G650, just like the Rock Stars flew.

While the aircraft looked normal enough, packed inside it were a myriad of different intelligence, surveillance, and reconnaissance ca-pabilities, along with a complete small-arms arsenal hidden in its walls. The Mossad kit had been pretty good, but I was looking for-ward to flinging our capabilities in Shoshana's face, especially since, beyond the one Browning pistol Knuckles had used at the armored car, Shoshana and Aaron had no lethal tools, and the weapons in the Rock Star bird would solve that problem.

Finally, Kurt was spinning up the reachback assets, recalling the hackers and intel geeks who'd been shelved along with everyone else in the Taskforce, but I had nothing for them at the moment.

My plan had been to capture both men in the target house, either tonight or tomorrow, but it looked like that operation had just hit a snag. Nothing was ever easy.

I keyed the radio, saying, "You got them on tape? Are they talking?"

"Roger. They're chatting on the front portico. I'll shoot you what I have as soon as I can."

I watched our feed from the camera hidden in the parked car, seeing the discussion playing out. About a minute later, the two shook hands. Simon moved to the black Mercedes that held the luggage, followed by two security men. Mikhail waited until Simon was seated before going to the Volkswagen he'd arrived in, only now he also had two security men. The final bodyguard walked back to the house.

I said, "Okay, Koko, Aaron, pick up on Simon. Carrie and I will be right behind you. Knuckles, you provide backup with the camera car when it's clear to approach it. Let Mikhail go."

I didn't want to force our luck with Mikhail after our surveillance the previous day. We were more than likely good, but Simon was the ringleader. If we bagged him, we could definitely cause some damage to whatever they'd planned.

Jennifer came back, "Pike, I've got the transcript. He's headed to Vienna. You want to track him all the way there? I don't know if he's driving, flying, or what, but we aren't going to locate a bed-down here."

Well, crap. Conducting surveillance on him all the way to a different country was a nonstarter. No way could we accomplish that with the small team we had. We'd be compromised for sure.

"What's Mikhail doing?"

"Apparently talking to a diamond merchant, probably the one who held the crate, then taking a train late tonight. Appears he's going to Vienna as well."

I asked Shoshana, "How many train stations here in Bratislava?"

"Only one."

So we can interdict him later.

I got back on the radio. "Okay, let them go. Here's the plan: Knuckles and I will stake out the train station, then pick up Mikhail tonight. Koko, Carrie, and Aaron will conduct a B and E on the house. Break in and search it for anything related to either the attack or those two knuckleheads. For now, head back to the hotel once they're both clear, and we'll do some detailed planning."

47

★★★

M ikhail exited the cab, moving slowly to the rear for his luggage, giving him time to survey the entrance to the Bratislava train station. He saw nothing out of the ordinary, the harsh fluorescent light providing plenty of illumination in the night. People coming and going, dragging luggage or buying snacks and coffee at an outdoor kiosk. Nobody paying him any mind. He opened the trunk and handed out carry-on rollers to his new security, telling them to go purchase tickets to Warsaw. He watched them drag the roll-aboards inside, paid the cab, then followed.

The train station was surprisingly compact, given that it was the only way to catch a train out of the capital of Slovakia. One entrance lobby with a big digital board dictating the next departures, and a single stairwell leading down to the platforms, with hallways left and right to a small snack shop or offices for the various train lines.

He looked at the board, saw the time for his train—and his decoy—then met the two security men at the ticket counter. "Get first class?"

"No. All they had left were two sleepers in coach."

Mikhail held up the first-class ticket he'd purchased earlier, shook his head, and said, "Too bad. Get ready to sleep with your suitcase. Let's go to the platform."

Pavel said, "The train doesn't leave for an hour. Let's go get chow."

Mikhail said, "No. There's a reason I want to wait on the platform. I want people to see us."

Pavel looked confused, but picked up his suitcase. They went down the stairs, walking under the platforms until they reached the fifth one. Mikhail started going up and Pavel said, "Wrong one, boss. Warsaw is platform six."

"I know. This one is going to Austria in thirty minutes. We'll hang out here until it leaves, then pop over to the Warsaw train."

"Why?"

"Just a precaution. Something that's allowed me to live as long as I have."

Mikhail saw Pavel grimace at his partner, and didn't fault him. He had no knowledge of tradecraft, no skill at evading anyone. His whole worldview was predicated by a closed fist—something he was well versed in, and something Mikhail would leverage if he had to.

He stopped at a bench, placed his roll-aboard against it, and sat down, waiting, as he had plenty of times in the past. Most tradecraft involved nothing more than waiting. He thought about the upcoming meeting, tossing around how he would employ his two security men.

According to Simon, both of them had served in the Russian FSB, the inheritors of the defunct KGB, but neither showed any skill at tradecraft. Although they'd shown plenty of skill at pure violence.

Earlier, when Mikhail needed to confirm that the diamond merchant had not told the authorities anything, the two security men had proven up to the task, surgically taking apart the poor man piece by piece and showing no qualms about it at all. They were efficient and unemotional. The best combination. But they held little concern for what could happen to them if someone were planning against them, convinced their strength in the moment would prevent any catastrophe. Mikhail knew better.

The team that had hit the armored car was still out there. Still tracking. And he understood their skills, having once been a member of an organization that did the exact same thing.

The death of the diamond merchant bothered him not at all. It had been grisly, but necessary. Just like the deaths he'd caused in the name of a state. Necessary. If he had to take such actions in the future, he would.

But it would be better to slip the net with tradecraft rather than violence.

Knuckles said, "So you think she's an issue?"

"I don't know," I answered. "This guy Mikhail is bringing out bad things, and she's dealing with it, but she's most definitely not on her A game."

"What, like PTSD?"

I hesitated, picking my words carefully. PTSD had a clinical definition that was pretty broad, but meant something specific to men who'd seen combat. "Yeah, I think so, but it's more along the lines of a battered wife or something like that. It's combat related, but not because of what she's seen or done. It's what was done to her, against her will."

Knuckles nodded and said, "Your call. I trust your judgment. You think she can hack this, I'm with you. Might be the best thing for her. Get her over the hump."

"I appreciate it. I just wanted to make you aware. I think she's good for specific tasks, but she can't be involved in any takedown of Mikhail."

"You know that transcript also talked about the Torah. You think they're really in this to help us?"

Before I could respond, we saw a cab pull up and we sagged in our seats like a couple of kids hiding from the cops. The passenger door opened, and I said, "That's him."

Knuckles relayed via cell to the hotel, putting it on speaker and saying, "Target acquired."

Aaron came back. "Good to go. We have a couple of hours before we penetrate. Let us know where he's headed and we'll meet you there."

I said, "Don't get compromised in there. Find what you can, and get out."

Jennifer came on. "Pike, we got it. You already approved the plan."

Which was true, but it didn't mean I wasn't worried. I glanced out the window, seeing the three men disappear inside. I said, "Okay, we're on the move. Call you in a second."

We exited and walked up to the entrance like we were catching a train. I'd worried about following Simon to a different country using automobiles, but in this case we knew Mikhail was using the rail system. Boarding the same one wouldn't look odd. We could track him for the duration as simple passengers, and when he got off, so would we.

Once inside, I paused, glancing at the big board as if I was looking for a train, but really giving Knuckles a chance to clear the area with his eyes. He said, "We're good. They're gone. What's leaving next?"

"Train to Vienna. That's where Simon went. Makes sense."

"Come on. Let's check."

We took a right from the board and went into the little snack shop, finding a table near the window. I went to the counter to get a couple of Cokes, letting Knuckles find a seat. By the time I'd returned, he'd located our targets.

He stood and said, "Track five. The train to Vienna. We should get our tickets. It leaves in a few minutes."

It took less than two minutes to book seats, the ticket counter deserted. We went underground, walked down the tunnel, then exited on platform five. Going up the stairs I said, "If they're still standing, just board. Don't pay them any attention."

Just as we reached the top, he said, "Do I look like an amateur?"

We entered the train, studiously ignoring the party of three. I moved to the back, taking a seat where I could see them on the platform. We waited, and the time ticked down. One minute before we were to leave, they stood up, but didn't board.

What the hell?

Our train lurched forward, the schedule for departure met, and I saw them go back down the stairs, dragging their luggage with them. They popped out next to a train on platform six, and I leapt up, slapping my hands to the window, knowing immediately what Mikhail had done. As we pulled away, gathering speed, I strained to see the station on the digital display next to the train they were boarding.

Warszawa Centralna, leaving at eleven P.M., thirty minutes from now.

48

★★★

We slowly pulled away, and I knew I'd just fallen for the easiest trick in the book, making me feel like a fool. Nothing I could do about it now. Leaping out onto the tracks would only highlight our stupidity. Might as well hold up a neon sign reading OKAY, YOU GOT US as we jumped.

Typical Knuckles, he watched the platforms recede in the distance and said, "Aren't we supposed to be on that train?"

I said, "Did you see the station?"

"Yeah, Warzawa Central, or something like that."

"Call the Taskforce. Get the intel shop working. Figure out where that is, and figure out how long it'll take to get there."

I called Aaron, really not wanting to admit what had happened. He answered on the second ring. I said, "Mikhail pulled a duck on us. We're on a train to Vienna, but he's boarding one that leaves in about twenty-five minutes to a place called Warszawa Centralna."

"That's the main train station in Warsaw, Poland. I don't have enough time to get to the station before he rolls."

Knuckles said, "They're saying Warsaw."

I put my hand over the mouthpiece and said, "Reroute the Rock Star bird. Get them moving to Warsaw instead of here." I returned to the phone. "Okay, change of plans. No more B and E. Meet us at the first place this train stops. I don't know where that is, but you can figure it out. Bring everyone with you. We'll haul ass on the roads and meet Mikhail at the far end."

"What if he doesn't get off on the far end?"

"What do you mean? That's the train he's on."

"He used tradecraft on you just to board. What makes you think he won't with his destination?"

Shit. He was right.

He said, "Hang on."

Five seconds later he said, "I found the train on the net. The first stop is in Kuty, about forty-five minutes away. I can get there before it arrives."

"And do what?"

"Insert Jennifer and Shoshana. Then I can run back to you, pick you up, and leapfrog again. We can then just track the train by vehicle, using them as early warning if he leaves it."

I liked the plan with the exception of one thing. I said, "No Shoshana."

He said, "Pike, I wouldn't advise a singleton on this. Two heads are better than one, and Shoshana is smart. Inserting Jennifer alone is placing her in danger."

"Putting Shoshana on that train is *asking* for danger. You go with Jennifer."

"Yes, that would be best, but we're on a very tight timeline. I know the highways. I know where your train is stopping and how to get there right now. I know where Kuty is and what roads to take. When I was on Samson, I worked this area enough that it's like the back of my hand. Before I got Shoshana, she spent most of her time in the occupied territories and the Middle East. Over there, I rely on her for navigation. Here, she relies on me. If Shoshana drives, she's going to be using a GPS, which may not get her there in time."

"Mikhail knows her on sight."

"Look, that's a problem either way. Quite possibly he knows Jennifer as well, but he's in a sleeper car, I promise. He only travels first class. I was going to place them in the back, in the cattle section. All they need to do is keep eyes on who exits the train at the various stops. Most everyone will be taking the train *to* Warsaw, so the extra stops will be people boarding, not exiting. If he leaves, we'll know it just by watching the platform. Meanwhile, you and I will be shadowing the train. When he exits, we pick up the follow."

"So my choices are to put her on the train for a long-look or use her in a vehicle for a short tether? Is that what you're saying?"

"Yes, except you three will be screaming at a GPS to give you directions."

"What if she goes nuts?"

"She won't. She won't get close enough to do that."

I said, "Is she standing there?"

"Yes."

"Put her on."

The phone fumbled and I heard "Yes, Nephilim?"

"You ready for this?"

"Of course."

"Okay. Listen closely: no Pumpkin King unless I ask. You understand? No running into the funnel of fire if you see Mikhail."

She laughed, putting me at ease. She said, "I'll have Koko with me. Don't worry, she won't let me go berserk."

"Then you guys get moving. You've got a train to catch."

49

★★★

The small train station—more what I'd call a train stop—was deserted at this time of night, so when I saw headlights flash, I stood up. Sure enough, I saw Aaron behind the wheel of a minivan. We'd only been on the train for twenty minutes before we got off, just on the other side of the Danube, now in Austria.

I said, "That's what we're going to speed up and down the roads in?"

He smiled and said, "Train's only doing about a hundred kilometers an hour, and it's stopping a lot. We can do at least one-fifty in this, and it'll blend in better on the open road. It looks like a service van. Besides, I'm carrying everyone's luggage."

I took the passenger seat and Knuckles piled into the back. Aaron wheeled out, riding on surface streets, jigging left, then right, until he hit a four-lane freeway running parallel to the tracks.

I said, "That's it? You're going to run a freeway right next to the tracks? You really think we couldn't figure that out?"

He laughed and said, "It'll separate after Kuty. We'll have to take a different freeway to reach Otrokovice in the Czech Republic. That's the train's next major stop."

Knuckles said, "How'd the insertion go?"

"Fine, as far as I can tell. I didn't wait around. The train is spending twenty minutes there. Jennifer called after she boarded, saying they had seats that provided visibility outside the train, and the car was pretty much empty. Lights are off to let people sleep. They're okay. She said she'd call when they left."

I nodded and said, "How long to get there?"

"At speed, about thirty minutes to Kuty, then another hour to Otrokovice. Hour and forty-five minutes, max."

He had the train schedule up on his tablet, and after looking at it, I said, "That's going to be close."

"Yeah, I know, but the train's making two stops in between Kuty and there. I had to take a risk that he wouldn't get off at them because they're practically nothing more than a concrete slab. Nothing at either stop, and both are still in Slovakia. He's at least crossing the border, or why else take a train?"

I tended to agree with him, but it was still going to be close.

My phone rang, Jennifer on the other end. "Pike, we just left the station. No issues so far. He didn't get off here. I'll call at each stop one way or the other."

I said, "Sounds good. How's Carrie doing?"

"Fine. She's bugging me with questions, as usual."

"Don't give out any secrets."

She laughed and said, "I won't," then hung up.

We drove in silence for forty minutes, past Kuty, then past another small station. I said, "Was that the one the train was supposed to stop at?"

Aaron said, "Too dark to tell. Must not have been. They didn't call."

I dialed Jennifer's number. It rang for an eternity, then someone answered. I heard nothing but breathing. I said, "Jennifer?" and the phone went dead.

I dialed Shoshana's number, with it going to voice mail.

Aaron saw my face, and understood that something terrible had happened. I tamped down the human urge to start freaking out, saying to Knuckles, "Keep trying Jennifer."

He heard my voice, unnaturally calm, and realized we had a situation. To Aaron, I asked, "Did they take in earbuds?"

"Yeah, but we don't have the range to use them."

"Catch the train before we have to split off the tracks. Get me near that fucker."

Mikhail cracked the window shade of his sleeping car, seeing the train slide into Kuty. He shut it again, then heard a knock on his door. He opened it, seeing Pavel outside. Speaking Russian, Pavel said, "Hey, boss, we never got any dinner. I sent Adam into the station for a sandwich. You want anything?"

"What do they have?"

Pavel dialed his phone, spoke for a moment, then said, "A bunch of different sandwiches and rolls. He's sending a picture. You can pick what you want from that."

The phone dinged, showing a slanted photo of the display case, wraps, subs, and other sandwiches within. Mikhail zoomed in to pick a meal, then froze.

Pavel said, "What's wrong?"

Mikhail manipulated the screen, dragging it left and zooming in even farther. He held the phone up to Pavel and said, "What do you see?"

Pavel stared, confused, valiantly trying to see what the fuss was about. He said, "You want the salami?"

Mikhail snarled, "You see the woman in the background? The one at the ticket counter?"

"Yes . . . So?"

"She's a fucking Israeli assassin. She's here to kill you. I don't know how they found us, but the Israeli team is here."

Pavel looked at Mikhail as if he were losing it. "Hey . . . she's just buying a ticket. Are you sure?"

Mikhail grabbed his ear and twisted, forcing his face into the phone. "You fucking neophyte, she is a *killer*. I know because I worked with her. I *know* because I trained her."

He let go and said, "Adam stays. Watch what they do. If he has to miss us leaving, he does so. He stays. If they board, we deal with it."

Pavel rubbed his ear, shocked at the ferocity. He said, "Okay, okay."

50

★★★

Jennifer took a seat in the back of the last car, Shoshana sitting next to the window and Jennifer on the aisle. They sorted themselves out, then sat in silence, until it grew too long.

Shoshana said, "Pike doesn't believe in me."

Jennifer said, "Yes, he does. He just needs you to execute what he wants."

"Is that how you work with him? You do what he says?"

Jennifer considered, then said, "Yes and no. Pike is . . . a little different. He wants you to follow his orders, until he wants you to forget them. I've learned to just do what I think is right. He'll always follow that, without fail."

Shoshana took that in, then said, "So you can do whatever you want? In your relationship?"

Jennifer turned to her and said, "Shoshana, the relationship has nothing to do with the mission. Can't you see that?"

Shoshana said, "There is nothing but the mission. How do you separate it?"

Jennifer shook her head and said, "I think you need to really look at what you want. When you say 'the mission,' that's not a relationship. You deserve more than that. The job is not your life."

Jennifer saw her brain working, actually considering the words like they were something new. She said, "How can it not be? That's what we do."

The train started to move, and Jennifer said, "Time for an update." She pulled out her phone, glad to get away from the conversation, dialing Pike. When she was done, she looked back at Shoshana, saying, "They're on the move. Easy day. All we have to do is make sure Mikhail doesn't leave."

Shoshana said, "If it came down to it, would you kill for Pike?"

Jennifer had no idea where the question was going. She said, "No. I wouldn't kill *for* Pike. But I'd kill. And I have. There's a difference, and Pike is usually right. And so is Aaron. Why do you keep bringing this up?"

Shoshana glanced out the window and said, "I kill because I'm told to. I was never asked if it was right or wrong. I'm good at it. Better than most."

Jennifer said, "But you don't have to. It's your choice."

Shoshana slid her eyes away and said, "It's easy to say that. Much harder to live it."

Jennifer had no answer for that, wondering how on earth anyone could even believe that killing simply because someone ordered it was a normal thing, as Shoshana seemed to. Like it was the natural circle of life.

Shoshana said, "I'm through killing."

Jennifer started to answer when the door to their car opened and a beefy man walked in. He looked vaguely familiar. Jennifer tightened up, pretending to work a sudoku puzzle, allowing the man to pass without acknowledging him.

Another man came through the door, and she thought she recognized him as well. She lowered her eyes, and Shoshana said, "Those are the two from the video."

Jennifer said, "Let them go. Let them walk past us."

Shoshana tensed her body and said, "They aren't here coincidentally. There's no one else in this car, and nothing behind us."

"No. Don't. Let them go. They don't know who we are. They've never seen us."

The first man walked down the aisle, ignoring them both. He

reached their row, and Jennifer saw she'd made a mistake with her command. He pulled out a small pistol and jammed it into Jennifer's chest. He said, "You two are invited to first class. There's a man who wants to meet you."

Jennifer stiffened, waiting on Shoshana to explode. The second man leaned over the row in front of them, small pistol in hand, and said, "Mikhail said to tell you hello. He's looking forward to talking."

Everything Shoshana had said about killing faded away. For the first time since she'd known her, Jennifer saw fear on Shoshana's face.

Mikhail waited in his cabin, going back and forth about how he would handle the confrontation. He knew he needed to understand exactly what the Mossad had learned about him and, most important, how they'd found him, but part of him wanted to spend time with Shoshana.

She was the prize. He had broken her once, and she'd somehow rebounded, destroying his career. She had always been a flower he could never have. Someone who had defied him. He now had a second chance.

He'd felt the familiar warmth in his groin the moment he'd seen her digital image. Part trepidation and part lust. He despised her, a hatred borne of fear of what she was capable of. But he could destroy that fear, if he had her. And now he did.

He heard a knock, and opened the door. The first thing he saw was Shoshana, obediently walking in front of his security. He studied her face, waiting on the satisfaction of the moment when she recognized him. He got it.

She saw him and began to tremble.

51
★★★

The man pushed the barrel against Jennifer's back, forcing her into the sleeping cabin behind Shoshana. She was shoved into a chair. Shoshana remained standing in front of the man they knew as Mikhail. Jennifer swiftly analyzed the small cabin, looking for the way out. Looking for the seam she could exploit, confident that with Shoshana, she could persevere. The men with guns had no idea of the violence she and Shoshana could perpetrate, choosing to treat them like weak women, which was a mistake.

The first security man threw a bag on the table, containing the contents of what they'd found on Jennifer and Shoshana. Mikhail reached inside and poked around, eventually pulling out Jennifer's cell phone.

Jennifer glanced at Shoshana, trying to communicate with her eyes, and was shocked at what she saw. Shoshana was a shell of herself.

Guided to the bed, she sat down without resistance.

Mikhail set the phone on the counter, pointed at Jennifer, and said, "Secure her." The train began to slow and the men glanced at him. He said, "It's the three-minute stop. Don't worry about it."

He approached Shoshana and she recoiled. He leaned into her face and licked her cheek like a cat, saying, "Oh, how I've missed you."

The two men pulled out wire coat hangers from the closet, and in short order had wired Jennifer's legs together, then bound her hands at the wrist. By the time they were done, the train was moving again.

Jennifer gave one feeble attempt at innocence, saying, "Why are you doing this?"

Mikhail glanced at her, then spoke in Yiddish. Jennifer looked confused, and Mikhail smacked Shoshana on the side of the head, hammering her on the ear and slamming her skull into the wall. Punishing her for Jennifer's perceived insolence. Jennifer alone saw her earbud fly out. Shoshana rolled upright, still frozen in fear, taking the blow as if it were what was expected in life.

Mikhail asked Jennifer another question in Yiddish. She once again looked confused, and it broke through. In English, Mikhail said, "You're not Mossad. Interesting. Very interesting. We'll get to the bottom of that, I assure you. I don't know you like I do Shoshana, but I will. Biblically, if you want." He smiled at his joke and said, "That can be fun, or it can be painful. It all depends on you."

A phone started buzzing, and Jennifer realized it was hers, lying next to the bag on the counter. Mikhail went to it and picked it up. He let it ring a couple more times, deciding, then answered, saying nothing. He listened for a second, then hung up. A minute later, the other phone in the bag began ringing. He ignored it.

Jennifer gave up feigning innocence, trying intimidation instead. She said, "We have a team tracking us. Harming us would not be wise."

He laughed and said, "Tracking you on a moving train? Yes, I'm sure they are, but all they have is a cell phone. What I need to know is how you found me. And how much you know about my plans. I will learn that soon."

He turned to Shoshana and leaned into her. She recoiled, and he held her head in his hands. Unlike Jennifer, her own arms and legs were free, but she showed no willingness to use them. He kissed her lips and said, "I've missed you so much. Remember the fun we had between missions?"

She nodded hesitantly. He slid his hands up from her cheeks and gripped her hair hard, pulling until a gasp escaped her lips. He said, "This will be nothing like that."

He released her and said something in Russian to the men. He left with one, leaving the other in the room holding a small Walther PPK pistol, the man glowering at Jennifer from under thick eyebrows.

Jennifer fervently stared at Shoshana, trying to get her attention and failing. Shoshana was mentally shattered. Mikhail had left her unbound, and yet she did nothing but rock back and forth, her eyes unfocused.

Jennifer looked at the man on the chair, wondering how she could get to him. The thought was ridiculous, with her hands and ankles wrapped in wire. Shoshana was the only chance.

She said, "Shoshana, you all right?"

Shoshana glanced at her in an offhand, glazed way. She repeated, "Shoshana?"

The man in the chair leaned forward, putting a finger to his lips. Jennifer realized he didn't speak English.

How that would help, she was unsure. She knew they had only minutes before the other two men returned. Which meant one shot to get Shoshana back.

She shouted, "Shoshana!"

Shoshana jerked at her name, and the man in the chair leaned forward, lightly smacking Jennifer in the face, saying, "*Nyet*."

The roughness of the man brought home her lack of choices, the fear now closing in like the debilitating cloak that Shoshana wore.

Way out. Gotta be a way out. Always a way out. Think.

Her earbud crackled, and she thought it was from the slap. Then she heard her mentor.

The way out.

"Carrie, Koko, Carrie, Koko, this is Pike. You copy?"

She was electrified at the words, but couldn't respond.

It came through again. "Carrie, Koko, Carrie, Koko, this is Pike. Come back."

She did, glancing at the guard. She mumbled, as if she were just talking to herself. "Pike, Koko. We're in deep shit. Need help. Now."

The man looked at her, and she realized her first assessment had been correct. He didn't understand English. She kept her head bowed, mumbling. He let her go.

Pike came back, speaking as calmly as if he was ordering a pizza, which meant he understood how bad things had become.

"Need info. What's going on?"

"We've been captured. I'm bound. Mikhail is coming back any second. He's going to torture us for information."

She heard nothing, then, "Tell him everything. Don't hold back. Give it all to him. Fuck the mission. Where's Shoshana?"

"She's here. Mikhail hit her in the head. Her earbud is gone."

"Tell her the same thing. Buy time. Tell them whatever they want to know."

"Pike, I don't think that'll be enough."

"Can you escape? Did they put regular handcuffs on you? Something you can pick?"

"No. I'm wrapped up in clothes hangers."

"Shoshana?"

"She's free."

"What? Say again?"

The guard leaned into Jennifer and tapped her on the head with the barrel of his weapon, saying again, "*Nyet.*"

She moaned, then muttered something as if she were as subdued as Shoshana. He leaned back, satisfied.

She said into the radio, "Pike, she's lost it. She's done. She took one look at Mikhail and shut down. She's no help."

She heard "What are you saying? Are you talking about Shoshana?"

"Pike, it's like Cougar in *Top Gun*. She's catatonic. I need you here. She's no fucking help. Get your ass here."

She heard the worst words she could imagine. "I can't get there. I'm tracking the train right now, but there's no way for me to board."

She was like an astronaut in a space capsule, hurtling out of control to Earth, death on the horizon, knowing there was nothing mission control could do to prevent it. She felt the tears in her eyes and hated them.

She said, "Pike, he's going to kill us."

She heard nothing, knowing Pike was tearing himself apart at his inability to do anything. Then he came back, with a different tone. "Jennifer, we're about to have to turn off. The road is going to leave the tracks and we're going to lose radio comms. Tell Shoshana something from me. Tell her loudly. Shout it."

"What?"

"Tell her Nephilim wants to see the Pumpkin King. Tell her she *is* the Pumpkin King. Tell her she holds her own destiny."

"What the hell are you saying?"

"Just *do* it. Tell her . . ."

The radio broke contact, and the door opened. She had no idea what Pike meant by his words, and was now on the verge of becoming catatonic herself. Mikhail entered alone, saying, "I think we've figured out how to handle this. Once we're through with our interrogation."

He moved to Shoshana and said, "But before we start with the rough stuff, let's do what we used to enjoy."

He turned so his belt was in front of her and said, "Remember?"

Resigned, Shoshana began working the buckle. To Jennifer it was surreal. Like she was watching a show outside of her body. Seeing the strongest woman she'd ever known succumb over nothing more than a given command.

52

★ ★ ★

Shoshana continued obediently, and Jennifer realized she wasn't going to fight. The thought brought a blast of panic. She jerked her wire bonds sharply, trying to break them open, screaming for help. When that failed, she leapt out of her chair, falling on the ground and writhing toward the door. The Russian guarding her slapped her in the face, then pulled her upright, sitting her back in the chair. He leaned forward, and she regained her view, seeing Shoshana looking at her with pity.

Jennifer bored into her eyes and said, "Nephilim talked to me. On the radio."

She got a response. A flicker. Jennifer continued, "He told me to tell you he wants the Pumpkin King. He wants it right *now*."

The Russian slapped Jennifer in the face, hard enough to knock her out of the chair. Shoshana continued working the buckle.

On the ground, Jennifer felt the blood in her mouth, spit it out, and said, "Shoshana, Nephilim said you *are* the Pumpkin King."

There was no discernable difference in the room. None that the men could see, but the world they were in shifted on its axis. Jennifer recognized it, mystified as to why, but knowing she'd finally reached her. A twisted smile spread across Shoshana's face, and the dark angel appeared, Shoshana changing in front of her eyes. A cloak of death enveloped her, and she set about doing what few on earth could.

With her right hand inside Mikhail's pants, she viciously squeezed. Mikhail screamed and flailed at her arms. She released her grip and went at him, all elbows and sharp edges in the confining space, battering his head over and over. Mikhail fell backward and the Russian security man rose, bringing his weapon to bear. Shoshana slapped the pistol aside and hammered him in the temple. He ignored the blow, wrapping her up in his arms and bringing her to the ground.

Mikhail stumbled out of the room hunched over, his pants around his thighs, slamming the door behind him. The Russian rolled on top of Shoshana, trying to get his weapon into play. Her entire body contained within his embrace, she whipped her head forward, hammering him between his eyes with the hard mallet of her forehead, then tore into his nose with her teeth, savagely ripping.

The Russian wailed and pounded her with the butt of his pistol. Jennifer flopped over the both of them, grabbing the pistol between her bound hands. She fell backward, using her weight, and the pistol came free. She rolled over, trying for a shot without killing Shoshana.

She shouted, "Shoshana! Fall off!"

The Russian realized what was about to occur, and bear-hugged Shoshana, crushing her spine with his enormous strength. Shoshana grunted loudly, reached up with her thumbs, and plunged them into the man's eyes. He screamed and released her, bringing his hands up to his destroyed orbs. She curled her fingers at the first joint and speared his throat, crushing his larynx.

He collapsed on the floor, writhing in pain. His lungs screamed for air, but his larynx swelled with the shattering blow, cutting off his oxygen. He began wheezing, until he could no longer even do that. In seconds, he was dead.

Breathing heavily, Shoshana looked up at Jennifer, a savage smile on her face, a trickle of blood running out of the corner of her mouth. She said, "I *am* the Pumpkin King."

Seeing the man's destroyed face, his nose hanging by gristle, both eyes leaking fluid, Jennifer said, "I have no idea what that means. I'm just glad I didn't ask for something greater than fruit royalty. Lock the door."

Shoshana did, right before someone rattled it to get in.

Jennifer said, "We need to get the hell out of here."

Both of them jumped as someone on the other side began shooting into the lock. Jennifer fired three rounds through the door, ceasing the attempt at entry.

Jennifer said, "Help me with these."

Shoshana went to work on the makeshift binds, saying, "He'll be back. Should we hunt him, or run?"

Jennifer broke the wiring to her hands and said, "Run."

Shoshana separated the ankle bonds and said, "We should kill him. Right now."

Jennifer saw the dark angel still there. The hatred. She said, "There's one more Russian out there with a gun. I say we take this as a win."

Shoshana looked up at her, and the dark angel receded. "Okay, Koko. You saved my life tonight. And I will save yours."

She turned to the window, and bullets began slamming through the door. Jennifer leapt on the bed, getting out of the line of fire. Shoshana did the same, rolling underneath the bunk. Jennifer fired three more rounds through the door, and the weapon locked open, the magazine empty. The shooting stopped from the other side.

Shoshana rolled out and grabbed the window's emergency exit lever, flipping it up and flinging the glass into the night. The air rushed in, the noise of the train exploding inside the small enclosure.

Shoshana said, "You first."

Jennifer said, "Search that body. Get anything you can," then exited out into the night.

She clambered up the side of the train, using the window ledge, bolts, and seams to get to the top, the wind whipping at her, trying hard to peel her away. She pulled herself to the roof and looked below, waiting on Shoshana, the clanking noise of the wheels pounding in her ears. Shoshana appeared, clambering out the window. She was halfway to the roof when the second Russian's head popped out. He looked up, then brought his arm through, a pistol in his hand.

Jennifer shouted, and Shoshana kicked, knocking the weapon into the darkness. Shoshana climbed as fast as she could, and the man followed. Shoshana made it to the top and the man grabbed her leg. Jennifer jerked Shoshana's arms in an insane game of tug-of-war, breaking her free. They rolled on the roof of the train, the wind threatening to whip them off, the car rocking back and forth.

The man made it to the top and stood up, yelling something in Russian. Shoshana and Jennifer scrambled away. He followed, trying to run, but was reduced to a shuffle by the motion of the train.

Shoshana stood up and the man waved her forward, like a prize-fighter taunting an opponent. Shoshana let loose a banshee wail and dove right at him. She hit him in the middle of the gut, knocking him backward. His eyes flew wide in shock, his arms flailing for contact to prevent the inevitable. They both hit the top of the train within inches of the edge.

He slipped over the side, holding on with one hand. Shoshana remained on top. She pounded his hand, then peeled the fingers back, and he fell screaming under the wheels.

The train kept barreling along, the wind still whistling over them. Shoshana eventually rolled over, sliding to the middle of the car. Jennifer bear-crawled to her, wrapping her in her arms.

Jennifer looked into her eyes and said, "You okay?"

Shoshana hugged her back and said, "Never better. Never."

Jennifer laughed and said, "What about Mikhail?"

Shoshana said, "He's no threat. I saw his soul. Saw him for what he is. He's afraid." Shoshana let slip a smile of pure venom. "Afraid of *me*. And because of it, he's a dead man."

The train rocked forward for a few moments, then Jennifer said, "Now what?"

Shoshana held out a cell phone she'd pulled from the man she'd killed in the cabin. She said, "Now? Now it's time for Nephilim to earn his pay. The Pumpkin King can only do so much."

53
★★★

Mikhail waited in the passageway, hearing the overloud clanking of wheels coming from the open window in the cabin but no other noise. He felt the train slowing into the second three-minute stop. He nudged the door open with his pistol, seeing a foot on the floor. He swung the bullet-riddled door wide.

The first thing he saw was the destroyed face of Pavel, the blood congealing underneath his hair. He swept the tiny cabin with his pistol and found it empty. He went to the window and looked out, wondering if the two females had simply jumped for their lives.

But if they did that, where is Adam?

He dialed Adam's number, but the phone simply rang out, going to voice mail. Mikhail looked at Pavel, and realized Adam was dead as well. *Shoshana.* He wondered if it had been as violent.

He had made a major mistake with her. He'd lost his professionalism, letting his personal feelings dictate the mission. He'd assumed he still had control over her—and he *had*. Then something had changed. He caught his reflection in the mirror, seeing the bruises forming from her attack. From her absolute savagery. She had almost ripped his dick off, and then had mutilated a former member of the Russian security services.

His choice to toy with her had been clearly ill-advised, but she'd been subservient when he'd seen her. The Shoshana of his past. The one who had obsequiously let herself be used, over and over again. The one who had recognized him as the master. The role reversal was shocking, not the least because he was now the one in fear.

He had sent Adam into the room alone, saying he would provide cover for any train officials who attempted to interfere, but that had been a lie. He had been afraid to go in. Afraid of Shoshana's capabilities. She had looked at him with a hatred that bordered on the supernatural, and he had felt her penetrating his soul. And then she had set about destroying everyone he'd brought with him.

It induced a deep-rooted terror he had never experienced in all his years working in the blackness of his profession, and he despised it. He had killed many men who thought they were better than him, but they had all been human.

Shoshana was not.

He felt the train stop and realized the first thing he needed to do was get the hell off. Get lost into the landscape, before whatever hit team was tracking him managed to reacquire him. Not to mention get the hell away from the bloodbath before the lax authorities on the train discovered it. The noise of the wheels had overshadowed the gunfight, but it was only a matter of time before a conductor came through.

Which brought up another problem: He'd have to resort to using his real passport for travel. The one that had purchased this ticket was definitely burned, and he was out of alias documents.

At the very least, he'd managed to break up their surveillance of him. The action had been an unmitigated disaster, but he was fairly sure they had no idea where he was going. If they had, they'd have simply waited at the far end instead of boarding early.

No, they knew he was on the train, but that was about it. If he disappeared now, he could regain the initiative.

Initiative for what, though? Continuing the mission, or fleeing the continent?

He flicked off the lights in the cabin, then peeked out the gaping hole where the window used to be. The train was stopped at a concrete open-air platform with a long roof spanning the length, the cars themselves only inches away from both. His cabin was in the front, off the platform. Below him was dimly lit track. To his right, the locomotive.

Did the engineers in front have rearview mirrors? If he left now, would they see him? He decided to wait. It was only a three-minute stop.

He saw the conductor wandering the platform, then glance above him, rotating around trying to see between the sliver of air between the roof of the train and the roof of the station. He stared for a second, then shook his head, waving to the engine and boarding the train. The wheels began to move.

The train picked up speed rapidly. Mikhail waited until the car had rolled about four meters before leaping out the window. He hit the slope on his feet, rolled, then scampered quickly into the shadows as the cars went past.

He waited until all the cars were gone before moving again, ensuring he wasn't spotted by an insomniac rider gazing out the window.

With the end of the train receding in the distance, he stayed low, only exposing himself to get over a chain-link fence. He circled around the small train station, reaching a car lot with a sprinkling of vehicles parked randomly. He saw a flash of headlights enter the lot and slammed up behind a Dumpster, waiting on them to disappear.

He thought again about his problem, wondering if he should just flee, run back to Israel. But that would be a problem in and of itself. Shoshana was Israeli. She knew who he was, and she was still Mossad—he was sure of it. And the American on the team worried him. If the United States had paired up with Israel to track him, it would prove a formidable combination. But why would the Americans care about a gold shipment from the Holocaust? Was there something about that chest that Simon had kept from him?

The Israeli connection he could manage, but the American interest was a serious concern, and it dictated his decision.

He peeked around the trash container and saw a minivan waiting on a passenger. Soon enough, the headlights washed over the ground as it left. In the darkness, he made his choice.

America was interested in him because they had that luxury. They had the ability to dedicate assets to chasing him. It was time for them to become interested in something else. Something that would consume their ability to chase thieves from a small-time gold heist.

Something like Putin and World War III.

54

★★★

Inside the Oval Office, President Hannister had started to become comfortable behind the old Resolute desk. Kurt saw that he was coming to terms with the fact that others could provide advice, but *he* was the man in charge. The one who ultimately made decisions. Kurt was pleased, because he'd seen "decision by committee" in the past, and it was never pretty.

Holding a CIA cable, Hannister said, "So is this independent confirmation of what Simon is up to?"

Kerry Bostwick said, "No, sir. It's not independent. It's from the same source as before, but it *is* additional information confirming the original reporting."

Working with Kerry, the director of the CIA and an Oversight Council member, Kurt had "laundered" Pike's report through CIA channels to allow it to be presented to members of the national security team who had no knowledge of Taskforce activities. As a result, President Hannister had become confused, believing it was a second report from a different source.

Hannister finally connected the dots and said, "When did this come in?"

"About six hours ago."

General Durham said, "Can I see it?"

Hannister handed him the cable, a redacted transcript of a recording between two men.

Subject One: *You're getting your damn war. You're getting Putin overthrown. I'd say that's a damn bargain*

> *for all that. I told you, I'd handle the diamond*
> *merchant. You don't have to leave now.*

Subject Two: *Oh, yes, I do. Have you seen what the United*
States is doing? I need a buffer country between
me and the fault line.

Subject One: *I saw, but they're just recovering their dead.*

Subject Two: *Right now, yes. But they won't be in a few days,*
will they?

Subject One: *No, I suppose not.*

Subject Two: *When you go, I want you to take some security*
with you. Pavel and Adam will travel with you.

Subject One: *Why?*

Subject Two: *Let's just say I don't trust my contact as much*
as I should. He wants the money, but he's also
connected to the Russian machine.

General Durham said, "What's this mean?"

Kerry said, "We have a source who believes the tensions in Europe are being deliberately stoked, and that these men are trying to start a war. The source believes that President Warren's plane was brought down by someone outside the Russian government specifically to create a war between NATO and Russia. The subject, for reasons unknown, wants Putin gone, and believes a war will do it, but he's growing impatient, and there are significant indicators that another attack is on the way. One that will guarantee a NATO response against Russia."

"Who's this 'source'? A Russian?"

"I'm not going to discuss sources and methods."

"Well, no offense, but the CIA wasn't exactly Johnny-on-the-spot for the whole Crimean takeover. Putin played you then, and he's playing you now."

"General, the source isn't Russian, and his reporting comes with high confidence."

"When and where is this supposed attack going to occur?"

"We don't know. We're working on it."

Aaron was blasting down a back road, driving dangerously fast for the conditions, headed toward the next stop the train was going to make. His decision to drive had proven correct, as he continually ignored the GPS, using his own knowledge of the roads. We didn't have a lot of time to beat the train to the stop, and if I'd have been forced to rely on the GPS, we never would have made it.

Then again, if it had been Shoshana in the vehicle and Aaron on the train, we might not need to be speeding at all. But that was all hindsight, and doing me no good now.

Initially just following as backup for surveillance in case Mikhail left early, Jennifer's call had changed everything. I was boarding at the next available stop, and I was ready to kill.

I refused to think about what I might find, concentrating on the mechanics of clearing the train. Focusing on what we, as a three-man team, could accomplish with a single firearm, which, given the skills of the men in the van, was still significant. In the end, it didn't matter what we found. I'd already designated Mikhail and his men as a DOA force for this mission, and whatever damage was onboard wouldn't alter that.

I was going to kill him. Along with anyone who tried to stop us.

I looked at our constantly recalculating GPS and saw we were about three kilometers out, four minutes ahead of the train. With only a three-minute stop, we were cutting it close, but I thought we'd make it.

I kept flipping my knife open and closed, and Knuckles said, "Never cleared a linear target with only a blade before."

I said, "We'll have weapons soon enough. After the first contact."

He saw the bloodlust in my eyes and grimly nodded.

Aaron said, "About one minute out," and then, strangely, my cell phone began vibrating. I looked at the screen and saw an international number. *Mikhail.* Clearly, Jennifer had given my number to him. I didn't want to think what that had required. I focused on one thing: Vengeance.

Knuckles said, "Who is it?"

"I don't know. Probably Mikhail."

The phone buzzed again, and he said, "You going to answer it?"

I flicked my blade open again and said, "I think I'll wait to talk to him in person."

Knuckles said, "You'll get that chance, but answering can only give us intelligence. You'd be giving us an edge."

As usual, he was right. I did so, putting the phone to my ear and hearing nothing but a giant rushing sound. I narrowed my eyes and said, "Hello?"

I heard someone shouting about Shoshana. I put a finger in my other ear, having a hard time hearing. I said, "Let me speak to her."

Through the wind, I thought I heard, "You are, idiot."

I said, "Shoshana?"

"You are speaking to Shoshana."

"I can't hear you."

"I'm on top of a train."

"Top of a train?"

"Why do you keep repeating everything I say? Are you drunk?"

I looked at Knuckles, amazed. He mouthed, *what?* Into the phone, I said, "I fucking can't hear you. Who is this?"

"It's the damn Pumpkin King."

I heard *Pumpkin King* come through the phone loud and clear, and relief flooded through me like a patient hearing a doctor say the test had come back negative.

55

★ ★ ★

General Durham said, "So your 'source' *thinks* an attack is going to occur, but has no idea where or when?" He turned to President Hannister and said, "Sir, even if it's true, it doesn't alter our need for preparation. If anything, it means we should redouble our efforts. Instead of a game of brinksmanship, it's now just a race to be first to the punch."

Hannister nodded reluctantly, saying, "What do the Joint Chiefs recommend?"

"Full-on support for NATO. We don't want to trigger anything, but we have to be prepared. The NATO response force is a single brigade, and it's run by Spain now. Nothing against them, but we are the eight hundred–pound gorilla. We need to take charge."

"But didn't we agree to the response force rotation? How are we going to run in and assume command? It's *their* continent."

Durham said, "Sir, we front most of NATO's costs. This isn't a time to pretend that our allies' feelings are worth more than the outcome we seek."

Tired beyond belief, Hannister rubbed his eyes and said, "Can anyone else in this room give me a response that doesn't involve pissing off everyone we know?"

Oglethorpe said, "Sir, the enemy gets a vote, and Putin may not wait. Hell, look at it this way: If this supposed attack occurs, and it's a big enough spark, we're going to war whether we want to or not, because *NATO* will. We need to manage that, and doing so requires a commitment of forces. Stake in the game."

Hannister nodded and said, "But if I escalate, forcing him to do the same, we both drive to a resolution neither one of us wants."

General Durham said, "Sir, *he's* the one who's escalating! I don't want to go to war, either, but I also don't want to fight from a position of weakness."

"What if he's escalating because he's got someone on his side yelling at him like you're yelling at me?"

General Durham snorted and said, "Sir, you have two brigades in Putin's fire sack right now. He's moved two armored divisions and an artillery brigade into range across the border. If he wants to destroy them without warning, he can. And that will be on your head."

Hannister was incredulous. "Did you just accuse me of putting lives in danger, after you accused me of cowardice for not doing so? Do you think I'm too stupid to see what you're doing? Why did the artillery and armor move to the border?"

Oglethorpe tried to defuse the situation, but only got as far as "Sir" before Hannister cut him off with a glare.

They waited in silence for a moment, then General Durham said, "I'm not sure what you're asking me, sir."

"I'm asking for your assessment as to why Russia has now moved two armored divisions and an artillery brigade to the border with Ukraine."

"Sir, it's obvious why. Because of our airborne operation for Air Force One."

Hannister said, "At least you understand cause and effect. Fine. Pull them out. Get them back, right now. Defuse the situation."

Oglethorpe said, "Sir, they aren't finished with the body and document recovery. That'll take another couple of days. They need the time to scrub the wreckage for anything of intelligence value. Pulling out now will send a horrible signal."

General Durham said, "Showing weakness is not the way to go here. The Marine armored battalion is en route right now, traveling overland. They'll be there soon and provide the protection our men need."

"Or they will provide the excuse for Russia to finally unleash its forces. Maybe we won't have to wait for another instigating attack. Maybe you'll do it all by yourself."

Kurt wasn't sure which way he leaned on the discussion, then he heard words he never would have expected from the chairman of the Joint Chiefs of Staff. General Durham got political.

"Sir, have you seen the news? The population is screaming for vengeance. You *must* show strength."

Dennis McFadden, President Warren's chief of staff, and thus President Hannister's by default, said, "Sir, that's true. All the polling shows that the public wants a forceful response."

Durham continued, saying, "You have two brigades within range of both Russian artillery and armor. *You* put them there. Now you need to back them up."

Enraged, Hannister drew up and said, "*You* demanded that, and now you want to force my hand."

General Durham said, "Sir, I recommend. You execute. I agree with the decision, but I only recommend, like I'm doing now."

The room grew quiet. Kurt was embarrassed to say he wore the same uniform as General Durham, wondering how on earth he'd reached the highest military position in the United States arsenal. He was disgusted at the political display with lives on the line, and wanted to interject, but could not. He needn't have worried, because there was a greater leadership in the room. One no one expected to rise to the occasion.

Hannister locked eyes with the general and said, "Okay, then, we know where we both stand. Remember those words. You *recommend*. I execute."

And then a mild-mannered economist, forced into a situation beyond his asking, began to take control. General Durham looked at the secretary of defense, wanting backup, but not getting it. He turned to Hannister and said, "Sir, I told you I was hired by the president for my unvarnished opinion. President *Warren*."

Hannister said, "Warren's dead. I'm not sure that's sunk in for you. I'm making the decisions from now on."

Standing at attention like a cadet at West Point, General Durham nodded his head, finally backing down, but Hannister wasn't finished. "Right now, my decision is that you get the hell out of my office."

General Durham looked like he'd been slapped. Hannister said, "Go."

Durham left, along with most of the air in the room. Hannister said, "We're done here. The armor package holds up. Don't make it look like we changed our minds. Just hold them up in Kiev for a day until we can figure this out."

He looked around the room, sizing up who was left. He said, "Mark, Kurt, Kerry, and Palmer, stay behind. The rest of you, good night."

After the room had cleared, leaving only Oversight Council members, Kurt finally spoke. "Sir, this isn't the way to run a crisis. We can't have the divisions. We'll need rapid responses and consensus based on trust."

Hannister leaned back and said, "Yes. I think I just engendered that."

Mark Oglethorpe said, "Sir, General Durham *is* your senior military advisor."

"Then tell him to advise instead of manipulate. He's about to be shitcanned. Jesus, he actually brought up polling."

At a loss to defend the man, Mark said, "Yes, sir."

Hannister turned to Kurt and said, "What's the update?"

"Sir, Pike was planning on taking out both men as soon as his team arrived, but they split up right after the transcript was made. Simon went to Vienna and Mikhail is taking a train to an unknown location."

"So you're tracking Simon?"

"No, sir. The team made the call to track Mikhail. Simon presented complications that would lead to compromise with the team."

"Can't we do both? Can't we send someone to Vienna?"

Kurt considered, then said, "Yes, sir, that's actually a good idea, but let's do it aboveboard. We don't have a handle on where he'll end up, but if I could recommend, I'd get the FBI LEGATT at the embassy rolling. Simon is on our Ten Most Wanted list. Get HRT over there and let the FBI start working it with their contacts. Arrest him in conjunction with the Austrians. Even if they don't get him, it might create enough pressure to disrupt what he's doing."

To Palmer, Hannister said, "Get it done."

Palmer nodded and Hannister said, "Tell me that Pike can stop this attack. I can prevent us from doing something unforgivably stupid, but that's about it."

"Sir, Pike's working the problem, but there are no guarantees. He's got very little to go on. He's currently tracking the man who's conducting the meeting. Still no idea why or what that meeting is about, but it's tied to the attack."

"Tell him from me, the president of the United States, that the fate of Europe may depend on his success."

Kurt smiled and said, "Not sure that'll have an effect. No offense, but the last time Pike dealt with you, you had him arrested."

Hannister pinched the bridge of his nose as if he were warding off a migraine. He said, "Well, tell him we all change perspectives once we change jobs."

He removed his hand from his face and said, "Wait a minute. I have a better idea: Tell him I'll arrest him again if he fails. Pissing that guy off seems to bring out his best."

The tension in the room finally broke with the Council members' chuckling. Kurt stood to leave, saying, "You might be right on that."

56
★ ★ ★

It finally penetrated my brain that I really *was* talking to Shoshana, although the circumstances were beyond bizarre. I said, "What the hell are you doing? Where's Jennifer?"

"She's right here next to me. We're on top of the train."

"On top of the train?"

"Yes, on top of the train."

"You're actually on *top* of the train?"

"You're repeating things again."

A smile split my face, and I saw Knuckles relax. I said, "Where's Mikhail?"

"I don't know, but his men are dead. Look, we're rolling into a stop. We're getting off here. We'd like a ride."

Her nonchalance was amazing. I chuckled and said, "We're thirty seconds out from that stop. Where do you want to meet?"

"Standby. I can see the station."

I heard the wind recede as the train slowed, and Aaron said, "Station is in sight. What do you want me to do?"

"Hold what you got. It's now an exfil, not an assault."

I saw him smile as he pulled into a turnout, shutting off the lights.

I waited, then Shoshana came back on, now easy to hear, the area so quiet she whispered. She said, "We're going across the roof of the platform. Koko's moving to check it out. I'll call you back."

And she hung up.

I had no idea what had occurred on the train, but I knew if

Shoshana was talking to me, Jennifer had convinced her to fight, and it had probably been ugly.

Aaron turned around and said, "What happened?"

I said, "I don't know, but I'm pretty sure your little demon saved the day."

When he'd heard the earlier conversation, he'd been ripped apart by how bad things had become, knowing it had been his decision to put Jennifer and Shoshana on the train. He smiled, saying, "Thank you. Thank you for believing in her, like I do."

I said, "Are you nuts? I didn't believe in her at all. I'm the one who was against her boarding in the first place."

He said, "No, I don't mean before. I mean during. Nobody else could have gotten to her. Nobody else could have reached her. Not even me."

My phone rang again, and he said, "One of these days, I'm going to ask what the hell the Pumpkin King is, but I'll wait."

I answered and Shoshana said, "Coming down the east wall of the station. Right next to the bus terminal. Drive up and park."

I relayed the instructions, and we rolled into the parking lot, sweeping it with our headlights and seeing just a scattering of cars. Aaron pulled to the east side, right up next to a pillar of brick bulging out of the facade, a line of decorative trim that ran all the way to the roof. He cut the lights and a figure appeared. I leaned out and saw someone helping another get a grip on the brick facade. The figure began coming down, made it halfway, then slipped, falling the last seven feet to the ground.

Not Jennifer.

I leapt out to help, recognizing Shoshana just as another figure cleared the roof. I grabbed Shoshana's hand and pulled her to her feet at the same time that Jennifer came down like a monkey. She flung herself off the pillar at the same level as Shoshana and landed on her feet next to us.

I said, "Impressive."

Jennifer said, "No way. You're helping up Mrs. Impressive. You haven't *seen* impressive, trust me."

I pulled Shoshana to me and whispered in her ear, "Thank you. Nice to have you back."

She smiled at the affirmation. "Thank you for reminding me who I am."

She seemed to mean it, and it was good to have her return to normal. Well, normal for her, meaning she was predictably crazy instead of just plain batshit.

We climbed into the van, me giving Shoshana the shotgun seat so I could talk directly to Jennifer. We started to roll out of the parking lot and Shoshana leaned into the back, looking at me. Knuckles said, "So what the hell happened?"

Jennifer said, "I have never been so scared." She glanced at me and said, "Those assholes are seriously bad. They have no compunction about killing. They're just like the Russian guys in Istanbul."

She started gushing words, the story spilling out in almost incoherent sentences, and it was brutal. She fake-laughed at something about her binds, then her eyes welled as she recounted what Shoshana had been forced to do, but she continued talking, letting it all out. When she was done, there was silence in the van.

Knuckles broke it, patting Shoshana's arm. "Remind me not to cross you."

Shoshana said, "It was Jennifer who saved us. If she hadn't been there, I would be dead."

Jennifer didn't even hear the words. She was looking at me for absolution. Wanting me to wash away the blood and fear with a word. I couldn't do that, but I could come close.

I brushed a tear from her face, finally saying what I'd feared I never would again. "I'm glad you're alive."

She ran her hands over her cheeks, dealing with the emotional aftermath now that she was safe. I said, "You did good. You both did."

She finally smiled and said, "I'm glad you can read a situation, even through a radio."

I saw Shoshana staring intently at us. I said, "What the hell took so long for the Pumpkin King? I ask for it, I get it. We agreed on that."

I was trying to bring a little humor and break the talk of death, but she shrunk in, and I realized I was poking a sore that I had no right to touch. I said, "Hey, I was kidding. There is no one else I would have wanted in that situation."

She said, "Do you mean that?"

I could see she was vulnerable, on the cusp, wanting to believe my words. I said, "Yes. Yes, I do."

She glanced at Aaron to see if he thought the same. He reached over and cupped her chin, saying, "I'm glad you're alive as well, but I have to agree with Pike."

She craved his affirmation more than anyone's, but she still didn't look convinced. She knew what had happened in the train. Knew how she'd succumbed to Mikhail. She wanted to believe she was better than him, but she didn't. Aaron put that to rest.

He said, "Shoshana, you keep questioning yourself, but you shouldn't. Ever. You're pure, and you always have been. Mikhail can't take that from you."

Curled in the seat, the words washed away her doubt. She hesitated for a brief moment, then leaned over the console and kissed Aaron on the cheek. He reacted like he'd been stung by a bee, swerving the van over the shoulder of the road. She recoiled, sagging back like she'd broken a rule. Jennifer scowled at the reaction, ready to rip Aaron's head off. But he was quicker than that.

He gained control of the van, saying, "Sorry. That was a surprise. I wasn't expecting it." He patted Shoshana's hand, and her face lit up.

He said, "We can talk later. If you want."

She nodded rapidly, saying, "Yes. I'll *show* you later. Just like Jennifer does with Pike, when they're alone."

Jennifer's mouth opened in surprise, and the words hung in the air, the van silent. I closed my eyes. *Crazy is as crazy does.*

Knuckles said, "Enough of this shit. I want out of the van."

Shoshana looked at Jennifer for support, saying, "What did I do wrong?"

Jennifer grimaced. "You don't *tell* them," she said. "You just *do* it."

Shoshana nodded slowly, her eyes scrunched like she was actually computing what Jennifer had said. Factoring it in like she'd been raised by wolves and was just learning basic human social skills.

Which was probably true.

I said, "Great. You guys are the best. Mic drop. Lovefest over."

Jennifer poked my shoulder. I ignored her, continuing, "We still have a mission here. We need to get rolling on Mikhail."

Shoshana turned serious and said, "Yes, we do. Nephilim, I looked into him tonight, and I saw fear, but also fire."

I wanted to ignore her usual psychobabble, but I . . . well, I believed. I said, "What do you mean?"

"I don't know. I just saw fire. He has something very bad planned, and he's close. He knows he's close. I could see it."

I leaned back and said, "Shit. If that's true, we don't have a lead to stop him in time."

She pulled out a cell phone and said, "Yes, we do. I called you on this."

I said, "And?"

Jennifer said, "It's from the dead Russian, and it's tied to Mikhail."

Knuckles said, "Well, that's more like it. Let's go hunting."

57

★ ★ ★

The squeaking of the springs in the bunk against the window started again, and Mikhail clenched his teeth. He looked at his watch and saw it was almost five A.M. The stamina was impressive, but the irritation of keeping him awake was turning on the dark side of his personality. He waited, hoping the noise would end with the groaning of the springs, but that hadn't happened the previous two times. And like clockwork, the springs were overshadowed by a frenzy of thumping.

Wump, wump, wump. In between, groans of pleasure—or maybe pain, since it sounded like the guy was driving her head into the wall with each thrust. Lord knows this shithole didn't waste any money on headboards.

He thought about just walking across the room and murdering the both of them. He could probably get away with it, since the hostel was decidedly seedy and had probably seen its fair share of violence, but the last thing he needed was undue focus on the tenants. Especially since he had an important meeting in a few hours, and he'd wasted valuable time just getting to Warsaw. He needed the small amount he had left to prepare, not dodge the law.

Forced to abandon the trains, and unwilling to use his true identity to rent a car, it had taken him a day and a half to get here.

As soon as he'd cleared the parking lot of the train station, he'd hit several ATMs in the little town, putting his hand over the camera and maxing out his alias credit cards. He needed the money, for sure, but he couldn't be on camera. Right now, the only thing they had was a name. No way did he want to give them a face to go with it. After getting the money he destroyed the cards, hopefully leaving behind a trail that said he was still inside Slovakia, once the police determined whose ticket was tied to the carnage in the sleeper car.

He'd holed up in a cheap, by-the-hour hotel, paying in cash, then set out for Warsaw the following morning, after four hours of sleep. Using euros and his language abilities, he'd managed to reach Warsaw riding shotgun with four separate long-haul truckers, completely covering his tracks and giving himself a clean break.

Dropped off in the city center at the giant communist monstrosity known as the palace of culture, he snagged a cab, asking for a cheap hotel near the old town that would take cash, the implied statement being that they also wouldn't ask any questions.

The cabby stopped at a brick turret, looking like it had been built ages ago, but that was actually a modern construct, as was most everything in Warsaw. World War II had not been kind to the city. The Poles had refused to submit to their Nazi occupiers, and as a result, the German war machine had demolished every single building, the fighting a brutal house-to-house slugfest.

The cabby pointed through the turret and gave instructions in broken English, giving landmarks and left and right turns. Mikhail exited and began walking, weary and rumpled. He followed the directions, tripping on the cobblestone streets, looking for a bell, or maybe a plaque. He was unsure what the cabby had actually said.

He reached a square and was pleasantly surprised to find an old bell in the center, kids rubbing its top and walking around it in circles. He glanced at the walls of the nearest building and saw the plaque, now realizing what the cab driver had been trying to tell him by repeating the word *strong*. The plaque was for a man code-named Jack Strong, a CIA asset who had helped bring an end to communist rule in Poland.

Mikhail cared not a whit about any of it. Wishing bells or Cold

War heroes. He only wanted to sleep, and the hostel was down a tunnel right next door. He found it under an arch of bricks, a small sign out front. He entered, seeing a claustrophobic lobby the size of a closet. Two other patrons were in front of him, one a twentysomething female with dreadlocks, the other a male with a backpack, a scraggly neck beard, and less than stellar dental work. They began kissing while waiting, and little did he know they would soon be the bane of his existence.

He paid for a room, went up the stairs, and was surprised to see he'd be sharing it with the greasy couple. They introduced themselves, stating they were from France and tromping around Europe, then began to probe why a single guy like him, an "old man," was staying there. He'd made up a story about starting a career too young, forcing him to miss out on the experiences of youth, and he was now making up for it. Impressed at the lie, they offered to share a bottle of wine. He'd begged off, saying he was too tired.

He'd taken the bunk closest to the door, laying down fully clothed. They'd moved off to the end of the room, near the window. And then the activities had begun.

The thumping started to increase in speed, and Mikhail rubbed his face, then set his feet on the floor harder than necessary. The noise ceased. He stood up, hearing whispering. He flicked on the light, and got "Hey, shut that off."

The man with the crooked teeth glared at him, incensed, hunched over the woman, her face turned away. Mikhail said, "Sorry. Gotta go."

The man said, "Turn out the fuckin' light."

Which was enough to push Mikhail over the edge. He walked slowly toward the couple, and his approach was enough to indicate to the man that he'd made a mistake. Mikhail squatted down, getting eye to eye with him, ignoring the woman.

Speaking in a low tone, he brandished a folding knife, flicking the blade out. "You say one more word and I'll cut your fucking tongue out." He used his index finger to punctuate the last four words, jabbing it into the man's forehead after each one.

The man's eyes were so large, it was comical. He nodded, but remained mute, afraid to test the threat. The girl began to tremble underneath him, hiding her face in the pillow as if that would prevent the bogeyman from finding her.

Mikhail rose, then left the room, not even bothering to look back.

58

★★★

I was awakened in our vehicle by Jennifer poking me in the shoulder. It was her turn on watch, but if she was waking me, something had happened.

She said, "Veep's got him. Leaving the hostel right now."

I looked at my watch. *Five in the morning. Early to leave for no reason. This must be it.*

We were all running on about two hours of sleep, because it had taken quite a bit of time to find the phone associated with Mikhail. People thought the evil NSA could listen in on every phone call on earth, but that was woefully untrue. They needed a focus. A target. And then they needed time.

I'd fed the entire database of Shoshana's phone to Kurt, and he'd had to get the data washed through the CIA and into the NSA system because we, as the Taskforce, had been restricted from duplicating NSA capability. It was a conscious decision by President Warren and Kurt to prevent us from becoming an overarching Gestapo that everyone in America believed was alive and well anyway. Because of it, we now had to trickle our information into the beast and hope that someone had the power to redirect assets to act on our information.

Luckily, we also had the commander in chief in our corner.

The NSA, without having a clue why, had analyzed the recent call logs of the Russian phone, then necked down the numbers to four based on metadata. Through a process of elimination, the Taskforce intel cell had discarded three and had told them to focus on one single number. Like the machine they were, they did. People had a fantasy that the NSA actually made decisions on what to do and whom to target, but that was largely false. Others on the ground made that decision. They only executed what they were told.

The analysts had taken a look at the numbers, and using our input on what we knew about Mikhail's historical locations—in Slovakia, on the train, and at the Castle—had determined which number was his. From there, the NSA, using what was, in fact, a breathtaking capability to parse data once they had a target, had located the phone in Warsaw. They could only get it down to a cell provider in the city, but that was close enough, because we now had the Rock Star bird, and that thing could pinpoint the phone to four meters. All we had needed was a plot of ground small enough to start looking, and the NSA had found it.

By the time the rest of the team had landed, Kurt had sent the NSA information on the Warsaw location. We'd unloaded the bird with whatever kit I thought we could use—along with some lethal tools, finally—and I'd launched it into the air again, using its ISR capability to pinpoint the phone. It had finally done so at one in the morning, tracking the phone to a block of buildings in the ancient downtown section of Warsaw. From there, we'd done Internet research and had found a youth hostel, the only place anywhere near the target grid where Mikhail could be staying. And we had started the surveillance, running on fumes and coffee.

It had been a frenzied amount of work, and I was proud of the intelligence community's ability to actually accomplish what we needed—for once not getting bogged down in food fights. Then again, from Kurt's last call, I knew this was about much more than stopping a single attack. That was our mandate, but this time, Kurt had seemed genuinely worried.

Veep came on the radio, sounding bored, which I knew was a front. His real name was Nick Seacrest, and he was the vice president's son—make that the president's son. He'd only done one mission with us, and I'd called him forward not because of his skill, but because he was an unknown for Mikhail, and I knew he was nervous as hell about screwing up.

Well, that's not exactly true. He was pretty good. Just relatively untested, unlike Retro, the other member of the team. Someone I'd done many, many operations with.

"I got him. He's walking toward the main square. He's showing no tradecraft."

Perfect.

Sitting in the minivan at one of the few exits from the area, I said, "No vehicles?"

"None. He's walking. No luggage. No support. He's got a day's growth of beard, and I think he slept in his clothes. He looks pretty ragged."

I thought, *Seeing Shoshana turn into the dark angel will do that to a man.*

I said, "Roger all. Keep tracking. Bumper one, Bumper two, you copy?"

Aaron came on, saying, "Bumper one, roger all. I'm up and waiting."

Knuckles followed, "Bumper two. Got it."

Retro came on, saying, "I got Veep's backup on foot."

And now we would see if my call was correct.

We'd had the chance to take him down inside the hostel, penetrating with a device called Growler that would allow us to lock his phone and pinpoint his room, but I'd opted not to. For one thing, while we could find his room, we couldn't determine who else was staying with him, and the last thing we needed was to subdue a couple of civilians, then have them talking afterward. For another, I couldn't get the fidelity for an assault plan inside the hostel without risking burning the last two clean team members I had. But that was always a hard choice.

It was a question I'd experienced many times before. Something that the counterterrorism architecture had tussled with since 9/11: develop or strike?

Everyone wants the simple answer—the one Hollywood feeds you—but it rarely ever happens. Each time you hunt a terrorist, you're forced to make a choice: take that guy out, or track him, developing the situation. All terrorists are tied into cells, and the longer you watch them, the more cells you end up exposing. Unfortunately, while you're watching a target, he's planning further attacks. He's working. I sometimes lie awake at night wondering, *If I'd taken out Terrorist X earlier, could I have prevented further deaths?* But then I think about the guy he led us to, someone who wasn't a cog, but ran the entire terrorist wheel.

I'd decided to develop here. I wasn't sure Mikhail was a single point of failure, and didn't know if the plan was already in motion. Taking him out might not stop it.

I didn't know yet if I'd made the right decision, but at least we had him in our sights.

59

★★★

Mikhail retraced his steps, walking by the square with the bell and plaque, now deserted at the early hour. It was just after five in the morning and the sun had already started to crack the horizon, but had yet to provide any summer heat. The air was brisk and smelled faintly of smoke. He took that as a good sign. Someone was baking breakfast pierogi for the early risers, which meant coffee.

He took a right, went through a small tunnel, and popped out onto a new street, right next to a large cathedral. He saw a neighborhood bakery and walked toward it, then did a double take when he recognized the cathedral.

It was St. John the Baptist. The location of his meeting. From the map, he thought it would be down the street a block or so.

Perfect.

The meeting wasn't until seven fifteen, right after the morning mass started, but he wanted to watch early. Wanted a chance to determine what he was up against, and the bakery offered the perfect spot to simply sit and do that.

He pulled the door and found it locked. He peeked through the window, seeing a man in a stained apron working a large brick oven. He knocked, and the man shouted something at him in Polish, pointing at his watch, then holding up six fingers.

Thirty minutes away.

He wandered past the cathedral, looking for another spot, when he saw someone come out of the large double doors. The cathedral was open, which meant he could conduct reconnaissance of the meeting site.

He forgot about finding a coffee shop and went straight to the church, cracking open the doors and peeking inside. He saw it was empty, but not completely so. He could get in without arousing questions.

When Simon had initially asked him where he wished to meet the Russians, Mikhail's mind had gone to two things: protection and escape. He'd initially wanted to use an airport, as that would definitely prevent any weapons from coming into play, but it would also prove problematic for transferring the radioactive material. He'd researched restaurants, hotels, and bars, knowing he needed someplace crowded, but had come up with nothing satisfactory. And then he'd hit on a church.

The Poles were overwhelmingly Catholic, and each church held mass several times a day. If he could find a cathedral with the correct characteristics, it would work, because there was no way that the Russians would attempt anything inside a church, for one simple reason: The Poles despised Russians, in a visceral way. If they tried anything in a house of God, they'd be ripped limb from limb by the churchgoers attending mass.

The problem with his scheme was precisely that the protection would hinder the transfer. It wasn't like they could do it in the pews. He'd searched for a church with something unique, and had found it in St. John's. It had been demolished in World War II, but the destruction hadn't reached the crypts. When it was rebuilt, the crypts were left in place. Or at least Mikhail's research had said so. Now he'd know for sure.

Mikhail pushed through the doors, entering a foyer where a gray-haired lady stood smiling at him. He smiled back and walked into the nave. He glanced to his left and saw the stairs to the crypt. No gate, nothing stopping his entrance.

He glanced at the sanctuary on the far end, seeing someone lighting candles and a few scattered souls in the pews. He entered the
stairs, winding down below the church. He hit a landing and saw
several sarcophagi arrayed in a row, the lighting muted, the brick
clearly old, unlike the church above. He stalked down the tunnel,
listening for anyone following. He heard nothing.

He explored the depths of the crypt, seeing a staircase at the end.
He took it, and found himself at the altar in the front of the church,
a cleric looking at him curiously.

He waved and smiled, retreating back down the steps. In seconds,
he was outside.

He walked to the bakery, finding the owner willing to let him in
even though it was still some minutes before opening. He bought a
cup of coffee and took a seat, watching the doors to the church
through the windows.

He sat for forty minutes, studying the growing traffic. He felt his
phone vibrate with a text. A short note from Simon, and an attachment. He opened it and found a picture of a captain in a US Air Force
uniform, then a listing of biographical data, including an address in
Lodz, Poland.

He called Simon, surprised when he answered on the first ring.

"You get the attachment?"

"Yes. He's the target?"

"Correct. He runs the security for the American side of the base.
Get him under control, and you can guarantee access."

"Is he married?"

"He is."

"Okay. I'll handle the prep with the Night Wolves, but I'm not
going on the base with them. If they screw it up, it's on them. I'm
headed straight to Vienna."

"Good enough. Are you prepared for the transfer?"

"I'm here, but I'm not so sure about being prepared. You have anything on the team tracking me? How they found out about the train?"

"No. My contacts in Israel could turn up nothing. They have no idea why a composite American/Israeli team would be hunting us."

"You mean hunting me."

Simon laughed and said, "Yes. I suppose that's true. Their assessment is it's something like you—not official."

"Simon, the tracking concerns me. They put a lot of effort into it, and it wasn't because of some gold."

"Yes, it concerns me as well, but the answer to the problem is the same one as before. Only now it involves you as well as me. Get the sample and meet the Night Wolves. Cause enough chaos and they'll choose to leave instead of follow."

Mikhail saw people beginning to enter the church, the crowd for mass beginning. He said, "I'm not so sure I want to follow through. I've lost my security team. Now I have to meet these guys alone."

Simon said, "It'll be good. I talked to him yesterday. He wants to deal and is afraid of Putin trying to stop him. He's scared Putin is going to turn on him much like he did me."

"Did you pay?"

"No, of course not. He's bringing you a sample of Cesium-137. He'll show it to you, and you say you need to check it out with our capability. Tell him you want to make sure it's pure. He'll set up another meeting for the transfer of the total load, and we won't be there. Done deal."

Mikhail said, "Cesium? I thought I was getting uranium?"

"No, I was mistaken. It's something called Cesium-137. A castoff from nuclear waste in Russia. It's very deadly, but not useful for anything other than a dirty bomb. He'll have a quarter kilo of it. That's not enough to do any real damage, and he'll expect you to meet him for the rest. We won't be doing that."

"What's the problem with Cesium? Is it going to hurt me?"

"No. It'll be shielded, but it's very, very dangerous when exposed. It's not like you could build a nuclear bomb with it, but you can certainly spread it around with some explosives, which will cause a serious panic. The fingerprints of the Cesium will point back to Russia, and it'll give us the result we want, I promise."

Mikhail watched the church doors swing wide, the people streaming in, mass close to beginning. He said, "But it's on my back if the meeting goes wrong."

Simon said, "It won't, Mikhail. Just get it done."

"I'm looking at the front of the church, and thinking hard about that refund."

Watching the crowd, Mikhail saw three men who stood out. Two had crew cuts and overcoats, burly guys. One was older, wearing a fedora and carrying a briefcase. He had no doubt who they were. The man with the briefcase was an ex-KGB Russian known only as the Colonel, and he'd been attempting to sell radioactive material since at least 2010. His activities in Moldova had been broken up by the American FBI on four separate occasions, and yet he'd walked free each time.

Mikhail thought, *Three men.* He could handle that. He thought about the crypts, and the way out from the stairwell he'd found.

He said, "They're here. I just saw them go in."

Simon said nothing for a moment, then came back. "Mikhail, we are a team. If the refund means so much to you, I'll let it go. I need this attack, or I'll be hunted forever. Go meet them."

"Have you seen the news? The Americans are stirring things up all on their own."

"Yes, they are, but they always back down when push comes to shove. Tensions are heating up in Poland. Putin is stacking forces close to Kaliningrad, and the Poles are growing fearful. Unlike America, they cannot retreat with the wolf at their door, and your attack will guarantee American involvement as well."

Mikhail looked at his watch, seeing he had three minutes. Resigned, he said, "Okay. I'm going in."

"Get it done, and the money from the Torah is yours. Remember, all we need is a spark."

"I can't help but wonder if the United States won't give us what we want without all this bullshit risk."

"They aren't willing to fight. All they do is rattle sabers and threaten."

"You forget: It takes two to fight a war. Those threats might be enough."

60

★★★

Lieutenant Colonel Quinton Straight watched the refueling operation, and wondered if they'd have enough gas to complete the mission. As the battalion commander of the 2nd Tank Battalion, 2nd MARDIV, he'd been told—and had planned accordingly—to be self-sustaining for four days, but then had been ordered to hold up in Kiev, where he'd burned fuel sitting around waiting to move forward.

He understood the political dimensions of his advance, and would follow whatever orders he'd been given, but seriously, didn't the National Command Authority understand how much fuel these beasts used?

The M1A1 Abrams tanks he'd pulled out of stocks burned an enormous amount of JP-8 AVGAS, literally getting a half mile to the gallon, a sum so paltry that fuel usage was determined not by miles, but by hours. The average M1 used about three hundred gallons every eight hours—and he'd computed what he'd need for the mission based on the OPORDER he'd been given. Now he wondered if this two-day stay counted against that. Did he have four *more* days to go? And what if he had to fight at the end of it?

The two tank companies he'd brought with him, comprising thirty steel-clad weapons that were the most deadly armor ever to enter the battlefield, had spent the last two days in a tactical perimeter, the men half on and half off security, all wondering why the holdup had occurred. They'd secured a perimeter, living on their awful field rations and plying their limited skills on the women who came to watch the show, never thinking the operation they were on had any consequences greater than the training mission they'd left.

Kiev was peaceful, and the population appreciated them coming, showing enough gratitude that it should have penetrated there was something in front of them they should fear, if only because the natives that lived there did.

After twenty-four hours of waiting, the men had become restless. Why should they live in the woods when the town was right next door? They began to surreptitiously slip out, using official business as an excuse.

Quinton let them go, turning a blind eye to the supposed "resupply runs." A Mustang, he'd been one of them once, and understood that a blanket clampdown would be counterproductive. Let them pretend to sneak out. As long as they had a senior NCO with them, he knew they'd be okay, because he'd fostered a layer of trust in his battalion. The NCOs, like all NCOs from the beginning of time, took that trust to heart. They'd go out, but they'd sure as hell bring everyone back. And because they were professionals, they wouldn't allow any gap in security.

He'd actually begun to think this diversion into Ukraine would be good for the battalion, giving the two companies he'd brought a taste of anticipation without the threat, sharpening their edge. And then he'd received the intelligence reports the night before. The Donetsk airport, held in rebel hands and utterly destroyed, had shown movement on the runway. Someone had begun to prepare the demolished area for reception. Nobody knew why, but it couldn't be good. He was ordered forward, into the rebel-held Luhansk territory, to provide support for the evacuation of the dead from Air Force One.

He'd had one night to prepare, and was now late on the LD time he'd set for the battalion, the refueling taking longer than expected. As Clausewitz once said, *Everything in war is very simple, but the simplest thing is difficult.*

Only this wasn't a war. Was it?

The refueling finished, and the tactical assembly area broke down, with all tanks lining up in order of march. He gave the command, and they began rolling east, in radio contact with the Stryker brigade and the 82nd Airborne.

He spent the majority of time while they moved coordinating exactly that—the movement. One would think just driving a caravan of tanks would be easy, but it wasn't. Every ten kilometers there was another call. Another reason to pull over. Another problem to solve.

During the march, he didn't give a lot of thought to deploying for a fight, but it was there in the back of his mind. Always present, hovering just on the outside of the current decision, like a bad hangover that shrouded his brain.

He knew there was a reason he'd been held up in Kiev. He just didn't know what it was. He hadn't been told anything specific, only having been given the order to laager. He'd done so, and then had been given the order to move out literally four hours ago. He'd responded that he couldn't turn on a dime, getting exasperation from the Black Sea Rotational Force commander—someone who clearly had no armor experience. The beasts required a windup. They were called Iron Horses for a reason.

The abrupt call to move concerned him, not the least because it had happened in the middle of the night, with no warning. He'd asked if it had anything to do with the Donetsk airport, and had been told they didn't know, because this wasn't a Black Sea NATO mission. This had nothing to do with NATO. He was controlled by an organization that actually had no control. He couldn't be NATO. He was the United States, pure and simple. In the hodgepodge creation of his mission, his command in Europe had become nothing more than a radio relay, simply because they had the architecture. That would change once he made linkup with the 82nd Airborne. He'd fall OPCON to them, leaving the rotation force for good.

Quinton was a student of history, as most military officers were. He understood the application of force, but also the deterrent threat that force implied. He was willing to go toe-to-toe with anyone on earth, but understood his true purpose was exactly to prevent that. To keep someone from even wanting to fight. He knew the Russians were watching his advance. In the new world of satellites and drones, he had no doubt about that.

He was rolling forward with more firepower than an armored division in World War II, facing a threat that had more firepower than the entire armies of Patton, Montgomery, and Hitler combined. He understood that he'd been held up in Kiev for political reasons, giving the Russians time to capitulate.

And now he'd been ordered into the Luhansk Oblast.

He was afraid to question why that was.

61
★★★

Mikhail waited until the men had disappeared into the crowd before crossing the street. He held the door for an old couple, then entered the nave and quickly descended the stairs. He reached the landing, finding one of the overcoat wearers at the base. A man two inches taller, with a thin layer of blond hair cut razor close, stared at Mikhail with piggish, marble eyes.

In Russian, Mikhail said, "Mass has started. You're going to be late."

The Russian showed a flicker of recognition at the bona fides, and responded, "I'm attending the later one."

Getting the correct response, Mikhail moved past him into the hallway, saying, "Where is the Colonel?"

"Go to the first intersection, then take a right."

Not good. Not his plan. The intersection led to a dead end with an alcove housing skulls cut into the rock. Once in, with the beefy Russian behind him, he'd be trapped, his stairwell exit useless.

He started down the arched tunnel and felt the Russian fall in behind him. *Keep cool. They want the money more than they want you.*

He reached a T intersection, the tunnel to the right much more narrow than the one he was in, with barely enough room for a single man to pass. The other pipe-swinger was standing just inside. Beyond him, he saw the fedora-wearing older gentleman, holding a briefcase.

The second pipe-swinger stepped out, leaving one in front of Mikhail and one behind. He held his hand out, as if he were inviting him down the narrow passage. Mikhail hesitated, and he said, "Don't worry. We'll prevent anyone from interfering."

Mikhail nodded and entered the tunnel. He walked about forty feet, and the man in the fedora turned, a smile on his face. Speaking in Russian, he said, "Simon, I presume?"

"No, Colonel, I'm his representative."

The answer made the man's smile falter. Mikhail could swear he saw a flicker of fear, but was unsure why. He said, "I was told Simon would be here."

"Simon *is* here, for all practical purposes. I'm empowered to transact on his behalf. You are speaking to him when you talk to me. Is that the sample?"

"Yes." The man bent down and opened the briefcase, exposing a cylindrical tube two inches in diameter with a thick glass window about an inch square, covered with metal mesh. Inside, Simon could see a white powder that appeared to glow. The Colonel said, "It's pure. As promised."

"We'll need to test it."

"I know. I brought the necessary equipment."

From the briefcase, he withdrew what looked like a voltage meter with a rubber cord hanging out. He plugged the cord into a valve in the top of the cylinder, cinching it tight, then twisted a control knob, and the needle spiked into the red zone.

"See?"

Mikhail said, "Colonel, no offense to you, but Simon has stressed that we must test it with our own equipment. We've been burned in the past with the seller providing the testing."

The Colonel scowled and said, "That's not happening. And Simon must be at the transfer of the rest of the Cesium. Him, and him alone. I'll give you an address to pass to him. It won't be here in Poland."

The statement crystallized what this was about. The Colonel wasn't trying to sell Cesium. He was selling Simon. Somehow, Putin had gotten wind of the purchase, and he'd rightly determined that it wasn't for something benign. He might have even put together that Simon was behind the death of the United States's president.

And now he was fighting back.

Carefully, Mikhail said, "Okay. I'll talk to him. But I need to take the specimen. He'll be here for the transfer, but obviously, he can't be here now. And he's not going to arrange a meeting for the rest if this doesn't prove worth it."

"No. The specimen stays here. I've showed you the worth of it."

Mikhail realized he was losing the race, and decided to back out completely. "Okay, okay. Where do you want to meet for the transfer?"

The Colonel's demeanor shifted, and Mikhail knew he'd capitulated too early. The man didn't believe him. He said, "We're done here."

He snapped his fingers, and the crew-cut beast closed in, now showing a suppressed pistol. The Colonel said, "I don't know who you are, but there are powerful men who would like to talk to Simon, and you will lead us to him."

Mikhail saw the pistol and realized he'd been mistaken. The stakes at play far outweighed any fear of being a Russian security man in Poland.

He held his hands up and said, "Wait, this is supposed to just be an exchange."

The second thug searched him, finding the Browning Hi-Power against the small of his back. The Colonel said, "You can call it that. You're exchanging your life for Simon's. You will tell us where he is, or you will suffer the consequences. Let's go."

They exited the crypt in the middle of mass, nobody paying them a bit of attention.

After being loaded into a sedan, sandwiched between the two bricks of muscle, Mikhail kept track of their location as they left the old town, driving through the steel of the city. When they stopped, he couldn't help but feel the irony.

They forced him out in front of a dilapidated tenement house, with makeshift clotheslines dangling out of windows, the concrete blocking all light.

Outside the tenement was a plaque delineating the buffer zone for the Jewish Ghetto that had seen a valiant uprising in World War II. They were taking him into a location where the Jews had fought to the death against Nazi Germany. He hoped that was a good sign, even as he realized they had no idea he was of the same faith.

The pipe-swinger to his left said, "No talking. No quick movements."

They left the sedan on the street and walked through an entranceway into a center courtyard. Built by the communist regime after the war, the structure was falling into ruin. The courtyard was designed to provide light for the people in the building, but whatever had been bright and happy here had long since departed. The concrete was grimy and soiled, and trash littered the ground. On the left side were the skeletons of four bicycles, still chained to a rail, all missing their seats and wheels. They were an apt analogy for those who lived here.

Shells of life.

A woman on the fourth floor looked out a window, the glass long since gone, her body backlit by the illumination of candles behind her. She saw them and scurried back into the room.

The man to Mikhail's right nudged him, pointing to a darkened doorway lacking an actual door. They went up dilapidated stairs, the wood so old he thought it would give way, stopping on the third floor. One of the men opened a door, and they entered a small den with a threadbare rug. In a kitchen off to the left, the vintage appliances sat rusting, telling him it had been a long time since anyone had lived here.

He was led through the kitchen into a back room smelling of urine, then searched more thoroughly. His cell phone, wallet, and passport were placed on the table, then his right hand was handcuffed to an old iron bed frame, the mattress long gone.

The goons faded back, and Mikhail finally said, "Colonel, we had a deal."

The Colonel said, "We never had a deal. Simon had a deal, and he's pissed off too many people to complete it. Some men will be here soon. They will question you, and they'll get the answers they want."

Fighting for leverage, Mikhail lied, saying, "I'm willing to pay you right now. Give you the money. And you can keep the Cesium."

Setting the briefcase on the ground next to the dresser, the Colonel said, "This is about more than money. It's about the future of Russia."

Mikhail saw the conviction on the Colonel's face and knew he was done. No amount of pleading or negotiation would help. When the interrogators showed up, they would pry him open like a can of beans, learning Simon's location. It wasn't that he wanted to protect Simon out of goodwill. If he thought giving Simon up would allow him to walk away, he'd do it in a heartbeat, but he'd been on the other side of the knife, and he knew as soon as they located Simon, he was useless to them. Meaning dead.

In the old days, with the Mossad, he could at least hope a rescue force was on the way. But there was no such hope here.

62

★ ★ ★

Pulling my turn on radio watch, all I got from Retro was *no change*. He'd now been watching the building for close to ten hours, and nothing exciting had happened. I killed the time watching the BBC in our suite, and saw the beginnings of the television broadcasting of the events our intelligence community already knew. Kurt had called earlier with a report that added serious urgency to our mission: The Russians were attempting to surround our forces in Ukraine.

From the small den, I heard Jennifer ask, "Do we really need a sniper rifle?"

Knuckles replied, "Depends on what Retro says, but keep it out just in case."

Sorting through equipment, they were preparing for an assault on the bed-down we'd located for Mikhail and his merry band of men. We'd tracked them from the church to a broken-down commie tenement house right next to the boundary of the old Jewish Ghetto on Walicow Street, and because of its location, it was looking like the best place to interdict them.

Retro and Veep had given us photos of the sedan they were using, and the rest of the team, split into three vehicles, picked it up and followed it from the church to the tenement. I'd left Aaron watching the squalid building for the short term, and had returned to pick up Retro and Veep. I'd given them a surveillance kit, then swapped them out with Aaron.

While I was positive this was the viper's nest and that our wait last night had paid off, Retro wasn't so sure and recommended we develop the situation a little further. He had some good points:

First, Mikhail had been sandwiched in the back, between two men who could only be described as paid muscle. The older man had driven, and the passenger seat had remained empty.

Second, and more important, Retro pointed out that if you were going to a tenement house for planning, why meet up in a church first? Why not just linkup in the tenement? If it really was the safe house, why meet in public first?

In his mind, it smelled a little, and maybe we were misreading the whole thing. His thoughts made sense, but I still believed this was the final stage before an attack. Maybe Mikhail had chosen to sit in back to discuss whatever they were planning, using a map or computer as he did so. And maybe he didn't know where the tenement was and had tasked them to find a secure area, planning a linkup meeting beforehand to take him there. Or maybe *he'd* found the tenement, but didn't know the men he'd eventually use and wanted to vet them first before taking *them* there.

Retro's comments held weight, though, and I'd decided to watch for a little while instead of rolling right in, hopefully gaining a little clarity on what was happening. That choice had become moot after Kurt's call.

While we were establishing a static observation post, I'd had Jennifer and Shoshana locate the first hotel she could find with a suite large enough for us to plan and prepare in. She'd settled on the Inter-Continental Warsaw, only about four minutes away. She'd given Aaron and me the room number, and we'd left Veep and Retro for the static surveillance, letting them figure out how they'd do it. Retro—who had earned his callsign because he was a miser and habitually wore clothes that were years out of date—would blend in fine. Veep would have to learn on the fly.

We'd checked in and had begun the mundane work of mission planning, shuttling the equipment up from the Rock Star bird—suppressed break-down rifles in .300 Blackout, Glock 27s, miniature battering rams, various electronic devices, you name it—and then had settled in to wait for information from our observation post.

And then Kurt had called on the VPN.

I was surprised, because it was my responsibility to initiate contact with him, not the other way around, but I learned quickly why he'd done so. Things had changed, and not for the better. When the screen cleared, I'd thought he had the flu. He looked like he hadn't slept for a week. He ignored any perfunctory questions about the team, digging right into the mission.

"What's your status?"

"We found the bed-down, but we want to develop more." I explained what we'd seen, and the competing theories of what it meant, ending with, "Bottom line, if they stay, we can hit it, but we might still be wrong, missing the operational team."

Kurt said, "Story of my life. But it's irrelevant now. We can't risk losing Mikhail. Hit them tonight."

Which took me aback. I said, "Sir?"

Kurt rubbed his eyes and said, "This isn't a developmental target anymore."

I said, "Sir, you realize that this operation is bigger than we thought, right? This isn't a single strike. This is more like a full-blown conspiracy. We need to sort it out."

He sounded weary. He said, "Pike, the United States's path is getting beyond our ability to control. Tensions are high, and all it will take is a single spark."

"What's going on?"

"The Russians cleared the airfield at Donetsk. The rebels have held it forever, but it was literally destroyed in the initial fighting and useless without a lot of work. It's why we jumped into the Severodonetsk airport instead. We saw them working on it, and now we're watching them fly in armor. A BMP battalion so far, but they're still coming in. It's to the west of the airfield we seized, which means they have a lodgment behind our own and can cut off our supply lines. They're creating an encirclement around the two brigades we have in-country."

"What are we doing?"

"We had a Marine armor battalion in Kiev. They've now gone forward, and we've repositioned some artillery. It's not enough to protect them if Russia is determined to attack, but hopefully it'll be enough to give the Russians pause about offensive action. We are on the cusp of a major fight, and if it culminates, we're going to lose."

Lose? I had never heard those words spoken about the United States's might in the entire time I had been in the US military. I wasn't even sure I'd heard correctly. I said, "What do you mean?"

"I mean this is about to be a shooting war, and not like Iraq or Afghanistan, where we owned the monopoly of violence. We go to war here, with what we've got, and we're going to lose. We're trying to build up, but it won't happen quickly enough. Those brigades will be wiped out, and Russia will roll through, taking the Baltic states without much of a fight. We can't stop them."

"What about NATO?"

"They just don't have the combat power. They can keep the Russians from overrunning Europe—mainly through stretching out the Russian supply lines—but they can't prevent a massacre in the ring states bordering Russia. We don't think Russia wants that, but we're reaching critical mass where it won't matter what anyone wants. We're working the issue here, tamping down the trigger, but if those fucks you're chasing do anything, we won't be able to stop the outcome."

I took that in, sitting in a hotel surrounded by residents who had no idea how close they were to fleeing for their lives. Wondering if the people in Warsaw in 1939 had been just as unknowing. I said, "So hit Mikhail tonight, regardless?"

Kurt rubbed his eyes and said, "Yeah. Hit them. Hard. But not hard enough to trigger your own international incident. The last thing we need is a conspiracy theory spreading in Poland that Russian sleeper cells have invaded. The Poles are on a hair trigger."

I said, "Sir . . . you're putting me in a tough spot here. I mean, it's looking pretty optimal for an assault—but it might not be."

He nodded, saying, "I know. Take them off the board."

I said, "Roger all, sir, but if I get this done, President Hannister had better buy me a beer at a place of my choosing."

He laughed and said, "You prevent World War Three, and I think I can arrange that."

63

★★★

The time had passed slowly for Mikhail. The man guarding him had shown no inclination to talk, and in fact had only moved once, to turn on small battery-powered lanterns once the sun had set. Mikhail had asked for food, and then water, and had been ignored both times. He was about to try again when he heard movement outside the room. The guard heard it too and went outside, closing the door behind him.

Mikhail strained to hear what was happening. Conversation floated through the door. Greetings, then murmured discussions. The interrogators had arrived.

Left alone in the room, Mikhail frantically began to work the handcuff on his wrist. He'd been trained on defeating restraints, and had jammed his hand forward when the cuff began to close on his wrist, driving it up into the meatier part of his arm, but he hadn't gained much space. He checked the other end, finding the bed frame solid. Whoever had made the frame had intended it to outlast the concrete of the building. The iron would require a welder to get through.

He stood as far as he could, stretching out, reaching toward the dresser for his phone. If he could get it, he could call the Night Wolves. They were currently in the suburb of Praga just across the Vistula River, sitting and waiting on the briefcase here in the apartment. He could let those suicidal maniacs shoot it out with the Russian intelligence men. It wasn't a perfect solution, since he'd probably get shot in the crossfire, but it was better than waiting for Russian interrogators to peel him open.

He came a foot short from the dresser. He stretched forward, and the bed refused to move. He tore the skin on his wrist and gave up. His mind running through options, he focused on the window above the bed. He leaned toward it, now stretching in the opposite direction, and saw a rusting fire escape. He hoped it was as sturdy as the bed, but with his luck, it would be made of low-grade steel and would collapse at the lightest touch.

He frantically studied the bed frame, looking for a weakness. He found none. He heard the door to the room open and whirled around, seeing two new men entering. One was short, about five foot four, with eyes set close together, making him look like a ferret. The other was of average height, but obese, his gut spilling out over his belt. Hunched over, his manacled hand preventing him from standing upright, Mikhail warily stared at them.

The obese man said, "Don't bother attempting to escape. We made sure to find a secure place. Don't make this hard on yourself. Sit down."

He did so, causing the old bedsprings to groan in protest.

The short man surveyed the top of the dresser, flipping through Mikhail's passport. He turned and said, "Israeli. That is a surprise. How do you speak Russian?"

Mikhail said, "I learned it in school."

"And what school would that be?"

Mikhail remained mute.

The man lashed out, smacking him in the face, saying, "This isn't a give-and-take. It's only a take. You need to understand that early."

I called Retro as soon as I hung up with Kurt, saying, "We're going in tonight. Give me an assault plan."

He said, "Pike, I haven't seen anything since they entered. We're going in without any further information. What's driving the change?"

I ignored the question. "Have you seen enough to get us to the apartment they're in? Without any reconnaissance from the team? Can you get an assault force to the door?"

"Yeah, I've got a target package built. Veep's sending it now, but like I said, I don't know anything more than I did when you dropped us off. What's happening?"

I told him what I'd learned. The bottom line was, we were assaulting tonight, and like the good soldier he was, he didn't question. I ended with, "Can you get us in?"

All he said was, "That depends. Are they designated a hostile force?"

The definition of that term held a specific weight, much more than the benign words would indicate. In the law of land warfare, it meant we didn't need to discriminate when we found a target. We didn't need to determine if the individual was friend or foe, as we did with hostage rescue. For all practical purposes, it made the apartment like fighting the Germans in World War II: See someone in a German uniform, and you could kill him. The difference here was that nobody was wearing a uniform—which is why someone had to make the official call that the force we were going against was hostile. And Kurt had done so.

Knuckles came in, holding another laptop. He said, "Got the target package. From thermal, it looks like one on the first-floor landing, the rest inside the apartment. Third floor, south tower."

I nodded and said, "That still accurate, Retro?"

"Yes. Two of them are in a kitchen next to the courtyard window, neither of them Mikhail. You get me the Punisher, from my position I can definitely eliminate one, possibly both, depending on reaction time. I can't get a shot at the guy inside the landing."

The Punisher was a custom long-gun built on the AR platform in 6.5 Creedmoor, a round with extreme accuracy that could reach out past a thousand yards. It broke down at the stock, making it portable, and was muffled by a Gemtech Dagger suppressor, leaving only the supersonic crack of the bullet to worry about. It was a bit of overkill, given the distance between Retro and the target, but with its surgical precision and our need to ensure one-shot placement, I'd get it to him.

Knuckles said, "Punisher's already packed for transport, along with a .300 Blackout for Veep."

I said, "Okay, Retro, be prepared to linkup in an hour. You got a spot for that?"

"Yeah. There's a disco just up Walicow called Club 70. It's hopping right now, with people spilling into the street. Pull into the parking lot on the south side. I'll send Veep to meet you there."

"Atmospherics?"

"Good. Everyone here is a squatter, and there sure as shit aren't any phone lines. Nobody's going to interfere. You keep it at least half-way quiet, and we can be in and out without trouble."

"Okay, give us thirty and I'll call—" He interrupted me. "Break, break, Pike, another vehicle just rolled up. Two men exited. They aren't dressed like the squatters here, and nobody in this place could afford a car."

I waited for a moment, and he came back on. "The landing guard just came outside and talked to them, then they went in. The vehicle's staged just outside the courtyard. It's a van. I think they're packing up to leave."

Crap. "Okay. We're rolling. I'll radio when we leave the parking lot. It's about five minutes to you. Keep eyes on, then start Veep moving to linkup when I call."

64

★★★

The weasel-eyed man set the passport on the dresser and picked up Mikhail's cell phone. He nodded to the obese one and they left the room. Mikhail knew why. They were going to analyze it first, then build a list of questions off what they found.

Mikhail spent the next ten minutes looking for something he could exploit, searching the bed frame for a rusted bolt or gap, examining each link of the handcuff, and testing whether he could remove his hand. His efforts ended with him ripping his skin enough to draw blood, but the bones of his hands prevented further movement.

He was considering shattering them with the frame of the bed, turning his hand to jelly, when the door opened again. This time, the fat man held a roll of duct tape, and Weasel-Eyes was carrying a satchel. He said, "Interesting mix of information on that cell phone, but nothing on Simon's location."

He opened the satchel, and Mikhail saw several syringes, full of liquid. The man nodded to his partner, and the fat man stripped out several lengths of duct tape, draping them onto the dresser. Mikhail outwardly showed fear, but felt some hope.

Please let me out of the handcuffs.

The weasel placed a wooden chair in the center of the room, withdrew a Makarov pistol, and centered it on Mikhail. Fatman released Mikhail from the handcuffs and sat him in the chair, saying, "The procedures we're going to do don't work well with you chained." He smiled and said, "The metal could become a threat to your life, and we can't have that. Hold your wrists out."

Mikhail did so, absolutely not resisting. He put his hands together as if he were praying, palms facing each other, fingers extended out.

The man strapped the duct tape around Mikhail's wrists. Mikhail remained still to ensure that none of the folds tucked under, leaving the wrapping pure, and he succeeded. Now he had an out.

Duct tape was an effective restraint that had been used on many, many terrorist victims. In Israel, they'd once found an operative wrapped in duct tape and shot in the back of the head. The Mossad had set out to defeat the restraint. To give a man some ability to escape. After some research, they'd found a way. When wrapped around the arms at the wrist, with the hands together, it could be broken as easily as the captor tearing the strip of tape to perform the wrap. The key was that there could be no folds, no underwraps or contortions in the binding. If someone wrapped the arms leaving the edges clean, as if they were simply wrapping the tape back onto the roll, it could be torn using leverage.

Mikhail had been forced to practice the escape over and over, hating it at the time, but now silently thanking his instructors.

The satchel man showed Mikhail the syringes and said, "I would like to use these right from the beginning, but unfortunately, it has a tendency to fry your brain. Once I have the information, I have no capability to go back. I'll get what you know, but I have to ask the right questions, and I'm not even sure what they are at this point, which leaves me in a quandary. I *must* have Simon. Failure here will bring me the same fate I'm bringing you."

Mikhail started to say something, and the man held out his hand. "No. Don't bother. I have done this many times. You can tell me all you know freely, but I can't trust it. You know that. I have to be sure."

I gave orders on the fly, which would seem to be risky, but really wasn't that much of an issue, because this wasn't a complex operation.

Our primary problem was the guard on the first floor. We needed to eliminate him before he could alert the others in the apartment. If we did that, we could initiate the assault with Retro's sniper shot, overwhelm them with violence of action, and capture Mikhail alive. Although that was truly a side note.

If he chose to fight, he'd be dead. Simple as that.

I said, "Aaron, Knuckles and I will assault. Jennifer drives for exfil. Shoshana provides rear security. I'll go in singleton, taking out the man on the landing. Once he's down, we'll flow to the third floor." I looked at Shoshana. "You come in with them, and remain behind on the landing."

She said, "I should go in first."

I started to snap at her but she interrupted me, saying, "You won't get within five feet of that landing before the guard calls you in. Even if you kill him, the damage will be done. I can reach him without that. I'm no threat. He'll think I belong there."

What she said made perfect sense, on the surface. I said, "You sure?"

She knew what I was asking. She said, "Yes, Nephilim. I'm sure. I *know* who I am. I'm no different than you."

I didn't like the sound of that. I asked, "And? What's that mean?"

"And you take a life only for the good. I have no problem killing here."

Whew. "Okay, but you're not coming up with us. I need someone on the landing, and I'm not swapping out Aaron for you again."

"You're just scared of me."

I nodded and said, "Yeah, yeah I am."

That brought a smile. I turned back to the group and said, "The apartment is the farthest to the west. Once Shoshana's got her man down, we'll move up the stairs and stack on it. I'll call Retro, and when we hear the shot, we'll breach. Knuckles, you got the Bam-Bam. Hostile force ROE. You see anyone besides Mikhail, take them out."

Knuckles said, "And Mikhail?"

"You see him and he presents a threat, kill him too."

As I finished my sentence, Jennifer pulled into the small parking lot adjacent to Club 70, threading her way to the back. The club entrance on Walicow Street was crowded with young men and women either waiting to enter, or just hanging out, drinking beer and smoking cigarettes. She parked in the corner where the club building met a wall and I said, "Stand by here. Listen close on the radio. When I call, you come running. Drive right into the courtyard and stage nose-out for exfil."

Knuckles said, "There's Veep."

I glanced toward the club entrance and saw Nicholas Seacrest threading through the cars, a lit cigarette between his lips. I said, "Break out his pack."

Knuckles slid a duffel bag forward, saying, "All in there."

I pulled open the side door of the van and said, "Your dad know you smoke?"

Veep smiled and said, "Just bummed it from a guy who asked me a question. Blending in."

I said, "You speak Polish?"

"Uhh . . . no. That's why I bummed the cigarette."

"Some blending." He looked embarrassed, then realized I was just ribbing him. I slid the bag forward and said, "You got the Punisher in here for Retro and a 300 for you. How long will it take you to get back?"

"No longer than four minutes. We found a stairwell that leads right to the roof. The only climbing is into a window on the back side of the building."

"Then get going. You call set, and it's showtime."

65

★★★

Ignoring the command to remain silent, trying to buy time, Mikhail said, "I have no idea where Simon is. We do business occasionally. He asked me to make this purchase, and I agreed."

Weasel-Eyes turned to the side of the dresser and picked up the briefcase. He flipped open the latches, then turned it around, facing Mikhail. "Yes, I'm sure that's true. You agreed to buy a deadly amount of radioactive waste just because he asked you to, and you have no idea what it's for or how to get it to him."

Mikhail said, "I was supposed to pass it to another man, tomorrow. He'll know where Simon's located."

The man held up a finger, saying, "Unfortunately, I don't believe you. We'll have to start with the old methods. And they can be brutal."

He sat the briefcase down and pulled out a long, thin filleting knife. The fat man placed a digital recorder on the dresser, turning it on. The weasel with the knife said, "I ordinarily ask a couple of questions first, to establish a baseline, but after seeing your passport, I'm fairly sure that would be worthless."

He cut the buttons off Mikhail's shirt, popping them slowly, one after another. He was halfway down when a muted crack split the air.

We waited for what seemed like an eternity, me looking out the window every five seconds to see if anyone was paying attention to us. They were not. Finally, Retro came on. "I'm set. Target acquired. Only one in the scope right now."

"And the guy on the landing?"

"Still there."

I looked at Shoshana and she nodded. I said, "We're rolling."

Aaron slid open the door. Knuckles grabbed our own duffel bag and stepped out. Shoshana and I followed. We reached the crowd and Shoshana slid her hand into mine. Just another couple of folks headed to the disco.

We passed through the crowd without incident, then crossed the street, getting back into the darkness, all the lamps either shattered or burned out. Two blocks down and we were at the entrance to the courtyard, the van from the two unknowns blocking the view of any-one watching from the street.

Knuckles bent down and began handing out our weapons. Shoshana took a suppressed Glock 27, and the rest of us got short-barreled, integrally suppressed assault rifles. Built by Primary Weapon Systems on the AR platform and chambered in subsonic .300 Black-out, they were an overmatch for whatever firepower the men upstairs had. In combat, there was no such thing as a "fair" fight.

I called Retro. "We're at our last covered position. Target still in-side the landing?"

"Roger."

I said, "You got thermals on him?"

"Veep does. I'm on the scope."

"Veep, Shoshana's about to commit. Give me a rundown."

"Roger that."

I looked at Shoshana and said, "Showtime."

She chambered a round, and the dark angel fluttered awake. Aaron grabbed her arm and said, "No crazy shit. Just put him down."

She smiled, looking feral, and said, "Okay. For you."

She disappeared around the corner and he said, "She'll do as she's told." But he didn't look convinced.

Veep came on. "Got her. No movement from the target."

I waited, convinced I was going to hear some primal scream as Shoshana killed him with her teeth. Instead, Veep said, "Target down. I say again, target down."

We rounded the corner at a trot, running right up to the landing and entering the foyer. Shoshana was over the body, searching him. She looked up, a childlike innocence on her face, wanting approval. Truth be told—with her standing over the steaming carcass of a man she'd just killed—it was more terrifying than seeing the dark angel.

I whispered, "Good work. Stand by right here. Nobody comes in behind us."

She nodded, and we went up the stairs two at a time. We hit the third floor, got our bearings, then began tracking west. We reached the apartment door, me on one side, Aaron and Knuckles on the other, Knuckles holding a small battering ram we called a Bam Bam. I clicked my radio twice.

Veep said, "I copy I have control. Standby. Five . . . four . . . three . . . two . . . one."

On the utterance of *one*, a sound like a bullwhip cracking split the air, and Knuckles swung the battering ram with both hands, shattering the door inward. He flattened against the wall, and we flowed into the room. I saw an older man wearing a fedora standing over the body of someone in a small kitchen, shouting hysterically. I shot him in the face.

I cleared my sector and heard Aaron's weapon cycle, hitting a man attempting to hide behind a ratty chair, his head flying back and a small pocket pistol clattering to the floor. Knuckles stacked on a door and I ran up behind him, Aaron keeping his weapon focused on the kitchen.

Knuckles kicked in the door, and we found a bathroom, too small to hide anyone. For the first time, I heard gunfire that wasn't suppressed. Someone else was shooting.

Aaron returned fire, then slammed back into the entryway, seeking cover behind the brick and saying, "Back room. Off the kitchen."

We slid down our wall, seeing the rounds slap into the top of the stove. I said, "Hi-low." I took a knee, and then Knuckles squeezed my shoulder. We both turned the corner, firing controlled pairs into the doorway."

66
★★★

The weasel-eyed man heard the snap, sounding like a firecracker, then screaming from outside the bedroom from someone losing control. The fat man loosened his hold on Mikhail's shoulders, and then they heard the apartment doorjamb splinter, followed by footsteps pounding in. The fat man ran to the door and peeked out, then took a knee, pulling out his pistol and shooting into the kitchen, shouting, "We're under attack!"

The weasel turned to the door, drawing his own weapon, and Mikhail went to work.

He broke the palm-to-palm hold he'd been maintaining, twisting his right hand over his left, forming an X with his hands and arms, and putting significant tension on the tape. He slammed his hands into his chest, pulling outward, and the top part of the tape split a quarter of an inch. He threw his hands out again, then repeated the procedure. The tear grew larger, like a dam with a hole in it, the water flowing out.

The weasel caught the movement and turned back to him. Mikhail saw him raising his pistol and repeated his attempts a third time, and the top part of the binding split through.

Mikhail leapt out of the chair, ripping his hands free and hammering the weasel with his shoulder, knocking him to the ground. The fat man turned from the door, and Mikhail saw his head explode, a round hitting the rear of his skull and exiting from the top of his forehead, the blast showering Mikhail in brain matter.

The body collapsed forward, the hand with the pistol outstretched.

Mikhail grabbed it, then jammed the barrel into the weasel's temple and pulled the trigger.

He heard movement outside the door and slammed it closed, then fired twice more through it, the weapon locking open. He grabbed the weasel's gun and punched bullets through the door again, drawing a fusillade of suppressed fire in return.

He knew what was coming. They were planning an assault, and by the skill with which they'd killed the entire Russian cell, he knew it wouldn't be a ten-minute conference full of dithering. He had seconds.

He snatched his passport and wallet off the dresser and fired two more rounds through the door, giving them pause. He grabbed the briefcase of Cesium and smashed the window over the bed. He crawled out onto the fire escape, gingerly placing his feet onto the rusted steel. It held.

He slid forward, and the bolts affixing the old metal to the concrete wall let go, plummeting half the fire escape toward the earth. He felt the fall and desperately held on, dropping the briefcase and pistol so he could clutch the rails in a vicelike grip. The stairs continued to drop, then hit the platform below, jarring his hold. He was thrown forward, and the second-story rails ripped out of the wall as well, a domino effect bouncing him down the platform, causing him to roll inexorably into space.

He pitched over the side, grabbing the bottom rung of the platform with his hands, the briefcase tumbling into space. He hung for a moment, the bolts loosening and groaning. He glanced down and saw he was about fourteen feet off the ground.

He let go, hitting the concrete hard and rolling. He looked up and saw a man staring out the window, searching for him.

He grabbed the briefcase, stood to run, and saw movement out of the corner of his eye. He recognized the threat, and felt more fear than he had inside the room, handcuffed with a knife at his breast.

It was the devil.

Shoshana was rounding the corner, and she was bringing death with her.

Shoshana heard the crack of the sniper rifle and crouched in the doorway, wanting to join the fight, but doing her duty. The radio came alive with calls, and she recognized that they'd achieved surprise. Mikhail would be dead, or facing her in a van soon. She heard unsuppressed gunfire, meaning the men in the room were fighting back, and considered running up the stairs.

She did not.

The calls came, fast and furious, and she could almost track the movement of the team: Aaron pinned down, Pike suppressing a doorway, fire coming back, then a final assault.

Then quiet. No jackpot call, but then again, no calls of wounded. She waited, letting them do their work. Then she heard, "Carrie, Carrie, this is Pike. Got a squirter."

She was electrified at the words. She said, "This is Carrie. Send it."

"It's Mikhail. He's escaped out the back, off a fire escape. He's just around the corner."

She press-checked her pistol and took off out of the alcove, saying, "What's my mission? What can I do?"

And heard exactly what she wanted.

"Kill him."

She ran up the street, seeing the crowds still in place in front of Club 70. She turned the corner and saw Mikhail on his knees, a briefcase next to him, dazed by his fall. He saw her coming and leapt up, grabbing the briefcase and running to the street right in front of her. She took a knee and settled the front site post, squeezing off a round.

She felt the recoil, then saw him fall. She stood, and he did too, holding the side of his head. She saw the terror on his face, and he sprinted into the crowds. She raised the pistol, but held off the shot.

She followed, the blood lust raging. She watched him barrel his way to the entrance, and she was there thirty seconds later. She tried to bull her way through, and was stopped by a man already angry about Mikhail's pushing. She raised her Glock and snarled, "Get the fuck out of my way."

The Polish millennials parted like the Red Sea.

She entered the club, blasted by the music and the cloying, claustrophobic mass of people. She pushed through the first layer and saw the writhing bodies on the dance floor, along with the three-deep layer at the bar. She wanted to continue the search, knowing her enemy was cowering within, but none in the club were looking askance, as if something weird had just passed by.

Unlike the way they were looking at her.

With her pistol out, the people behind her were pointing and talking. It was only a matter of time.

The professional in her defeated the dark angel.

She retreated.

67

★★★

Kurt Hale saw George Wolffe poke his head in the door. "Sir, we gotta go. Meeting in forty minutes, and rush hour is still going on."

Kurt held up his finger, talking into a headset, saying, "So he got away?"

Pike said, "Yes, sir. He did. To make matters worse, the men we killed are Russian. I think they were trying to stop him. Putin must know that Simon is behind what's going on, and our assault was a rescue for him. If we'd have sat back, we'd have let them destroy the plan."

"How do you know?"

"During SSE we found duct tape, handcuffs with blood on them, and syringes with some type of drug in them. Mikhail was being held against his will for interrogation. Our assault gave him the chance to escape."

Kurt cursed under his breath, then said, "That's not something I can bring to higher. Where do we stand?"

"One of the men we searched had two smartphones. We think one of them is Mikhail's. We just don't know which one, but if we can neck it down, we might be able to get something off it."

"Okay, good. We'll take a look. Let Taskforce intel drain both phones. They'll figure it out."

Pike said, "Already done."

"What's the status of the apartment?"

Pike knew what he was asking. "We sterilized it, but had to leave the bodies. If they're found it'll look like a gangland hit, without any indication they're Russian. It was the best we could do."

"And you got in and out clean?"

"Yes. Well, Shoshana spiked a bit at the club across the street, chasing Mikhail, but we got out clean. She had the presence of mind to simply keep going, away from our operation. We picked her up on the street a mile away from the target. No police interference."

"Okay. At least that's something."

"What's my next move with the team? Are we still okay to operate?"

Kurt rubbed his face and said, "Yeah, for whatever good that will do."

Pike said, "Hey, sir, that assault was a correct call. We're under pressure and we had to execute. It didn't work out, but if I had to do it again, I'd do it."

Kurt said nothing, then heard Pike ask, "Sir?"

"I hear you, Pike. I do. It was my call, and for the record, you were right. We should have developed the target. If we had, Mikhail would be dead."

Kurt was surprised at the vociferous response. "*Fuck* that. You know how these operations go. Sometimes you make the right call, sometimes you don't. Don't let the stakes here become a judgment on your decision-making."

Remembering his position, Kurt said, "Pike, I wasn't asking for forgiveness. Just that I should have listened to you. Look, I have to go to a meeting with the president. I'll get you the information from the phone as soon as I can. I expect you to continue the hunt, but pull off the Israelis. They're done. I can't report their actions without political fallout."

Pike said, "Sir, I can't do that. I need them on this."

"Pike, I can't brief the president on this disaster *and* have Mossad involved."

"Sir, it's not a disaster. Just a setback. Look, if we move anywhere else, I'll leave them here in Warsaw. I won't cut them free, but I'll only use them if I have to, as a reserve. Will that work? The mission is what's important here. We can deal with the fallout later, but if we miss on this, it won't matter."

Hearing Pike's argument, Kurt remembered that trust was the cornerstone of Taskforce existence, and clearly Pike trusted the Israeli component of his team. As for him, Kurt had learned long ago to trust the man on the ground.

"Okay, Pike. That'll work. I'll call when I have something."

He heard "Call soon, because Shoshana wants to kill someone."

He hung up, not wanting to learn if that was just a joke.

George said, "What happened?"

"They missed. My call, but it went bad."

"And?"

"And there's still a team out there trying to spark a war."

George nodded, the information enough. He said, "We gotta go. We're going to be late."

Kurt stood and put on what he had taken to calling his White House jacket, saying, "This isn't going to go well."

They received their badges, the staff inside the West Wing unusually quiet and subdued. They went past the secretary's gatekeeping position without a second glance, the woman known to all politicos as the Dragon Lady waving them forward, and entered the Oval Office.

Alexander Palmer was more agitated than Kurt had ever seen, flipping pages in a folder as if he were searching for a truth that wasn't being presented. Mark Oglethorpe, the secretary of defense, was leaning on a table doing the same thing, poring over intel reports. And the president himself was pacing back and forth in front of the window, as if he were deciding what to believe.

It didn't look good.

Kurt coughed, getting their attention. President Hannister snapped his head up from the window and said, "Tell me you stopped whatever they had planned, because we're looking at World War Three without it."

Kurt drew himself up, ready for the punishment. He said, "No, sir. We missed. Mikhail and Simon are still on the loose." He laid out what he knew, ending with, "The best we can hope for is that the assault scared them into quitting."

Nobody in the room said a word. President Hannister stared at the ceiling for a moment, then said, "So they're still on the hunt?"

"Most likely, sir."

Palmer thumped his fist and said, "Shit. We should have never authorized that operation. The press is going to have a field day if they learn we could have stopped this and didn't."

Kurt heard the words and had had enough. He'd lived in the world of politics before, but in the last five days he'd been immersed in it, like a man dropped into a septic tank. He advanced on Palmer and saw him recoil.

He got within inches of Palmer's face and said, "This isn't about optics, but like every other political fuck in this country, you can't separate the two. If Pike had done *nothing*, Mikhail might still be on the loose, and yet you look for someone else to blame to protect yourself from the nightly news."

President Hannister interrupted, saying, "Hey, this isn't helping. Back off, Kurt. Don't blame him for the tension. Things have taken a turn for the worse."

Kurt stepped back and said, "What's happening now?"

The SECDEF said, "Russia's begun to flex. They've split the border between Poland and Lithuania, building a land bridge to Kaliningrad. Poland and Lithuania, of course, are going crazy—as is NATO, because they're both members. Russia is saying they need a land bridge to Kaliningrad because of our 'provocation' in breaking the treaties NATO had against staging forces on their border. Meaning the forces picking the guts out of Air Force One that they shot down."

Hannister said, "Bottom line is, it's getting out of our control. We're about to be at war whether we like it or not. I can restrain US forces, but I can't do anything with Lithuania and Poland. They flip out, and it'll invoke Article 5 of NATO. We'll be at war."

Kurt said, "Tell them to back off. Jesus Christ, Mikhail escaped, but he did so from *Russian* intelligence. Putin *knows* what's going on. He knows that Simon is driving this forward. Am I the only one that sees this? Call him. Get him to stop."

"Yeah, we all agree on that, with one exception: We think the Belarus strike was under his orders, and then he lost control. He can't have that come out. He can't say it was all a crazy man if Simon's on the loose, because Simon might appear and say it was all *Putin's* doing."

Kurt said, "Are you fucking kidding me? The fate of the world has devolved into a seventh-grade he-said, she-said tiff?"

Palmer said, "Unfortunately, yes. That's pretty much what it is."

Kurt looked at Hannister and said, "Call him. Tell him you understand. Tell him you know what happened, and it isn't worth a war. He doesn't think it is, or he wouldn't be hunting Mikhail. He *knows* what's going on."

The SECDEF said, "He won't listen. He won't back down. He *will not* admit anything with Belarus, even if it means going to war. Remember whom we're talking about here. He doesn't answer to his people."

The room remained quiet for a moment, everyone realizing the truth of the statement. Finally, Kurt said, "What do we do from here? What do you want from me?"

Hannister turned from the window and said, "I want you to find Mikhail. I want you to stop that attack. Buy me some time."

Kurt started to say something, but Hannister cut him off. "I'm not done. Stop that attack, and then find me Simon. Get him in our hands. Give me something to use against Putin."

Kurt nodded, saying nothing.

"You can do that, right? Tell me you can. President Warren created the Taskforce. He trusted you. Tell me that trust wasn't misplaced."

Kurt realized the president of the United States was waiting on him to say only one thing. Wanting to hear nothing but confidence.

He said, "Yes, sir. I can do that."

But he didn't believe it.

68

★★★

Working with the dim light of a candle, Kirill peeled off the makeshift bandage affixed to Mikhail's ear, saying, "What the hell happened?"

Mikhail flinched at the touch, then kept his head still. "I got shot, okay? I got fucking shot."

Oleg said, "Shot how? What's going on?"

Knowing he could in no way intimate that the Russian apparatus was against what he was about to order the Night Wolves to execute, he said, "A disagreement with the seller of your product. I handled it, but it wasn't pretty."

His flight from the historical Jewish Ghetto was still fresh in his mind, and he knew he'd narrowly escaped by the sheer luck of the club being nearby. He'd raced through the throngs of dancers, searching for a way out, and had stumbled into a storeroom. He'd run to the back and crouched down, finally noticing blood on his right shoulder.

He'd remained, hiding in the corner, the fear of Shoshana actually getting her hands on him more terrifying than anything he'd faced in the room with the Russians.

After ten minutes, he'd begun to believe that Shoshana had given up. He'd cautiously explored the storeroom and found a bathroom. He looked in the mirror and saw that Shoshana had shot off his right ear, the lower portion simply gone, nothing but yellow, bloody gristle right below the ear canal. One inch to the left, and he'd have been dead.

He'd taken a wad of hand towels and pressed it to the wound, letting the clotting blend with the paper like a giant shaving nick. When he had the bleeding under control, he'd spilled out of Club 70 through a back door, running into the night.

He'd eventually slowed, getting lost in the concrete and steel of Warsaw, mildly surprised to realize that he still held the briefcase. He'd thought about his next move, the most urgent being to get away from the demon Shoshana no matter what it took, his primordial brain retreating to a fight or flight response. Once he caught his breath, out of danger, he reconsidered his options, and realized they were very few.

He now had not only Shoshana—attached to some American agency—chasing him, but he had the Russians as well. Putin was on the hunt to stop Simon, and Putin now knew who he was, and his ferocious bloodlust rivaled Shoshana's. As Simon had learned once before.

He'd decided that the only course available was to continue the mission. If he ran now, he'd be running for the rest of his life, but if the plan succeeded, he just might be able to survive.

He'd begun walking east, sticking to the shadows. He crossed the river, entering the suburb of Praga, the buildings becoming seedy and worn. He reached a narrow cross street named Brzeska and turned south, entering a ghettolike apartment area. He traced the addresses, warily keeping his eye on a pack of youths sitting on some steps. When he passed them, they rose and began to follow him.

He reached the end of the street, the youths still behind him, and realized he'd passed the apartment the Night Wolves were holed up in. He wasn't going to find it with a memorized address alone. He abruptly turned, confronting the men behind him. In English he said, "Can I borrow your cell phone?"

Taken aback, the leader said something in Polish, pointing at the briefcase. Mikhail said, "I don't speak Polish." He pointed at his ear, and they finally noticed the bandage and blood in the darkness. He held his hand to his other ear and said, "Phone."

Remarkably, the teenager handed him one. Keeping his eye on the group, Mikhail dialed and spoke. In short order, he saw a man coming out of a building a block away. The man waved, and Mikhail recognized Kirill. Into the phone, he said, "I see him," then hung up, handed the cell back, and speed-walked up the street the way he had come.

Now relatively safe, Mikhail had begun to calm down and reassess. He needed to get another cell phone, and he definitely needed to talk to Simon about what had occurred, but first things first: He wanted a proper bandage on his wound.

Pulling off the final piece of paper towel from Mikhail's damaged ear, Kirill said, "Is this disagreement going to cause us problems? Are you being chased?"

Remembering the shootout, Mikhail said, "No. The men I fought with look worse than me, I promise."

Kirill began to apply a real bandage, asking, "Is that briefcase the product?"

"Yes. Do you have explosives and weapons?"

"Explosives, yes, but we don't have any weapons. We go back for that tonight."

"You don't have guns? How are you getting weapons in Poland? They hate your ass here."

Kirill scoffed and said, "Yeah, they 'hate us,' but the old Soviet black market systems are still in place. Four blocks from here is the Bazar Rozyckiego. A flea market that sells everything. Out front are T-shirts. In back is whatever we need."

"You trust it?"

"Yes, because it survived in the old Soviet system. Today, it's even easier. In the new world, they've fallen on hard times and are willing to deal. The black market isn't as big now, and because of it, they don't care about nationality. Only money."

Mikhail nodded and said, "We need to talk about the target. How we're going to do it."

Oleg said, "Yeah. It's about time. We don't even know what the target is."

"It's really just like your mission in Belarus. Another airbase, this time in Lask."

"We're setting that bomb off on a Polish airbase?"

"Yes, but just like in Belarus, the target is different. The Americans have a squadron of A-10 close air support aircraft there. You will penetrate the base, find them, then emplace the bomb. Once it's on the ground, set the timer for however long you need to escape, and leave. It's actually easier, because you won't be in direct combat. You'll be gone before it goes off."

"How are we going to penetrate? In Belarus, we pretended to be Russian military. That worked because we *are* Russian. There's no way we can pretend to be American. Or Polish."

"I know, but there's someone who is going to help us. An American. Hand me your phone. I need to contact Simon. He has the information I need."

Kirill did, saying, "An American is going to get us on the base? Why?"

Dialing the phone, Mikhail said, "Because you're going to kidnap his family tomorrow."

69

Amy Tatum was stymied yet again in her attempts to get the hot water working in her apartment. The provider who'd shown up spoke no English and, after a discussion that went nowhere, had left, taking his equipment bag with him.

She went back into the bathroom and looked at the plywood that he'd haphazardly screwed into the wall, his makeshift temporary fix after creating a hole about four feet square. He'd done the same thing on the outside wall, but had left that open, the bricks piled up on the short patch of grass outside.

Frustrating, but there was nothing she could do about it. At least it wasn't wintertime, because they'd end up freezing in the apartment. She picked at the plywood, seeing it wasn't even properly attached, and began to regret following her husband here.

It was nothing like Germany, where the population was used to Americans and actually seemed to enjoy their presence. She knew when she'd married her husband that it would entail foreign assignments, but this was sliding into "a bit much" territory. The fantasy of seeing the world was taking a backseat to getting some basic services.

Unlike just about every other American military member in Poland, her husband had been permanently detailed here. A "PCS" move, in military jargon. The pilots her husband protected came and went on rotation, but her husband— the commander of a US Air Force base security unit—had been assigned for a year. They'd told him it was an unaccompanied tour, but he could bring his wife if he was willing to pay for her moving expenses out of pocket. He had, and now she was regretting it.

It wasn't like her last home, where there were multiple American families she could bond with, learning how to operate in a new society and having a small bubble to fall within when she was overwhelmed. None of the other married men in her husband's command had brought their spouses, and they all lived in an apartment complex in Lask, forty minutes away. She had nothing to anchor against, and her fledgling attempts at learning German at their previous duty station helped not a whit here.

But it was only for a year, and she was already four months into it.

She heard the doorbell to their small apartment ring, and thought, *What now?*

She went to the door and looked out the peephole. She saw two men, both rough, but not alarmingly so. She thought about her hot water and opened the door. She said, "Can I help you?"

The first showed a pistol in his waistband. The second, in heavily accented English, said, "Yes. You can."

She stumbled backward, her hand to her mouth, and both men entered. One stood at the door, waving down the street. The other said, "My name is Mikhail, and I know this is scary, but we mean you no harm."

Three other men entered the small apartment, all staring at her. She broke for the bedroom, but the man called Mikhail had expected this and cut her off. She tried to scream, and he clamped a hand over her mouth, saying, "*Shhhh*. Stop it. We aren't going to hurt you. If I remove my hand, will you remain quiet?"

She nodded.

When his hand dropped away, she said, "What do you want? We don't have any money." She was petrified about the answer, her mind conjuring horrific fantasies. His answer confused her.

"Simple, really. We want you to call your husband."

70

★ ★ ★

It was after eleven A.M. before we managed to leave Warsaw, but at least we were moving forward instead of sitting around our hotel room waiting. It took time, as all counterterrorism analysis did, but the Taskforce had finally completed their inspection of the phones and had necked down what they believed was Mikhail's handset, finding a couple of promising leads: first, a document detailing the military record of a United States Air Force captain named Devon Tatum. We had no idea why it was on the phone, but in the research, they'd found that he was currently the base security commander for the US squadron at the airbase in Lask, Poland. The same airfield that housed all US airpower in the current standoff with Russia.

In my mind, it wasn't too hard to figure out why: That bastard had decided to help the Russians.

The second lead was the cell number that had sent the document. Metadata analysis had provided a general map of its movements, and it mirrored what we knew of Simon Migunov. To cap it off, the phone was currently located in Vienna, Austria—the last place Simon had stated he was going.

Even with all the might of the Taskforce, the analysts could only get a general location of Simon's handset, with nowhere near the fidelity required for an interdiction. They'd done their best to locate him through entry control points and hotel databases, but had come up empty—meaning he was using an alias. Kurt had asked if I could run split-team ops—wanting to use the ISR package inside the Rock

Star bird just like we'd done in Warsaw, and I'd said of course—if I could use the Israelis.

He'd relented, saying I had probably planned the problem to get the Israelis back into action, and I'd sent Knuckles and Retro to Vienna with a twofold mission: one, neck down the location of the phone, and two, interface with the FBI tactical team that was currently spinning its wheels in Vienna, giving them the information for arrest.

Knuckles had worked with the FBI on a previous mission, so he was the natural choice—although that mission had ended with him wounded and most of the FBI team dead—and Retro was the best on my team working with technology. He'd been the one who'd pinpointed Mikhail's phone in Warsaw, and he'd jumped at the chance to do the same in Vienna.

While they were spooling up to leave, we'd had to plan just what the hell we were going to do about Captain Tatum. The easiest choice would have been to simply order his chain of command to detain him, but Kurt and I both knew that was fraught with risk. For one, it would be damn near impossible to wade through the inertia of the chain of command without him being alerted. Questions would be asked, resistance would be presented, and, in the end, he wouldn't be arrested simply because we'd found his data on a phone. We didn't know what he had planned, or how close he was to executing. If he got wind of the inquiry and fled, we'd lose our only lead.

The second problem was compounded by the first: The only way to guarantee his detention by his chain of command or host-nation forces would be to spell out our fears—and that alone might inflame an already tense situation. If word spread that we were attempting to interdict a Russian team intent on sabatoge, it might lead to rumors of Russian bogeymen being found everywhere—especially after the "spontaneous uprising" in Crimea had turned out to be interspersed with Russian Spetsnaz commandos—which might be enough of a catalyst for exactly what we were trying to prevent: Poland going nuts against Russia.

Working through the problem on a conference call with the Taskforce principals, Kurt had said, "We're wasting time pole-vaulting over mouse turds. Just drive down there and get him. How far is it from Warsaw?"

I said, "It's only about two hours. That's not the problem. How can I access the base? I'm a civilian. The Polish police on the gate will never let me in, and if you start coordinating with the American forces on the base, we're back at square one by alerting him. He's the one that will do the coordination. And before anyone mentions it, sitting outside hoping he leaves isn't a recipe for success."

Kurt said, "All we need is a reason. Some plausible deniability."

Kerry Bostwick, the D/CIA, said, "I can help there. The CIA is debating putting some UAVs on that airbase. We did a site survey a week ago, and it would be easy to plan a 'follow-up.' You know, maybe check out the security situation."

I said, "That would be perfect. I'd have to coordinate with the base security commander. You got someone on the airfield right now that can meet me?"

"Uhh . . . no. They're all forward, getting their jihad on for US intelligence."

And then I remembered. "That's right! You jerked Brett Thorpe off my team as soon as the president ordered the Taskforce stand-down."

"Where is he?" Kurt asked.

"Offhand, I don't know," said Kerry, "but he's either in Poland or Ukraine. Either way, I can get him to Lask before Pike arrives. He's definitely less than two hours away by plane."

I said, "Give him my cell. We're rolling."

With Aaron's knowledge, it took a little under two hours to reach the road leading to the Lask airbase. Well, that and the fact that he drove like a lunatic. Apparently, there weren't a lot of police in the

Polish countryside, and I found myself with both hands on the steering wheel just trying to keep up with his vehicle.

When he exited the S8 expressway, he pulled over, letting me take the lead. I drove about two miles down a battered piece of asphalt and saw a Mercedes van. Standing next to it was an African American fireplug of muscle with a decidedly irritated expression.

Brett Thorpe, the man we called Blood.

I pulled up next to him, rolling down the window. I said, "You need a lift? I doubt any Poles are going to help out a man with your demeanor."

He shook his head and said, "I swear, when they told me I was pulled from my assignment to help someone get on a military base, I knew immediately it was your sorry ass. You realize that I'm actually doing something important, right?"

I said, "Get in. Nothing is more important than what you're about to do."

71

★★★

Captain Devon Tatum hung up his cell, aggravated. His master sergeant saw the look on his face and said, "Trouble?"

"It's Amy. She's got a problem with the Polish plumbers and wants me to come home."

"You still working on the hot water issue?"

"Yeah, yeah." He rubbed his face and said, "I should have listened to you, Fitz, and come over here unaccompanied."

Master Sergeant Fitzgerald laughed and said, "I tried to warn you. Bringing your wife sounds like a good deal, but without the support infrastructure from big Air Force, it's always a pain in the ass."

"Yeah, not to mention the commute."

"Head on home. Nothing happening around here, anyway. I can handle the briefing tonight if you need me to."

Devon put on his cover and said, "No, that's okay. The last thing I need is someone asking why I'm helping my wife instead of attending a squadron update on base security. I'll be back before then. An hour or two max."

"Okay, sir. But if you need the time, take it. One less briefing you have to attend, and I'll get the pleasure of not listening to you bitch about cold showers."

Devon smiled and said, "I appreciate it. Call if anything comes up. I'll come straight back."

He pulled the keys to the duty sedan off the board and said, "This thing fixed now?"

"Yeah. Should be."

Devon said, "We'll see," and exited the Sprung temporary shelter, a marshmallow-colored cloth structure that had become synonymous with deployed American forces.

He drove down the flight line, past the hangars full of A-10 aircraft, reaching the US inner perimeter guard. He waved, and the man raised the drop bar, allowing him through. He reached the main outer gate, seeing two civilians at the visitors' center. One was short and black, the other tall, with crew-cut hair and a two-day growth of beard. Both were wearing civilian clothes.

Spooks.

He recognized the type, having seen them a few weeks ago during a site survey of his perimeter. He exited the main gate, driving to the S8 expressway and dialing his wife on his cell. He told her he was on the way, hating hearing the quaver in her voice.

He hung up and decided he'd fly her home. Not back to Germany, but home to Indiana and her parents. This was simply not working out.

Originally, bringing her had seemed like a great idea. Sure, they wouldn't have a US military base to shop on, and the military wouldn't supplement their income or pay for her to move, but it wasn't like they were going to China.

He'd even gone so far as to compromise on housing, once they'd seen the town of Lask, the closest village to the airbase. It had been industrial and small, so they'd settled on an apartment in Lodz, forty minutes away, finding a place within walking distance of a gigantic mall. An old Soviet manufacturing facility, it had been repurposed into a shopping area that would fit in any city in the United States. But it hadn't been enough.

The language barrier was the primary problem. He hadn't realized how much he had relied on the Air Force while in Germany for services like banking, telephone, cable television, power, and everything else.

Here, it required laborious phone calls until someone could be found to translate, then more laborious coordination once someone showed up at the apartment. And the strain was taking a toll on their marriage. While he saw his men each day, Amy spent the time holed up in the house by herself, which left him with the sneaking suspicion that Amy had called him home precisely because she was tired of being alone.

And that would only get worse.

Twenty minutes into the trip he saw a red warning light flash on his dash. The car was overheating.

What the hell? He'd discovered the sedan had a leaky radiator four days ago and had turned it in to the maintenance men, who'd then taken it to some Polish contractors. A jack-of-all trades sort of business that had been hired to repair everything from air conditioners to toilets, they'd worked on his sedan. Fitz had assured him it was repaired, but clearly it wasn't.

They'd probably just dumped in some radiator sealant and charged the US government the price of a new car.

He pulled over at a gas station, letting the engine cool and buying a gallon of distilled water. He called Amy and told her what had happened, and she seemed more upset at his delay than she was about the problem with the hot water. He sharply chastised her and hung up, feeling guilty as soon as he was done.

After forty-five minutes, he was back on the road, his "hour or two" detour home now stretching into at least three.

Twenty minutes more of driving, and he'd perfected his speech. He'd deal with the hot water issue first, then convince Amy to fly home. He knew she'd fight him, as it would be admitting failure, and she was strong willed. He exited the S8 and entered the outer perimeter of Lodz. He threaded down the streets, dodging cable trams and pedestrians until he wound through a traffic circle and snuck into a back parking lot, something he'd found after being frustrated by trying to locate street parking.

He locked the car and walked down a narrow alley to the front of his apartment building, a four-story monolith built in the industrial Soviet style. He'd found it intriguing when they'd first surveyed it—a bit of history they could tell their children about someday—but now saw it for what it was: a dilapidated slab of concrete that hadn't been built correctly to begin with, and was eroding with the passage of time.

He walked by a pile of bricks and realized it was from his own apartment. They'd actually split the wall to get access. He squatted down, seeing a gaping four-foot hole. He could see the light spilling out from the makeshift cover in his bathroom four feet away, the pipes and dust from forty years of communist rule in between him and the light.

It confirmed his decision to get Amy out of here. He could live with the less-than-stellar conditions, but there was no reason she had to.

He walked up to the front door and turned the knob. It was locked. *Another indicator.* If she'd taken to locking the door, she was afraid to even stay in the house. He pulled out his key, unlocked the door, and swung it wide, preparing to call out to his wife.

What he saw caused the shout to die in his throat.

Five rough-looking men staring at him with overt hostility. His wife was in a chair, one of the men standing next to her with a pistol to her head.

He stood in the open doorway in silence, unable to comprehend what he was seeing. The man next to his wife said, "Come inside, please."

He did so, closing the door robotically.

The man standing over his wife said, "My name is Mikhail, and I have a favor to ask of you. It will not be pleasant to you, which is why we are forced to use such drastic tactics."

Devon remained silent, staring into the eyes of his wife. Seeing the fear. Seeing the tears running down her face. Knowing he'd brought her here.

Mikhail snapped, "*Focus.* Focus on me."

Devon did.

"We need some information on the American squadron at Lask. You can give us that. We want you to get us into the base. All we want you to do is drive us around the perimeter. We'll film, and you'll drive. When we're done, you get your wife back and can scream to high heaven about what happened."

Still overwhelmed, Devon said nothing. He glanced around the room, seeing his coffee cup from that morning, his gym shorts on the floor, the magazines he'd promised to get rid of. All the things that caused friction in his marriage above and beyond the move. All now ridiculously small.

Mikhail said, "Hey! Pay attention. We're talking here."

Devon looked into his wife's eyes, and what he truly cared about came home. He said, "What do you want?"

"I just told you. We want on the base."

He turned to Mikhail and said, "I can't do that. Surely you understand. My entire purpose is base security."

Mikhail placed the pistol on a dresser and pulled out a knife. He held it to Amy's neck, causing her tears to flow and her breath to hitch. Devon crumbled.

"Just pictures? That's all?"

Mikhail said, "One lap. You go in, you drive a circuit, and you come home. After that, you can tell anyone you want that we were here. You get your life, and we get the information we need."

"Why? What do you want out of it?"

Mikhail said, "Don't be naïve. We're about to be at war. We don't want it, but you keep pushing. We have plans in place, and we need intelligence. That's all."

"But if you let us live, if you let us tell the authorities you were here, what good is it?"

"Can you alter the airbase? Can you alter the hangars and where they are? No. It's just some pictures. Don't sacrifice your family over this."

And Devon wanted to believe. Wanted to do whatever it took to save his wife, even as his instincts told him the man was lying.

He hesitated, then said, "Okay."

Mikhail withdrew the knife and pulled Amy out of the chair, pushing her to another man. He led her into the bathroom in the back and sat her on the toilet. Mikhail said, "Give me the keys to your car."

Thinking of the problems they would have, inadvertently helping them in their plot, he said, "My car has a radiator leak. If we take it, we're liable to break down on the airfield."

Mikhail scoffed and said, "Good try. No way are we going into an airbase without a recognized vehicle. Give me the keys."

Devon complied, saying, "It's the brown Ford. Four-door." Mikhail tossed the keys to another man, then said something in Russian. Devon said, "I need to call my work. Tell them I'm not coming back. They think I left because of some hot water problems."

Mikhail said, "No. That's not happening. Get in the bathroom."

Devon realized that his failure to check in might be a good thing, and Mikhail recognized the same thing. He said, "Hold up."

Devon paused. Mikhail said, "You call, on your phone, and I'll listen. You tell him whatever you need to, but you don't give any indication of what's happening. You understand?"

Devon nodded. Mikhail said, "If I think you've tipped them off, I'll gut your wife in front of you."

Whatever thoughts Devon had about alerting his command faded away.

Three minutes later, the phone call was done. Mikhail took Devon's cell phone, then shoved him into the bathroom with his wife, closing the door behind him.

Wiping tears from her eyes, Amy said, "What is this about?"

He hugged her and said, "I don't know. I honestly don't. I have the ability to get on base, and they want to use it. But they won't harm you. I promise."

She sniffled and said, "They're using me to get to you. You can't let that happen."

He looked at her, seeing the strength that had first attracted him to her and said, "Yes, I can."

72

★★★

Kirill watched Devon being led to the back, and waited until the door had closed before saying, "We need to discuss who's doing this mission."

Mikhail chuckled and said, "It isn't going to be me, of that you can be assured."

Kirill's eyes narrowed. He said, "Why not? Why should I risk my life if the Russian command is afraid? You work for President Putin, correct?"

Mikhail backpedaled swiftly, saying, "Don't get me wrong, it's not because I'm unwilling. I have to enable other operations that will leverage yours. In fact, I'm headed to Vienna today to do just that. Get the device out of our car and put it in his, and for God's sake, make sure those idiots don't tamper with the timing mechanism."

Kirill gave the order, still looking at Mikhail with distrust. When the men had left the room he said, "It will only take one man to accomplish this mission, but he needs to speak English, and we need to leave at least one English speaker here with the woman."

"And your point?"

"We only have two English speakers. Me and Oleg. I am fluent, but Oleg barely understands. He can order a meal, but he can't speak the language."

Mikhail nodded, thinking, *No way am I being drawn into this.*

He said, "You go with the device. Leave Oleg here with the woman. All he'll have to do is answer her calls for water. Leave her in the bathroom for the duration."

Kirill didn't look convinced. Mikhail said, "Hey, they're both going to die. If she gives Oleg any problems, he can kill her anytime after you leave. And once you're inside the perimeter, you can kill the American. Remember, all we need is for the bomb to go off. It doesn't even need to harm anyone. There's no reason to turn this into something greater."

Kirill said, "And yet you flee as if it is."

"You've seen what's happened. It's working perfectly. You're giving Putin exactly what he wants—the chance to devour NATO without being accused as the aggressor."

"Where is Simon? President Putin's supposed ally?"

"He's close. And watching. As is President Putin. Are you now second-guessing your commitment to Mother Russia?"

Kirill snapped, "No. Of course not, but I'm second-guessing *your* commitment."

Mikhail's trials of the last twenty-four hours flashed in his mind, the absurdity of what he was doing and the sacrifices he'd made to ensure the mission continued to a successful conclusion. Shoshana's visage bubbled up, and he felt a wave of unaccustomed fear slam into him.

He snapped out quickly, snatching Kirill's tattooed neck. To the right, Oleg jumped back, pulling out a pistol and aiming it at Mikhail's head. Bending Kirill over backward, Mikhail said, "You pull that trigger, you better not miss. Because I'll kill everyone in here."

Kirill gargled, and Oleg hesitated. Mikhail dug his fingers in and said, "Don't *ever* question my commitment. Make. This. Happen. Do you understand?"

Kirill nodded, and Mikhail dropped him on the floor. He looked at Oleg and said, "Save your energy for the enemy."

He backed toward the door, keeping his eyes on Oleg, then left, slamming it behind him.

Getting into the front gate of a foreign airbase proved a hell of a lot easier than I would have thought. But then again, I had the might of the CIA behind me.

I'd left the rest of my team on the cutout where we'd met Blood, and the two of us drove down the road leading to the base. Along the way, I'd had the enjoyment of listening to him bitch about being pulled off his primary assignment.

He'd said, "You know that the Russians have built a land bridge into the Kaliningrad Oblast? They've actually taken over NATO terrain? And you've got me here on some wild-goose chase?"

"Yeah. I know. But it's not a wild-goose chase."

He'd snorted, then remained silent for a moment. When he spoke again, it was with a conviction that belied his usual happy-go-lucky demeanor.

"Polish nationals have started firing mortars into Russian positions. They think they're defending their land, but they don't know what they're dealing with. It's small potatoes now, but it's growing. Russia has held off for the moment, but that won't last."

"I know. Trust me, I know. Everyone's looking for a spark, and I'm trying to prevent it."

He swung into the road leading to the front gate and said, "Pike, you know I'd follow you into hell and back, but you've just pulled me from the one thing that *may* prevent it. I can't provide the National Command Authority intelligence if I'm out here half stepping for you. I was on the border—in the fight. I've developed contacts in the breakaway Polish gangs trying to start the war."

I said, "There's a gang in play here that trumps anyone shooting a mortar."

And I told him what I knew. By the time we reached the gate, he'd become a believer.

He'd shown his badges, and after a brief phone conversation and a handwritten base-access pass, we'd gone through the gate, then had driven down the flight line, reaching the second circle of protection, guarded by Americans. He'd shown his badges again and said, "We need to speak to Captain Devon Tatum about force protection measures."

The guard radioed someone, then let us through, giving us directions to a temporary shelter.

We parked outside of a Sprung, one that looked the same as the ones used in Iraq or Afghanistan, and Brett had said, "What's your play here? If you think he's bad?"

I said, "Honestly, I don't know. Get him separated from his men, and then apply some pressure."

He opened the door with a grin, saying, "Glad to see your planning ability hasn't diminished."

We went inside, seeing a master sergeant named Fitzgerald behind a computer. He glanced up at our entrance, and I said, "Hey, we're with OGA, and we need to talk base security for a potential deployment of UAVs. Is Captain Tatum here?"

He squeezed his eyes shut like he didn't want the question, wondering what problems we were bringing, then said, "You just missed him. His wife called and he went home for some plumbing issues."

"Wife? Why is his wife here?"

Appearing wary, he said, "He's asking the same question, trust me. He just called and said he wouldn't be back on base tonight. Makes my life miserable because I've got to take the update brief tonight."

Trying for rapport, I said, "He's thrown you to the wolves because of some personal problem?"

He appraised both of us and said, "Yeah. You guys ex-military?"

I smiled and said, "Yep, and I've been involved in enough death-by-PowerPoint meetings to steer me clear of ever going back."

He laughed, relaxing, and said, "What can I help you with?"

We gave him our cover story, and he said, "Well, he'll be back tomorrow. Best I can do. If he was living with us, I'd say just drive on over, but he's forty minutes away, in Lodz."

He pronounced the town "Woodge," indicating he'd been here awhile.

Brett asked, "What time does he show up in the morning?"

I felt my phone vibrate, and saw it was Kurt. To Brett, I said, "Figure out a linkup. I have to take this."

I left him in the office and went outside.

73

★★★

Devon heard the shouted Russian and the scuffling of a fight through the door. Which meant they weren't focused on him or his wife. He knelt down to the plywood slapped over the hole in the bathroom wall and began to pull it, the wood popping in protest.

He stopped, looking for something to use for leverage.

He said, "Hand me your toothbrush."

Amy did, and he jammed the end underneath the wood, then pried out. The nail separated an infinitesimal amount. Holding the gap, he hissed, "Get me my toothbrush."

She did, and he jammed that one in as well, then began prying back and forth. He heard footsteps coming down the hall and stopped, turning around and hiding what he was doing with his body.

One of the Russians opened the door and said, "I am Kirill. It's time. Come with me."

Devon said, "What about my wife?"

"She stays. She'll be here when you get back."

He handed Devon the keys to the sedan and pointed toward the den. Devon turned around, kissed his wife, saying, "Be strong. This will be over soon."

She wiped a tear away and nodded.

Devon followed the Russian into the den. Before opening the door, Kirill showed him a pistol in his waistband, saying, "Do not, under any circumstances, attempt to escape or alert anyone. Or your wife will be the one to suffer."

Devon nodded, and they went to his car. He saw a briefcase in the backseat and asked, "What is that?"

"It's the camera I'm going to use."

"The gate might search it."

"For your wife's sake, I'd make sure that doesn't happen."

Devon started the sedan and began retracing his route back to the airbase in Lask, purposely using roads that would take longer than necessary to get out of the city. Eventually, he was forced to enter the expressway, and found himself doing a hundred kilometers an hour just to keep from getting run over. At this speed he would reach the base soon if he didn't come up with some plan to slow down.

And then the radiator warning light came on. Devon prayed that Kirill wouldn't notice, this time ignoring the warning, instead turning the air-conditioning on max.

Twelve minutes later, the first waft of steam floated out from under the hood. Kirill saw it, and said, "What's happening?"

"I told you I had a radiator problem. The car's overheating."

Kirill withdrew his pistol and said, "You fucking liar! What did you do?"

Devon took his right hand off the wheel, holding it up in surrender. "Nothing! I swear! I told you it had a problem. I didn't hide it from you. You guys demanded I take this car."

Kirill turned off the air conditioner, rotated the knob to heat, and said, "Get off the road before it seizes up."

A half mile down the expressway, Devon saw the Shell station he'd stopped at on the way into town. He coasted off the exit ramp and rolled into the parking lot, the motor coughing and sputtering.

He killed the engine and said, "This is going to take about an hour to cool down before we can put in some water."

Kirill said, "Get out of the car. We're going inside to buy coolant. If you try anything, I'll kill you and anyone else inside. And then I'll spend some quality time with your wife."

I watched Brett talking to Master Sergeant Fitzgerald through the glass in the door and said, "What's up, sir?"

"You got Captain Tatum yet?"

"We're on the base talking to his NCO, but he left early. He's got some family issues. Brett's finding out what time he's coming in tomorrow and setting up a private meeting."

"We don't have time to wait. We need to get him, right now."

"What happened?"

"We completed the analysis of the information from the Jewish Ghetto target, and we've identified two of the five dead Russians. It's not good news."

Before my team had left the apartment, we conducted a thorough site exploitation, retrieving biometric data from the dead men, a host of documents, and anything else we thought would be useful—down to the labels in the men's clothes—and had shipped all that, along with the phones, to the Taskforce.

I said, "What did they find?"

"One of the men was arrested in a joint FBI sting operation in Moldova. The FBI has his arrest jacket. The other is his boss—a man known as the 'Colonel' in the underworld. Both were former members of the Russian security apparatus, with the Colonel being the actual target of the sting. He got away, but he was trying to sell radioactive waste to terrorists. We think Mikhail is trying to make a dirty bomb."

Holy shit.

I said, "If the guy was arrested in Moldova, how is he running around Poland?"

"He spent less than six months in a Moldovan prison before being released. The Moldovans bungled the sting, getting the sample he brought, but not the mother lode. And they missed the Colonel as well."

"But these guys were about to torture the hell out of Mikhail. That doesn't make any sense."

"We don't know what went on in that apartment. We can only go with what we *do* know, which is that an attack is planned, and the planners met with a Russian group known for trying to sell radioactive waste to terrorists."

Needless to say, I was fairly sure that had the presidential administration's ass in a pucker.

I said, "I'm on it. I'll interdict him in Lodz, but I'll have to figure out his address. Where do we stand with Simon?"

"Knuckles has the phone pinpointed to the Ritz-Carlton in Vienna. We're currently trying to neck down his room, but it's a lot of information to go through, and we have no idea what name he's using. We're focusing on Russian passports right now."

I saw Brett heading my way and said, "I have to go, sir. I'll be in touch."

I opened the door and Brett said, "Zero-seven-thirty. We'll be the first on his agenda." He saw my face and said, "What happened?"

I said, "Hang on a sec." I turned to Master Sergeant Fitzgerald and said, "There is something else you can help us with. If we put drones here, besides the force protection issue, we're going to need a place for the maintenance team to stay. Do you have the real estate agency that Captain Tatum used?"

"You don't want to go to Lodz. Too long of a commute."

"Hey, no offense, but my days of sleeping in the dirt are over. We've already looked at Lask, and my guys are going to want a town big enough to have at least two bars."

He laughed and stood up, saying, "I don't have it, but it might be in his desk."

He rooted through the top drawer, then pulled out a card, saying, "Here it is. I remember he kept it because the lady he worked with could speak fluent English. He sometimes calls her for things that have nothing to do with real estate. I think it's how he found the plumber he's using now."

I took a picture of the card with my phone and thanked him, saying we'd see him tomorrow morning.

Once outside, Brett glanced at me, and I gave him the news. He said, "Wow. How do you always end up in the middle of a shit sandwich?"

We got in the car and I said, "Skill."

I sent the picture of the card to Kurt, then tried to call, getting his voice mail. We exited the base, going back to the turnout where the team waited. On the drive, Brett said, "You remember Iraq? In 2002?"

"Yeah."

"Remember when the world leaders were all looking for an out, and everyone was talking about inspections, UN resolutions, and the way to head off a war?"

"Yeah. I do."

"We reached a point—long before we crossed the berm—where the war was on its own trajectory, and nothing anybody was going to do would alter that. We'd built up so much combat power that it became a self-fulfilling prophecy. Somewhere we crossed a line where all the talk was wasted breath, and the only thing remaining was the timing."

He exhaled, the air leaking out in a resigned way. He said, "I think we're close to that here. This thing is going to take on a life of its own within forty-eight hours, and after that, nothing you or I do will change it."

I hoped he was wrong.

We exited the gate, finding the team patiently waiting on us. I briefed them on the status of Tatum, then where we stood with Simon.

Jennifer said, "Sounds like Knuckles is having better luck than us."

"Not really. All they have is a gigantic hotel. Simon's using an alias, and they don't know what it is. Only that it's probably Russian."

Shoshana said, "Tell them to look for Israelis. If he's using a false passport and Mikhail is involved, it'll be Israeli."

Of course. I felt like planting a giant face-palm. My phone rang, and I saw it was Kurt returning my call. To her, I said, "You're a damn genius."

Shoshana grinned and said, "I know."

I answered the phone, saying, "Did you get the card I sent?"

"Yes. What is it?"

"Devon Tatum's real estate agent. They've got a website, and I'll bet hacking it is child's play. We're headed to Lodz right now. Get the Taskforce on it. You have about an hour to get me an address."

I heard him say something to someone in the background, then he returned, saying, "They're on it. Give me an update as soon as you can."

I said, "Will do." He started to hang up and I said, "Sir!"

"Yeah, what? I gotta go."

"We think you're looking at the wrong passports for Simon. Screen anyone from Israel. There will probably be only two or three, and one of them is the target."

"Why would you think that?"

"Let's just say I have some people on my team who are pretty well versed in the target set."

"Shoshana?"

"Yeah. And she's right. I guarantee it."

74

★★★

On the portico of the West Wing, Kurt Hale hung up the phone and began giving rapid orders to George Wolffe. He passed the photo of the business card, gave him the Israeli information, then said, "Get back to the Taskforce and start working this. Pike needs an address in an hour or less, and give whatever you find on Simon directly to Knuckles."

George said, "My pleasure. You oughta come with me. Get out of that hellhole."

"I wish. If I leave here now, Lord knows what decisions will be made in that room."

George turned to leave, saying, "Good luck with that. Someday we'll have our normal life back, just chasing terrorists."

Kurt said, "Someday. If we're not all jumping into lead-lined bunkers shortly."

He walked back to the situation room, the place reeking of sweat, with the long conference table covered in a blizzard of reports and briefings, and staffers of all types clogging up any available space. He searched the perimeter, finally seeing Alexander Palmer at the head of the table, talking to someone he didn't recognize.

He slipped through the bodies, their armpits stained and ties askew, then sidled up to Palmer.

Palmer saw him and said, "Excuse me, Bill," then stepped away from the man he had been talking to without waiting for an acknowledgment.

"Tell me some good news."

"We got a handle on Captain Tatum, but we don't have control of him yet. We've also got Simon's phone necked down to the Ritz in Vienna, but we don't know a room."

"Well, shit. I can't take that to the president. Come back when you've actually worked a solution."

"What's the latest?"

"NATO's fully alerted. Poland hasn't invoked Article 5 yet, but that's because President Hannister has asked them not to. Doing so is basically a declaration of war, and when that happens, Putin's going to smash everything around him in a preemptive bid to keep NATO out. So far, they've listened to us, but they've got some nationalists who are making it very hard."

"What about our forces?"

"Hunkered down in a defensive perimeter. Putin's saturated the Luhansk province with his forces. In fact, they're still flying in."

"I thought we were finished at the crash site."

Palmer scoffed and said, "Yeah, we were." He flicked his head to the chairman of the Joint Chiefs, standing across the room and animatedly waving his hands about something. He said, "That jackass failed to take into account that jumping into combat is a one-way ticket. Once on the ground, the only way out is by foot, or by linkup with someone who can drive. The Marines and Army forces we sent in don't have enough vehicles to extract the two battalions of the 82nd on the ground. Which means the armor—that could have gotten out on its own—is staying behind for a defense."

"We need to tell the Russians what we have. Let him know about Simon and that we don't think Russia was behind the downing of Air Force One. Someone needs to tone down the tension here."

"President Hannister is talking to them, but they're belligerent," Palmer said. "And I mean *really* belligerent. Putin is not backing down at all. He's blaming NATO and the West for the entire escalation, screaming about the Polish nationals that are doing hit-and-run attacks on his forces—conveniently forgetting that he fucking built a land bridge to the Kaliningrad Oblast through Polish territory. He's not going to listen to anything we say without proof, and after what you reported about the Russians trying to take out Mikhail, we'd better find that proof before he does. If he kills Simon to protect himself, we're probably going to war."

Kurt said, "I'm working it, sir."

Palmer said, "I know. I just wish it were quicker." Kurt let him return to his work, then took a seat and listened to the various conversations occurring. After forty minutes, he was considering returning to the Taskforce headquarters, feeling he wasn't doing anything constructive here, when his phone vibrated with a call from George. He answered. "You got good news?"

"Pike's information panned out. Simon's got an Israeli passport, and it took us about fifteen seconds of sifting to find his room. Knuckles is asking where the hell the FBI tactical team is. He's ready to hit, right now. He needs to linkup with them."

Kurt smiled for the first time. He said, "I can make that happen."

Amy Tatum had been sitting still for so long, her legs had fallen asleep. Every so often, a man named Oleg looked in to make sure she was behaving, causing her to tremble, but she gathered a little more courage each time after he left without harming her. It appeared they weren't going to rape or kill her outright. She began timing the visits, finding they were between eight and twelve minutes apart. After the last one, she hesitantly decided to do more than simply sit.

She slid off the toilet and tentatively worked the two toothbrushes still under the plywood. She pried them back, gaining a space between the wood and the wall, but she couldn't slide the toothbrushes higher to increase it. Every time she created a gap, she lost it. She needed

·something larger to prop open the wood before trying to move closer to the nail.

She heard footsteps on the tile outside, and scrambled onto the toilet. This time, when he opened the door, she asked for a glass of water. He muttered something incomprehensible, but brought back what she wanted: a glass.

She waited until the footsteps retreated, straining her ears to be sure he'd gone, then dumped the water into the sink. She levered open the plywood, gaining the same space she had before, but this time, she jammed in the glass, keeping it open. She slid the toothbrushes higher, and levered again, gaining more space. She slid the glass upward and repeated the procedure until the nail popped out of the gypsum board wall.

She rotated the piece of plywood counterclockwise on the remaining nail, until the hole in the wall was exposed. She bent down, now knowing she was committed, but not wanting to be so. If someone came in to check on her and saw the hole, she'd probably be killed.

But if she tried to run and was caught, she most definitely would be killed. And she was sure they would catch her. She could see the daylight coming from the hole in the brick of the outer wall a mere four feet away, tantalizing her.

She went back and forth in her mind, considering the risk and feeling the seconds tick away. The man would return in five minutes, and the longer she sat there, the less time she had to run for freedom.

The fear overwhelmed her courage. She started to rotate the plywood back over the hole, then held it for a moment. She thought about what her husband would do, and she took that path. She flung the plywood back and squeezed into the small opening, worming her way through the pipes, feeling the grit of forty years digging into her skin. She reached the opening in the brick and cracked her head on a cinder block, seeing stars.

She fought through the pain and wriggled the final meter, spilling out onto the sidewalk next to her apartment complex. She leapt up and began running, looking for anyone to help her.

She went north, toward the mall, and hit Staromiejski Park. She saw a woman walking a dog, and sprinted toward her across the boundary street. The woman took one look at her dirty appearance and began walking rapidly away. Amy caught up to her and said, "Help me, please! I've been kidnapped!"

The woman shouted in Polish, scooped up her dog, and scurried away. Amy looked behind her, checking to see if she was being chased. She was not. She thought through the problem. She needed people. If they didn't speak her language, they would at least understand that she was being threatened if one of the men came after her.

She saw the giant Manufaktura mall in the distance and remembered the food court. Most of the people working the counters spoke English, and the place was always crowded. It was her ticket out of this nightmare.

If she could get there.

75

★★★

Knuckles walked into the lobby of the Ritz-Carlton, his eyes scanning for his contact. He had been told to look for a man reading a newspaper with a cup of coffee in front of him, but when Knuckles saw the contact, he didn't need any bona fides.

Like every other Operator in the United States arsenal, the guy couldn't stop the hard edge from leaking out. Knuckles tugged the knapsack on Retro's back and said, "That's him."

They walked up and said, "Marty Cressfield?"

The man stood and said, "Yeah, but it's Martin." He pointed to a man on his right and said, "This is Crutch."

He shook their hands and said, "You can call me Knuckles. This is Retro. Where's the team?"

"Not so fast. I was told to meet you, but I'll be damned if I know why. Who are you?"

Exasperated, Knuckles said, "Look, we don't have time for a dick-measuring contest. I work for another government agency, and we have the intel on the location of Simon Migunov's room. I was told you'd have a team. That you'd already coordinated with the Austrians for an arrest."

He said, "CIA, huh. Just up front, you need to know that this is a law-enforcement mission, not some James Bond intelligence collection op. You give me the information, and we'll take it from there."

"So you don't have a fucking team here?"

"No, I don't. Did you expect me to bring in a bunch of guys all kitted up, sitting around the lobby waiting on you? Give me the information, and like I said, we'll take it from there. We'll need to do some development first. Tap the room phone, get some intel from the staff here, emplace surveillance, that sort of thing. There's not a rush on this. We expected a month or more of investigation."

And Knuckles realized that he thought he was doing nothing more than arresting someone on their most wanted list. He didn't understand the connection between the man they were hunting and the war about to break out.

Knuckles said, "You two *are* special agents in the FBI, correct? You can arrest somebody, right?"

Taken aback, Martin withdrew his badge and surreptitiously showed it, believing he was providing proof of his position and not understanding the reasons for the question. He said, "Yeah, we're FBI."

"And you've already coordinated with the Austrians for the eventual arrest? They're expecting it?"

Now confused, he said, "Well, yes, but they'll be the ones doing the heavy lifting. We'll accompany them, but it's their arrest on our warrant."

Knuckles said, "Not anymore. You guys are about to be the heroes, because we're going to that room right now."

He filled them in, and Martin's expression went slack at what he was being told. When Knuckles was done, Martin said, "I can't unilaterally barge into a foreign hotel room. I need to get permission."

"Is permission from the president of the United States high enough for you? Because that's who sent me."

"Wait, wait. There are too many unknowns. What if your intelligence is wrong?"

"We apologize to whoever's there, and leave. But it's not wrong."

"What if he has a protective detail?"

"I've been tracking this guy across Europe. Last time I had him, he had two meatheads protecting him. We're four against two, and it's his room, trust me."

At the back-and-forth, a thought occurred to Retro. He asked, "You guys *are* armed, right?"

Martin said, "Of course, but I still need to clear this with higher."

Knuckles knew if he allowed the operation to be briefed to Martin's chain of command, the assault would be delayed by at least twenty-four hours, possibly more, because they would defer to a joint Austrian/FBI operation. And that alone had a chance of getting bungled, just like it had in Moldova.

"Did you hear what I just said? This guy is the key to stopping a war. We don't have time for some giant Mafia surveillance operation or cross-regional coordination. Why don't you think about the problem instead of your career?"

The words hung in the air, a deliberate insult that Knuckles hoped would penetrate. It did.

Crutch said, "Hey, Martin, we already got permission with the Austrians when we landed. I say we go."

Knuckles threw down his final card. "I wanted to do it officially, with an FBI warrant, but I'll do it myself if I have to, right now. This guy is going to cause the deaths of a lot of people, and I can't look in the mirror afterward simply because you haven't coordinated."

And that was enough. Martin said, "Okay, okay. Where is he? What's your plan?"

Relieved, Knuckles said, "He's on the sixth floor in a club suite. It has one connecting bedroom, which we think is where the security is staying. I want to do this clandestinely, without firing a shot. We go in through the connecting bedroom, taking out whoever is there, then hit the suite. We overwhelm them with speed and violence of action. Simple."

"How are we going to get in?"

"Well, honestly, I was told all that crap was in your ballpark, and you would have already coordinated with the hotel. I take it none of that has happened?"

"No, but it can. It'll take some time, because we'll need to get our

Austrian counterpart over here, and he'll probably need to get authorization from the Austrian government. Get them to serve the hotel their version of a warrant."

Retro shook his head, saying, "I told you so." He walked away, heading to reception.

Knuckles said, "Don't worry about it. We rented some rooms on the sixth floor. When he gets the key, he'll recode it for the suite."

In a few minutes, Retro returned, and they took the elevator to the sixth floor. Knuckles glanced at the room direction placard and said, "He's to the left. Where are we, Retro?"

"Right."

They followed him, Crutch saying, "How are you going to reprogram the key?"

"I have a portable encoder. All the keys work off a central system, but they aren't centrally connected. Each lock is just run off a battery, but it keeps the last key used in memory. The next key wipes the authorization of the last one, if it presents the correct code."

"Yeah, so?"

"I rented two rooms adjacent to each other. What I'm going to do is read the keys of both rooms. There will be an access code assigned to each. I'll get them, then match up the access code to the room number. Once I have that, I'll simply do the math to his room, because they're run sequentially. If the first code is something like 123, and the next is 124 or 122, I'll know which way to count. I'll enter the access code, reprogramming my key for his room."

He reached the first room, swiped, and entered. He sat on the bed, opening up his knapsack and pulling out what looked like a portable credit card reader seen all over Europe. He started working, saying, "The key—no pun intended—is the encrypted security code that tells the lock the card is legit. I can't duplicate that, but fortunately, it's the same code on every keycard in the hotel. Which is why I needed to rent a room."

Crunch said, "Maybe we should just knock."

Martin glared at him, and he said, "Just kidding. How are we entering? What's the order?"

Knuckles let Retro work, thinking about it. On one hand, they *were* the FBI. On the other, he was much more comfortable with Retro's skills. He said, "Retro and I will lead into the connecting room. If it's empty, we'll continue to the main suite. If there's someone there, we'll clear it and you enter the main suite. Get guns on anyone in there. We'll flow in behind you and clear whatever is left."

Crutch nodded, but deferred to Martin, his boss. Martin said, "You guys ever do anything like this before?"

Knuckles said, "Yeah. Trust me, we've got the skill."

"Why didn't you take him down before, if you were tracking him?"

"We didn't know what he was doing then. By the time we figured it out, he'd slipped our net."

Retro interrupted. "I'm done. I've reprogrammed one key for the connecting bedroom, one key for the suite, and the spare key for the first room I rented with the code for the second. Let's go test."

They entered the hallway, and Retro went to the room next door. He inserted the card, saying, "Drumroll, please." Nobody obliged, but the reader light turned green. He opened the door a crack and said, "Looks like it's showtime."

Knuckles could see the pace was a little bit fast for Martin. He said, "You guys good? We get in, and you start throwing those badges around. Nobody gets shot who doesn't deserve it."

Overwhelmed with how quickly the operation was progressing, but gaining confidence in the skills of the man asking the question, Martin nodded, saying, "Let's do it."

Knuckles smiled, and said, "Okay, then. Let's go."

They walked past the elevators, took a left, then continued down the hall toward a large double door at the end. Knuckles said, "That's the main suite."

They speed-walked toward it, Retro stopping at the last room on the right, mouthing, *Connecting bedroom.*

Knuckles checked the hallway behind them, finding it empty. He withdrew his Glock 27, and the other men followed suit. He moved to the right side of the door, next to the handle. He waited until the other men stacked behind him, then nodded at Retro. Retro stuck the card in, and the light went green.

He flung the door open, only to feel it slam into the U-bolt latch after an inch of travel. Retro's eyes popped open in surprise, and someone inside shouted in Russian.

Retro slammed his shoulder into the door, ripping the U-bolt out of the wall and flinging the door open. It hammered into a man walking forward from the other side, knocking him into a wall. Retro dove on him.

Knuckles jumped over the fight, shouting, "Bathroom!" Martin broke that way, and Knuckles entered the main suite with Crutch directly behind him. He went left and Crutch went right. He swept the main living room, crossing his fields of fire with Crutch, but it was empty, with a bathroom on the left and a bedroom on the right. Knuckles pointed at the bedroom, and Crutch started running to the door. Knuckles caught movement out of the corner of his eye, and turned, seeing a bear of a man coming out of the bathroom, barreling at him and screaming.

The man leapt through the air like he was tackling a fullback running to the end zone, but Knuckles was no longer where the bear had intended.

Knuckles rotated out and down, tucking at the waist. The man landed on his back, and Knuckles gained control of one of his arms, then used the man's own momentum against him. He sprang up, flipping the bear off his back and sending him crashing through a glass table in the center of the room, controlling the fall by leveraging his arm.

Knuckles held on to the man's wrist with one hand, aiming his pistol with the other. The bear groaned, attempting to get up, and Knuckles shook his head.

Crutch shouted, "Jackpot!"

Martin entered the room and Knuckles said, "Other target?"

"Down."

"Cover this shithead."

Martin leveled his pistol and Knuckles went into the ornate bedroom of the suite. He saw Simon Migunov sitting on an ottoman and wearing a robe, showed not a whit of concern.

Before Knuckles could speak, Simon said, "American FBI, I presume?"

Crutch said, "Yes," then began to read him his Miranda rights. Simon waved his hand and said, "Don't waste your breath. My lawyers will keep me from being extradited."

Crutch finished anyway, then looked to Knuckles for guidance. Knuckles said, "Mister Migunov, let's not talk of lawyers just yet. I have a deal for you, and when I'm done, I'm pretty sure you're going to want to play ball with the United States."

"And why on earth would I do that?"

"Because if you don't, your lawyers will be pleading with President Putin, and I'm pretty sure you know how that's going to end up."

Knuckles waited, and knew he'd won when the blood drained from Simon's face.

76

★★★

President Hannister said, "How long before we know?"

Kurt said, "He just took him down ten minutes ago. Let Knuckles work on him a little bit."

"And you believe this will work?"

"Yeah, I think so. He's feigning complete ignorance of any planned attack in Poland, but he's admitted knowledge of both Belarus and the downing of Air Force One. He's blaming Putin, but that should be enough. No way will he want to go back to Russia. Because of that, I'm pretty sure it'll work on Simon's end, but getting Putin onboard will be up to you, sir."

Alexander Palmer, Kerry Bostwick, and Mark Oglethorpe entered the Oval Office in a rush, followed by George Wolffe. George said, "Found them."

Palmer said, "What's this about Simon?"

Kurt said, "We got him."

Kerry said, "And you think you can turn him? Why would he do that?"

"Because he'd much rather face American justice than Russian. Hell, with our justice system, he's liable to get off, claiming Russian persecution."

Palmer said, "So what's the deal you're giving him?"

"Pretty simple. A, if he keeps his mouth shut, refusing to play ball, we hand-deliver him to Putin. Or option B, he admits that he—and he alone, without Putin's involvement—attacked the Russian airbase in Belarus and instigated the shoot-down of Air Force One."

"How does that help us?"

"Well, if he agrees to play ball, we then turn the story around on Putin, telling him we *know* that Simon was working for him and that he set up the Belarus hit—and we can prove it with information Simon's providing. We also know that he had nothing to do with Air Force One."

Kerry interrupted, "Do we know these two things?"

"Not yet, but I strongly believe that's the case. Anyway, we tell Putin this through back channels, then tell him we're willing to forget about Belarus if he's willing to pull the hell back. Basically, tell him we'll make a splash about arresting Simon, and Simon will take the fall. We can both blame it on 'terrorism,' just like he did initially. It gives him an out, and gives us a way to diffuse the situation. If he refuses, we threaten to expose the Belarus operation on the world stage."

Palmer said, "That's a pretty risky gambit."

"Yeah, and it just might work."

Mark Oglethorpe said, "We're forgetting about Captain Tatum. You guys are talking about a two-man decision, but if that attack occurs in Poland, it won't matter one damn bit what we or Putin want. We'll be going to war."

77

★★★

I made Veep slow down so I could study the apartment buildings on my right. The GPS was saying Tatum's address was two hundred meters away, but that didn't mean much. The only thing I trusted from it right now was that it had me on the correct street.

We'd already reached the outskirts of Lodz before the Taskforce had called with an address and description. They'd managed to crack the web server of the real estate agent, but had then had to scrounge up someone who spoke Polish to translate. Luckily, there weren't a lot of Americans renting from this agent—in point of fact, only one—so it hadn't taken long to find the correct address.

We'd pulled over, plugged the address into the GPS, and reorganized. I'd decided that the males would bird-dog the apartment, and then the females would approach. They could knock on the door without any fear of retaliation and then get a read of the atmospherics. From there, it was up to them. Either enter, or back off and wait on us.

Veep said, "We just passed the GPS coordinates. It's supposed to be behind us now."

I said, "Yeah, but the description in the file states it's a corner apartment with views two ways. That GPS grid doesn't fit."

We reached a cross street and I saw a pile of bricks on the ground from a hole in the wall of the last apartment. I said, "That's it."

"How do you know?"

"He came home because of a plumbing problem. The real estate file says it's a corner apartment, and we're on the right street. Pull over."

He did so, and I radioed the rear car, "Koko, we have it. It's the last apartment on this block. Go ahead and park. We'll keep eyes on."

She acknowledged and Aaron said, "Pike, movement from the apartment."

I turned around and saw two men leap out, comically look left and right, then bolt across the street into a park. The shirttail of one flapped up as he went across, and I saw the butt of a pistol.

What the hell?

I said, "Change of plans. Koko, Carrie, dismount and follow those guys. Find out what they're doing."

"Roger all."

"Careful. They're armed."

To the car I said, "Kit up. We're going in hard."

Ten seconds later we were jogging up to the front door. Veep tried the knob, then nodded at me. I nodded back, and he swung the door inward, allowing me access.

I raised my weapon and saw a man talking on a cell phone, his back to me. The rest of the team came barreling in, clearing the apartment. He turned at the noise, dropped the phone and reached for his belt. I closed the distance and hammered him across the bridge of his nose with the suppressor of my Glock. He fell to his knees.

Veep came from the back, saying, "It's clear."

Aaron picked up the phone, seeing it was still connected. He said, "Hello?"

He waited, listening, and I saw him smile. He began speaking in Yiddish. He turned to me and said, "He hung up. Can't imagine why."

Confused, I said, "Who was it?"

"Mikhail. I recognized the voice."

"What did you tell him?"

"He asked who I was. In Yiddish, I said, 'I'm the bill collector. I'm coming for the payment.'"

"No shit. I didn't think you had that sort of humor in you."

"That wasn't humor. I *am* coming for him." And for the first time, I saw a little of the dark angel that hovered so close to the surface with Shoshana, floating deep within him.

I replied, "You should have said, 'I want my two dollars.' "

"Huh?"

"It's a joke from a movie. . . . Never mind. Veep, start SSE. Turn this place upside down and see what you can find."

I turned to the Russian at my feet and said, "You speak English?"

He just stared at me with his pale eyes, uncomprehending, and I knew I was out of luck.

Aaron said, "He speaks English. He would have at least understood that question and shook his head. He's faking."

Aaron squatted down, saying, "If he doesn't have that capability, he'll be able to speak my language, I promise. Everyone understands pain."

He was five inches away from the Russian, and the dark angel blossomed in him, just like it did with Shoshana, scaring even me. It finally dawned what the connection was between the two of them. She wasn't the odd one out. She was *him*, only he kept it hidden deep. It caused a serious reappraisal of everything I knew about the two.

He bored into the Russian, and the man cracked, just like that. "I speak English."

Without breaking his stare, Aaron said, "We have some questions for you, and an answer of 'I don't know' will not suffice. Do you understand?"

78
★★★

Jennifer and Shoshana managed to keep the men in sight without spiking even as they ran through the park. They were clearly searching for someone and, because of that, spent just as much time running parallel as moving forward. Eventually, they reached the top end and began arguing between themselves. One of them pointed to the west, and Jennifer saw a large brick building with the word MAN-UFAKTURA on top. On the walkway leading to it were multiple sculptures painted in bright colors, and throngs of people coming and going.

A shopping area?

The men took off toward it, no longer outright sprinting, but jogging with their heads on a swivel. Jennifer and Shoshana fought to keep up without showing a signature that they were, in fact, trying to keep up. The men were caught at the pedestrian crossing for a four-lane road, both sides building up with people waiting to cross. Jennifer and Shoshana joined the crowd, watching the light.

When it changed, the men jogged across, then slowed to a walk, glancing all around, trying to find someone in the crowds.

Jennifer and Shoshana followed, still with no idea whom they were looking for. They walked past the sculptures, then entered the building at the end of the brick promenade, and Jennifer found it *was* a shopping area. A gigantic, three-story mall not unlike the kind found in America, with even a few American brand stores sprinkled throughout.

The men discussed, and one took the escalator to the second floor, while the other pressed ahead. Without needing to use words,

Shoshana split off, taking the escalator. Jennifer followed the man who'd stayed on the ground floor.

They began to wind through the mall, him still craning his neck at each store entrance, and her earpiece came alive.

"Koko, Carrie, this is Pike, you copy?"

She acknowledged and heard "We caught a guy here, and he's talking. They're after Amy Tatum, Devon's wife. She was being held hostage and managed to escape. They're using her as leverage to force him to give them access to the base."

Her phone vibrated, and he said, "Just sent a picture. I don't know how old it is, but Devon's in uniform, and he's wearing captain rank, so it can't be that off."

She looked, seeing a bright, cheerful woman a little on the heavy side, but with a beaming smile.

She said, "Got it."

"She's the key to stopping Devon. Find her before they do."

Shoshana came on. "What's Devon doing?"

"He thinks he's facilitating them taking pictures, but he's really transporting a dirty bomb."

Jennifer said, "Tell the base to stop him."

"I'm afraid to do that. I'm afraid with his wife's life in the balance he may do something stupid to gain access. We also have no idea how that thing is triggered, or whether his passenger is on a suicide run. Remember Secretary of State Billings? His captor had the detonator on his body. Billings would be alive today if we'd realized it, and I'm not making the same mistake twice. I've got Blood prepared to interdict at the base, but this is much more than simply preventing an attack against our aircraft. If they trigger anywhere on the base—even if it's at the front gate—it could be catastrophic. We need her to contact him. Give him a way out."

Shoshana came on. "Break, break. I found her. I say again, I found her. She's in the food court. The other guy is tracking her."

"He's found her too?"

"Yes. He just closed in. He's sitting right next to her. He's holding her arm, and I'm pretty sure he's got a weapon on her."

"Shit. The guy here says they're going to kill her the first chance they get."

Jennifer saw her man answer his cell phone. She said, "My target's on the phone. He's turning around."

Shoshana said, "Pike, he just stood her up. What do you want?"

Jennifer heard "What do I want? I want the fucking Pumpkin King."

Amy reached the top of the escalator and went around to the side, where she could get a view of the entrance. Drawing in deep breaths, she began to calm down when the two men chasing her didn't appear.

In the park, her small bit of safety vanished the minute she finished with the dog-walker. She'd made the decision to sprint to the mall and then had seen the two men who'd held her breaking into the park, scaring the life out of her. She should have had at least another five minutes on the loose before they discovered she was missing.

They must have heard something.

She crouched behind a bush, the option of sprinting now lost to her because it would highlight where she was. Luckily, it was easy to keep track of the two chasing her precisely because they were running back and forth like a couple of dogs chasing a ball.

She kept the bushes between her and them and managed to slink four feet at a time to the far side of the park. She circled a building, now blocked from view of the park, and began speed-walking toward the mall. She reached the four-lane road at a bus stop, and waited for the light to allow her to cross. It did, and she was halfway across before she glanced at the large crowd on the main crosswalk a hundred feet to her left.

She saw her hunters and almost froze.

She kept walking, getting to the far side, once again putting a building between her and the men. She'd taken off running at that point, trying to gain entrance to the mall while they searched the crowds on the primary walkway. She reached the building and sidled toward the entrance, scanning the crowds. She didn't see the hunters. She ripped open the doors and immediately took the escalator to the second level, then wound around to watch.

She waited for another couple of seconds, becoming calmer, then the two entered the lower level. She immediately crouched down, afraid they had some magical method of seeing her.

The men split, one moving to the escalator that would lead him directly to her. She faded back in a panic, entering the food court. A large area ringed with various vendors selling the usual American fast food, along with some Polish fare, it was crowded and loud. She ran to the far corner and sat at a table behind a pillar, cautiously peeking out around it.

She decided to wait until the man came through, playing the same hide-and-seek game she had in the park. She peeked out again, and felt a bolt of adrenaline when she couldn't see where he'd gone. She craned to her left, looking around the pillar the other way, and locked eyes with him. She bolted upright, and he closed in on her, seizing her arm and forcing her into a chair. He shook his head left and right, showed a pistol in his waistband, then said something in Russian.

He dialed his phone, spoke into it, then tilted his head toward the door. She sat still. He pinched her arm and, holding the skin in his hands, stood. She did as well.

He marched her to the escalator, and the glide down felt like a mini-movie detailing the end of her life.

When they reached the bottom, the other man was waiting. He positioned himself on her left side, and they exited, but they didn't go down the main promenade. They steered her to the left, toward the parking garage in the distance, the sidewalk deserted.

They began walking, and she realized they weren't taking her back to the house. They were going to kill her, right here, in broad daylight. Her husband was more than likely already dead.

She began to cry, stumbling forward, and the man to her left said, "*Shhhh*," shaking his head.

She tried to stop, but couldn't. The man on the left jerked her arm and sat her on a bench, off the gritty sidewalk and behind a maintenance shed. He sat next to her, and she thought, *This is it*.

He put a finger to her lips, and she realized they were simply waiting on some pedestrians to pass. Two females were coming down the walkway, talking animatedly.

They drew closer, and she recognized that they were speaking English. One was definitely American, with a blond ponytail. The other had an accent she couldn't place, with black hair cut in a pageboy.

For a fleeting moment, she thought about shouting at them to get their attention. But she knew she couldn't. All it would do was get them killed, and she couldn't be responsible for that.

They came abreast, and in the span of a second, she realized she had feared for the life of the wrong people.

Without warning, the two women turned toward the bench. The man standing in front of her, pretending to be engaged in conversation, made a half turn before his head exploded, spraying the man seated to her left in gore. The sitting man made it halfway off the bench before he suffered the same fate. He collapsed back, making more noise in the fall than the weapon that had caused his death.

Her mouth opening and closing in shock, she looked at her new enemies. The women were both holding pistols from an action movie, with large, bulbous barrels that showed a trace of smoke. The pageboy haircut said, "Make this quick," then retreated to the walkway, looking back the way they'd come. The blonde said, "Amy, my name is Jennifer Cahill. Are you all right?"

She nodded dumbly, her mouth still open in shock.

The blonde said, "Good, because we really need you to call your husband."

She fainted.

79

★★★

United States Air Force Captain Devon Tatum recognized the landmarks, and knew he had about five minutes before he reached the exit to Lask. Five minutes to figure a way out of the death spiral he was caught in.

He'd found a radiator leak kit in the Shell station, and had managed to stretch the stop to an hour and a half because the kit required not only a completely cool engine, but also thirty minutes to solidify. During that wait, he'd thought about what these men had planned, and knew it wasn't simply picture-taking. It made no sense.

If you wanted to know the location of the hangars, why not use Google Earth? If you wanted a bird's-eye perspective of what was on the ground, why use him for access when they could have simply tortured the information out of him? As the commander of base security, he had a hell of a lot more information than a simple circuit with a camera could reveal, and yet the men hadn't asked a single question. In fact, they seemed unprepared to do so.

They wanted base access for something else. And he had to find a way to stop it.

He considered just driving the car at high speed into the fourteen-foot noise reduction barriers that blanketed the expressway, as he knew he was a dead man anyway, but found he couldn't sacrifice his wife.

And then the true fear came home: If they were going to kill him, she might already be dead.

The thought brought a bolt of rage. He tried to contain it, but the man called Kirill noticed and said, "Don't get any thoughts. This is easy. One lap, and you're on your way."

Devon knew that was a fucking lie. If he let this killer on the post, more men than just him would die. He prayed to God for an answer, and was given one.

He heard the distinctive ringtone of his phone, the song "Wild Thing" by The Troggs filling the car. Kirill pulled the phone from his front pocket, looked at the screen, then held it out for Devon to see.

He didn't recognize the number, but said, "It's my command. If I don't answer, they'll just keep calling. Better if I did so, since we're about to enter the gate."

Kirill handed him the phone, saying, "I'm listening. You say anything suspicious, and your wife is dead."

Devon took it, hitting the green button at the bottom, and said, "Hello?"

And heard his world flipped upside down. "Captain Tatum, my name is Pike Logan, and I work for the United States government. I need you to pretend that this is an official call, and I need you to just listen. I know who is sitting next to you. Do not say anything to alert him. Okay?"

Devon said nothing. The man on the phone said, "You can answer the damn question with a yes or no."

He said, "Yes."

"Good. First, your wife is alive and fine. She's with my team. The men who held her are dead. Do not, under any circumstances, ask to speak to her."

He felt a bolt of adrenaline at the news and fought hard not to show anything. Robotically, he said, "Okay."

"Good. You're doing good. The man in the seat has a dirty bomb in your car. He's planning to set it off inside the American perimeter of the Lask airbase. Confirm you understand."

"Yes. I got it."

"Say something about the flux capacitor, like you're talking about work."

"What?"

"Say something related to work. Make it sound like you're talking about your job."

Devon glanced at Kirill and said, "Yes, I have the oil for the flux capacitor. I can bring it tomorrow."

"Jesus, man, I didn't mean actually say 'flux capacitor.' Listen, I don't want you to try to do anything. We don't know if this guy is a suicide bomber or what. He might have a detonator on his body. Under no circumstances are you to try to stop him. Do you understand?"

Confused, Devon answered, "Yes. I understand," but thought, *If not me, who?*

"Good. Listen, you go to the airbase just like he expects. When you get to the American perimeter, you'll be met by a guy you don't recognize. I need you to show him your ID card upside down. Do you understand?"

"Yes. I can do that."

"How far out are you? You can answer that, but do it in a normal way."

"Sure, that'll only take about five minutes. It's easy."

"Okay, got it. Remember, don't show any surprise at a man on the gate you don't know. His name is Brett Thorpe. Roll up and say a greeting. He'll do the rest."

"Okay. Talk to you soon."

"Good answer. Because you will. Hang in there. It's almost over."

He ended the call and said, "Some bullshit from work, but I can deal with it tomorrow." He handed the phone back and said, "I will be able to do that, right?"

His suspicions belied because of the question, Kirill said, "Yeah, sure. One lap, and you're back to your normal life."

They exited the expressway, Devon fighting to control the adrenaline racing through his body. They reached the street that dead-ended into the base, and went down the pitted asphalt to the main gate. He rolled up to the outer perimeter, seeing the same Polish man he'd seen when he left earlier, fearing that he'd be stopped and questioned about his passenger. Wondering if he was about to feel a fireball. The man didn't even ask him to roll down the window, waving him through.

He exhaled and Kirill said, "Good. Very good. Keep it like that, and you'll be home with your wife soon."

They rolled down the flight line, and Kirill made no attempt to retrieve his "camera" from the back. Devon realized everything the man on the phone had said was true. He saw the temporary American inner perimeter ahead, and felt the spike of adrenaline again.

This is it.

He slowed, seeing a short African American man he didn't recognize, wearing a uniform that didn't fit. He prayed that Kirill wouldn't notice. He rolled down his window, struggling to remember the last name of the man, but couldn't. He spit out, "Hey, Sergeant Brett. Just running in for something I forgot."

Devon held out his CAC card, upside down.

The man called Brett leaned in as if to study the card and said, "Hey, how's the wife?"

Stunned, Devon stuttered, "She . . . she's good."

He said, "I know."

He jammed a pistol past him, slamming it right up against Kirill's head, then pulled the trigger.

80

★★★

So they really have him?" Putin asked.

The head of the FSB, Ilya Kozlov, glanced around the table, not meeting the eyes of the men sitting, and said, "Yes, sir. They most definitely have him."

It was Kozlov's first time visiting the Black Sea Estate, and he was clearly awed not only by the grandeur of the structure, but also by the power of the men around the table.

"Can we get to him?"

"Not anytime soon. He is under incredible security, an outer ring of Austrian special police, and an inner ring of United States FBI. Maybe when they move him, but short of blowing up the building, there is no way to currently effect any lethal operations against Simon."

Putin took that in, then said, "And our team in Warsaw? What of them?"

Kozlov shuffled from foot to foot, then said, "Dead, sir. They were found in a tenement house by Polish police. Gunshot wounds."

"The Americans again?"

"We don't know. Odds are it was Simon, sending a team to rescue the man we were going to interrogate."

"What about the Cesium the Colonel was trying to sell?"

"It has disappeared, along with the man named Mikhail."

Putin slowly nodded, then said, "You may leave."

Putin waited until he'd closed the door to the ornate dining room before returning to the men around the table. Powerful oligarchs, not politicians, they were the true heart of the Russian machine, and had been privy to the attempts to annex Belarus.

Alex Romanov, a thin, white-haired man sitting to Putin's right, toyed with his cane and said, "Perhaps we should take the offer."

"Then we lose Belarus. We lose everything we were attempting to gain."

"We go to war, and we will lose much more than that."

Putin knew the men around the room were growing skittish at the rattling of sabers. They had stood with him on the machinations with Belarus, but had become alarmed at how it had spiraled out of control. They had interests that went far beyond politics, and feared the financial repercussions of a war.

They could not tell him what to do, of course, but he held no illusions as to their power, and neither did his personal staff. Before flying here from Moscow, his most trusted aide had said one thing: *Beware the Ides of March*. Putin may be the emperor, but like Caesar, it didn't make him invincible.

Putin said, "What if Simon begins talking? How can we guarantee he won't raise the truth at a later date?"

A younger man with a scar on his cheek, seated farther down, said, "Each day that passes makes him less believable. The president of the United States said he would announce Simon's sole culpability. If Simon says something at a later date, it will look like a desperate man attempting anything to save himself. It will mean the United States is in on the conspiracy." He smiled, showing yellow teeth. "And who would believe that?"

Romanov said, "Don't forget, he's charged in the death of President Warren. It's not inconceivable that we will get the opportunity to take care of him. Remember what happened to Lee Harvey Oswald? The Americans have no love for assassins."

That thought made Putin smile. In truth, part of his reticence was purely to punish Simon. No man on earth had ever dared to cause him so much trouble. Maybe patience would allow that punishment to occur.

He went around the room, seeing the concurrence on each man's face.

He said, "So be it."

Private First Class Joe Meglan was one of the last to board the MC-130, having been tasked with the final scrub of the perimeter. He drove around it in an RSOV, looking on with a small bit of nostalgia, because at one point, he was sure they were going to war and that he would die inside the hole he'd dug.

They'd had the radio reports coming in every ten minutes, and had known that if the Russians wanted to take their airfield, they would do so. Unlike some of the press reporting coming out of America, he understood that they were but a trip wire for commitment of United States forces, and resented the people who screamed at the president to "show strength."

Show strength, my ass. You pick up a gun and get your ass over here.

It was the difference between involvement and commitment, like ham and eggs. The chicken was involved, but the pig was committed.

One thing was for sure, he'd never make fun of the FBI again. Who would have thought this whole crisis would be precipitated by some crazy Russian with a grudge against President Putin? It was surreal, but he'd listened to President Hannister announce the arrest, and the tireless work from the FBI that had made it happen.

He would now come home a hero for his actions, but those guys were the ones who deserved the praise. If they hadn't broken open the case and tracked that nutjob down, there was a good chance he'd be coming home in a box.

He remembered the relief they'd all felt when President Putin agreed with President Hannister's statement, following up with a press conference of his own. Of course, he'd demanded the extradition of the instigator to his judicial system, but—as he was implicated in the death of a United States president—nobody saw that happening anytime soon.

When the Russian armor began to roll back to the border, they'd spent the last three days bringing in vehicles to extract the 82nd paratroopers from the Air Force One crash site. And now, it was time for him to go home.

He swung back to the tarmac, telling his squad leader he'd seen nothing of note. The squad leader replied, "Let's go. First in, last out."

They loaded the vehicle, cinching it down in the aircraft, then he'd buckled into the webbing of the MC-130, his squad leader next to him. He said, "If this wasn't combat, what was it?"

His squad leader considered for a moment, then said, "Just the new world order."

The bird lifted off, and Joe said, "So no combat infantryman's badge?"

His squad leader laughed and said, "Don't worry. I'm sure we'll be catching our original deployment to Afghanistan."

81
★ ★ ★

I rolled over and cocked my eye at the clock, seeing it wasn't yet ten A.M., which meant I wasn't getting up. A pillow hit the back of my head, and Jennifer said, "I see you're awake. Come on! This is getting old. You've caught up on your sleep."

I rolled over and said, "Not when you keep me up at night."

She put a hand on her hip and said, "Okay, if that's what's causing the issue, I can fix it. Starting tonight."

I laughed and sat up, saying, "Don't you ever want to sleep in? Just stay in bed until you have to tell the maids to go away?"

"Not when I'm in Vienna. We only have two more days here before our flight home, and I don't want to spend them in a hotel room."

Which was a poke in my eye, and she knew it. The Rock Star bird had come for the team in Warsaw, delivering us to Vienna, and we'd been suitably rewarded with rooms at the Ritz-Carlton, then conveniently separated from Taskforce control.

I understood why, given our connection over here with the Israelis and the always-present concerns over cover, but it was still a little shitty. We'd had to buy our own tickets back, and I'll be damned if Jennifer hadn't been upgraded to business class. Which didn't make me want to get out of bed any sooner.

She said, "You've got no excuse. We weren't roped into Simon's interrogation. You should feel lucky."

She did have a point. Knuckles and Retro were tied into Simon and the FBI, and because Retro had flown across the pond on the Rock Star bird with Veep, so was the vice president's son. All of them now connected by a lease agreement for an aircraft, affecting a cover that had to remain secret. They'd go home together. I'd fly coach.

Jennifer tried one more time. "Hey, Shoshana and Aaron are leaving tomorrow. We should at least go out with them once."

Growing wary, I said, "What's that mean?"

"You know, go out together. Like a double date."

I knew it.

I rolled out of bed, saying, "I'm not so sure that's a good idea. Shoshana's . . . a little loopy."

She said, "No, she's not. You should get to know her. She's really trying, and Aaron is . . . a little weird himself."

I remembered the house, and Aaron's transformation. I said, "Yeah, they only seem to click when they're killing people."

She threw a towel at me and said, "I'm trying to break them of that predilection. Get cleaned up."

And then my phone rang.

I saw that it was Knuckles, and said, "What's up, you looking for a coach seat?"

He was all business. "Pike, I got some information on Mikhail. He's here, in Vienna."

Jennifer saw my face harden and started to ask a question. I held up a finger and said, "How do you know?"

"Simon's trying to rope him into the conspiracy, but the FBI doesn't give a shit, because he's an Israeli citizen and not on any lists they have. They took notes, telling me they'd give it to Israel, but they don't seem to really care, what with Simon tied up in a neat bow and all."

"You got those notes?"

"Better. I went back in to Simon by myself. Mikhail's here in Vienna, and he's trying to sell that damn Torah. He's got a buyer, and I have all the information on him. The FBI doesn't have any of it."

I said, "No shit. I was just telling Jennifer we should double-date with those assassins."

I heard him laugh, then, "Yeah, I figured that's what you'd say."

I hung up, and Jennifer said, "What was that about?"

"Exactly what you wanted. We get to go on a date with the Israelis."

I dialed the phone, Aaron answered, and I heard "Tell me you aren't getting hammered by Jennifer for a double date."

"As a matter of fact, I am, but I've been resisting until now."

He laughed and said, "They're colluding, but I'm not sure Shoshana's ready. It would be embarrassing."

"Well, that depends. I'm calling for the bill collector, and I think she's ready for that."

82

★★★

Carrying a leather messenger bag over his shoulder, Mikhail window-shopped up the street, burning off his time while running a surveillance detection route. He passed by the Hofburg palace, the grand structure overlooking the Michaelerplatz circle, and took the roundabout to the west, heading toward the glitzy shopping section of downtown Vienna. He paused at the Demel pastry and chocolate shop, going inside and browsing while occasionally looking out the window to see if anyone was on him.

He wound through the store, using the choke points and narrow pathways to ensure he was clean. He determined he was.

He exited back on the street, checked his time, and saw he was close. He walked up Kohlmarkt, passing Tiffany's jewelers, then took a left on a smaller pedestrian path called Naglergasse. He walked past the turn he wanted to enter, glancing down it. He saw nothing of concern.

He did an about-face, entering a narrow alley with a few eclectic shops. At the end was the Bockshorn Irish Pub. His meeting spot for the transfer of the Torah.

He'd had a rough few days, but now, he'd get the cash he needed to escape the nightmare that had sucked him down like a spider flicked into a toilet.

Simon's name had been splashed all over the news, but so far, Mikhail hadn't seen anything about himself. The attack in Poland had not occurred, which meant it wasn't going to, although there had been absolutely nothing on television talking about breaking up any terrorist actions. The last he'd heard was a phone call from Oleg saying the woman had escaped.

And then the voice of the bill collector.

But now, it would all be behind him. He'd take the fifty thousand euros he was getting from this sale and travel to South Africa, where a man of his skills was still valued.

He pushed into the small pub, letting his eyes adjust to the dim lighting. He saw the narrow bar snaking away from him to his front, two drinkers leaning over it, the entire place cluttered with memorabilia from one event or another, a scattering of lamps providing the only light. It was almost like a cave, and a little bit claustrophobic, which is exactly what he wanted. He'd be able to control anything that happened in here. Not that he'd need to, dealing with a seventy-year-old man.

He glanced to his right, toward a small room, seeing nobody. He surveyed the main bar for a threat, saw none, and nodded at the bartender. He went right, looking for his contact.

The room was really nothing more than a hallway with tables running down it. At the far end he saw a man with a full beard, a fedora hiding his face. Next to him was a briefcase.

He walked up, getting the man's attention. He said, "You can find the most interesting things shopping these small alleys."

"So I've heard. But they don't sell what I'm looking for."

Satisfied with the answer, proving the man was his contact, Mikhail sat down, saying, "I don't want to spend any more time here than I need to. Inside this bag is the Torah. Look at it, satisfy yourself, but don't take forever."

The man raised his head, and Mikhail recognized the eyes. Recognized *him*. He snapped his hand to his waist and, in Yiddish, said, "What, are you going to try to kill me right here? In the bar?"

Calmly, Aaron said, "No, don't be silly. I'm not going to kill you. That wouldn't be right. I'm not the bill collector."

Mikhail caught movement behind him, and turned.

Aaron said, "But I brought her with me."

He had a brief flash of recognition just before the blade penetrated his ribs. Shoshana above him, the dark angel expanding out of her, enveloping them both.

He gasped in shock, grabbing her arm. The knife bit deeper and he felt the rage coming through the steel. She twisted, expanding the wound channel, excising every horrible thing he had forced her to do. He tried to stand, but she bore down, spearing him in place.

He fought against her, weakly batting at her arms. She said not a word, working the knife. Aaron refused to move. Never even raised a hand, content to simply watch.

And Mikhail succumbed to the inevitability of Shoshana's rage, the demon inside her consuming him. He dropped his hands and sagged back, his last vision on mortal earth the dark angel, extracting the payment of his soul.

Sitting at a small outdoor café, our work done, Jennifer was growing concerned. She said, "What's taking so long?"

"I don't know. Let 'em work. We did our track. The rest is up to them."

She glanced at me and said, "You don't feel responsible at all?"

"For what?"

"I'm just thinking about . . . Never mind."

"No, what were you going to say?"

She leaned forward and took my hands, saying, "We just set a man up to be killed. Doesn't that affect you at all? I mean, even if it's right. Don't you think about it?"

I squeezed her hands and said, "What I thought about was *you* telling me a horrific story in the back of a van. That's *all* I thought about."

She took that in, then said, "Yeah . . . but . . . it's not the same thing. We just killed a guy in cold blood."

"No, we didn't. We killed a parasite. Just because you happen to be born with a human body doesn't make you human."

She said nothing. I said, "If you'd have killed him on the train, would you have second-guessed yourself?"

"No, of course not."

"Then why are you doing it now? That fuck was trying to cause the death of half of Europe in a world war. And he sure as shit screwed up Shoshana."

She cocked her head at that and said, "That's what this is about, isn't it?"

I took a sip of my beer, saying nothing. She said, "It is, isn't it? You *do* care about her, and she told you something. She opened up to you, and you wanted to make it right."

I said, "Look, all I did was facilitate their operation as payback for helping us. That's it. We owed them for their help, and I honored that."

She squinted her eyes and said, "That's bullshit."

I was saved by seeing Aaron walking down the street, Shoshana next to him holding a messenger bag. The same bag I'd seen Mikhail carrying twenty minutes ago. I waved, and Shoshana waved back, a childlike grin on her face.

They sat down, Aaron pulling off the fake beard and Shoshana opening the case. I said, "Looks like it went okay."

Shoshana held out the Torah and said, "Yeah, we bring this back and we'll get more work than we can handle."

Jennifer said, "What did you do to get it?"

Shoshana seemed to shrink a bit in the chair. She said, "I did what was required."

I started to interrupt, scared that Jennifer would take away what Shoshana had just achieved. I needn't have worried. Jennifer leaned forward and said, "Shoshana, I don't ask because I fear for him. I fear for *you*."

Shoshana absorbed the words, believing she had earned Jennifer's disapproval, and I could see it hurt. Like Aaron, Jennifer had somehow become the dark angel's mentor. She remained silent for a moment, then defiantly spit out, "I killed him. And it was *good*. Is that what you want to hear?"

Jennifer saw the change in demeanor, the statement bringing closure for someone she held dear. She said, "Yes, Pumpkin King, that's *exactly* what I wanted to hear."

Shoshana was shocked at the response, not expecting it from Jennifer and her strict moral compass, and because it had come from her, it meant all the more. Her face lit up in a smile, and I said, "Well, this is pretty much what I thought a double date in Vienna would be like with you two. Me and Jennifer tracking a guy, you and Aaron killing him. Much better than dinner and a movie."

I saw my sarcasm take a small slice of her newfound sense of purpose for her life, and I immediately backpedaled. I leaned forward and said, "Shoshana, I'm going to let you in on a little secret. After all of your 'research' into my relationship with Jennifer, looking for the perfect answer, you missed the most obvious thing: We're *all* Pumpkin Kings. We're all trying to find our way."

She said nothing, but her eyes told me all I needed to know. She was good. I changed the subject, saying, "Will they pay the contract?"

Relieved at the turn of conversation, Aaron said, "Maybe, but we made more from just retrieving it."

"What's that mean?"

"Let's just say that the man who was going to purchase it is from an old Jewish family, and he was more than willing to lose the money to keep his name out of the press."

I said, "Devious. What're you going to do with your newfound largess? Outside of paying us, I mean?"

Shoshana said, "Pay *you*? Why on earth would we do that? After all the crap you've dragged us through?"

I said, "You got the Torah, correct? And through my work. Sounds like the contract was fulfilled."

She wound up, and I cut her off. "I'm teasing, Carrie. Jennifer says you want to go on a real double date. You know, one where you don't slaughter someone."

She glanced at Aaron, afraid I was mocking her. Tentatively, she said, "Yes?"

"How would you like to do that with the president of the United States?"

Jennifer scrunched her eyes and said, "What are you talking about?"

"We saved the world, and Kurt told me that the president would have a beer with us at a place of my choosing."

83

★★★

Talking into a speakerphone centered on the conference table, Kurt Hale said, "Have you lost your damn mind?"

George Wolffe hid a smile, waiting on what that lunatic Pike Logan would say next. The voice came out tinny, but the request was valid.

"Sir, you said if I saved the world, I could have a beer with the president at a location of my choosing."

"Yeah, we were just bullshitting. And anyway, I thought you meant coming over to the White House or something. Not in Charleston."

"It's *my* choosing, and he's running through the damn state campaigning. He's coming to Charleston anyway."

"Pike, he's busy trying to win election to the highest office in the land."

"How's that going anyway? I haven't seen the news."

Kurt recognized the deception immediately. Pike knew very well how the campaign was going. President Hannister was leading in every single poll, crushing all opponents. The *Washington Post* had written an exposé on the crisis, and Hannister's actions were being held up as a cross between JFK at the Bay of Pigs, showing strength in the face of overwhelming domestic military opposition, and JFK during the Cuban Missile Crisis, showing strength against an existential threat and making nuanced decisions in the face of potential nuclear conflagration.

And the JFK theme was resonating on both sides of the aisle.

Kurt refused to bite, saying, "He's doing pretty well."

"Really? I wonder why that is?"

George laughed. Pike said, "And what about us? The Taskforce?"

Kurt knew what he was asking. "Okay, Pike, so you've heard."

"Heard what?"

Kurt looked at George with an expression that said, *Do I really have to put up with this arrogance?*

George grinned and said, "Yes, you do."

From the phone, Pike said, "What was that? George, did you say something?"

Kurt said, "Pike, the president greatly appreciates what you've accomplished. In fact, he called the Oversight Council together and chastised them for their reticence in using the Taskforce. It was a complete turnaround. We're back in business, at least until the election. Like I'm sure you know."

He heard "Yeah, I know. I happen to have his son on my team, and he gave me a quote from the old man: 'Out of all the elements of power that I wield, only one had the ability to preserve the security of this nation.' Is that true? Did he say that?"

Kurt wondered how Hannister's son knew what had been said in a classified meeting of the Oversight Council, but said, "Yeah, he said that."

"Okay, I'm just wondering how all of those accolades don't translate into a beer in Charleston when he comes through."

Kurt exhaled and said, "You're really testing me."

"I think we've earned it."

Kurt looked at George, who said, "Can't hurt to ask."

Pike said, "Yeah, sir. What's the harm in asking? From what I hear, you're his right-hand man now."

Kurt bristled, saying, "I don't want to hear that shit, you understand?"

Pike said, "Whoa. Touchy. Sorry."

George hit the mute button and said, "You know, they really *do* deserve it. It's the least he could do, and he'd probably jump at the chance. The Taskforce is like his praetorian guard now."

Kurt unmuted the phone and said, "I'll see what I can do, Pike."

"Sounds good, sir. It'll be at the Windjammer on the Isle of Palms. You just tell me when. Let the president know there'll be a couple of Israelis in attendance."

Kurt started to respond and realized that Pike had hung up before he could. He looked at George and said, "That guy is the bane of my existence."

George laughed and said, "That guy is the *reason* you exist."

ACKNOWLEDGMENTS

People ask me all the time where the ideas from my books come from, and usually, they're from interesting news reports—tidbits that catch my eye, leading me to dig down. This time, it was a really obscure story, because I was desperate.

I was on a security contract and had just typed the final correction on the copyedits for *The Forgotten Soldier* when I received an e-mail from my editor politely asking for the title and plot of my next book. I literally had no earthly idea. I knew two things: One, I wanted to move away from Islamic terrorism, and two, I wanted to bring back Shoshana and Aaron. I remembered a strange story I'd read about a motorcycle gang in Russia that had fought in Crimea and something about a Russian gas company with mob ties. Since I had limited connectivity at my location and seriously constrained available time due to the contract, I shot my wife an e-mail asking her to do some research and then went to my day job. By the time I'd returned to the barracks, she'd completed her research, and it was a doozy.

She sent me a data dump on the Night Wolves and Gazprom Industries—both real entities—and they had done things that made a fiction writer like me shake his head because nobody would believe it if I'd have made it up. And there was one cool tidbit: A guy named Semion Mogilevich owned a majority of the gas lines coming out of Russia—and he was one of the biggest mob bosses on the planet, having hit our own FBI top ten list. The capstone? He was a dual Russian–Israeli citizen. The story began to write itself.

This being the tenth book, I decided to go big. Forget about a single terrorist attack. What about taking on the fault line of the old Iron Curtain? And so my wife and I were off to Eastern Europe. Once again, I'm indebted to her for coordinating the entire trip—yes, I made her drive all over Poland. She might need it operationally one day. . . .

For the background and set pieces of Bratislava, I'm indebted to Mgr. Denisa V., a local national who took us all over the city, including finding some pretty neat pubs and giving some unique insight that would never have been discovered on the Internet (like the fact that the parking garage next to the US Embassy had to relocate its entrance after 9/11).

Ksiaz Castle is real, of course, as is Project Riese. Unfortunately, the only way for a person to see the tunnels is through a paid tour guide—and the only tour guide they had spoke no English. So, we took a two-hour group tour of the castle listening to some guy drone on and on in Polish, having not a clue what was being said, but eventually I got to explore the tunnels on my own. The elevator shaft that Pike and Shoshana use in the book is real, and I probably could have included some serious history as to why it was behind a bookshelf, but I have no idea what that guy was saying. . . .

The fabled "gold/ghost" train (depending on who's writing the story) is real as well. So far, it's amounted to nothing but rumors and legends, but it might be found someday.

While on the surface the Marines and Army would appear similar, there are distinct differences, and I'm indebted to Neil S. for giving me some insight into a Marine LAV platoon. A Mustang himself, he stood up MARSOC and was the commander of the first MARSOC Battalion, with an interesting history involving more than just the Marine Corps. As such, he also helped me with the unclassified reorganization of the CIA, including their new "Mission Centers."

I'm indebted to Joe M. (yeah, try to figure out what that letter stands for) for working with me on the airfield seizure scene. A close friend and veteran of the 1st Ranger Battalion, he's done just about every job on an airfield seizure in between deployments to combat, and he provided insight that I would have never gotten accurate on operational template, airflow, and, most important, the RCT. It's a skill that the Rangers have perfected like no one else on earth, and they continue to perfect it even as they serve in harm's way in distant lands. Any mistakes, of course, are mine alone. Oh, and Joe M. isn't a private first class in real life.

This publication marks the mighty 10th Dutton title for me. A milestone I never would have imagined possible when I typed the first (long since deleted) sentence for *One Rough Man*. Through it all, I have had nothing but support and professionalism from the Dutton team. From my editors, Ben Sevier and Jessica Renheim; to my publicist, Liza Cassity; to Carrie Swetonic in marketing. From day one, the team—along with my agent, John Talbot—has worked tirelessly to assure the success of the Pike Logan series. I can't thank all of you enough for your work ethic and dedication.

ABOUT THE AUTHOR

Brad Taylor, Lieutenant Colonel (ret.), is a twenty-one-year veteran of the U.S. Army Infantry and Special Forces, including eight years with the 1st Special Forces Operational Detachment—Delta, popularly known as the Delta Force. Taylor retired in 2010 after serving more than two decades and participating in Operation Enduring Freedom and Operation Iraqi Freedom, as well as classified operations around the globe. His final military post was as Assistant Professor of Military Science at the Citadel. His first nine Pike Logan thrillers were *New York Times* bestsellers. He lives in Charleston, South Carolina.